THE THINGS WE KEEP IN THE ATTIC

KRISTEN LANE

this one's for me

CONTENT NOTE

While I would love to send you into this book blindly, I feel an ethical responsibility to mention potentially triggering content. This story explores grief and trauma in an intense and personal way, as well as what it looks like when we become proponents of our own pain. You can expect:

- childhood neglect + abuse
- death of family member
- portrayals of alcoholism, anxiety, depression, + self-harm
- mention of miscarriage and infertility
- mention of childhood sexual assault (this does *not* happen on page)

ONE

NOVEMBER

There is something deeply unsettling about the silence that threatens to suffocate me as I sit in my new therapist's office. The sun beams through the windows that line the walls, the warmth wrapping around me in what would be a comforting hug—if it wasn't for Marjorie, the shrink, eyeing me from the oversized, olive-green beanbag she was perched on.

We've been sitting silently in this godforsaken room, neither of us uttering a word outside of the formal hello's we'd exchanged 15 minutes ago when I first crossed the threshold. It was my second session—my second attempt at trying to talk and, as I sit, lost in thought, I keep coming back to the same question. *Why the fuck am I here?*

I cast my eyes around the room, trying not to judge the overwhelming color preference that fills every corner. Everything from the beanbag to the rickety couch I was sitting on —was some version of green. From the deep emerald of the walls to the sage pen in Marjorie's hand, hovering over the open pine-colored notebook in her lap. A glance outside did nothing to ease the strain on my eyes, seeing as the office was surrounded by trees. I blow out a frustrated breath and finally turn my attention back to the woman in front of me.

Marjorie seems to be around my same age, exuding a childlike quality that I can't quite grasp. Maybe it was the fact that she hadn't dropped her small, phony smile since I'd settled into the uncomfortably thin cushions of the itchy, moss-green couch.

I clear my throat, tilting my head at her in defiance, and watching as she shakes hers—her pin-straight, auburn hair dancing with the movement—letting out a small chuckle. She reaches for one of the two water bottles that wait on the coffee table between us. She's slow with her movements—methodical and deliberate as she unscrews the cap, the satisfying click of the seal breaking fills the awkward air for a moment. Her eyes don't leave mine as she pulls back a steady drink, the action laced with challenge.

I huff a laugh as she sets down the open bottle and clicks her pen twice. "We can start whenever you're ready."

I stare at her, hoping she can feel the virtual heat radiating from my place on the loveseat. I let another minute pass before I shift in my seat, extending my legs before crossing them again.

"Listen. You have an opportunity here and you're the only one who can decide to use it. You and I? We have a clean slate. I don't know enough about you to judge you and you're not giving me much to work with. The first thing you need to understand is that you're safe here. Nothing leaves this room unless I'm concerned you're going to become a danger to yourself or others." She pauses, her gaze flicking past my head toward the wall, where I can only assume a clock—green, if I had to guess—hung in place. "Work with me for these next forty minutes and we'll see what happens. Okay?"

You're safe here. The words echoed in my head as my eyes glossed over with tears. I let out a small cough, blinking them away. "Nothing leaves this room?"

"*Nothing* leaves this room, Asha."

"I don't even know where to start."

"How about you start at the beginning," she says, surprising me as her tone slips away from the accusatory judge and back into—what I'd assume was—the comforting lilt of a therapist. "Or wherever you feel most comfortable."

I hesitate, torn between a thousand different beginnings. Guilt, shame, and fear mix in my stomach as I war between the hundred different reasons for why I exist in this...shell. I didn't miss the fact that I could be sitting outside, sipping a cup of coffee right now. Instead, I decided to torture myself with an hour of explaining my life story—to a stranger with an unnatural obsession with the color green at that. *And I'm the one with issues?*

"I guess it starts with Armatta."

Marjorie clicks her pen once more, flipping her notebook open with ease. She scribbles a single word down before turning her focus back to me. "And who is Armatta?"

"My..." I nearly gag on the word, "mother."

"Hmm," she hums, the sound reminding me of the opening note to a song I couldn't recall at the moment. "Do you have any siblings?"

"A sister, AnaMarie."

"Hmm, okay," she starts, her pen already in motion— quick, vigorous strokes that scratch at the paper, as if she couldn't get her thoughts out fast enough. "And are you close with your sister?"

"No."

Flashes of my most recent fight with AnaMarie rushed through my head—harsh words screamed between us under the flickering lights of her dingy apartment. My skin prickles, a layer of sweat starting to coat my lower back as the memory crawls under my skin. I shift under the oppressive sun rays blasting against my back—weighing down on me just like Ana's suffocating words had. I catch my bottom lip between my teeth, biting into the skin as I lose focus for a few seconds.

"Okay," she says, huffing a small, frustrated breath—clearly annoyed by my lack of response. "Why don't you share a memory that stands out to you. Something that would help me get a sense of what your family dynamic looked like while you were growing up."

I fall farther behind invisible walls, wringing my hands together as my throat locks up. A thousand words sit on the tip of my tongue but none of them were strong enough to break through my hesitation.

"Look," she starts, folding the notebook closed—a page filled by my twenty minutes of silence alone—before slamming it on the table. "I can't make you talk. I can't force you to tell me why you came here in the first place and I'm not going to try because you have to pay me for my time regardless. Just know that the time you waste is time that someone who *actually* needed my help could have had. Ball's in your court."

I feel my eyebrows arch in surprise as her words—surprisingly curt daggers from a therapist—gave Marjorie what she was probably looking for. A reaction.

"Okay," I start, wiping my, now sweating, hands against the smooth fabric of my sweatpants. "I guess there was this one time when Matta had been gone for a while, longer than we were used to. Ana and I were usually okay for a few days, but this time we'd run the grocery budget to the ground and were waiting on our mother to come home to pay the water bill. Ana had gotten so worried that she called our Auntie Aisha and asked for help..."

"She left me with a twenty and told me to watch Asha but I'm starting to feel scared, Auntie. She's been gone a couple days now. We only got one more frozen dinner left and just got the third notice on the water bill."

My sister's voice filled the entire one-bedroom apartment, her fear touching everything in sight. She leaned against the kitchen counter with her head in one hand, the pressure of raising me sitting squarely on her shoulders. I could hear our Aunt Aisha's mumbled response through the receiver as the knot of anxiety built in my stomach.

AnaMarie's eyes squeezed shut as she listened to Aisha on the other line. Her thick dark curls hung past her shoulders, effortlessly coiling around her head. I watched as she ran a frustrated hand through the strands, jealous at how flawlessly they fell back into place.

I snuck from behind the kitchen counter and pulled myself onto the worn-out couch we'd found on a street corner earlier this year. It was our first real piece of furniture in the apartment aside from the bed we three shared. My excitement lasted through the days Ana and I had to spend cleaning it. Momma had said something to Auntie over the phone about the 'smile that was stuck to Asha's face over a threadbare couch' while she delegated from the kitchen.

Ana's sixteen-year-old hands frantically scribbled something onto a piece of paper as our aunt continued to talk. What I could see of her face looked like it was about to crumble as they exchanged goodbyes. I jumped at the sound of the phone slamming into the receiver but kept my eyes pinned on my sister. She let out a huff of frustration before walking over and plopping down beside me, "Auntie can't come till the morning...I think it's just you and me again tonight, little monster."

A small smile tugged at my mouth at the sound of my nickname but fell just as fast. It wasn't unlike Momma to leave us alone for a few days but, most of the time she'd call. Of course, half the time she was calling just to demand that we clean up the house because she was bringing home a man. I doubted this time would be any different. A big part of me wished she would call and fuss at us—if it meant she was finally coming home. The other part of me, a tiny part, hoped she'd stay away. I didn't know where she went, but it hurt knowing she'd rather be there than with Ana and me. My hand found a loose thread on the couch and I tugged on it while I tried to remember the last time she was home in time to eat with us without one of her "friends."

Just the week before, she'd made it home for dinnertime but with someone in tow—a tall, thin man whose light brown skin seemed washed out as he stood next to our beautiful dark-skinned Momma. His green eyes reminded me of slime and the way his smile curled to one side made me think of a snake. I didn't like him. And I didn't like how Momma waved her hand toward Ana and me and told the green-eyed snake man not to mind us. She made it clear to all of us that we wouldn't bother the two of them as she pulled him into the bedroom—our only bedroom—leaving Ana and me to sleep in the living room that night. The pounding of his heavy footsteps woke me up as he left the next morning, the creak of the front door as it shut sent me running to the bedroom to check on Momma. I found her lying in bed, asleep. The reek of cigarette smoke clinging to the room seemed to be the only sign he was there in the first place.

In the last year, Ana and I met three potential dads—and Momma made sure we called them as such. Paolo couldn't be a *father even if he managed to keep away from his 'special bottle', Grant couldn't keep his hands off of Ana's money jar, and Anthony couldn't keep his hands off of Momma. None of that ever stopped her from trying again with the next guy. Her promises for 'something better' always rolling off my back.*

Ana reached over and pushed a loose curl out of my eyes, her own tears threatening to spill over. The comforting touch was fleeting as Ana turned away to wipe her face and take a few deep breaths. She reached for the remote and I wondered where the universe got it wrong. Why couldn't Ana or Aisha be my momma? How did I get stuck with Armatta Arlington?

The TV clicked on to static and Ana changed the channel. She flipped through every station we got on the basic cable package, each displaying the same salt and pepper screen. I used to beg Momma to get us more channels, but my pleas were met with a swift slap across the cheek and a reminder to be 'grateful for what we already have.' I finally stopped asking when Ana told me that Momma couldn't afford the pressure of another monthly bill.

I stayed cuddled on the couch slipping in and out of sleep until Auntie Aisha showed up the next morning. At some point, Ana must've gotten up to get me a blanket because I was wrapped up tight when I awoke to the sounds of hushed voices in the kitchen.

"I don't know when she's coming back. She won't call me." I heard my aunt say.

"Last time she was gone this long she was smoking that stuff. You can't leave us here with her if she's like that again," my sister said, begging my aunt to take us with her.

"You'll be fine," Auntie said.

"You always say that, and nothing is ever fine."

"What do you want me to do about it, girl? I ain't your mother. It's her job to raise y'all. I'm just here to help where I

can." A sigh escaped, filling the room just before her promise. "If she ain't back by tomorrow, you call me and we'll come get y'all for dinner. Here's a twenty for the rest of the week."

Footsteps, the door slamming, and the powerful quiet of understanding.

After Aisha left, Ana sat back down next to me and we waited. I didn't know what we were waiting for until we heard the keys jingling outside. Not until she walked up to us, crouched down to my level like she hadn't abandoned us for a week and planted kisses on our faces like she actually missed us.

Her cold hands rested on my cheeks as she looked me in the eyes and said, "Momma's got it all figured out now, baby. You're gonna change the Arlington women's fate forever."

"Hmm," Marjorie starts, the sound bringing me back to the virid room. "And what exactly did Armatta mean by that?"

My focus shifts to Marjorie, our eyes meeting across a sea of green, "Exactly what she said."

I wrap my arms around myself in an attempt to fight off the chill that was settling around me—a voice in my head telling me to run far, far from this woman and the conversation that was currently choking me. I shift in the seat, my back—stiff with anxiety—screaming in protest as I try to find a sliver of comfort.

"I can see you're a little hesitant to talk about it and that's okay. Let's talk about what brought you in *today*."

The kindness in her tone feels processed, stale. Warning bells clang through my head, reminding me to look for deception hiding between honeyed words. *Safe,* she'd said. Nothing about this is safe, especially not when the walls are pressing in with every wobbled breath I set free.

"I keep pushing everyone away."

"And when do you think you started to push people away? Is this a recent behavior?"

I open my mouth to answer but snap it shut as the words catch in my throat. My eyes jump from the floor to the water bottles to the jungle of plants scattered around the office—anywhere but Marjorie, whose heavy gaze now pins me to the couch in judgment. Tension stretches, thick and relentless, as memories flood my mind. It was funny, in a cruel way. I know exactly when my perfectly tailored life began to unravel.

Two

MAY, SIX MONTHS BEFORE

The sounds of my latest conquest—attempting to slip out of my apartment before the morning sun could shed light on his shameful night—kept me from the sleep I so desperately needed for the day ahead.

Late last night, I called Jaxon, the latest hire at Arlington Nannies, hoping he'd be eager to meet his new boss for drinks. We talked for a couple of hours, tucked in the back corner of a bar in the business-riddled streets of Clayton, before I led him back to my apartment. A part of me hated him for how easy he was to lure in, but the other part of me—the broken and power-hungry side—relished in the ease of the game. For years I'd diminished myself, accepting hurried excuses from men who couldn't elicit an orgasm from a woman if their life depended on it. It seemed like most of the guys I met were the same—detached, boring, and incapable of making me feel anything, in or out of bed.

"Sneaking away? Cold, Jaxon. Just cold," I said, my voice cutting through the darkness. A metallic clang sounded through the room—Jaxon's belt falling to the floor in surprise, if I had to guess. I turned, my curls never leaving the pillow as I tried to pick out his frame in the darkness of my room.

"I, uh…didn't mean to wake you," he said, his voice trembling as hard as the scrawny man in front of me.

"I'd have to be asleep for someone to wake me up, Jax," I said before blowing out a sigh. "It's tragic really."

"What?" His whispered words barely reached me, but I smiled anyway.

"That you couldn't put in enough effort for me to get even a wink of sleep," I let my words drip with the same honeyed tone, an ensnaring smile pulling at the corner of my lips. If the lights were on, I'd surely see his face heating under the pressure of my claims, his hands fumbling for the fallen belt. Like Armatta used to say, *'Men don't like it when you point out their inadequacies.'*

I sighed, pulling my phone from under my pillow, squinting against the glare of the screen. It was only two in the morning—nine hours until I had to meet my family at the church. Jaxon cleared his throat, directing my attention back to him. I looked up, not entirely surprised to find him in the same spot by the door. "Do you need me to dismiss you?"

He shook his head, rows of tight plaits swinging in the moonlight and bolted—the movement comical, like the Looney Tunes soundtrack should've been running in the background. I waited for the sound of my apartment door slamming closed before a bitter laugh let out from my chest.

Yes, after years of being manipulated, I was finally in control.

"Funeral's at eleven, Asha. Don't be late or Aisha will hang me by my toes." AnaMarie's face was plastered with a withering look—half dread, half exasperation. Only my sister could pull it off while still looking utterly beautiful. I couldn't help but roll my eyes at her and the irrational idea that Aisha would do anything to harm her favorite niece. I propped my phone against my bathroom vanity, checking to make sure I was in the frame before dangling two different earrings in front of the camera. I was hoping to get an opinion from Ana who'd been in charge of organizing the ceremony for our Uncle Charles and Junior—Aisha's husband and son.

"Aisha would never," I said, glancing at the time on the screen. *Shit. It's already 9:45.* "That is if my sister would help me choose some earrings so I can get downstairs in time."

"Definitely the black pearls," AnaMarie said, her eyes rolling in the opposite direction of mine. "You haven't worn anything different for like the last ten funerals."

"I haven't even been to ten funerals..." I said, trying to tally them all in my head before shooing away the distraction. I punched the earrings through their holes before making sure they were secured. "I'm on my way. Save me a glass of the good wine!"

"You're starting to sound like Matta. Just hurry up!" AnaMarie whined—her first-born arrogance palpable through the phone—before she hung up. I felt my face tighten at the mention of Matta. Nothing cut deeper than being compared to her—especially when I was trying so damn hard to become everything she wasn't.

According to the story, our mother had met my sister's dad on a random excursion—one of many—to New York but things didn't last. Matta always told us that he was the closest she ever got to actually loving someone, but not for her lack of trying. Nine months later, AnaMarie was born and instantly had my momma and auntie wrapped around her finger. That's what my Aunt Aisha would say. Sometimes I wondered what Ana's life was like for those first few years. Was I the reason that Matta had changed or was it always just as bad?

Armatta met *my* dad on one of her wild excursions overseas. She spoke about him once when I was young and, even then, I knew not to ask again. Aisha said whatever light Matta had before that trip went out the moment she returned. I always just assumed that whatever spark my auntie had seen in Matta's eyes, had died the second she held me in her arms.

Even though Matta's fire had dimmed, there were moments of hope—small sparks of joy that kept us going, like the day my niece was born. Hadley graced us with her unearthly presence when I was just shy of fourteen. Aisha and I passed her back and forth for hours, waiting for her to cry even once, while Ana rested in the hospital bed. From the moment she was born, Hadley filled the room with a quiet strength—even as AnaMarie's heartbroken sobs echoed around her, my truly regal niece just stared up at her with those big, curious eyes.

It had been six years since I'd seen Hadley. And, honestly, I was half-hoping Ana would leave her at home instead of dragging her to such a morbid affair. If I was being honest, the idea of facing my niece, and her weighty, assessing stare after so much time apart was the last thing I wanted to do today—and that's counting the double funeral.

I glanced in the mirror before ordering a car. Ana was right—my dress was the same black number I'd pulled out for every funeral I'd been to in my adult life, the skirt cutting off just above my bony knees. The black pearl earrings Ana helped me choose cascaded down, reaching for the matching string of pearls at my collarbone—the last gift I received from my grandmother and the only one my mother failed to get her hands on. The warmth of a woman I barely knew rushed through my fingertips as I traced over the grooves between the cool spheres. I double-checked my makeup, making sure that every detail was *exactly* how I liked it—a swipe of dark eyeshadow to enhance my mourner's mask, deadly-sharp wings of eyeliner, my last set of eyelashes, and a light layer of gloss all working together to bring out my favorite parts of my face. Half of my natural curls were pinned on top of my head, the rest hovering above my shoulders, coiled and ready to bounce through the day.

A week ago, Aisha was in France visiting Matta—a part of my mother's aggrandized apology plan to spoil her with *my* spoils. She'd started with my aunt, inviting her on an extravagant trip—no charge to Aisha, of course—to atone for her past sins. Ana and Hadley were likely next which, naturally, saved me for last. That's what she'd been doing. Attempting to drag the Arlington women back into her tangled web one expensive excursion after the other.

But, while Aisha was away, Charles and Junior had gone to sleep and never woke up.

Carbon monoxide poisoning, Ana reported when she called to tell me. It was the first time we'd spoken in years, and our conversation ended in silence—neither of us willing to hang up first.

I ran my hands over my dress, smoothing wrinkles that didn't exist. The cut, modest though tight, did its job of accentuating what little curves I possessed. So unlike my sister and mother whose shorter, filled out frames had been a point of jealousy of mine for years. I texted Ana to let her know I was on the way before swapping the stilettos I'd chosen with ballet flats—the black heels sliding perfectly into the burgundy tote bag I'd reserved for funerals.

Turning back to the mirror, I studied the familiar reflection. High cheekbones, a pointed chin, and full lips from my mother—everything else, thankfully, came from the man she refused to talk about. I carefully placed loose curls back in line and wiped away the smudges from around my eyes, the full costume of the day coming together as I practiced my "mourner's smile." A calculated mix of fake pity and restraint—eyebrows pulled together, lips forming a tight, pathetic line. Behind it, the hollow version of me stared back. A honk from outside pulled me from my rehearsal. *One breath in, one breath out.*

A few hours of family chaos and then I could retreat to the security of my apartment. Glancing at the mirror one last time, I dragged myself to the elevator, that smile still firmly glued in place.

❧

I stepped out of the car trying to ignore the anxiety, a near-constant pressure twisting through my stomach, as I looked at the white steeple towering over me. The funeral was, of course, held at our family church—a place vehemently avoided ever since I was forced to spend hours here each week after Ana got pregnant. It was my mother's backwards attempt at proving there was at least one pious and virginal daughter in the family—a stretch to enhance her image of being a perfect person, with a perfect family, who had a perfect life after years of failing to be a decent mom.

Aisha let out a sob when she saw me, pulling me against her chest in a tight hug. I stumbled as her knees buckled, her weight shifting onto me. I tried to help her stand and began scanning the small crowd around us for help. I was just starting to push her toward a chair, desperate to keep both of us on our feet, when a strong hand met my back. I turned to meet a set of blue eyes and dimples that most women would trip into bed for. I let out a breath of surprise as Matthew Scheffter, my business partner, slid into action, gently easing her off of me and into the chair I was aiming for. He sent a wink my way before taking Aisha's hands into his, his eyes meeting hers with a genuineness he normally reserved.

"I'm deeply sorry for your losses, Miss Aisha. I can't imagine what you're going through. Please, if there's anything I can do, don't hesitate to make that grouchy niece of yours give me a call," Scheff said sincerely. I frowned at his choice of description, my arms unconsciously crossing in front of my chest.

"I'm not grouchy, and you're not supposed to be here," I mumbled, the words dripping with irritation. Aisha, oblivious to my tone, pulled Scheff down, wrapping her arms around his shoulders—tighter and longer than the paltry hug she'd offered me—murmuring her thanks. He met her sincerity with a kind smile, sidestepping my glare as if I wasn't even there. *Always one to play a game.*

As he slinked through the ornately carved doors, I couldn't help but wonder why he was in town. His unexpected presence so close to our annual business dinner set my nerves on fire. We'd had the meeting on the calendar for months, and it wasn't like him to be early for anything.

The shift in energy was palpable as we made our way inside the sanctuary, an usher taking Aisha's arm, gently leading her to the front pew. No one mentioned my mother. There seemed to be an unspoken understanding that, even if she was on this continent, she still wouldn't have the time or desire to show up for her sister.

Scheff had found a seat among the crowd, a few rows from the pulpit. Ana and Hadley sat near the back of the church so Ana could quietly direct the ceremony—proof that her incessant need for control hadn't waned in the years since we'd last been close. That left me, the next closest family member, seated beside Aisha. Her frail frame trembled with sobs, guilt and grief radiating from her in waves. I tried to match her sorrow but quickly found myself bored, hiding my face in her shoulder as she cried.

The pastor offered promises about heaven and freedom, preaching about a better life where Charles and Junior could "fly free." I fought the urge to roll my eyes at the sanctimonious crap. Life is shit and then you die. That's all I'd ever been shown.

Afterward, Ana asked me to stand at Aisha's side—my sister on the other as a stream of distant family, friends, and community members passed by, shaking our hands and murmuring their condolences. The stuffiness of the church on such a humid spring day seemed to amplify the musty smell that had been embedded in the carpets since Armatta first dragged us here. Even with the stained-glass windows cracked for ventilation, nothing seemed to quell my burning desire to leave before someone asked me to stay for the reception. Aisha wasn't immune either, her body shaking violently now and then with a bout of coughs.

It wasn't until Scheff, ever the knight in a black Armani suit, made his way to the front of the line that I caught a chance to breathe. I watched as he embraced Ana with a firm squeeze, gave Hadley a polite side hug, and lingered with Aisha in a long, comforting embrace. His mask of sadness melted when he reached me, replaced by a rakish smirk that sent a ripple of something sharper than annoyance searing through my body. Some would say that we were merely close business partners, while others would claim it's much, much more than that. *I* would say it existed on a toxic plane somewhere in between.

"Asha," Scheff said, taking my hand in his. "My condolences." He raised my hand to his lips, lingering just a moment too long.

"Oh, stop it. You're gonna give them something to talk about," I said, swatting his chest before pulling him into a hug. The warmth of his hands on my back and the slight smirk on his face felt dangerous.

"Should I offer to steal you away, or would that be looked down upon?" he asked into my hair, his hand brushing my lower back.

"Please steal me away," I murmured, pulling back as his fingers laced through mine.

"Excuse us," he said with an easy smile, throwing a wink in my direction before turning to the group of mourners. "I need to pick Asha's brain about something. I promise to bring her back soon."

A small twinkle lit Aisha's eyes, though it sputtered out just as quickly. "You know she doesn't want to be here anyhow," she said, waving her hands at us. "Go on. I'll be fine."

Something like regret tightened in my chest as I looked at her frail form. Aisha, Ana, and I used to be inseparable. I shook my head before old memories of sunlit afternoons could claw their way in. A brutal cough wracked her frame, and before I could react, Ana was looping an arm around her to steady her fragile body.

"Thanks for coming, Ash," Aisha said, her words muffled behind a tissue.

"Of course," I replied, watching her trembling hands pull another tissue from her purse. My eyes flicked to Ana, her glare promising a future conversation. "I'll see you soon, Aisha."

Scheff gave my hand a slight tug, guiding me through the dense crowd still gathered at the front of the church. As we weaved between familiar faces and strangers alike, I let my gaze wander. Call me a cynic, but there was no convincing me that everyone in this room truly cared about my uncle and cousin.

We eventually made our way outside, and I sucked in a deep breath, grateful for the fresh air clearing the lingering heaviness from my chest. A light breeze blew between us, and I gently pried my hand from his. "Why are you here, Scheff?"

"Is it so wrong for me to check on my business partner after a family tragedy?" he asked, lips twitching with amusement. Classic Scheff—always answering a question with another question.

"No, but I wasn't expecting you for a month. I don't have any reports ready yet," I said, my eyes drifting back toward the church as the faint strains of the organ floated through the cracked windows. It wouldn't be long before everyone started filing out.

"I'm just here to see you, Asha. I heard about everything and wanted to check in. Sue me for being a good friend."

"I don't know if I'd consider us friends anymore, Scheff. Good to know you can be one, though," I said dryly, my tone laced with an edge.

"Funny." He shot me a playful glare, his hands sinking into his pockets. "I planned to stop by the office tomorrow. Think you can make some space for me?"

"How long are you staying?"

"Depends."

Nothing was ever solid with Scheff. Our business was the only constant—he'd always been upfront about that.

Fucking Scheff. Matthew Scheffter intrigued me from the

moment I noticed him at freshman orientation. We wound up standing next to each other in the back of the lecture hall, his towering frame drawing my attention. When I finally felt brave enough to sneak a glance, the shadows under his eyes only amplified the discomfort that seemed to seep from his pale skin. His awkwardly long limbs were swallowed by an oversized black sweatshirt, doing a disservice to the attractive boy underneath.

I hadn't been with a white boy before but couldn't deny the pull I felt toward him. Maybe it was curiosity more than genuine interest, but I needed to find out what was behind those tired eyes.

We shared a few classes that first semester but never spoke. Occasionally, I'd catch him staring, and, still nervous about starting college and taking the opportunity to reinvent myself, I'd look away quickly, heat rushing to my cheeks. A few weeks in, I started finding small silver flowers left at my seat. Gum wrappers, folded delicately into intricate shapes—a daisy, a rose, even a stalk of lavender.

It was daunting—trying to maintain a calm demeanor while he stared from across the room. Still, I found myself eager to discover which flower would appear next.

Months into the semester, he finally sat beside me. I watched as he slowly reached over, his fist trembling slightly, and dropped a handful of those tiny gum wrapper flowers onto my desk. They scattered, some slipping to the floor. I rushed to pick them up, only to knock heads with him in the process.

"Sorry," he mumbled, cheeks flushing pink as his eyes darted everywhere but my face.

"I'm Asha," I whispered, trying not to smile too much.

"Scheff. Well, Matthew Scheffter, but everyone just calls me Scheff."

Up close, I noticed the sandy highlights threading through his bright blonde hair as he nervously ran a hand through it. He wasn't just awkward—he was endearing.

It wasn't long before we were inseparable.

Four years later, I'd come to know him as a take-no-shit, business-minded man—a perfect match for my ambitions and his father's trust fund. Together, we spent a year building the foundation for the company that became everything I'd dreamed of.

We even tried dating, once. Although, neither of us thought it would last, and we ended things with an amicable dinner followed by a very passionate night together. Since then, we'd existed in a strange in-between: definitely my best, and only friend, definitely business partners, and occasional fuck-buddies.

However temporary I intended our connection to be, he ended up helping me lay the foundation for Arlington Nannies which solidified his place in my life. With his financial backing came the lifelong commitment to an annual dinner in order to ensure things stayed in "tip-top shape"—his words, not mine. In reality, our arrangement was two old classmates grabbing dinner, pretending to chat about business before fucking each other senseless then proceeding to ignore the other's existence for the rest of the fiscal year.

I took the time to look him over, noticing the subtle changes that a year could bring. Long gone was the boy who gifted me gum-wrapper flowers freshman year. On second thought, after all of my failed sexual encounters this year, I might even be happy to have him home early.

"You changed your beard up a bit," I said, reaching for his chin. The last time I saw him, he was letting it grow free and wild. The sandy blonde hair was now cut close to his face, barely more than a shadow.

"It was starting to scare people off," he said with a smirk, grabbing my hand and pulling it to his lips.

"*Scheff,*" I hissed, pulling my hand away. "Stop being so touchy. Why…What…How long are you here?"

"So many questions, Asha. Why don't you join me for dinner tonight and we can get into the messy details."

"I can't tonight. I have plans." *Lie.*

"Hmm—" his phone buzzed and he quickly pulled it from his pocket—always tuned in to work. "Then I'll text Kate and have her set something up for us."

"Perfect. She'll be happy to know you're in town." *Lie.*

"You really should consider giving her some time off now and then. You know, before you run her ragged."

"She knows what she signed up for. I gave her a trial period."

Kate had worked as my assistant for three years and hadn't complained once. She always spoke her mind without hesitation and I doubted she'd keep any discontent from me.

Scheff laughed, the sound stirring something deep inside me—memories of late-night pizza runs and planning for the future. I couldn't help but smile at him.

"It's good to see you." I said, pulling him in for one more hug, breathing in the alluring smell of his cedar shampoo and the cologne he refused to tell me the name of. He claimed I would turn around and give it to the first man I found, rendering Scheff 'inconsequential which would break' his heart. His dramatics aside, I did miss him.

"The pleasure, as always, Asha dear, is mine. We'll talk soon." Scheff offered me a final wink before slipping into a car that seemed to materialize out of thin air.

I turned, taking one last look at the church, silently hoping it would be years before I had to set foot inside it again. Pulling my phone from my purse, I requested a ride and swapped out my stilettos for the worn flats tucked away at the bottom of my bag. Relief spread through my aching feet as the car pulled up just in time to save me from awkward small talk with people I didn't care about as they spilled out of the church.

As we drove away, I spotted Ana and Hadley gently guiding Aisha down the steps, each one supporting her frail frame. A pang of guilt racked through me as Hadley's focus snapped to me—her all-knowing gaze finally finding time to pin me down. I focused on the rumble of the car engine and the comforting hum of distance growing between me and the church instead of the judgemental curiosity in my niece's eyes.

I stripped out of my dress as soon as I locked my apartment door, leaving it in a heap on the floor as I beelined for the bedroom in search of my nightshirt. The comforting fabric brushed against my skin like a balm, but before I could even think about washing off my makeup, the violent buzz of my phone shattered the brief moment of peace.

Evil Incarnate. The screen practically sneered at me.

I groaned, dragging my finger across the screen. "Hello, Armatta," I said, letting sarcasm lace my tone. I hadn't called her *Momma* in years, and the idea of doing so now felt like a joke.

"Asha, so good to hear your voice." Her words were lacquered with her signature false sweetness, the kind that usually heralded a favor or concealed an insult. She paused, leaving a space wide enough for me to drive the conversation wherever I wanted. I took the bait.

"It's late there. What do you want?" I replied, my annoyance crackling through the line.

"Oh, sweet girl, it's a beautiful night in Paris! I start my days late here—so much easier to enjoy all the beauty my Parisian companions offer into the wee hours."

Ah, yes. Armatta Arlington, my mother, the Parisian princess, living off the fruits of my labor—no doubt racking up charges on the credit card attached to my account.

I put the call on speaker and unlocked my phone, eager for a distraction against Armatta's rambling. One new text from Jaxon and at least eight emails I had no intention of reading until morning.

Jaxon: I really didn't mean to offend you, Asha. Please, let's just talk about all of this.

He wasn't a bad guy, and I couldn't blame him for wanting to clarify things. But that didn't change the joy I felt in playing with a man's emotions. *I can't imagine losing you, my ass.*

My reply? *Don't fuck up at work, and we won't have anything to talk about.*

I walked into the bathroom, setting my phone on the counter beside the sink as my mom droned on about her calorie count and how she "simply can't stop eating these lovely croissants."

Closing my eyes, I let my head sink into my shoulders. Maybe if I pretended to fall asleep, she'd hang up. I was mourning, after all—someone had to.

"Asha, I really think you should fly out and see me for a while. When was the last time you had a proper adventure?" Armatta's voice snapped me back from whatever half-sleep I was pretending to be in.

"Matta, no. I'm busy. Two new employees are onboarding this week, meetings already scheduled for the month, and every bit of free time in between is accounted for." My words spilled out matter-of-factly, the truth of my constantly in-motion life. Between client meetings and media obligations, my existence had long since become a stream of tasks. I ate in Ubers, drank coffee while walking, and handled calls with new clients while onboarding staff. My mind had always run on six cylinders, so it made sense that my life did too.

"Why must you take that tone with me? What have I done, Asha Marie?" she replied bitterly.

"It's just been a long day, Matta." I sighed, setting my phone on the bathroom vanity. "That's all." My voice echoed through the tiled space as I waited for her reply.

"Mmm," she drawled, her tone dripping with disapproval. "Well, I just wanted to see how you were holding up. I'm sorry I couldn't make it for the funeral. A tragedy, of course." The pause in her voice made it unclear whether she was referring to the funeral itself or her absence.

"Yes, I feel so sad for Auntie. All of her family just...gone. She's been through so much in the last few weeks." The rehearsed niceties I'd deployed all day easily repeating, as though they were truly meant for this moment.

I poured a measure of powdered cleanser into my palm, watching it mix with the water, turning into a thick scrub. Pressing it into my skin, I let the grit bite into me, tiny claws scratching away the residue of the day.

'*Harder*,' the voice in my head urged.

I pressed harder, like I could sand down the layers of frustration Armatta always managed to coat my skin with.

"Yes, so hard. Sometimes I wonder if it's for the best that I never found a father for you girls. Less heartbreak in lovers," Armatta said with a wistful sigh.

I laughed, the sound amusingly dry. "Don't act like you never tried. You had a new man in that apartment every weekend, and you know it."

I took a deep breath and leaned toward the faucet to rinse

the scrub from my face. The bubbles swirled around the drain, rushing down as if they couldn't escape fast enough. I wished they could take me with them.

"Oh, hush. You're all grown up now. *Let it go*, Asha," she replied coolly—as if she weren't responsible for most of the scars etched into my childhood. "Maybe if you ever had a relationship of your own, you wouldn't act so brash when I muse. All you need is someone to shove his–"

"I'm hanging up now! My ears are bleeding!" I cut her off, my finger hovering over the red button, desperate to end the call before she could dig further into my love life.

"Hold on! I called you for a reason," she said sharply, halting me mid-motion. My shoulders slumped as I rested my hands on the counter, staring at the mirror. I blew out a heavy breath, frustration tightening my chest. The reflection staring back at me was razor-edged, cutting straight through me.

"What?" I asked flatly, already bracing for her latest favor. Knowing her, it could range anywhere from a new outfit to a fully customized Range Rover with chromed-out rims.

For once, it seemed like asking me for something actually bothered her. I could practically see the way her face must have pinched in disgust—not at needing help, but at whatever task she was about to ask *me* to do.

"I called for someone to go out and take a look at Aisha's house. I don't think it's a coincidence that Charles and Junior passed while she was visiting. I fear there is something... amiss. He'll be over Thursday at five. Do you think you could handle it? I don't want to bother Aisha while she's... grieving," she finally sputtered out, her voice tight with something that almost sounded like concern. Almost.

I frowned, already wondering why she wouldn't just ask AnaMarie. Of all the people to step in for something like this, "Why me? I just told you my schedule is jam-packed, Matta.

How am I supposed to fit this in when you didn't even think to ask about my time or commitments?"

"He came highly recommended, and I didn't want to wait for something to happen to her. She's my only sister, you know. You'd think you'd want to help, considering you only have one sister yourself."

Oh, the guilt. Obligation, frustration, and guilt. The holy trinity of being Armatta Arlington's daughter.

"Fine. Whatever. Send the details to Kate, and she'll try to fit it in. Next time, call someone else," I snapped, hanging up before she could add another impossible favor to her list.

I rinsed my face one last time, grabbing a small towel from the dwindling pile next to the sink. I patted my skin dry, making a mental note to start a load of laundry soon. Tossing the towel into the bin of used linens, I reached for the light switch—pausing as I caught my reflection in the mirror.

'Ugly,' the voice, alive and unrelenting in my mind, hissed through the void. *'Ugly, hideous face. Why couldn't you have skin like Ana's? Why does everything about you scream worthless?'*

Rage shimmered in the empty eyes that glared back at me. The intensity burned holes through the fragile facade I'd spent years perfecting. I closed my eyes slowly, letting the overwhelming weight of dread curl around me. The sharp, tight heat that came only when the voice rattled through my brain twisted deep in my stomach—a nauseating truth I couldn't escape: *ugly, hideous, worthless.*

My breath hitched as I reached again for the light switch. The faint click echoed louder than it should have, the bathroom plunging into darkness. But even as I left, I swore those hollow eyes followed me.

THREE

Being my own boss theoretically meant I could start the workday whenever I felt like it—but theories didn't pay the bills. A comforting heat warmed my face as I blinked against the haze of sleep, a low groan slipping from my lips as blood prickled back into my limbs. I squinted toward the clock on the pristine white wall, its hands edging toward eight in the morning.

Rolling onto my side, I reached blindly for my phone teetering on the edge of the nightstand. Once in hand, I pushed myself upright, blinking at the glowing screen as I scrolled through the few emails that had landed in my inbox overnight. The usual suspects: anxious parents vying for a spot on the Arlington Nannies waitlist, and Kate, the saint that she was, corralling the chaos of my week with her carefully worded plans. After skimming each message, I reached for the glass of lukewarm water beside my bed and drained it in a few unceremonious gulps, eager to soothe my parched throat.

As founder and CEO of Arlington Nannies, my days followed a reliable rhythm. Wake up. Drink a cup—or three—

of coffee. Waste twenty minutes choosing a power outfit to project the right balance of control and charm. Sweep my curls into a perfectly slicked back ponytail and sprint out the door to meet Kate for our daily coffee meeting. She had a knack for sniffing out quirky cafes tucked into unsuspecting corners of the city, turning our morning meetings into a caffeine-fueled scavenger hunt. I didn't mind—it gave us a quiet reprieve from the noise of the office and a chance to align on the day ahead.

Kate had come into my life about a year after I started the company. Just three years younger, she shared a sharp wit and no-nonsense attitude that made her indispensable—a welcome change from my first hag of an assistant, who insisted on being called "*Miss* Tabitha" and refused to perform even the simplest tasks. Miss Tabitha didn't last, quitting in a dramatic flourish, citing me as "too demanding." Enter Kate, my saving grace in a sea of mediocrity.

"Play 'Asha's Morning Mix,'" I called out, my voice echoing through the quiet. Hidden speakers hummed to life, and Bill Withers crooned about a "lovely day," the soulful notes filling the stillness of my home. I let the music set the tone, rinsing the empty water glass and slotting it into the dishwasher.

I danced down the hallway and twirled into my bedroom's walk-in closet—a space so expansive it dwarfed the living room and kitchen of the apartment I grew up in. Kicking off my slippers, I let my toes sink into the cool plush carpet, savoring the sensation. The high ceilings, a staple throughout my apartment, truly shone here, drawing attention to the custom shelving units wrapping around the room, measured to the millimeter of perfection. On one side, sleek black cabinets concealed my work attire, formal gowns, and collection of comfort wear. But my destination lay on the opposite side, where the closet opened into a small sunroom. The morning light poured through the glass, warming the space like a personal invitation from the sun itself. I lingered in the glow, allowing it to soak into my skin before the music drifting through the apartment lured me back into motion.

I pulled out a black satin pencil skirt I'd thrifted years ago, a particularly lucky find, pairing it with a classic plum-colored short-sleeved silk blouse from Neiman Marcus. My favorite black stilettos and a simple blazer rounded out the ensemble. I laid the outfit over the sunroom couch and, satisfied with it, I waltzed back to the kitchen, greeted by the rich aroma of freshly brewed coffee.

I took a sip, the liquid sliding over my tongue with a satisfying burn that barely registered anymore. *My Way* crooned through the speakers, Frank Sinatra's voice tangling with the melody in a way that felt like a dance. I let the rhythm guide me into the bathroom, coffee still in hand, as I turned on the shower, cranking the dial as hot as it would go.

The steam swirled around me as I washed away the residue of yesterday, the grime and weariness swirling down the drain. I stepped into the humidity, the air thick against my skin, and wrapped myself in a towel before returning to the closet. Dressed and ready to tackle the day, I finished my makeup—swiping a final coat of mascara over my lashes just as my phone dinged, signaling the arrival of my ride.

By the time I reached the meeting spot—a small café fifteen minutes from the office—Kate was already hard at work. Through the window, I saw her perched at a corner table, her laptop open and two lattes placed strategically on either side. Her pen moved frantically over the pages of her ever-present notebook, pausing only when she swiped at the rogue curl tumbling onto her face. The rest of her loose, blonde curls framed her sharp features, tucked behind her ears and resting on her squared shoulders. Her brows furrowed as she reached for her phone, typing feverishly—no doubt fine-tuning my calendar or addressing an employee slip-up I hadn't yet caught.

Kate made the world turn and managed to look astounding while doing it.

I thanked the driver and stepped out into the muggy embrace of St. Louis's unpredictable May weather. The month always felt like an enigma—either sweltering heat pressed onto your shoulders or a cool breeze sneaking into your lungs. Today, the air was heavy with the promise of summer, wrapping itself around me like a weighted blanket as I made my way toward Kate and the day ahead.

"Good morning," I said, sauntering up to the table with a practiced ease.

"Good morning!" Kate chirped, far too energized for the hour. Her eyes sparkled with mischief as her brows arched into a question. "You must've had a visitor over the weekend. What has you in such high spirits?"

"Oh, stop it. I can do as I please...and whomever I please." I smirked, dropping my purse into the open seat next to me and punctuating the statement with a wink.

Her groan was instant, perfectly manicured hands flying up to cover her face. "Oh God, tell me it wasn't a staff member again. Please! I had to do *so* much damage control last time."

"It was just Jaxon," I said with a laugh, waving her concern away like a pesky fly. "He'll be fine." I reached for the menu, but Kate's head fell dramatically onto her folded arms, earning another burst of laughter from me. The sound was a bit too loud for the café's subdued hum, drawing startled looks from nearby tables. Across the room, a waiter fumbled a tray of dishes, his honey-toned cheeks flushing a deep shade of red when our eyes met. I gave him a small wave before turning back to Kate, whose over-dramatic sigh of exasperation rivaled the crash of broken plates.

"Do you ever get tired of leading men around like dogs?" she asked, her eyes glued to her phone as her fingers flew across the screen.

"Now, *that* is a question I might entertain if it hadn't come from my assistant," I replied smoothly. "But don't you think you're a little too busy to delve into my personal life?"

Kate's fingers paused mid-typing as she glanced up, her honey-brown eyes locking on mine. "Funny enough, my job has *everything* to do with your life—personal or otherwise."

"Well, good thing you're compensated fairly, right?" I quipped, studying her over the edge of the menu.

Her lips curved into a knowing smirk as she leaned back in her chair, her posture as confident as ever. It was moments like these that reminded me how much Kate thrived on keeping up with me—not just in work but in wit.

When I first met Kate, I'd been struck by her effortless beauty. The kind that didn't demand attention but commanded it anyway. Her hair coiled and tucked in perfect spirals that framed her high cheekbones, and she had a figure that made her stand out in any room she walked into. I once overheard her casually mentioning she'd had a "glow-up" after high school, but I couldn't imagine a version of Kate that wasn't radiant. She rarely wore makeup—some mascara here, a gloss across her full lips there—and still managed to look flawless. It was a beauty so understated it could make you forget she was just as sharp as she was stunning.

Kate and I had met entirely by accident—just minutes after I fired Miss Tabitha and decided to finish the day at a nearby coffee shop. It wasn't the best place for beverages, and the interior carried an odd smell—something between burnt eggs and peanut butter—that always required an adjustment period, but its proximity to the office made up for it. The cramped dining room was a blessing in disguise; it kept most patrons from lingering, turning it into my unofficial workspace when I needed a breather.

I was checking emails on my phone when I collided with someone significantly shorter than me, her silky curls bouncing into my face as the tray of drinks she was holding tipped forward. A stream of liquid spilled down the front of my shirt.

"Oh my gosh, I am so sorry! Let me get you cleaned up," she *stammered, her words stretching out in a syrupy southern drawl.*

Annoyance pulled my brows together as I stood there, cold coffee seeping through the fabric of my blouse. Before I could protest, she darted to the bar and returned with a towel, dabbing at my shirt with more enthusiasm than precision.

I sucked in a slow breath, biting back my irritation, and gently grabbed her wrist. "It's fine," I said, forcing a laugh.

Her face brightened, tears glistening in her wide eyes. "Thank you. It's my first week, and I'm so clumsy, and I really don't want to get fired and—"

"We all gotta start somewhere," I said, offering a tight smile.

She sniffed, wiping at her eyes, and motioned for me to sit. I tugged my cardigan tighter around myself, trying to ignore the cold, sticky stain spreading across my chest.

"Can I get you something to drink? On the house, of course," she offered, pulling out a notepad and a fuzzy-tipped pink pen from her apron pocket.

"Just a vanilla latte, please." I opened my laptop with the intention of salvaging what was left of my afternoon.

"Coming right up!" she chirped, practically dancing away

on her toes. I couldn't decide if her boundless energy was endearing or grating—maybe both.

For months after the spill, I returned to that café and watched Kate. She was everywhere at once, moving between tables with effortless charm, greeting new patrons while somehow still managing to scribble in her ever-present notebook during stolen moments. Curiosity got the better of me.

"What are you always writing?" I asked as she passed by my table.

Kate's cheeks turned the faintest shade of pink. "I wanna be a writer," she admitted, her voice soft. "It's better to jot something down real quick than let it get away from me."

"Then be a writer," I replied, tilting my head. "Don't hide it."

She glanced toward the café's gruff owner, perched at the bar with a scowl. "If the boss man catches me, he'll probably fire me," she said, her fingers twitching toward the notebook tucked in her apron.

"Then let me be your boss," I said before I could second-guess myself. Her eyes widened, mirroring my own surprise of the offer.

Kate's gaze flicked between me and the owner, her lip caught between her teeth. Then, as if the realization hit all at once, she squealed—actually squealed—and threw her arms around me in a hug that knocked me off balance.

"When can I start?" she asked, her bubbly personality fully on display.

I shook the memory from my head, returning my attention to the present. Across the table, Kate's leg bounced anxiously as her phone vibrated against the woodtop, the persistent buzzing filling the space between us until the call dropped.

"You could've answered that, you know?" I said, setting the menu down on the table with a soft thud.

"It's okay," Kate replied, her lips pressing into a tight line. "It's nothing important. Probably just Gretta checking in about dinner or something," she said, referring to her long-time girlfriend, Gretta, who owned a restaurant in Ucity called TEMITOPE. She was a huge reason as to why I hadn't died of starvation these last few years. They'd been together as long as I'd known Kate, Gretta being the fiery contrast to my assistant's quirky yet calm composition.

"It must not be if you can't stop staring at it and it won't stop ringing," I said, letting an edge of sarcasm thread through my voice.

"It's *nothing*, Asha. Leave it at that." Her hand darted out to snatch the phone off the table, shoving it deep into her bag. *Weird*.

"Oh, so now we're shutting down? The week's just starting, Kate. Talk to me."

"When have you *ever* wanted to talk?" she snapped, her voice low but biting. The buzzing phone had been replaced by the rhythmic knock of her leg bouncing against the table, as relentless as a car blinker left on in rush hour traffic.

I made it clear to Kate when she started working for me: she was my assistant, not my friend. Our arrangement was simple—she worked around my demanding schedule, and in return, I gave her the time and resources to write. It was a clean, professional agreement. Or, at least, it was supposed to be.

Her words struck a nerve, and I felt my shoulders tighten, my body bracing instinctively for a fight. But instead of snapping back, I exhaled slowly—a technique Ana drilled into me when I was younger, one of her many unsolicited "calming exercises." My shoulders eased as I spoke again, my voice measured. "I want you to feel comfortable telling me things, Kate. As long as—"

"'As long as it pertains to work and helps us build toward a better working environment.' Yeah, I get it," she interrupted, her tone clipped.

That same loose chunk of hair slipped over her face, but this time, she didn't bother brushing it away. Her leg stilled under the table, but the tension radiating off her was palpable. If she didn't want to talk, I wasn't going to force her.

"Cool. Maybe it's best for us to just meet in the office today," I said, pushing my chair back and collecting my things. "I'll be in by eleven. Have my breakfast and coffee waiting. Maybe you'll be ready to talk when I see you next."

As I turned for the door, I heard her mutter something under her breath. Something like, "treating employees like children." I stopped mid-step, my heel grinding against the pristine checkerboard floor. Slowly, I turned back.

"What did you say, Kate?"

Her honey-brown eyes met mine, and for a moment, I was back in that crummy café, staring at a nervous twenty-year-old girl with tears brimming in her eyes. But this time, there was no bubbly energy or frantic apologies—just sadness. My chest tightened as the realization hit: this time, maybe *I* was the evil boss in her story.

I rubbed a hand over my heart, trying to brush away the guilt clawing at me as I waited for her response. Hoping, foolishly, that she'd give in and tell me what was wrong.

"Nothing, Asha," she said quietly, her voice barely above a whisper. "I'll see you in a bit."

I turned again, my heels clicking against the tile as I headed for the door. Kate had a strict no-grime policy when it came to eateries; even the faintest hint of a sticky floor would send her—and me—scrambling for a better option. Even the spotless floor couldn't distract me from the sinking feeling in my chest.

I hovered by the front door, glancing back to see her slumped over the table, her usually sleek curls looking dull under the harsh overhead lights. There were deep shadows under her eyes, and the warmth I'd usually find there had dimmed—like someone had turned off her light all at once. My mouth twitched as a thousand possible words ran through my head, none of them feeling quite right. What comfort could I offer without breaking the walls I'd so carefully constructed?

I offered her an awkward wave before bolting for the door, desperate for fresh air and a break from the whirlwind of emotions my loyal assistant stirred in me.

I stepped outside, greeted by the steady hum of morning pedestrians weaving through the city. As I waited for the light to change, I ordered a car, debating which park to visit before heading into the office. Mondays were always packed—meetings with families and potential caretakers, tech updates, and all the other typical bullshit that had made its way to my desk. A quiet moment before the chaos felt necessary today.

The red flashing hand finally gave way to the white outline of a walking figure, signaling my escape. I'd barely taken three steps into the street when the blare of a horn shattered my focus. An old, beat up truck skidded to a stop beside me, the driver throwing his hands up in exaggerated frustration. I shot him a middle finger, added a chorus of insults for good measure, and deliberately sauntered across the street, using the full thirty seconds allotted for my crossing. *What the fuck is happening today?*

A sleek, black sedan pulled up as I checked my phone for updates. The window rolled down, revealing an older man in a plaid flat cap. "Asha?" he called, leaning over the console.

I nodded, double-checking the license plate before sliding into the cool leather seat. The sudden drop in temperature was a welcome relief from the oppressive heat outside. I sent my live location to Kate—another subtle reminder that she needed to be in the office before me—and tucked my phone into my purse. Outside the window, the city blurred into motion as we headed toward Shaw Park, a small, lush space just across from the Arlington Nannies building.

I'd come up with the exact idea for the company back in undergrad. Scheff and I had just finished babysitting his sister's kids—a gig we'd take sometimes for extra cash—when the thought struck me. At first, I'd planned to work independently, finding families, building my resume, and carving out a career. But Scheff, ever the strategist, pushed me to dream bigger. Together, we dissected the industry: shadowing established agencies, attending interviews, and picking apart contracts. We learned what worked, what didn't, and how to bridge the gaps.

Our model was simple: national rates for families, above-average pay for childcare providers. It was a win-win, and the pride I felt every time I approached our building was undeniable.

Scheff had found the office space himself, surprising me one night by claiming he'd found the "perfect apartment." He paid the first year's rent, insisting I focus on launching the business; and every year since, he'd returned to write another check. The five-story building, though modest in height, stretched across half a city block. The ground floor housed a dentist, an accountant, and a law office. Arlington Nannies took up the top floor, complete with a rooftop "tranquility zone" Kate had masterminded, turning it into a haven for the staff. I often suspected she spent more time there than anyone else, but I didn't mind. Even I found solace in its quietude.

The car pulled into the lot, and I stepped out into the sticky morning air, the humidity wrapping itself around me like a damp blanket. I inhaled deeply, hoping for relief, but the thick air barely budged. Shaw Park, just a short walk away, called to me, and I let my feet guide me toward the walking paths.

The park never failed to quiet my mind. Verdant greens surrounded me, the chatter of birds mingling with the rustle of trees. Two squirrels darted through the branches above, their playfulness pulling a smile from me. By the time I reached the waterfall, its steady flow bouncing off the rocks, my pulse had steadied. I found my usual bench beneath its partner tree, brushing away any debris before settling down.

This was my favorite spot—*my* sanctuary. From here, I could people-watch and find a reprieve from the turmoil in my head.

Today, that elderly couple shuffling down the hill? They're celebrating 42 years of marriage, though she'd loved his brother first. A life of resentment later, they'd found each other again and tried to make it work. Those two boys racing their bikes behind me? They don't know one of them is adopted, the other a byproduct of a one-night stand. The high schoolers sneaking through a hidden maintenance path to make out? One will leave for college, desperate to forget, while the other clings to what they thought they'd share forever.

Sometimes I wonder—does someone ever sit on a bench and make up a story about me?

'You wish you were like them, but you never will be. Freaks of nature don't fit in anywhere.'

I walked into the office, the comforting smell of fresh coffee and a toasted bagel drawing my eyes to the desk where both waited for me—a testament to the benefits of sharing my location with Kate. I hung my purse on the hook by the door, then rounded the desk to pull out my chair. Kicking off my heels, I let my feet sink into the soft rug Kate had insisted on putting under my desk. Small luxuries in those early days, but ones I'd come to appreciate.

After a few steadying breaths, I reached for the intercom to summon her, but before I could press the button, a soft knock sounded at the door.

"Kate?" I called hesitantly, lowering my hand. The door eased open, and my assistant appeared, her arms teetering under the weight of an unwieldy stack of files. The pile tilted precariously and then, inevitably, collapsed in a flurry of papers.

"Shit!" she hissed, making a frantic attempt to catch the falling files, only to send them scattering even farther.

A giggle bubbled out of me as I rounded the desk, crouching to help her gather the mess.

"Oh, hush," she snapped, her cheeks flushing a deep pink. "I didn't want to make two trips."

"There are too many people here for you to refuse to ask for help, Kate," I teased, shoving papers into random files with no regard for their order. "And they like you."

She huffed, stacking the files that remained intact onto my desk. "These were supposed to be the match list for the entire year. Families, nannies, case managers—all perfectly organized. I spent hours on it." Her voice was tight, and her hands trembled as she shuffled papers into a semblance of order.

I glanced at her face, catching the subtle swipe of her hand under her eye, and felt my stomach twist. Whatever had been weighing on her earlier was still there. She plastered on a smile—a forced expression as fake as the plastic flowers she'd arranged on my bookshelf months ago in a misguided attempt to "brighten up the space." The real bird of paradise plant in the corner fared better, thanks to Kate's diligence and its stubborn will to live.

"Thank you, Kate. I'll take a look at these later today," I said softly, unsure of how to offer her comfort. Another awkward wave wouldn't do much good.

I sank back into my chair as Kate sank into the one across from me, her trusty notebook and her beloved, fuzzy pink pen balanced on her lap.

"Okay," I began cautiously. "Let's get started. But first—about this morning—"

"Of course, Asha. It won't happen again," she cut in, her eyes fixed on the chipped corner of my desk.

"No, that's not what I—"

"You don't have to worry, and I'm sorry for my disruptive mornin'. I don't wanna do anything to jeopardize this job," she added, her tone clipped.

We locked eyes for a few seconds, and I tried to read the storm behind her gaze. What had happened over the weekend to rattle her so much? And was it just this weekend?

'Sounds like worries for a friend, Asha,' the voice in my head murmured.

I pushed the thought aside, though it lingered, and focused instead on the subtle shifts in Kate's demeanor over the past few weeks. How long had she been off-kilter like this?

Before I could find the words to probe deeper, she flipped open her notebook, her tone all business as she launched into the weekly report and calendar rundown. It was precisely what should've happened earlier in place of her...meltdown.

I jotted down key points, letting her words wash over me.

If she needed to outrun whatever haunted her, I wouldn't stand in her way—not yet. When she finally finished, her eyes studied me, searching for something I couldn't name before she gave a quick double-knock on the desk, stood, and turned to leave.

"Oh, Kate," I called just as she reached the door. She paused, her hand on the knob.

"Did my mother send over the details for that appointment on Thursday? Fit that in so I don't have to deal with the wrath of Armatta, please."

Kate nodded, her voice steady but detached. "I bumped your four o'clock appointment to next week and scheduled your dinner with Scheff for eight, so you'll have plenty of time to make it to Aisha's and back. Let me know if you need anything else."

She closed the door behind her, leaving me alone with the faint scent of coffee and a nagging sense of unease.

The week flew by in a blur of meetings, emails, and the monotony of routine. But, by the time Thursday arrived, I couldn't shake the feeling that the other shoe was about to drop. Despite the rough start with Kate, everything seemed to be running smoothly. Too smoothly.

I'd learned early on that owning a business meant living on borrowed time between crises. Just when things felt stable, a client would inevitably call, announcing that the nanny they'd handpicked—against my advice—wasn't the right fit. Then they'd insist I find someone new while ignoring every suggestion I made. Most of the time, I didn't mind; it padded the billable hours. But on days when the complaints came in waves, it felt like I was drowning in the endless demands of other people, my life slowly consumed by their needs.

Still, Kate and I had found a comfortable middle ground. Our conversations were shorter, devoid of any banter, and strictly professional. For all I knew, she was as boring as I was, and I intended to preserve that image for the duration of her employment. At least, that's what I told myself.

'Whatever you can do to make shit easier on yourself, huh, Asha?' the voice taunted, beckoning me toward another odious spiral.

The intercom buzzed, cutting through my thoughts. Kate's voice crackled through the speaker. "Asha, your car will be here in five minutes to take you to your aunt's house. I also sent a list of potential matches for the Peterson family to your email. If you get the chance, can you review them and send the go or no-go to the staff inbox before the end of the day?"

"Ah, you're an angel. Thank you!" I said, my voice brightening. Just as I was about to release the button, an idea gnawed at the edges of my mind. "Oh, and Kate... why don't you take off for the night? Hell, everyone can go home." I hesitated, debating my next words and how they would land. "Actually, enjoy tomorrow off too. I won't be coming in, and everyone already has their assignments. Maybe you and Gretta could do something fun."

I lifted my finger from the intercom, waiting for her response. I couldn't remember the last time I'd taken a day off, which meant Kate likely hadn't either. The thought of my upcoming dinner with Scheff had me preemptively nursing a phantom migraine—one that would inevitably transform into a very real hangover by morning. No work would get done tomorrow, so why force us both to pretend otherwise?

"Asha, are you sure?" she asked, her voice hesitant. "With

the Peterson account and onboarding wrapping up this week, I'm happy to step in while you're out."

"No need," I replied breezily. "I'll have Glen in HR handle the rest of the onboarding, and I'll meet the new staff next week. Can you pencil them in separately? I don't want to mix up their names again. Last time was...less than ideal." I laughed softly, remembering the disaster.

When I'd hired Kate, I ambitiously onboarded five new employees in one go. After their orientation, I made the rookie mistake of asking them all to introduce themselves at once. The flood of information left me hopelessly confused, and I resorted to calling them by numbers instead of names. Glen, the sole survivor of that group, had stuck around; the others left, citing my "inability to perceive them as people." In my opinion, they just couldn't handle a young boss who didn't tolerate nonsense. I didn't mind losing the dead weight.

The intercom buzzed again, breaking my reverie. Kate's tone was as cool as ever. "Got it. Have a great weekend, Asha."

"Thanks, Kate," I replied, glancing toward the office door, half-expecting her to walk in and say goodbye. The moment passed and my phone buzzed with a reminder about the inspector. By the time I left for Aisha's house, Kate was already gone.

Four

Aisha lived just over half an hour outside the city and the drive wasn't terrible. I planned to use the time to finish up some nanny placements but that didn't stop me from requesting reimbursement from Armatta—an amount substantial enough to sting—as I left the office.

'Even though it's your own money,' the voice chimed in.

I didn't even feel bad about it. It was her fault I was headed for Aisha's house of misery.

I nudged my office door shut behind me with a quiet click. The silence crept in, an unwelcome guest that made my skin prickle. My staff was small, but their usual buzz—a mix of low chatter, rustling papers, and the occasional burst of laughter—was the kind of white noise that kept me tethered to the present. Without it, the place felt hollow, like a shell after its occupant had long since scuttled away.

'That's how you know they don't like you,' the voice snickered. *'They can't leave fast enough.'*

I walked through the maze of cubicles, trailing my fingers along the edges of desks as I passed. Little pieces of their lives were scattered everywhere—framed photos of laughing couples with gap-toothed kids, and trinkets from faraway vacations. One desk had a mug proclaiming its owner the *World's Okayest Employee*. It was my staff that made the place feel alive.

I paused, glancing back toward my office. White walls and a desk so barren it might as well come with a Corporate Soullessness Starter Pack. If it weren't for Kate's intervention—things like the tiny succulent now gasping for life in the corner—it would have stayed that way. Another sound from my phone reminded me I was well on my way to being late.

I took one last glance around the large room, letting my pride swell—the tiniest of smiles on my face. Locking the doors, I stepped into the elevator bay, swiping the reminder from my phone screen before dialing Aisha's number.

My chest tightened as the call went straight to voicemail. Aisha usually answered within the first three rings—it was practically her signature. I eventually convinced myself that nothing would happen to her in the next thirty minutes.

I threw a wave toward the building receptionist without looking back, resigning myself to the evening heat that clung to every inch of me. I reached into my purse, fumbling for the pair of sunglasses I always kept stashed inside. The blinding sun rested on my face as my fingers sifted through everything —a mostly empty pack of gum, my headphones, a small notebook, a horde of pens, my wallet, some loose change—but no sunglasses. Finally, my fingers grazed the plastic frames as a honk sounded from the street. I looked up, squinting, only to be greeted by a familiar face.

"Hello, Miss Asha!" the driver called, the 'i' in *Miss* stretching into a long 'e.' "It is me! I am to drive you again!" Rather than waiting inside the car as he had before, Mr. Flat Cap jogged around the vehicle, lunging with dramatic flair to open the back passenger-side door for me. I gave him a nod and a confused smile, sliding into the cool refuge of the car as he jogged back to the driver's seat, wiping a bead of sweat from his brow.

"Did Kate schedule you on purpose?" I asked, unable to keep the corners of my mouth from twitching upward.

"Oh yes, Miss Kate is very nice. She mentioned you might be looking to hire a private driver." *When did we talk about that?*

"Oh...okay." I slid the sunglasses over my face, sinking back into the seat.

"My name is Vladimir. I can be very quiet, very discreet. I would be so happy to have an hourly job, Miss, you have no idea."

I bit the inside of my cheek, weighing the idea of a driver —much less one who promised discretion while chatting nonstop. Vladimir pulled away from the curb, a huge smile plastered across his face as we merged into traffic, heading toward Aisha and her potentially infected house.

"Do you feel comfortable, Miss? Would you like to stop anywhere before we arrive?" Vladimir asked, glancing at me in the rearview mirror.

"No, not unless you know of a bar along the way," I said, half-joking.

"I can take you to the casino off Interstate 70," Vladimir offered, his tone perfectly earnest.

For a fleeting moment, I considered it. A shot before facing the investigator wouldn't be the worst idea. But showing up late to Aisha's house would snowball into being late for dinner, which would lead to Scheff delivering a lecture about "punctuality" and "how it reflects in the business world"—a performance I wasn't willing to endure tonight.

"Probably shouldn't," I said, pinching the bridge of my

nose. A migraine was already forming, and I still had an entire evening ahead of me. "I need to stick to my schedule, but I appreciate the offer."

"Of course, Miss," Vlad replied, catching my gaze in the mirror with his hazel eyes. I quickly looked away, focusing instead on the city blurring past. Prolonged eye contact always felt like an intrusion, as though someone were peeling back layers I wasn't ready to share. Nobody needed to know the truth I kept buried—that my entire being was borderline unstable.

When we first moved to the city, I was always getting lost. The patchwork quilt of neighborhoods—held together by the fragile threads of history, politics, and those city lines that often seemed invisible—made it easy. I'd wander through the brick-exposed roads of Soulard or get caught in the cramped avenues of the Central West End. Ana and I would ride the bus down the county line on Skinker Boulevard, splitting St. Louis City from St. Louis County. But as I grew older, it all started to blur together. I began to see the city for what it really was: a tangle of over ninety different cultures and neighborhoods, each one uniquely beautiful in its own way, rooting itself along the base of the Missouri River Valley. It was always fun to guess who lived where—debating whether the glaring, expensive-looking white woman in her Porsche came from Clayton, or if she was a little more suburban, farther out in Des Peres.

I turned my attention back to the window as we crossed the Missouri River and passed the Ameristar Casino, St. Charles coming into view. "Actually, Vladimir—"

"Call me Vlad. Or Vee. I've always hated my proper name," he interrupted, his directness earning a small nod of approval.

"Okay, Vlad," I began cautiously. The impulse to flirt

flickered for a moment before I remembered that I might want to hire him. "I'll take that drink after I finish up at the house. I might need it before my next stop."

"Of course. I'll have the car waiting, but I need to get some gas after I drop you off. Would you like me to wait or take care of it while you're inside?"

"Go ahead. I'll be in there for about an hour."

We pulled off the interstate and into the suburban hell— an area that always struck me as a relic of a community's desperation to keep Black families from building lives within the city. Aisha had lived here for the past fifteen years, and it suited her—a small-town feel that barely concealed its population of seventy thousand.

For someone like Aisha, raised in a place with less than a third of that, it probably felt big enough. She and Uncle Charles had started out in an apartment a few blocks from the river, raising Junior there for ten years before finding the house they wanted to call home.

It was modest, with a big backyard and a front porch perfect for summer evenings. I'd listened to her excitement drain when Uncle Charles told her it was out of their budget, my heart aching with her. That ache had curdled into resentment when he suggested she ask me to co-sign—a gesture that somehow managed to honor and irritate me all at once.

Still, I'd been proud of her. For the first time in years, she'd made a decision without Armatta's input. But, of course, it came at a cost to me.

It had been her first big purchase, other than the beat-up Toyota Rav4 she'd been clunking around in for years. Without my signature, they probably wouldn't have gotten the house. A smile crept onto my face as I remembered how excited she was when they got the approval.

"Asha! We got it! We got the house!" Auntie's voice burst

through the receiver, so loud I had to pull the phone away from my ear.

"Auntie, slow down! We got what?" I asked, the sound of her excitement tugging a smile across my face.

"The house... Asha, we own a house." Her words were followed by a deep, shuddering sigh, as if she were exhaling the weight of the entire approval process. I heard a soft sniffle on her end, and while she was crying, I knew these weren't tears of disappointment. They were tears of comfort—of joy.

"You got it, Auntie. I'll be by soon for the full tour. Let me know if you need anything, okay?" I said, feeling the edges of my patience retreating. My tolerance for other people's emotions was nearing its limit.

"Aisha and Asha own a home," she murmured to herself. I could hear the pride swelling in her voice, filling the space between us.

"It will always be Auntie Aisha's home," I replied quickly, trying to keep my tone light. "We'll talk soon!" I added, hanging up before her tears could reach through the phone and unsettle the thoughts tethering me to the job that helped make this moment happen.

The memory faded as the crunch of gravel under Vlad's tires signaled our arrival.

Aisha's house stood two stories high, framed by a wide front porch that practically begged you to sit and stay awhile. Peaceful gray siding and ornate columns greeted me, while the driveway and walkway overflowed with lilacs, peonies, and rose bushes, their blooms—waving in the breeze—beckoned me closer. The heady fragrance hit me as soon as I opened the car door, and I couldn't help but think of all the times Aisha had called to fuss about her "flowers just not acting right."

I shut the door behind me and exchanged farewells with Vlad, who promised to return in an hour. Turning back, I made my way down the blossoming path, crouching to touch a velvet-soft rose petal when a buzzing caught my attention.

I froze, my eyes scanning the flowers until the culprit emerged—a thick-bodied bumblebee landing on the bramble beside my hand. We both stilled, sizing each other up. Me, watching his graceful pollen retrieval. Him, deciding if I warranted a kamikaze mission. I waited, tracking the bee's movement as pollen coated his legs.

Sunlight filtered through the trees, scattering golden streaks across my skin. For a moment, crouched there among the blooms, I felt something rare: peace.

I lingered, letting the warmth and quiet breathe around me, until the sound of footsteps crunching on the gravel yanked me back into reality. Auntie approached slowly, her grief a mask she couldn't take off. Her already small frame seemed to disappear under a loose housecoat, and I couldn't help but wonder if she'd lost weight since the funeral, trying to hide it so I wouldn't comment. I hadn't thought about how lonely her house must feel now.

"Aisha," I said with a small nod. The gray siding suddenly felt oppressive—its muted tones casting a shadow of sorrow over the place that used to feel so warm.

"Asha. Thank you for coming. Your mother didn't think I'd be able to handle all this," she started, smoothing invisible wrinkles down the front of her coat.

Armatta always said she'd named me after her little sister, hoping I'd inherit her bullheadedness, but dropped the "i" in hopes I'd be less selfish. The irony, of course, was that my mother was more selfish than all of us put together.

"You know how she gets, Auntie. Matta needs to control everything, no matter where she is in the world," I replied, brushing nonexistent dirt off my hands as I stepped forward to pull her into a hug.

We stood there for a moment in the front yard oasis, the garden's scent weaving through the air between us. When Aisha finally let go, I felt the cold settle in her absence. Clearing my throat, I glanced at the open door behind her. "Is the inspector here yet? I've got a dinner to make tonight, and I pushed it back for this," I said, already regretting my tone.

"Always rushing to somewhere new, huh?" she replied, one eyebrow arching above a judgmental glare that landed squarely on me.

"I'm not *rushing* anywhere," I said, my voice tightening with defensiveness I'd perfected over the years. "But I wasn't expecting to be stuck in the car for half an hour before a dinner I've had on my calendar for months."

She studied me from head to toe, her eyes sharp, like she was searching my body for a lie. It was her superpower, sniffing out a fib just by looking at someone. AnaMarie and I hated it when we were kids, but as I got older, I realized how much you can learn from a human lie detector.

"He's in there, all right. Started digging around about five minutes before you got here. Just running up my bills looking for something wrong," she said, turning to lead me toward the front steps. She paused before climbing, her gaze finding a crack that ran the length of the step. Her hand gripped the banister for support.

Her back looked so small, hunched under the weight of years and loss. The creases around her eyes, once earned through laughter, now seemed etched by something heavier. I reached toward her instinctively, my hand hovering, unsure of what comfort might even look like.

She coughed into a tissue, startling me.

"You okay, Auntie?" I asked, pulling my hand back and stepping closer.

She nodded slowly. "Your uncle meant to fix these damn

stairs but never got around to it. Every time I look at this step, I think of all the things we said we were going to do but never did. Every time," she said, frozen in place.

Her grief was suffocating. It mingled with the sharp scent of lavender in the air, wrapping around me until I couldn't do anything but put my arm around her shoulders.

"I'm so sorry," I murmured.

I've had my fair share of grief, but never the pain of losing someone before their time. If it weren't for Armatta, I'm convinced Aisha would've sat in this house, alone and withering, waiting to succumb to whatever stole her family from her. But how could I remind her she still has family when I barely want to be around? I shook the thought from my head and took Aisha's hand, guiding her up the weathered stairs.

As we crossed the threshold, the smell of freshly baked bread wrapped around me. "You've been baking, Auntie?" I asked, forcing a smile.

"Just to keep my mind off things," she replied softly, then added, "I have a box for you to take home."

I nodded, setting my purse down before taking in the stunning house once more. High ceilings, walnut floors, and white walls stretched out endlessly in the dim evening light. A chandelier greeted us in the entryway, its cascade of crystals shimmering faintly. To the right, the sun bounced off dust particles drifting through the family room, landing on the couch where I'd last seen Junior.

"Sounds like he's upstairs," Aisha said as the creak of floorboards broke through the stillness. "You go on up. I'll be here." She turned back toward the open door, her eyes locking onto the cracked step we had just climbed. *I really don't want to be here.*

As I climbed the stairs, imaginary spiders ran down my spine. The wall along the staircase, once filled with photos of

Aisha's life, was barren now. Only a few nails remained, jutting out as lonely reminders of what used to be.

I ascended slowly, trying to conjure personal memories of this family home. When I reached the top, I paused and took it in. Four rooms stretched out along the hallway: directly to the left was Aisha and Uncle Charles's room, its massive windows overlooking the garden. No wonder Aisha chose it —her paradise greeted her every morning. At the far end of the hall was Junior's old room, now empty. Between them were two smaller rooms. One had served as an office when Uncle Charles was still alive; the other, meant to be a nursery, had been locked for years. It was a shrine of sorts—a preserved space weighted with the pain of miscarriages too painful to keep track of.

I'd only been inside the nursery once. Years ago, Aisha had asked me to grab some books from her room, but my curiosity led me elsewhere. I'd turned the nursery's cold doorknob, hoping to glimpse what was inside. As soon as the door creaked open, a wave of sadness seemed to pour out. I slammed it shut, startled, and Aisha had rushed upstairs, worried I'd fallen.

The amused smile on her face vanished when she saw my expression. She knew. We never spoke about it. I felt the urge to try the door again a year or two later, but the knob refused to turn.

I shook off the memory, forcing myself to focus. Embarrassment churned in my stomach and heated my cheeks, but I pushed it down. Now wasn't the time.

"Hello?" I called out, my voice breaking through the house.

"Uh, down here! Room to the right!" came the reply.

The anxiety that had gripped me earlier faded, replaced by an odd calmness. I glanced down the hallway toward Junior's old room and noticed a light spilling from the slightly ajar door. I took a deep breath and walked toward the voice, allowing myself one last moment to collect my thoughts before I pushed the door open.

Standing a few inches taller than me was a man with a mop of dark curls that looked too perfect to be real. His copper skin gleamed where the sunlight managed to sneak through the curtains, and the industrial mask covering the lower half of his face left me nothing to focus on but his deep brown eyes.

He reached up, tugging the dusty mask down around his neck. A smile broke across his face, and for a second, I forgot how to breathe. As he stepped closer, I moved to cross the threshold but miscalculated, tripping instead. Embarrassment flared in my cheeks, and I scrambled to recover, reminding myself that I didn't get "weak in the knees" around anyone.

I ran my hands down the front of my skirt, stepping fully into the room with what I hoped looked like confidence.

He extended a hand. "Hey. Grayson. Nice to meet you."

I nodded, taking his hand in mine. My skin tingled as his rough palm met mine, and I debated lingering just a moment longer, curious about the texture of his grip.

'A perfect fit,' the voice purred.

I ignored it, offering him a small grin instead. "A pleasure," I said, pulling my hand back and dropping it to my side.

I stepped past him, letting my eyes wander around the room. Junior's bed sat untouched except for a small body print on the edge—one that could only belong to Aisha. Photos of Junior lined the walls, chronicling his childhood, while shelves sagged under the weight of trophies and medallions from countless sports. He would have turned seventeen this year, if not for the...*incident.*

I turned toward the window next to his bed. The backyard stretched out below, a tranquil space with flowers swaying gently in the breeze and three proud oak trees standing tall, their branches offering comfort and shade to anyone seeking solace.

"I'm just finishing up," Grayson said, pulling the mask back into place. I bit back a frown, already missing his face. "I'm confident in saying your mother needs to move out for a while. This house is *full* of carbon monoxide."

"Shouldn't I have a mask or something too?" I asked, the corners of my mouth curling in distaste at the thought of lingering toxins. I let the thought distract me from his confusion and the childish wish that Aisha *was* my mother.

Reaching for my phone, I fired off a quick text to Kate, asking her to find a hotel in the city. It looked like Aisha would be trading in her suburban retreat for the fast life for a while.

"You should be fine," Grayson replied, his voice muffled. "Head down whenever you're ready. I'll finish up here."

"Okay..." I mumbled, turning to leave the room.

I barely made it three steps before the thought hit me like a punch to the gut: Aisha's been here for the past week. Wouldn't that mean she's already affected? My breathing grew shallow, and I clenched my trembling hands, willing myself not to panic. Standing in my dead cousin's bedroom, the air felt heavier, as if grief and worry had seeped into the walls alongside the poison.

"Shit, what do we do next?" I asked, my voice breaking slightly.

Grayson didn't flinch, his tone calm and measured. "First, we evacuate the house. I believe the leak is coming from the water heater, which hasn't been checked since the house was built. That will need to be replaced. After the replacement, we'll run another inspection. If the levels check out, she can move back in. I'll finish up here and go over a full course of action with your mother."

"She's not my mom," I said quietly, cutting him off as I headed for the door. "We'll meet you outside."

In the hallway, I started mentally listing what Aisha would need for a few nights away. Stepping into her room, I searched for some kind of luggage and finally pulled a ratty old duffel bag from under the bed.

I moved methodically, folding items I knew would bring her comfort—slippers, sweats, and a few of Uncle Charles's shirts she liked to wear at night. Each piece felt like a small offering, a way to steady myself as much as her.

I nearly collided with Grayson as I left the room, his attention fixed on his phone.

"Excuse me," I mumbled, gripping the bag's handle as I tried to push past him.

"Let me get that for you," he said, his hands gently closing over mine on the strap.

The warmth of his touch sent a jolt through me. I pulled away quickly, hugging the bag to my chest as if it were a shield.

"Thanks, but I've got it," I said, rushing down the stairs. Distance—I needed distance from the walking distraction standing in Aisha's house. "Thank you," I called over my shoulder as I made my way to the kitchen.

I found Aisha bent over the sink, her head low, her shoulders trembling.

"Auntie," I said softly, reaching out to touch her back. "Grayson's all finished. He thinks there's a carbon monoxide leak, so I'm going to take you back to the city with me tonight."

She turned toward me, her face streaked with tears.

Nodding, she wiped at her cheeks, shuffling closer to me as Grayson came down the stairs.

He took a few minutes to walk her through his findings, outlining an action plan. He'd found a replacement water heater and just needed her approval and the house keys before heading out. As they talked, I stepped outside, spotting Vlad in the driveway, bobbing his head to a beat I couldn't hear.

I waved him over and passed him the duffel bag, explaining that we'd drop Aisha at a hotel before heading to my apartment. He nodded, tossing a quick reassurance about a comfortable ride over his shoulder as he headed back to the car.

I turned back toward the house, freezing at the sight of Aisha locked in a hug with Grayson. Fresh tears streamed down her face as she clung to him, her small frame trembling against his.

"Thank you so much, baby," she murmured, her voice thick with emotion. Jealousy stabbed at my chest but I didn't let the feeling linger.

"Really, no trouble at all," Grayson replied, his tone warm and steady. "I'll give you a call once I've got the replacement. We can go over the timeline then."

Aisha nodded, patting his chest before making her way down the stairs. Vlad met her at the car, offering an arm, while I remained rooted to the spot.

"Thank you," I said, turning my attention back to Grayson. His curls framed his face perfectly, and I admired the way his eyes crinkled when he smiled.

I started toward the car, but a gentle hand on my arm stopped me. A jolt shot down my arm, and I turned to him, eyebrows raised.

"Yes?" I asked, my eyes darting from his hand back to his face.

"I'm sorry, but I'd be beside myself if I didn't get your name," he said, his warm smile softening my glare.

"That sounded old as hell," I said with a laugh, my teasing earning a quick flush of disappointment on his face. "No, it was cute. I'm sorry," I backtracked quickly. "My name is Asha."

His smile returned, and I couldn't help but notice the way his muscles shifted under his shirt as he reached for his tool bag.

"Well, Miss Asha, I'd love to take you to dinner sometime. Can I get your number?"

"How about you get my auntie all fixed up first, and we'll see?" I replied, daring him to play along.

He crossed his arms, raising an eyebrow. "Now how am I supposed to let you know it's done if I don't have your number?"

I hesitated, a smirk tugging at my lips. Finally, I pulled a pen from my purse with ease, grabbed his hand, and scribbled my number onto his palm like a teenager.

Grayson studied it with a grin that outshone the setting sun. "I guess you'll be hearing from me soon, then," he said with a wink.

I simply winked and headed to the car, sliding into the backseat beside Aisha. Her knowing gaze and Vlad's playful smirk greeted me instantly.

"Oh, shut up, you two," I said, pulling out my phone to check on the hotel reservation. Vlad laughed, the sound filling the car as we pulled out of the driveway. Aisha shifted in her seat, clasping her hands tightly in her lap.

"I wasn't even saying anything," she muttered.

How could I forget how easy it was to be around my auntie.

FIVE

The warm glow of the streetlights welcomed us back into the city, passing shadows crawling over Aisha. I studied the light playing with the lines on her face—the deep, withered valleys around her eyes and lips that held her laughs and smiles over the years. I wished I could trace my finger over them. Did the joy still live there? My phone buzzed, forcing me to tear away from the timeworn canvas that was my auntie.

Unknown: By the way, your aunt definitely needs to be checked out at a hospital as soon as possible. Her vacation saved her life but there's still a questionable amount of time in which she could've been exposed.

My heart sank a bit as I looked toward my passenger. "Aisha, we need to get you checked out by a doctor. I'll have my assistant find a private to come and assess you at the hotel."

Her already weak smile dropped into a thin line as her eyes locked on mine. "I don't want to see a doctor."

"Let's get you settled at the hotel and then we'll worry about that, okay?" I said using the same saccharine tone I would with a child.

"I said I'm not going to see a doctor, Asha, and I meant it. Just because you got all this money to play around with doesn't mean that I want to use it."

"That didn't stop you from using me to get that house I just rescued you from, did it?"

"Then take me to the hospital!" She raised her hand with a dismissive wave. "What do I look like paying for a damn concierge doctor?"

"You shouldn't feel concerned about that when *you're not paying for it*," I snapped. Aisha's spine straightened.

"Listen to me, girl, just because you think you got your shit together doesn't mean you get to go around telling your auntie what to do. The only way I'm going to see a doctor is if it's the mortician examining me at the morgue." Her words were punctuated by a harsh cough.

Aisha opened her purse as the rasps continued, each one racking through her body harder than the last. I reached over to rub her back, but she scooted away abruptly—her frame crammed against the door of the car made her look even smaller as she tried to put as much space between us as possible. She looked out of the window, her eyes filling with tears and focused out on the world passing us by.

I created this—her unease around me. Hell, she hugged the fucking inspector, a man she had just met, longer than she ever hugged me.

"Are you okay?" I asked, my hand still frozen mid-air.

"No, Asha, I'm not okay. My husband and my child are *dead,* and I've been forced out of the one place I feel closest to them. It feels like my heart is beating somewhere else. You want me to get checked out by some fucking doctor when I already know what he's going to tell me, and I don't want to hear it. I know you've seen my bloody tissues, you ain't a fool. If God can steal my family away from me, he can take me too, damn it."

"You don't get to give up, Aisha."

"You don't get to decide, Asha." Her glare burned through me as she pulled a fresh tissue from her purse and wiped at her nose.

"So, what? You're just going to give up and leave us here?"

"Leave *us?* Who is 'us'? You've avoided all of your family for years. Don't go acting like you give a shit now."

Her words slapped me across the face. I drew in a sharp breath before turning away from her. "My family has done nothing but take from me, Aisha—you included—since I was ten years old."

She huffed out a laugh, "And now you've grown. You've made a life for yourself and *choose* to hold onto the bits that molded you into the person you are today. *You* choose to keep all that shit bottled up inside." She steered her glare away from me, her eyes once again settling on life outside of the four-wheeled prison.

Tears poked behind my eyes as I squeezed them shut trying to remember how to breathe like Ana taught me.

'You can take as many breaths as you'd like, it won't change the fact that she's right.'

"And I'm still not seeing no damn doctor."

❧

We sat in the car, the only sounds were the soft beat of Vlad's playlist coming from the speakers and Aisha's occasional cough. How could I convince her to go to the doctor in the short time it would take to get her situated at the hotel? I didn't want to reschedule dinner with Scheff, especially with him coming into town unannounced. I could just drop Aisha at the hotel and have someone come check on her in the morning. It was the easiest way to make it to dinner on time and avoid another argument. I really didn't have time to worry knowing Scheff was most likely on his way to the restaurant already.

I was out the car door running into the lobby to check Aisha before Vlad fully pulled up to the curb. When I returned, she and her bag were waiting to be taken up. She buzzed with energy—her hand rubbing her arm as if she were cold, her anxious eyes looking anywhere but at me, and her damn toe tapping on the floor. A clear sign she was annoyed too. I sighed before leading the way to her room.

We stood quietly as the elevator slowly dragged its way to the eleventh floor, each annoying beep that signaled our climb did nothing to dissuade the impatient *tap, tap, tap* of my fingers against the rail.

The doors opened up into the suite itself, and I quickly deposited the old duffel onto the bed before clapping my hands together. "Well, I will talk to you in the morning. Try to get some rest."

Something between a snort and a 'humph' came from Aisha as she turned toward the bed, her hands gently tugging on the zipper of the bag. She pulled out Uncle Charles's shirt, her hands shaking as she lifted it up to her nose.

"Aisha," I took a step toward her before remembering the way she jumped away from me in the car. "I just want to say that I'm sorry."

"We both know damn well you meant every word you said in that car." She huffed out a laugh.

"True."

"Ain't never been able to lie to me, Miss Asha Marie. You and me, we're one and the same. Your momma knew it when you were born and, well you know the story 'bout your name. There's some big differences though. You," she paused to swipe a tissue over her eyes before sitting down on the bed. "You're way tougher than I ever knew someone so young could be. You shouldered so much, and I let you and *I'm* sorry for that. I don't blame you one bit for how you've treated any of us, Asha, and I think it's time you knew that."

I felt like I was being torn in two as I slowly walked toward my heartbroken aunt, the weight of the moment pressing down on me. I crouched down in front of her, my hands reaching for hers as I caught her gaze. "I–"

"Another time, baby," she said, her hand cupping my cheek. "Another time."

She leaned forward, placing a kiss on my forehead. I squeezed my eyes shut, surprised when a single tear dropped onto her hand. We sat like that for a few minutes, her arms wrapped around me while my head rested in her lap. I reached for her hand and slid my fingers through hers, letting the comfort of the moment wash over me. I ran my finger over her wedding ring, the simple act making me feel much, much younger.

A text from Vlad reminding me of the time broke the embrace, and I had to stop myself from fighting to stay when Aisha started pulling me toward the doors.

Before I reached to call the elevator, I turned and looked my Auntie over, head to toe. I reached to touch her curls, the once deep-brown hair taken over by gray and silver strands. My hand clasped the small, diamond encrusted cross she'd worn on her neck my whole life—the same way I would when she'd hold me in her lap during church—and a small giggle found its way out from my cracking chest.

I pulled her into a hug and held her tightly for a few seconds before swiftly turning and smashing the elevator button. I stepped in, holding my breath until the elevator door closed, surrounding me with the privacy I'd been craving for the last few hours. I let my body rest against the wall as my head fell to my chest, a single sob jolting my entire body. The eleven-story descent allowed me to try and set the tension free from my chest, breathing out hard and begging for the air around me to enter back into my lungs. *One breath in, one breath out. She's fine. She's going to be fine.*

As the small red light marked the fourth floor, I sucked in one last breath before pulling a tissue out of my purse to wipe my eyes. I flipped open a compact and made sure I looked like the woman everyone saw walking in, thankful we still had time to stop by the apartment so I could add some finishing touches to my carefully crafted camouflage.

By the time the elevator car hit the first floor, marked by a long beep signaling my arrival, I was able to shake my head and walk out like nothing ever happened.

*

I walked into The Boom Boom Room, Scheff's chosen venue for the night, seven minutes after our designated meeting hour. I looked around the dimly lit room for the blonde head of hair that waved proudly like a flag in the night, catching a glimpse of it at the bar. A sly, purely sexual grin curled the corners of my mouth as I sauntered up to his side, dancing my hand along his ribs.

I leaned close, my lips dusting over his ear as my hand

made its way to his thigh, gently squeezing before seductively whispering, "Matthew."

I pulled back in time to see a small smile on his face, my eyes locking on his full lips—two soft pink pillows that only enhanced the pale blue ocean of his eyes.

"Asha," he said, his own hand wrapped around my waist as he leaned in to place a small peck on the corner of my lips —close enough to my lips to be considered a kiss, but far enough away that someone else might mistake it for a peck on the cheek. "Always a pleasure, my dear. I've gone ahead and ordered you an amaretto sour with double cherries. I hope you don't mind."

"And my mother wonders why you're my favorite." I replied, giggling.

Before I could climb onto the stool next to him, he gestured toward an empty booth tucked away from the burlesque stage that held most of the room's attention. I grabbed my drink, nodding my thanks toward the bartender before grabbing Scheff's hand, letting him lead the way to solitude. We cozied into the same side of the booth, our bodies fitting together as easily as two puzzle pieces. I took a sip of my drink before sliding my bare legs over his lap, shivering as he ran his fingers along them in a slow, languid circle.

"Should we order a bottle?" I asked. We both knew how this night would end so we might as well enjoy ourselves now.

"Eager tonight, are we?" he replied, a suggestive look weaved between his eyebrows.

I leaned forward to tussle his hair and we both laughed. He shook his head, the blonde strands falling back into place before motioning for a server. I rolled my eyes as he ordered a disgustingly expensive bottle of wine and some appetizers, his body relaxing as he spoke. One arm rested comfortably on my thigh while the other held the menu firmly. Confidence lingered in his eyes, on his face, and in the breath he let out after he finished ordering. I took a sip from my drink, trying to hide behind the glass as I looked over the man who had wormed his way into my life.

Scheff was always one to show off his style, no matter the venue. His wide, muscular shoulders looked spectacular in his plain, white button-down. The top was open, hinting at his impressive chest, with rolled-up sleeves exposing his forearms —veins shifting with each half-yelled word of our order. His favorite dark-wash jeans—the ones that hugged his ass *just right*—gently rubbed against my bare legs, the friction adding even more excitement to the night. I finished my drink in one gulp and slid the glass towards my business partner. He picked it up, sending his signature, roguish smile my way, as he asked the waiter to bring another.

The server walked away, and Scheff's attention found its way back to me, his eyes burning with desire as I felt his right hand creep up my leg.

"Buy me dinner first?" I joked. I reached for his hand and brought it to my mouth. I ran it across my lips gently before pulling his index finger into my mouth, causing a low groan to escape his throat.

"I'll buy you whatever the fuck you want." He groaned before pulling me onto his lap to kiss me for real this time. Yeah, I *definitely* missed Matthew Scheffter.

I pulled away, looking behind him toward the menagerie of bodies melding together on the dance floor. We tried to catch the beat of the music but it was drowned out by the sounds of the crowd surrounding us. His lips found my neck, his nose pressing into the sensitive spot just beneath my ear. A soft gasp passed over my lips right as the server appeared with an off-balanced tray. At least six plates lay across it with two empty wine glasses and a full bottle of Pinot Noir. My mouth watered in anticipation as I nudged Scheff's shoulder—directing his attention to the young man struggling to carry the tray of refreshments.

Scheff turned *too* abruptly, his elbow knocking into the man's arm. We watched with a mix of horror and amusement as the bottle of wine, about three hundred dollars on its own, teetered on the tray—slowly deciding if it would just dance or topple completely. We all waited as the bottle tilted to the left and back to the right, settling itself safely back on the platter. The server looked relieved that his tips wouldn't be going towards a wasted bottle of wine, and quickly saw to putting our food on the table.

"My bad, man!" Scheff said as we giggled together and let Artie—if his name tag was correct—pour a generous amount of wine into each of our glasses. We raised them to him, an extension of our gratitude, before turning to each other and tapping our glasses together—the clink signifying the official start of our yearly meeting.

We spent a couple hours in the bar catching each other up on the goings-on of the last year, flirting, and discreetly fondling each other in the dark booth before Scheff suggested a late-night stroll through the grounds of the Arch—the giant, touristy, metal eyesore of St. Louis. The heat of the day had leached through the night and the humidity seemed to stick to me as we walked under the soft, yellow lights flanking the path to the riverfront. I slipped my hand into Scheff's and let the hum of crickets weave between us.

The considerable amount of alcohol flying through my system left my body buzzed but I let myself relax into the comfort that I only ever felt with Scheff. I looked up to the sky and stared up at the Gateway Arch—a monument built in the 1960s as an ode to westward expansion, I'd learned once when I was younger—lit in the darkness and standing proudly in the night sky. At six-hundred and thirty feet in the air, I'm not sure anything else—aside from my mother—had ever made me feel so inferior.

When I was seven, after Armatta had, yet again, disappeared for a week, Aisha dragged me all the way to the top, trying to keep my mind off of the fact that my mother was essentially missing. The truth, of course, was that she wasn't missing; she chose to abandon us for her little adventures. Aisha made sure to explain how the ride would work with the least amount of detail possible—cramming me inside a small tram pod with three strangers. A gravelly voice spoke through hidden speakers sharing bits of history surrounding the Arch's creation. I tried my hardest to listen but couldn't pick up any words until the voice called out 'doors closing.' Once they shut, I felt like I was choking on the thick air trapped in the pod with us, anxious thoughts about the tram ride running wild in my head.

When we made it to the top of the 'gateway to the west,' Aisha lifted me up to the window and I froze in awe. I felt like I could see the whole city as my eyes scoured the skyline. We were so tiny, tucked high into the sky. I could just barely make out our neighborhood straddling the horizon, before my eyes started blending shapes and colors together. When I realized the building swayed with the wind, I clung to Aisha's leg. She simply chuckled, running a hand over my head.

The chill from the evening breeze stole the memory from my head. I took in a breath and slowed my steps, eager to soak in the park and how much it had changed since the last time I was here—on an utterly miserable date a few years ago. The symmetrical design of the area had always satisfied me—trees planted evenly along the pathways, ponds sitting on either side of the monument, deceivingly large sets of stairs that lead down to the riverfront drive.

As we walked, my focus was pulled across the interstate to the abandoned buildings sprinkled in between apartments, hotels, and restaurants. When the idea for the Arch was proposed, the riverfront was riddled with 'slums,' as the leaders of the city deemed them. They thought that building a monument to Thomas Jefferson and Westward Expansion would be the perfect way to eradicate the local businesses that remained in the forty blocks of buildings. After a rigged vote, city leaders went ahead with the idea, set to demolish the riverfront—wiping out the livelihoods of hundreds in a hail-mary to earn some federal construction money. What better way to *thank* the citizens of St. Louis than by forcing them out of their homes, razing forty blocks of businesses and buildings to the ground, and building a giant, shiny, 'fuck you' monument over the ashes of what remained? To me, the Arch served as a symbol of the city's wasted promise for a better future.

"Do you think the earth remembers history?" I asked Scheff, unable to tear my focus from the disgustingly blue color of the pond as we walked past it—whatever chemicals pumped through the water always made me worry for the geese that decided to land for a cool swim. The moon danced on the surface, the only light visible in the sky aside from the occasional, late-night airplane flying overhead and winking stars.

Scheff stood silent for a moment, his left eyebrow scrunching like it always did when he was trying to work something out in his head. "I think it would be impossible for it not to. Look at the Grand Canyon, or how long it takes for life to return to a forest after a wildfire. I think it scars just as we do."

I nodded my head in agreement, lightly shouldering him back on the path and toward the lot we asked the driver to meet us in. The evening heat sank with the sun and the breeze that wrapped around us caused me to shiver. Scheff pulled me closer, his hand abandoning mine to wrap around my shoulders instead. I leaned into his side, breathing in the cedar smell that always seemed to encompass him.

His body shook with laughter, "Are you really smelling me right now?"

"Yes, and I will keep smelling you until you tell me the name of your goddamn cologne," I replied, taking a deep breath in through my nose to accentuate the point.

"Guess I'm never going to get rid of you then, huh?" I looked up at him and wondered if that was what he wanted— for me to stay by his side forever.

'Nobody wants that from you.'

"Don't tell me you're trying to keep me around now." I laughed, slowing our steps so that I could take a second to look out over the Mississippi River. The moonlight reflected off the water, dancing in the ripples of the waves.

"What if I was?"

I reluctantly pulled my eyes away from the water to look at him. The lighter strands of his blonde hair looked silver in the cover of night. I reached up to tuck the longer strands behind his ear, my hand stopping to rest on his shoulder.

"Why are you being so sweet to me? Usually it's, 'Hi, Asha. How's the business? Ready to fuck so I can leave for another year? Cool,' and suddenly you're all...touchy and stuff." The question that had been at the front of my mind since the funeral finally laid out to play.

A sly grin pulled at Scheff's lips as he softly chuckled in

response. He tilted his head to the sky, his hair falling back in a pool of blonde waves.

"Okay, different question." I've known Matthew Scheffter long enough to know that, when he laughs instead of pausing to formulate an answer, he's not going to answer. "Why did you come back early? Really?" I asked as his arms snaked around my waist, his nose nuzzling into the crook of my neck.

"Do you really want to know?"

"Yes. No lies, *partner*," I said, the ease of the conversation made possible only with my liquor consumption in the last few hours. My overbearing anxiety was a quiet thrum in the back of my head, miles away from the exposed brick sidewalk we stumbled across.

He pulled his lips from my neck and contemplated me for a few seconds, his hand finding the small of my back, tracing the path of my spine. "I came back for a home."

I leaned back, matching my gaze to his. "You can find a house just about anywhere. Why here?"

"Ah, but I said a *home*, not a house," he started, his eyebrows raising in a silent challenge. "but maybe I missed the city." His shoulders raised in a shrug, his eyes turned to the parking lot, searching for the car.

"Maybe," I countered, "but you hated it here during undergrad. Try again."

"Maybe it's grown on me, Asha. Maybe I missed something about the quiet chaos that seems to brew here," he said, pausing to pull me closer. "Or maybe I simply missed you."

❧

We spent the ride back to my apartment huddled together, driven by Scheff's driver. A lanky man with long, black hair and a hooked nose, spooky in his silence, was waiting for us by the time we made it to the parking lot. The car was plenty warm, but it was easy to curl into Scheff's side again as soon as he was comfortable. I was asleep by the time we pulled up to the tall, brick apartment building I liked to refer to as my fortress.

Scheff pulled me off of him, gently caressing my cheek before sliding out of the car. I felt the door next to me open, the nippy air wiping the grogginess away.

"Come on, Beanpole," he said. A small smile tugged at his lips as he used the nickname—the first use of it had earned him a punch in the jaw.

"Why the fuck would you? Beanpole isn't very nice," I stumbled over my words, the alcohol finally hitting home after a twenty-minute nap.

He laughed and reached for my hand, pulling me out of the car. I groaned with the movement, the world spinning around us as Scheff tried to guide me up the stairs. I barely noticed Frank, my ever-present doorman, as we made our way to the elevator but managed to catch Scheff telling him that I was alright and that he would take care of me for the night. I threw my hand out in what I hoped was a wave goodnight toward Frank, and let Scheff pull me into the elevator bay.

"You fell fast tonight, didn't you? Couldn't last until we got to the real fun, huh?" he said, his hand swiping a loose curl from my face.

"I want my bed," I groaned.

"Soon, Asha dear."

I slumped back into his side and let my eyes close, the familiarity of the situation taking me back to college and the times we would stay out from sunset to sunrise, drinking ourselves under the table.

The annoying ding of the elevator sounded but I couldn't

bring myself to open my eyes, much less move. I felt a strong hand on my back while another one snaked around my legs, scooping me up. I tucked my head into Scheff's chest ready for sleep to pull me under. Rosy red flags waved in my head as I sank into a distinct feeling of peace. I felt *too* comfortable when his hand danced around my face, a thumb gently swiping over my bottom lip, before his kiss pressed against my forehead.

I didn't have any more energy to question his words or his actions, happy to let sleep take over.

Six

The thrum of a headache woke me early the next morning. The sun, still hiding beneath the horizon, wouldn't rise for another couple of hours or so. I groaned as I tried to shift from under the weight of Scheff's arm wrapped over me. It was a painfully slow process as I worked to avoid waking him up. The heat from him mixed with an overwhelming need to vomit had me jumping from the bed and running toward the bathroom.

"Come back," I heard him call from the room as I rid the contents of my stomach into the toilet. I rested my arm on the bowl, my head falling into my hand as I waited for another round of nausea to hit.

"Go back to sleep," I groaned knowing full well that he wouldn't. Scheff had seen me hungover enough times to not be fazed by the events that followed a night out—he'd make his way to me eventually, just like every time before.

I listened as his feet hit the tile, waiting until he was sitting behind me and his hand was rubbing along my back before I leaned into his touch.

"You'd think your body would be used to all of this by now, yeah?" he said, clear amusement in the words.

"I don't know," I said before another wave of nausea made me suck in a deep breath, "I think it would be crazier if my body was totally cool with me intentionally poisoning it, don't you?"

He laughed, the sound ringing through the bathroom, echoing off the marble walls of the shower. I let myself sink further into his body, my head resting on his chest while he wrapped his arms around me.

"I could stay here till the end of time," he murmured into my hair.

"Says the guy who couldn't stay in one place if his life depended on it."

His lack of response soured the moment as my joke fell flat. I'd asked him at our reunion last year why he couldn't seem to stick around for longer than a week and he'd given me a roundabout answer—saying something along the lines of it 'not being in the cards for him yet." I let it go at the time, a part of me understanding that Scheff was, and always would be, a mystery to me.

His reply was quiet though confident. "Maybe I want to this time."

I turned my head to look at him, my eyebrows pulling together in confusion. So, he didn't *want to* before?

"And what's that supposed to mean? What changed?" I asked.

"Oh, a whole bunch of things changed, Asha dear." *Matthew Scheffter and his fucking riddles.*

I pulled his arms from around me, turning my whole body around so I could study him—his eyes tended to look darker when he was sleepy, the usual sea blue irises replaced by two dark currants which were studying me too. "Like what?"

He reached up to tuck a loose curl behind my ear before resting his palm on my cheek. I leaned into the touch, craving the comfort hidden in the small gesture.

"Like...things," he said before placing a kiss on my forehead. "Now you either need to vomit again or brush your teeth because I can't keep sitting this close to you when your breath is blasting in my face."

I groaned before pulling myself up from the floor, the movements causing my head to start pounding again. I looked in the mirror, prepared to find a half-drunk monster looking back at me but was surprised to see I still looked fairly put together—or as put together as someone could be after a night with Scheff. My eyes followed him, tracking him in the mirror as he left the bathroom, his reflection disappearing into the darkness of the room.

"What time is it?" I asked as I reached for my toothbrush.

"Four," he called from the bedroom. I listened to the rustle of sheets as I brushed, letting the foam fill my mouth while I debated between staying up for a bit or crawling back into bed. The quiet pressed in on me and I started to think about our conversation from last night. Scheff had never shown interest in sticking around the city—he and Armatta were similar in that regard, always bouncing to the next adventure—so what changed? Why would he want to stay now?

"Do you want coffee and round two, or are you ready for more sleep?" he asked, clearly amused by my hungover state. I spit into the sink, watching as the toothpaste mixed with the running water, swirling down the drain.

"Round two, huh? I don't think we made it through round one," I said, before pulling my hair out of the bun I barely remembered putting it in before bed last night. I hesitated before stepping out of the bathroom, my eyes catching the half-used bottle of oil that mocked me from its spot on the shelf. I stared, debating if it was worth it to skip this step before snatching the bottle, turning it over in my hand before gently massaging the oil into my scalp. The relaxing scent of rosemary filled the bathroom as I worked my fingers through my hair, relishing the monotony of the moment. "Coffee, please!"

After chugging a glass of water that Scheff had waiting for me on the nightstand, I grabbed a sweater and walked into the kitchen where he had just started to grind the coffee beans.

"How are you so awake?" I asked as I tried to roll the tension from my neck.

"I'm usually up around this time anyway. I get my best work done in the morning." He made a performance of the process: gently laying a coffee filter into the basket, his hands dancing around the machine as he poured the freshly ground beans in, shutting the lid snugly before starting it. A fancy espresso machine rested on the counter next to the drip machine but even Scheff, culinary extraordinaire, knew that I preferred the simple stuff still.

"What work could you possibly need to get done when the rest of the world is still silent?" I scoffed.

Scheff, a playful glimmer in his eyes, silently reached out his hand. I tucked mine in his and let him pull me toward the balcony.

"Tell me again how quiet the world is, Asha dear." The latch of the door clicked, and we stepped outside. The soft, periwinkle glow of sunrise was just starting to climb on the horizon, "Seems alive to me."

I leaned forward, my arms resting on the cool railing of the balcony. I closed my eyes and listened to the symphony of sounds that surrounded us—the waking call of a robin in an oak tree rustling in the wind, the soft crunching as a squirrel nibbled on a fallen acorn, the flapping beat of bat wings as they dipped and dived around our heads. Winking stars waved goodbye as the world slowly woke up.

I let the music of the morning wrap around me as I leaned my arms against the railing. The cool dew from the morning found my skin while Scheff pressed against my back— the warmth of him surrounding me as he placed his hands on either side of me.

I focused on how Scheff fit against me, allowing that intoxicating smell of *him* to immerse myself in, what felt like, the magic of dawn. I turned in his arms, looking up at him before fully leaning in. My lips parted before I froze in his arms, too afraid to break the fragility in which this simple moment was grounded. The beep of the coffee machine and I let out a moan as I took a step back—the promising smell of caffeine working its way to my nose. Scheff coughed once before pulling away from me, the wind sweeping in to fill the void he left. I tightened my sweater around my body, the wool rubbing against my arms as I stepped back into the comforting quiet of my apartment.

"No business this morning, of course. Since you decided to pass out on me last night, consider it a continuation of our annual *meeting*," he said with a sly wink, his fingers emphasizing the final word with air quotes. He poured me a cup of coffee and I was eager to wrap my hands around the steaming mug.

"When was the last time you used this thing?" he asked, motioning to the oven as he reached to preheat it.

"Probably the last time I had a frozen pizza," I paused to take a sip of Scheff's perfect brew, leaving the mug raised to hide my smile. "So...a couple of years ago?"

Scheff's back stiffened, "Years, Asha? Actual years have passed since you turned on your oven?"

"I mean, between delivery and Kate's girlfriend being a chef, what's the point in me wasting my time cooking?"

"That's completely unacceptable." He turned to me with a huff, his eyebrows scrunched together while his eyes widened with shock.

While neither of us liked to talk about our childhoods, we each knew bits and pieces. I knew that, while he *was* raised with nannies and chefs and access to his father's chauffeur service, Scheff's parents valued knowledge and hard work above anything else. Scheff spent a summer at some fancy sleepaway camp for rich kids who wanted to learn to cook and it apparently 'ignited a fire' in him that 'one simply could not put out.' Whenever he deigned to visit the city, he'd find ways to sneak me his newest creations—he had a particular skill when it came to bread and pastries. So, my rarely used, state-of-the-art kitchen likely came as a shock to him.

"Maybe if you came to see me more it would get more use," I said, plopping onto a stool at the island.

"It's not my fault you usually opt for my hotel rather than inviting me home like a *real* lady would."

I choked on a sip of burning hot coffee as a laugh crawled up my slightly burnt throat, "And who gave you the impression that I would *ever* behave as a lady should?"

"Oh, you know how to behave just fine," he said, mischief pulling at the corners of his lips. His body relaxed as he moved around the kitchen—the bridge between comfort and enjoyment finally meeting in the middle—pulling utensils and random ingredients I didn't know I had from places I didn't realize existed. It was like seeing a poem set to motion.

"Do I? It's been so long since I've seen you, I think I might've forgotten," I said, setting the mug down on the counter, hard enough that Scheff jumped as the sound echoed through the apartment.

"And whose fault might that be, Asha dear? You and your silly little rules." He dipped a measuring cup into a bag of flour, leveling the excess off with a knife before sifting the rest into a bowl. He repeated the process a few times before moving on to a selection of other powders and...*things*.

"What're you making?" I asked, shamelessly changing the subject.

"If I remember correctly, you really enjoyed those orange-glazed scones from that café down in Soulard. Is that alright?" His eyes met mine and I gave him a small nod before hiding behind my ceramic barricade once more. Curiosity flamed anew as I wondered when he started paying this much attention to me, to what I liked.

I hadn't been to the coffee shop in months, opting for ones closer to my apartment in Clayton. In undergrad though, Scheff and I would find our way to Soulard, frequenting Protagonist Cafe every weekend, spending hours tucked in the back corner, working on schoolwork and drafting up grand plans for Arlington Nannies.

I let him focus on his task, my empty stomach growling in anticipation after expelling the alcohol I had overindulged in the night before.

I looked through my emails, surprised to see that nothing new had made it to my inbox overnight—a rarity. I closed the app before scrolling through my music library, eager to find something that fit this moment between my once-a-year paramour and I perfectly.

I fought against the smile tugging at the corners of my mouth as I cast the chosen song to the speakers. The acoustic strum of Daniel Caesar's *"Best Part"* filled the room, soft and bittersweet. I waited for recognition to flicker across Scheff's face. It came as he brought his hand down against a bowl, the crack of the egg blending seamlessly with the downbeat.

Memories from our freshman year flooded the space between us, unspoken but heavy.

His movements quickened, almost frantic now. He whisked the ingredients together with practiced efficiency, slapping mounds of dough onto the baking sheet in uneven piles. He slid the baking sheet in, and the oven door slammed shut with a metallic clang that sent darts of pain shooting through my skull. I winced as my migraine developed a stronger pulse but said nothing.

Scheff turned toward me, dough-caked hands frozen mid-motion, his gaze steady. Something unspoken hung in the air, as if the song itself had summoned it.

"Run," he said softly, his voice laced with mischief, before lunging toward me.

Laughter bubbled from my chest, spilling into the space and mingling with the music—the same song in the air the first time he kissed me. Scheff chased me around the apartment, our childlike giggles filling the air. Sticky fingers found my arm, pulling me toward him as the world around us blurred.

I rose onto my tiptoes, my hands slowly reaching behind him. Pressing a soft kiss to his lips, I felt his arms wrap around me, his intent to deepen the moment clear. But my fingers had already found their target—the flour resting on the countertop.

Before he could stop me, I grabbed a handful and pulled away, breaking free of his grasp. Smirking, I lifted my hand to my lips and blew him a kiss, the flour exploding in a white cloud that landed squarely on his face.

"Asha!" he yelled, but I was already gone. My laughter—rich and full of a joy I rarely let myself feel—filled the hall as Scheff's footsteps echoed behind me.

Scheff's dough-covered hand slipped into mine, spinning

me in a circle before pulling me close. His other hand snaked along my waist as we let the moment set in, slowly swaying around my apartment—the only sound, the beating of our hearts and the occasional exhale as I tried to catch my breath. I leaned my head against his chest, comfort gripping my heart.

'Don't get too comfortable. He'll be leaving you soon.'

"Where the hell did you find an apron?" I asked. I wouldn't be surprised if half of the things in here were because Kate and Gretta had bought them for me. The thought of Kate spiked my emotion, but I quickly shoved away my worries about her, hoping Scheff and I could stretch the joyous simplicity of our morning a little longer.

"I had my driver run and grab everything I needed last night," he said, resting his chin on top of my head.

"A little ambitious, weren't you?"

"As soon as you fell asleep in the car last night, I had the idea to invite myself over and make you breakfast in hopes you'd forgive my *intrusion*. I refuse to let your ability to drink steal the tiny amount of time I have with my precious Asha."

Precious. The last time I had been called 'precious' my mother was preening to a group of pageant moms, gloating over my latest win. She didn't care that, as soon as they left us alone—a group of ball gown-wearing children, competing at the behest of their self-involved mothers—I'd find myself in a modern rendition of *Lord of the Flies*. Of course, we all knew that it was every prepubescent, glory-craving girl for herself but that didn't stop them from teaming up on me once the doors locked our nosy mothers out. One girl—Betsy Colstram, a particularly bitchy contestant with a mother who made Armatta look sweet—once went so far as cutting holes in my dress. Guess who didn't care when I cried to her about it.

Nothing about me was precious and if anyone should

know that it was Scheff. I pulled away, refusing to meet his gaze as I looked at the mess we'd made in my apartment. Flour coated the counters and floor like a fresh blanket of snow, while blobs of dough clung to the walls. I dropped my head in my hands, regretting the decision to start a food fight.

"Don't worry," he laughed, the sound empty compared to the ones we had shared just minutes ago, "I'll clean it up." I shot him a look that suggested my doubt and he shrugged his shoulders, adding, "or I'll have someone clean it up. Either way, don't worry your pretty little head about it."

I stared at him, my brow furrowed while frustration crawled the length of my spine. I dusted the flour from the counter, the small specks falling gently to the floor. "Why are you here?"

"What do you mean? I couldn't just drop you off like a hookup after dinner. Not when you were so drunk," he said, his eyebrows pulling together.

"You could've, actually," I challenged. Scheff knows my rules—I rarely fuck someone twice, I won't *ever* commit to a relationship, and no one—absolutely no one—stays the entire night.

"Don't ruin this, Asha."

"Ruin what?"

"The moment. The first time in a long time that you've let me be around you—the *you* that you refuse to let anyone see."

I paused but the determination in his face made me quickly turn away. "You haven't seemed to mind that version of me every other time you're in town."

"Of course, I'm not going to mind the shreds of yourself you share with me when they're the only parts you share with me." His voice wavered. I could feel his glare burning into the back of my head.

I crossed my arms across my chest, intent on standing my ground.

"Why is it so hard for you to let me in?"

"You know why. Stop pushing, Scheff."

"Actually, I don't, Asha," he said, his jaw working as he ground his teeth together—a clear sign he was growing frustrated with me, "Add it to the list of things you don't trust me enough to know."

I let my silence feed his anger, as I hurried to the coffee pot, filling a clean mug before gulping it down like a shot of liquor. I relished the scorch that bit into my throat, the pain I probably deserved for the argument I started.

The oven beeped—the scones were done.

I went back to my seat at the counter, now flour-free, hesitating before brushing a stool clean for Scheff. I didn't miss the small grin that flashed on his face before his stone-cold mask slid back into place.

He iced the steaming pastries quickly, muttering something about how he *should* let them cool but it was "never good to keep a beast waiting." He set one of the luscious baked goods on a plate in front me and I leaned in, letting the steam drift to my nose. The smell made my mouth water— the cozy combination of orange and vanilla slowly filling the house.

I tried to suppress a moan as I bit in, hesitant to show Scheff how much better these were than the ones I would've snagged at the coffee shop. We ate as the light of the morning sun slowly crawled up the walls of the room—trying its best to warm the freezing tension that now surrounded us.

"I need to go check on Aisha," I said with a mouthful of scone. I forced myself to meet his eyes, letting him see the resolve that was steeled in my eyes—I wouldn't change my mind. *Not about this.*

I left for the bedroom without another word, carelessly grabbing clothes—a pair of sweats, a shirt proudly boasting a St. Louis University Billiken on its front, and two random socks. I looked about as chaotic as I felt but didn't really care when the only people who were going to see me were Aisha and Vlad.

"I'll take you," Scheff called from the kitchen.

"I don't think that's the best idea. I'll have Vlad come get me."

"Vlad?"

"My driver-by-trial as of now," I called, quickly returning my curls into a bun on top of my pounding head before walking back towards the kitchen. "Feel free to stick around. I don't know when I'll be back."

Scheff grabbed my hands, his eyes focused on our fingers as he laced them together. "One day, you're going to see how much I can help you."

I ripped my hands from his, "It's not about what you can do for me. I can't give you *anything*, Scheff."

"We'll see about that Asha, dear," he grabbed my hand once again, placing a kiss on it, "and do give Aisha my warmest wishes." I rolled my eyes before stepping around him, eager to break free from all of the feelings clouding my apartment.

SEVEN

Vlad rolled up to the curb of my building within minutes of me calling him—his eager, bouncing energy greeting me as he opened the back car door. He asked after my welfare and, after a couple minutes of one-word answers or silence from yours truly, gave up on talking altogether.

Scheff could dress up his intentions however he liked but I knew what he was alluding to. The pieces of the puzzle finally shifted together as I realized he came back to St. Louis to try and entice me into the idea of a relationship.

I shook the ridiculous idea out of my head as I walked into the lobby of the hotel, nodding to the front desk as I strolled toward the elevator. Time seemed to still as the doors of the elevator opened, goosebumps prickling my skin as I stepped inside. For once, my head seemed quiet—the pressures of my life left behind in the marbled entrance of the hotel. Maybe I could devise a plan in the next minute to get Aisha to the doctor.

I listened to the steady beating of my heart as I reached for the button that would deliver me to the penthouse. The thumping interrupted by the doors opening to the suite and, as I stepped in, a new wave of coldness pressed down on my shoulders. I turned the corner and realized it was intuition—the universe, God, whoever is in control of this twisted, sick life—that had eddied the thoughts into my head when I got here.

The sound came first—the loud bitter wail that exploded from my throat as I processed the scene in front of me. I could taste the blood second—the metallic taste of terror that coated my throat as I stared at my aunt's body, her hollow eyes burning through me. I slowly walked toward her, noticing the bloody tissues that littered the bed, one still crumpled in her hand as it hung off the side. I threw myself on top of Aisha's body, pulling her lifeless form up as I shook her.

"Wake up! Wake the fuck up, Aisha!" I pressed my fingers to her neck, praying to whatever god she believed in that I would feel the faint beating of her heart that simply wasn't there.

"You weren't supposed to die like this," I screamed at her. Tears were running rampant down my cheeks as I pulled her to my chest, hugging her tightly while I sobbed. "Help!"

'*You know this is your fault, right?*'

"Someone help me please," I screamed, before gently laying Aisha on the bed. I ripped my purse open, digging for my phone so I could call 911. Another scream—a cry of pure rage and frustration—rang out when I couldn't find it. I dumped my purse, shaking the menagerie of its contents as the items poured out over my aunt's body, my phone landing on her chest. I reached for it, barely able to dial the number as it jumped around in my hands.

After a few minutes trying to explain the situation to a kind dispatcher, I sent AnaMarie a text—I couldn't stand to hear her voice when I had so much to do.

I cleared my things away from Aisha, dropping them back into my bag carelessly. I went to the bathroom and ran a towel under warm water—she wouldn't have appreciated a cold one pressing against her face—tightly wringing it out before rushing back to her side. I wiped the dribble of blood that ran from the corner of her mouth down to her chest and carefully moved loose curls that had fallen onto her face. I gathered up the debris that surrounded her and watched as the blood-stained tissue bouquet fell into the small hotel trash bin, filling it up. I slowly made my way back to Aisha, dropping to the floor once I was back at her side. The carpet burned my knees as I collided with the ground beside the bed.

I reached for my aunt's hand, running her weathered skin under my thumb, "I was going to have a doctor come today. If you weren't so fucking stubborn, you'd be here to fuss at me about how you didn't need one. I guess I was right for once, huh?" I squeezed my eyes shut as hot tears escaped, my head leaning against her hand as the ten-ton pressure of guilt pressed down on my shoulders.

"If I wasn't in such a rush last night, I would've forced you to get checked out. I should've done it anyway."

'Selfish, selfish Asha. How fitting that you would be the cause of your namesake's death.'

"I hated you for so long for not saving us from *her*. I realized yesterday that I needed to apologize, but you wouldn't let me. *You wouldn't let me.* I could hate you for that too." My words came out between ragged breaths, desperate attempts to get air to my lungs before a panic attack set in. The faint cry of sirens echoed in the distance, the sound signaling the end of our time together.

"I'm so sorry, Aisha. I'm so fucking sorry. You deserved a better niece, and a better death. I should've been here." I reached for her necklace, knowing it would be the last time, rubbing the jeweled cross between my fingers.

"I forgive you, Aisha. I forgive you. Please forgive me." I choked on the words, bile climbing up my throat as my tears fell faster.

I stayed by her side, the sounds of a busy Friday in the city melting away as I reached up to close her eyes. I couldn't remember the last time I had prayed but I made sure to beg for benevolence on behalf of my aunt before the ding of the elevator pulled my attention away. Hands wrapped around me, trying to drag me away from Aisha as paramedics rushed to get closer—a whirlwind of bodies moving around the room as I kept a death grip on my deceased aunt's hand. I screamed and fought against them, a wild beast trying to protect her kin.

The cool metal of the wedding ring on her finger slipped against my hand. I tightened my grip on it, desperate to take a piece of Aisha with me. The ring slid off with a crack of her finger and I fell to the ground. I curled into myself, holding the small gold band to my chest as the overwhelming panic finally set in and I lost control of my breathing altogether. I laid in a ball on the floor—my chest rising and falling quickly as I sucked down shallow breaths—until gentle hands brushed the side of my face, stopping to pull up my chin.

Scheff's eyes, full of worry, met mine before he tucked me into his chest—the warmth of his body wrapped around me as he held every breaking piece of me in his arms. Hollow screams echoed through the room and, as I tried to breathe between the sounds, I realized they were mine. The wails twisted something in my heart, pushing the already fragile and guarded thing far past its breaking point.

Aisha was dead and it was completely my fault.

EIGHT

I relished the feel of scalding hot water biting into my skin, a thousand tiny burns. I deserved to be punished, to hurt. If I wasn't so damn stupid and selfish, Aisha would be here. I pressed the tips of my fingers into my arms, my nails sinking into my flesh as I dragged them down. Four trails followed the path, slowly turning red as blood rushed to the surface.

I didn't realize that I was crying until I started choking on air.

I hadn't really talked to Aisha in years—our conversations were rather limited after she bought the house and I was content to leave it that way.

Still, it didn't seem fair that I could close my heart off from everyone and still wind up feeling broken.

I continued to let myself burn in the shower, the weight of grief pressing down on me forcing me to cave, falling to the shower floor. I curled into my chest, a pathetic little ball, so encompassed by my own trauma that my vision started to blur.

'You know that part of you enjoys it. You know that you deserve *the pain.'*

I stayed under the scalding spray, letting it once again bite into my skin, my mind elsewhere. It drifted back to the hotel room, to the moment Scheff carried me away from my auntie's lifeless body. I'd spent the tear-filled drive to my apartment listening to the steady beat of his heart as he held me against his chest, gently rocking me as we cascaded through the city. I must have fallen asleep as the next thing I remembered was being led into my bathroom by his hand.

Everything felt numb but I allowed him to coax me into the shower, his overly encouraging voice made me feel like a toddler he was hired to handle. I let him turn the water on, unable to move as he peeled off my clothes, and took his hand when he offered it, following him toward the spray. I remember Scheff massaging my hands—the dried blood cracking under the water and the pressure of his thumbs rubbing in small deliberate circles until my hands were completely clean. He reached to turn down the temperature of the water, but I stopped him, my hand laying on his gently before I shook my head—two small motions that made my head pound even more. He looked at me, his eyes assessing—like he was scared to leave me for even a moment—before abandoning me in the bathroom filled with steam.

I didn't know how much time had passed—minutes or hours, it didn't matter—and I didn't hear Scheff come back in. One minute I was on the floor and the next I was sitting naked on my bed, Scheff running a towel over my legs. He took his time drying me off, finally pulling the soft, fluffy cloth around my shivering shoulders before running to the bathroom to grab my lotion. He gently rubbed it in, sparing no inch without making any advances—using a restraint with my naked body that I'd never seen from him. He grabbed the rosemary oil from my bedside table and rubbed it into my hair while he hummed. The tune was familiar, but I was too tired to place it and, honestly, I didn't really care to.

I sat on the floor in front of him, his hands working through my hair from his place on the bed. Tears clouded my vision as he gently tugged at my hair, separating sections before braiding it together. Between his hands weaving through the strands and his soft song, I found myself slipping back into reality—the heady smell of the oil worked into my nose first, the sharp, white corners of my bedside table coming into view, then the bottle of lotion, and finally Scheff behind me, his chest rising and falling and against my back.

When he finished with the tight plaits, he knelt on the floor in front of me, his hands latching onto the back of my knees as he fought to make eye contact. His thumbs danced along my skin, the gesture providing more comfort than I deserved.

"There is no timer set on getting over this," he said calmly.

I couldn't bring myself to say anything. All my thoughts were meant for someone who was dead.

A tear slid down my cheek as I pulled one of his hands to my face, leaning into the curve of his smooth palm. He pulled himself up onto the bed and wrapped his arms around me before laying us both down. I spent hours curled in a ball and cried into his chest. Eventually, he left my apartment, and I was forced to face the ghost of my aunt as I laid in my bed alone.

Aisha's haunting stare lurked in my dreams, each one starting in a similar way—I was always outside, enjoying the warmth of the sun beaming from the noon sky without a cloud in sight. I'd laugh as the bold rays danced through the branches of a tree I leaned against, and it was as if the sound called to her. Her short frame would just *appear* in the valley below me, slowly climbing up the hill and to the tree. She looked just like she did when I found her—hollow eyes, once brimming with life, pinning me down and a trail of blood down her chest, staining the gray shirt of her late husband. Her hand even clutched a bloody tissue. She never said anything, but she'd slowly make her way to me before sitting with her legs crossed under her—like she would when she was focused on a stubborn flower bed—in front of me. No matter how much I screamed at her, how many times I begged her to leave me alone, or how passionately I apologized, my stubborn Aunt Aisha just sat there, staring at me blankly. Sitting and waiting until I subconsciously broke every night.

Eventually, her eyes would crinkle at the sides as a half-smile tugged at her lips. Her mouth opened wide, her lips spreading into a circle. The motion appeared animatronic— her bottom jaw opening in a distinctly mechanical way before *my* screams erupted from my auntie's mouth. The constant loop of the same scream that tore through my throat when I found her in the hotel is what woke me every night.

After six days of sleepless nights, part of me was eager for the funeral that was waiting for us, merely a day away.

If it wasn't enough to see Aisha at night, I could feel her hovering around me—like her ghost couldn't make peace with leaving yet—the scent of her favorite perfume passing under my nose every once in a while. I'd silently curse her before audibly spewing apologies, worried *I* was the reason she couldn't move on. Some days, I'd shake away the feeling of her hand on my shoulder, reminding myself that it wasn't real.

I cried so much.

I cried for Aisha and the relationship I was too afraid to mend—for all of the opportunities that I had to fix things, all the time I took for granted. I cried for Ana and Hadley because I had failed them too—they loved Aisha. They would spend weekends together, working on that damn flower garden because that's what a family was supposed to do.

Apparently, AnaMarie and Hadley fought with Frank, telling him that if he didn't let them into my unit, his life would be hell. *Poor Frank.*

He let them up and Ana and Hadley had been here ever since—the two taking over the guest room in my apartment, sharing a bed far bigger than the one my sister and I had fought over growing up. Their constant presence grated on my nerves as much as it comforted me. In the span of a week, I had gone from having no one stay in my apartment to three different people. The thought almost made me as sick as the nightmares that sent me hauling for the bathroom every night. Hopefully *some of us* would find closure soon and make their way out of my apartment.

When the apartment quieted down at night and the only sound left was the dishwasher Ana started before going to bed, I let the hollow feeling in my chest crack open. Most nights I cried myself to sleep only to wake up with my pillow drenched in tears and snot crusted to my face. I'd spent most of my time locked away, only coming out to get tea when Aisha's ghost chased me from my room. I don't think I'd spoken to anyone outside of the police when they'd asked questions, opting for silently nodding or shaking my head when asked something. And, even then, I could only force out one-word answers.

Ana would try to spark conversation. Part of me wondered why she cared when I had barely spoken to her in the last eight years. Maybe she was just a better person than me—I was certain of it, even.

Scheff came to my apartment every day and was the only

one brave enough to actually come into my room. He'd knock on the door twice—gently, as if he didn't want to startle me—and then walk in, closing it quietly behind him. Usually, he had a cup of tea, columns of steam billowing from the top, in his hand. He'd ask, "how are you feeling?" and I would give him a series of noncommittal noises, and flat out ignored him when he'd encourage me to eat. I couldn't stomach the idea of food, not when the metallic stench of Aisha's blood—immediately cleaned from my hands when I got home—still lingered, haunting me alongside my aunt's ghost.

Scheff and I would sit, and I'd study the world from my windows. I felt frozen in time. Every harsh word I had thrown at Aisha over the years seemed to settle in my stomach like a bag of rocks—heavy and pointless.

When Scheff was tired of watching my mental struggle, he'd talk—about work, his various outings, new restaurants he was eager to try. If I had the energy to thank him for the distraction, I would, but there was little left for me to give.

On the day before Aisha's funeral, Scheff had been sitting with me for about an hour when I finally looked at him. I could see his worry—his eyebrows scrunched, and his bright eyes faded to a deeper, darker color. His mouth set in a thin line just like it was anytime he was trying to convince me to do something.

"Do you know how hard it is to cry silently?" My voice was hoarse after six days of not talking, the words grating through the room. I reached for my tea, hoping any remaining warmth would help my throat loosen up. It was the only thing I could think to say, the thought one of many that clouded my head over the last week.

Scheff didn't say anything, the only sign he heard me was the surprise found in his eyebrows shooting up. I reached for my tea again, then slid deeper into my pocket of the sunroom couch, wishing the cushions could swallow me entirely. I balanced the mug on my chest—I couldn't care less about how much it hurt to feel the burning clay against my bare skin, not when Aisha choked to death on her own blood.

Scheff scooted closer, pulling my feet into his lap. He ran his hand along my leg. The simple motion felt grounding—something I could focus on when everything around me seemed to be balancing on a stack of river rocks. I closed my eyes and let myself enjoy the small comfort.

'*You don't deserve it though, right? Not after what you've done. Selfish, selfish girl.*'

Tension filled the room, and I could tell he was waiting for more. I shouldn't have opened my mouth in the first place and yet, here he was, waiting to listen. I could feel his gaze burning into my cheek as I avoided his eyes, my focus locked on the trees swaying in the breeze. I had no interest in going outside when the flowers were just starting to bloom. Aisha would've been out there, happily digging in that damn garden of hers. I could see her bent over her flowers on a morning like this—her old, leather gloves covering her calloused hands, smudges of dirt on her clothes and face, and her favorite, wind-worn straw hat on her head.

The thought had me eager for another scalding sip of tea. I sat up to let it sink down my throat slowly, embracing the burning sensation.

Scheff reached over, his hand dragging slowly, gently down the side of my face. I wanted to snap at him, to tell him I didn't need his coddling but *damn*, it felt so good. I admitted, "It feels like my chest is caving in. Every day, I wake up and it hits me all over again. I *failed* her. She needed me for the first time in years and I let her die. *Alone.*" I swallowed the lump in my throat as I laid out the truth. I was too tired to keep my walls up, to play games.

"And then, no matter what I do, I feel like I can't breathe. If I did, my pathetic sounds would echo through the goddamn apartment and Ana and Hadley would know that I was crying."

He didn't say anything at first—like he was treading carefully, worried he'd push me back into my haunted reverie. "Is it so bad if they knew you were crying?"

"No one has to pretend that they care if I don't give them anything to care about."

"Do you really think we're pretending?" he asked, picking at a button on the couch.

"I know you are."

"How? How can you be so sure?"

It was my turn to pause. I didn't have an answer he wouldn't want to argue about, and I simply didn't have the energy for it.

"Just...just go, Scheff. I don't need you here."

"I *want* to be here for you."

"Like you've been here once a year for the past six? *You don't care.*"

"Don't throw that in my face like it wasn't your idea. *You* set the rules. I just play the game, Asha."

"If I make the rules, then leave."

"Nice try," he said with a small smile. "But even if I left, you'd have a much harder time convincing your sister that she should leave, stubborn thing that she is." He let out a breathy laugh when he noticed the small smile that pulled at my lips, the first one I'd let slip in days. Stubbornness ran rampant in the blood of all the Arlington women.

"I don't know why she's here either. No one's bothered to check on me in years and suddenly Aisha dies and it's like everyone remembers that I'm alive." The words came out with the ghost of a laugh.

"No one ever forgot about you, Asha. You shut us all out."

Part of me wished that I never engaged with the persistence of the man in the first place. Words and time wasted on someone who couldn't begin to understand.

He sighed, pulling my legs off his lap and laying them on the couch before standing up. "Kate was wondering if she could stop by. Apparently, you guys had some argument, and she didn't want to make you uncomfortable?"

I nodded before chugging the rest of my tea, relishing the pain again. *How long could my lips sit on the rim of the mug before I have to pull away?*

"She said Gretta wanted to bring you some food but wasn't sure what you would eat. Any ideas?"

Silence.

I could smell the memory—the distinct aroma of slow-cooked meat and an assortment of vegetables. The earthy combination had filled Aisha's old apartment building north of Delmar Boulevard, making my stomach grumble as we climbed the flight of stairs that led to my auntie's apartment.

"Hurry your lil asses up," Momma said from behind AnaMarie and me. Her voice was filled with frustration and annoyance—two feelings I was used to stirring in her. Someone was probably waiting for her.

My legs burned as I pushed them to go up the stairs faster. I hated when she was mad at me. I spent most of my time trying to do anything but get on her nerves. That's why I didn't remind her what day it was.

When we finally made it to Auntie's landing, I hunched over, trying to catch my breath. I felt just as tired going up those stairs with Momma pressing behind me as I did when the boys at school challenged me to a race. Like I was always trying to prove myself to someone.

Momma pounded on the door, the sound echoing in the empty hallway. Aisha didn't answer at first which only made Momma hit harder and faster. The neighbors were probably used to all her racket at this point. She'd dropped us off like this enough times for them to not care anymore.

Aisha eventually opened the door, baby Junior sitting on her hip. My auntie looked tired. I noticed the bags under her eyes and her t-shirt covered in white splotches—probably spit up from my happy, babbling cousin.

Ana stepped in and grabbed Junior from my aunt. She was thirteen and got her CPR license so she could babysit around the neighborhood. She told me she didn't really need it though—people were always desperate for someone to watch their kids.

I slid underneath Aisha's arm, eager to get away from Momma's anger.

"I can't keep taking them because of this bullshit, Matta."

"Just tonight, Aisha. I promise I'm turning things around."

Auntie huffed a laugh and shook her head, "One day, I might believe you."

She reminded me of the old ladies we'd see at church when we happened to make it to service—judgment clouding every movement and word.

Momma stepped away from the door, ready to bolt down the stairs and away from us again, before Aisha asked, "You don't even know what today is, do you?"

I looked at Ana whose eyes met mine, sadness lingering between us. Ana didn't forget. She gave me my present when I first woke up—a coloring book and a new pack of colored pencils. Only Momma forgot.

"It's your daughter's fucking birthday and you're running around like some stupid, reckless child. One day, you ain't gonna be able to hide from them, Matta."

I didn't hear Momma's response. I didn't want to. I turned back to Junior and my sister, the two of us trying to see who could make him laugh more.

I heard the door slam and tensed. I was used to Matta being mad, but it was rare for my aunt to get upset—I didn't know how to avoid her anger like I did Momma's. I knew that, if I looked at Aisha, her eyes would be squinted with frustration while her lips were puckered with irritation. So, I pretended like I couldn't hear the angry breath of air she released.

Aisha walked up to me, her footsteps creaking on the old hardwood floors. She crouched down, her arms circling around me, "Happy ninth birthday, lovey. I made your favorite—"

"Pot roast," I said before sinking deeper into the corner of the couch—leaning my head against the armrest, grateful for the thick cushion supporting me as I curled into myself. I let the warmth of the sun wash away the faraway memory of a birthday at Aisha's and welcomed the darkness of sleep.

NINE

I'm going to Aisha's funeral. Real.

It took every ounce of energy I could conjure to get into the shower but I managed. After climbing out of the suffocating heat, I wrapped myself in a towel and swiped a hand across the fogged over mirror. I stood still, watching drops of water cut through the rest of the condensation covering the glass. I caught my eyes in the reflection, dread pulling me closer to look at the shell of who I'd been a week ago. I didn't look *bad* per se—just like I stumbled in on a corpse and hadn't quite figured out how to process it yet. *Yeah, I look pretty fucking bad.*

Deep, purple bags had settled under my eyes, my chocolate-brown irises faded to the color of days-old mud. There was no sign of the little bit of sun I soaked in this spring, the slight glow that usually highlighted my shoulders had totally faded, and I looked *too* skinny—my head appearing too big for my body—like I was a living, breathing bobblehead.

All I had to do was make it through a couple of hours out in the real world and then I could return to the comfort of my bed. I didn't expect to sleep though—Aisha would be waiting to haunt my dreams soon enough.

I stalked out of the bathroom and into the closet, my feet dragging through the thick carpet. I hadn't been in here since I found Aisha. Scheff was on the bench, silently scrolling on his phone while I reached for my damn funeral dress, still hanging in the dry-cleaner's bag from the last one. I quickly ripped the plastic, the protective cover tearing as I dragged my fingers down. I pulled the dress off of the hanger, silently wishing it would get ruined and give me an excuse to stay home, away from the sadness and grief that would plague the church. The church I'd run away from just a couple of weeks ago when Aisha needed me most.

'*Selfish, undeserving,*' the voice crooned.

I hated how eerie it felt to pull it on when it had just made it back from the dry cleaners—not that it fit the same after a week of not eating.

I had just pulled the short, silky sleeves over my shoulders when Scheff stepped behind me, tenderly pulling the zipper up before I even had the chance to struggle with it. His fingers lightly brushed against my neck as he fastened the clasp at the top, his warmth surrounding me and gone in a second.

My chest dropped with a sigh, and I turned around, leaning my head against him. We didn't say a word. Scheff let me stand there for a minute or two before stepping back, his hands resting on my shoulders. "Are you ready?"

His smooth, powerful tenor was a rock in the sea of emotions swelling in my mind, grounding me against the worst of the thoughts that threatened to pull me under:

It's my fault.
She told me she was dying, and I ignored her.
I could've fixed this.
It's my fault.

I don't deserve this comfort from him.
I should be rotting instead of Aisha.
It's. My. Fault.

I nodded before pulling Scheff's hands off of me, the comforting swipe of his thumb now making my skin feel hot with the slick feeling of guilt. I stepped past him to look at myself in the mirror one last time. The same black pearls I'd worn two weeks ago dangled from my ears, the matching necklace resting on my pronounced collarbone and completing my funeral uniform. I put on a coat of lip gloss, slowly rubbing my lips together before wiping a hand under my eye—ensuring the mascara I had hastily thrown on wasn't staining my face. This was the most put together I'd looked in a week. I turned back to my friend, blowing out one more huff before nodding at him.

Scheff reached for my hand and I slipped it comfortably into his, letting him lead me out of the room. The click of my funeral-ready heels hitting the wood floors filled the hallway as we walked closer to Ana and Hadley's soft voices in the kitchen. As soon as we rounded the corner, Scheff dropped my hand—so quickly, it was as if the contact suddenly began to burn. Ana, with her toned arms leaned comfortably against my counter, smiled at him before pulling him closer. She yanked on his sleeves, pulling them down before securing the buttons on his cuffs for him. *Well, that's new.*

A jealous fire coursed through my veins.

'You don't deserve him anyways. Selfish, miserable, girl.'

I tore my eyes from them, directing my attention to the eleven-year-old girl who had changed so much in the six years since I'd last seen her. Her tawny skin was flawless, her hair a crown of chocolate-brown curls sprinkled with alternating streaks of copper and honey atop her head. She perched on the oversized couch, her tall, gangly frame nearly lost in its embrace. She'd grown *a lot*—her long limbs stretching out as the same big, assessing, almond brown eyes latched onto me.

Her eyes flicked from my face to my shifting feet, then found my hand—the one that had started twitching yesterday, each spasm rippling from my wrist to my fingers. Feeling the uncomfortable weight of her scrutiny, I quickly hid both hands behind my back. A wave of helplessness washed over me under her sharp, unrelenting gaze. I shook off the chill it left, forcing my focus back to my sister and Scheff.

"Are we riding together?" I asked, interrupting their rendezvous. Scheff fought to take his attention off of my sister, like whatever she was saying was the most important thing in the world. His head turned slowly, his eyes locked on her, waiting for every last word to fall past her perfect, plump lips before he could give me more than a morsel of his attention. *Typical. Why wouldn't he prefer perfect AnaMarie over the mess that I am?*

I pretended to clear my throat, the sound doing its job of bringing Ana's story to an abrupt halt. This time, their attention found mine with ease, a gentle tug pulled at the corners of my lips. *Triumph.*

"I asked if we were riding together."

Scheff leaned against the counter, looking away as he rubbed a hand behind his neck refusing to make eye contact with me, "We'll ride with Vlad, and Ana and Hads will meet us at the church." Ana and *Hads.* How close had they gotten in the week they'd spent together while I was holed up in my room in grief?

A smoky tension filled the room, everyone's eyes pinned to me, waiting for a reaction. Hadley pulled herself off of the couch, the sound of her black, taffeta dress cutting through the tension. "We can be awkward later," was all she said before walking to the door, the picture of poise and grace. She held her chin high, as if she was above my misery. I looked at Ana, my eyebrows pulled tight in question. She managed a small shrug before following her daughter out the door.

The front door closed gently, the latch securing before Scheff turned to me. "What's wrong?" he asked, reaching for my hand once more. I pulled away from the gesture, all while wishing to lean into it. Yesterday he had told me that he had been content 'just playing the game' in terms of my rules but what if I finally drove him too far? What if I pushed him right into my sister's hands?

"I'm headed to my aunt's funeral, Scheff. For fuck's sake, how do you want me to act?" I snapped, reaching for my clutch and turning for the door. I didn't bother turning around to see if he was following—a cruel part of me knew that he always would. *He should've just gone with Ana and Hadley.*

The elevator welcomed me with its cool, steel arms—an easy escape from Scheff and the gut-wrenching idea of him choosing someone else. He stepped into the bay with me, reaching for the ground floor button while blowing out a breath. I wondered if Ana taught him the breathing trick too.

'You don't deserve someone as calm and patient as him anyways. You'd drive him to his own death before you gave him even an inkling of happiness.'

As soon as the doors began to close, my throat started tightening—my body responding with an intense panic. The shaking in my hands doubled as anxiety and fear shot down to my toes. I leaned against the wall, sucking in desperate breaths, hoping Scheff wouldn't catch sight of my incoming breakdown.

The doors opened a second—that felt like an hour—later, and I all but fell out of the bay in relief, eager for the vast space of the building's lobby. Scheff threw a small wave towards Frank before leading me to the double doors. Vlad was waiting for us at the curb expectantly, the back door of the car already open. He was dressed in a deep, navy suit paired with a silver and navy striped tie—his funeral best, I'd say. I'd never seen him outside of a polo and simple pair of trousers, but he still donned his signature brown flat cap atop his bald head.

"Miss Asha, my dear," he started, his thick eyebrows dipped with concern as his sad eyes glanced over at me. I shifted under his gaze, shocked when he opened his arms wide. *He doesn't expect me to...hug him, does he?*

Before I could politely decline, Scheff's hand pressed against my back, gently urging me forward. Reluctantly, I stepped into my driver's embrace, his arms tightening around me in a hug that felt parental—a quiet assurance that everything would somehow be okay. For a few fleeting seconds, I let my mind wander, pretending that it already was.

I pulled myself away from the portly man, noting the affection on his face and wishing I could make it disappear. I didn't deserve any of this.

"Thank you, Vlad. And thanks for coming to the funeral."

"It is my pleasure, Miss Asha." The stretch of his vowels could've made me smile. I nodded my thanks one more time before sinking into the back seat of the car.

I sank back into my reserved silence, watching as we passed through the city, Vlad and Scheff talking about the current state of the St. Louis Cardinals—the baseball team that usually raked in more disappointment than fans. I made it all of a minute before the overwhelming vibrancy of the city boasting with spring forced me to focus my gaze back inside the car. I couldn't stomach the flowers blooming on the trees, in the bushes, even through the random cracks of dirt that managed to foster life in the middle of an interstate median.

"Beautiful things can grow in the most treacherous of places. You remember that now," Aisha had said once when I was younger, her hands weaving my hair into braids. At the time, she sounded so like a preacher whose voice boomed through church—full of authority, wisdom, and hope. *There's nothing beautiful that could come out of this, Aisha.*

⁂

Scheff deposited me in one of the front rows of the church, the pews reserved for Aisha's closest family members—the four of us who were still alive, at least.

The church crawled with the same nosy fuckers who had shown up at Uncle Charles and Junior's double funeral. The air was heavy—thick with counterfeit grief and the stale promises of faith—clinging to me like my ill-fitting garment.

Flowers were everywhere: an overwhelming array of blues, reds, yellows, and violets stretched from the entrance to the altar. It was as if the only thing anyone knew about Aisha was her love of the damned things. I kept my eyes pinned to the worn maroon carpet running down the center aisle, afraid that if I looked up, I'd drown in the sea of bouquets attached to each pew or the garlands draped from the sides of her open casket.

After what felt like an eternity of musty stillness, Hadley slid into the seat beside me. She must've felt my gaze burning into her cheek because she turned sharply, as if trying to catch me in the act.

"How're you feeling?" I asked, the words fumbling out of my mouth as anxious bubbles popped in my stomach.

She regarded me silently, her eyes darting over my face

with deliberate care, as though she were calculating the best way to handle me. "I'm starting to realize that a lot of grieving is making sure you're ready to take on other people's emotions," she said matter-of-factly.

I glanced at her—my niece, wiser than her eleven years, picking at the shiny, purple nail polish on her fingers.

"And how much do you know about grieving?" I asked, my voice quieter now, as though the question might unravel us both.

"I wasn't a baby when you told Mom that you weren't gonna talk to her again. I was five," she said, as if that was an answer to the question.

"I get it. You've grown up a lot since I last saw you. But that has nothing to do with grief."

"Have *you* grown up at all, Auntie?" The accusation—cleverly veiled as a question—was clear. Her child-like voice, spiked with authority and condescension, grated my nerves. But the cherry on the top was the way she used the title 'Auntie.' The sliver of ease I had found shriveled up and died. Walls began to rise in my mind, sealing me off from the world as stones—black as the pearls now strangling my neck—piled higher, blocking out the room around me.

I froze as the mental walls erected, panic seizing every atom in my body. I couldn't hear anything other than the high-pitched ringing between my ears. I lifted my head to look for Scheff, the movement sluggish, like I was trying to wade through a pool of molasses. I blinked, opening my eyes to a canvas of white, nothing and no one around me. I blinked again, trying to shake myself back to reality as terror seared through my veins. Another blink and I was back in the church, alone. The Aisha that haunted my dreams sitting upright in her casket, her hollow eyes pinning me to the pew.

I felt my lips part, a freezing cold breath passing over them before I tried to call Scheff's name.

A warm hand on my bare thigh shot me back into real life. Hadley was sitting next to me, still picking at her fingertips. I turned to find Scheff by my side, his eyebrows scrunched with worry as his lips curled into a smile that didn't meet his eyes—he didn't want to scare anyone, didn't want to scare *me*. His hand gently squeezed my thigh, reassurance that he was real.

"Are you okay?" His voice was low as he leaned closer, his eyes scanning my face.

My hand jumped to my throat, dry with fear and confusion. I felt dizzy, the ornate chandeliers hanging above us suddenly too bright. "Was I screaming?"

"No, but you looked like you were about to pass out. Do you want some water?"

I nodded, squeezing his hand once, assuring myself that he was here and that this was real.

I was sitting in the godforsaken church again. *Real.*

I was waiting for Aisha's funeral to start. *Real.*

Aisha was dead. *Real.*

Scheff disappeared behind the pews, quickly returning with a cool bottle of water. He sank into the seat and tucked me into his side. The remnants of my panic attack clung to my skin like a winter morning. I willed my body not to shiver and nestled deeper into him.

"A moment of silence for Aisha and her family members, please," the pastor said from his place on the dais.

Only seconds passed before a slam echoed through the chapel. The creak of the heavy, oak doors, and the sound of curiosity driving people to shift in their seats—eager to see who would *dare* cause a commotion at the start of prayer—filled the church.

I knew it was her before I could see her, even as I strained my neck to see over the sea of people here to grieve my aunt—the clicking of her red-bottomed stiletto heels echoed through the room before she let out a truly wretched cry. My mother—selfish, conniving, manipulative woman that she was—decided to drag her ass halfway across the world for the funeral of the sister she had belittled and controlled for most of their lives. I scoffed, rage quickly replacing every other feeling inside of me, my cheeks hot as she continued her show of dramatics. I noted how Scheff stiffened at the sight of her, his arm tightening around me as if he could protect me from her.

She stumbled down the main aisle, her steps interrupted by an occasional fall—in which she'd lean against the wide-eyed mourner closest to her. I sank further into Scheff's side, hoping to avoid any physical contact with Armatta Arlington. Tears spilled down her perfect face, her makeup an invincible shield against the pools that gathered in the few wrinkles she had earned over the years.

Only Armatta would require a dramatic entrance for a funeral.

We all watched—Ana, Scheff, and I in an embarrassed horror, while everyone else seemed genuinely moved by the display. Some people held a hand over their hearts, muttering words of prayer and comfort as Armatta made her way to Aisha's casket. She threw her body over the side, crying loudly.

"My sister," she wailed. "My poor, baby sister. I'm so sorry!" Her senseless yelling filled the nave of the church, ringing in the ears of the entire congregation. My poor aunt couldn't escape the theatrics of her older sister—not even in death.

I started to push myself up from the pew, ready to drag

my dramatic, bitch of a mother out of the building, but Scheff placed his hand over mine. Cool, soft eyes met mine as his lips tucked into a thin line. He stood, adjusted his suit, and calmly made his way to Armatta. One arm wrapped around her back while he rested his free hand on her shoulder. He leaned in to say something to her and, as if by magic, pulled her away from Aisha.

Scheff guided my mother to the family pew, helping her into the empty space on the other side of Hadley, before returning to my side. The pastor cleared the awkwardness of the moment with a soft cough before launching into his spiel about the heavens, a better life, and everlasting peace. I willed myself to focus on his words, the pew, even the floral abundance surrounding Aisha's casket instead of thinking about Evil Incarnate weeping into her tissue two seats away from me.

I scanned the room, my darting eyes eventually pinning to the casket. In the midst of Armatta's theatrics, a strand of peonies—a tidy row of dainty, white petals blooming around bright yellow stamens—had fallen to the ground.

Peonies were Aisha's favorite. When I was younger, when she still lived in that shitty apartment by the riverside, she would clip buds from the bushes of businesses and random houses—eager to see the balled-up petals unfold over the lip of an old wine bottle on her laminate countertop. She planted a few bushes behind the house after they moved in. I imagine she watched them bloom with the same joy pooling in her eyes.

The room went silent, a faint ringing in my ears as the pastor's mouth moved without any sound. Every thought slid from my mind, my fingertips digging into the wood of the pew in front of me as I pulled myself up—an overwhelming need to be near my Auntie forcing me from my seat.

I approached Aisha's casket with slow, measured steps, my arms wrapped tightly around myself as if that could stave off the church's haunted chill. My fingers found my sides, pinching and twisting the flesh until the sharp sting replaced the restless shaking in my bones. My knees burned as I stumbled on the final step and fell hard onto the threadbare carpet. It hadn't changed in decades.

I reached for the loose strand of delicate peonies, pulling a single blossom free before gently tucking the garland back in place. Every movement felt weighted, deliberate.

I sensed Scheff behind me—steadfast as always, likely with his hands clasped in front of him, head down as he waited. He stayed close but silent, a quiet pillar in the distance as I gripped the sides of the casket and peered inside.

Aisha looked peaceful in her lavender dress, the same shade as her favorite herb. Her face, relaxed in eternal rest, was framed by her dark, graying curls. Her left hand, now bare, drew my gaze like a magnet. I felt the wedding ring's absence like a fresh wound.

My hand trembled as I reached for the gold chain around my neck, the cool metal of her ring pressing into my palm. For the last few nights, I'd hidden it under my pillow, clutching it to my chest as nightmares chased away sleep.

"I'm sorry I took it," I whispered, my voice cracking. "I know how selfish I am. I just can't let this piece of you go."

A sob tore from my throat and echoed through the church, raw and untamed, rattling against the stillness around me.

"You were the light in so many people's lives, and I was so focused on being in the dark that I refused to let you shine in mine." I raised a hand to wipe a stray section of curls from her face, rubbing the thin locks between my fingers, trying to memorize the texture. I was eager to preserve *this* version of her death over the one that had been so insistent on haunting me—even as my tears dropped onto her light pink suit, my pain staining the front of her jacket. "It's *so dark* now, Auntie. And I'm *so tired* and I don't know where to find the light."

"I couldn't let her completely ruin your day like that. You deserve—" a hiccup cut off the words. I focused on blowing out a steady stream of air in order to continue. "—a beautiful, and perfect celebration. You deserve a sunny day, with just enough of a breeze to keep you cool...and the smell of all of your favorite flowers wrapping around you like your favorite blanket. With a big, fat, angel food cake, covered in sugared strawberries and whipped cream." A small laugh burst through my grief. It took me a second to steady my breathing again, wiping at the tears and snot starting to pool under my nose. My voice rose, exasperation freeing itself from my chest. "And peace. *God, Auntie*, you've earned some fucking peace."

A few gasps sounded from behind me, and I became painfully aware of all of the eyes currently pinned on me—my back ablaze from the judgmental crowd.

I leaned forward, the edge of the casket pressing into my stomach as I kissed my Aunt Aisha on the forehead—my lips lingering as I remembered all the times she would comfort me as a child with the same gesture. I slowly pulled away, wiping one of my tears away as it ran down her face. I placed the peony over her clasped hands, whispering in her ear. "Good-bye, Auntie. Rest well."

I turned to face the crowd, grateful for Scheff who was already stepping towards me, his arms open, waiting for me to collapse into them. He helped me down the aisle, basically carrying me as I sobbed into his side. The only thing strong enough to distract me was the brief burst of rage I felt as I met Armatta's cold, tear-filled glare that said, *How dare you take* any *attention away from me, your mother?*

I tore myself from the safety and comfort of my best friend's side, shoving a finger in my mother's face. I made sure the harsh words were whispered, loud enough only for Armatta to hear. "*You* don't deserve to be here. She may have forgiven you, but I will never forget how you treated her."

Her bottom lip began quivering, tears wielded like a weapon spilling down her cheeks as she leaned back, falling into Hadley's lap.

"Asha, come on," Scheff softly urged. I threw one more glare towards my mother before finally meeting his worried eyes.

"Take me home?" I asked. He nodded his head, guiding me down the aisle and out of the church.

As we crossed the threshold of the church, I glanced back to see Hadley, her stare burning a hole through me. Guilt pooled in my gut as our eyes locked, as she watched me walk away from our family once again.

Ten

I woke up to the sounds of hushed voices and muffled laughter coming from the direction of my kitchen. Confusion weighed down my eyebrows as I tried to shake the fog of sleep still clinging to my brain. Flashes from the morning passed through my head as I wiped my eyes, leftover makeup smudging on my fingers.

Once we made it outside of the church, Scheff had ordered a car and rushed me back to the apartment where I promptly stripped down and crawled into bed. I didn't even have the energy to run a wipe over my face before sleep pulled me into its exhausted grasp.

It was the comforting smell of pot roast and the echo of Scheff's laugh that finally pulled me from the bed. I slid into my slippers before reaching for the terry cloth robe that hung loyally by the door, and wrapped the oversized garment tight against my body, cinching it at the waist. I slowly pushed down the door handle, trying to prevent the sound of the lock releasing and the pull of the hinges from announcing my arrival.

Kate's melodious laugh rang through the apartment as

the door opened, and I could only assume the sound of the kitchen orchestra—steam rumbling the lid on a pot, the light clink of silverware being set beside plates, the sizzle and crack of something frying on the stove, and the steady beat of a knife chopping against a cutting board—was Gretta's doing. I doubted Kate or Scheff set aside their type-A personalities to work together in the kitchen, so the promised pot roast would be left in the hands of Kate's girlfriend.

Scheff was probably basking in the attention of an apartment full of women, combing his hand through his silky hair as Ana batted her eyes at him. I could hear my sister mumble something which filled the room with a burst of laughter— everyone's individual sound melding together into one. If it didn't make me feel completely sick with anxiety to have them all in my apartment, I might've found the moment...beautiful. I could only assume Hadley was close by, silently observing everyone's interactions and assigning judgements accordingly. I turned the corner to see the adults huddled around the island.

I had never had this particular group of people together at once—Kate stood comfortably next to Scheff on one side, their faces lit up with smiles as they animatedly talked with Ana, who mirrored their energy. Hadley lounged on the couch, completely at ease, while Gretta darted around my kitchen with a confident buzz. Her hands never stopped moving—cutting the pot roast, plating the side dishes, and somehow, at the same time, preparing cocktails.

I wasn't sure how long I stood there, watching from the doorway, but it was long enough for the scene to etch itself into my mind. Long enough for the sound of smooth jazz to crawl under my skin. Someone had connected their phone to the speakers, casting the obnoxious background noise over the odd group.

You would never have guessed that they just left a funeral service, all of them—even Scheff's uptight ass—wearing *loungewear*. Were they seriously planning on a pajama party?

'We can change that.'

I trudged past them all, heading straight for my liquor cabinet. I reached inside, my fingers tightening around a half-empty bottle of bourbon, grounding me as I reached for a glass. Their eyes followed me, the pity in their stares an excruciating weight—the tilt of Ana's head, the slight furrow of Scheff's brows, and Kate's doe-eyed concern, all screaming the same thing: *she's falling apart.*

I pulled the cork, taking a few gulps from the bottle before pouring a generous amount into the glass—the amber liquid rising faster than I intended, spilling over the rim. A sharp laugh escaped my lips, louder than I meant it to be. "Oops."

I sucked the excess liquor off the rim, ignoring the growing tension in the room.

"Asha, what the fuck?" Ana snapped, her voice sharp enough to cut through the thick air.

I turned to her, glass in hand, a lazy smirk tugging at my lips. "I haven't eaten in, what? A week? You can't blame me if I get a *little* tipsy, a *little* fast." I swirled the bourbon before taking another swig, savoring the burn as it slid down my throat. Two more of these and I guarantee even Aisha wouldn't be able to haunt me tonight.

"That's not an excuse," she shot back, her voice teetering on the edge of fury.

"I'm sorry." I laughed, swirling the last shot in my glass. "I seem to have forgotten whose house this is. Oh, right, Ana. It's mine. If you don't like my behavior, *leave.*"

"We're all here to be supportive," Ana snapped back. The

tension in the room was as strong as the alcohol working its way through my body.

"I didn't ask for your support. You assumed I needed it. You always assume, Ana." I turned the stool seat, looking for Hadley who was burrowed into what seemed to be her favorite corner of the couch. "Your mom ever tell you what assuming does, *Hads*? It makes an ass out of you and—"

"Asha, stop," Scheff reprimanded as he took place behind Ana. *Was it jealousy or the alcohol twisting knots in my stomach?*

I hated how they looked standing next to each other, how they looked standing united *against me*.

"Ooh, Scheff and Ana. The newest dynamic duo." At least they had the decency to look confused by the statement. "Like I said, if you don't like me, leave."

"Did you ever stop to think that maybe *we* needed support, Asha? You're not the only one who lost a fucking aunt, okay? We all deal with your dramatic shit but fuck. Hadley and I needed this. Kate and Scheff knew Aisha too. Why don't we get to grieve? Why is it *always* about you?" A loose curl fell, freeing itself from the bun crowning her head, framing the side of her face. Even in anger my sister looked utterly perfect.

I squeezed the glass in my hand, ignoring the tight strain that ran through my fingers. Everyone froze as the truth made its way around the room, only Hadley brave enough to move —and that was only to stalk into the guest bedroom, locking herself behind the door. Gretta and Kate turned their backs to us, pretending not to listen as they finished the food preparations—low, hurried whispers drifted from the corner of the kitchen, their voices too soft to make out.

A thousand memories ran through my head, arguments with Ana throughout the years as we battled wills. As each other's primary source of entertainment, petty fights were common. I tried to ignore the painful familiarity of her words.

"I didn't ask for you to host your support group in my apartment. Hell, I didn't ask for you to stay for the last week, but you invited yourself in anyway. What's wrong with your apartment, Ana? *You don't have to be here.*"

"You don't think I can't hear you screaming yourself awake every night? Puking, only to drag yourself back into bed. How do you think that's going to get better? By sulking in your room? Refusing to eat? Not talking to anyone? Making an ass out of yourself just to prove a fucking point?"

"And what do any of you do about that!? Wait till you're all together so you can discuss how I'm grieving? You lost an aunt, Ana, but *I found her fucking body.* Don't talk to me about *grief.*"

"Poor, Asha. Everybody dropped what they were doing to make sure *you* were okay. You couldn't even keep yourself together long enough to get through the funeral. If Armatta was ever right about one thing, it was you."

"Shut the fuck up, Ana!" I clenched my fist around the glass once more, instantly shattering it. I looked down at the constellation of broken pieces—a few had found their way into my hand, blood slowly pooling around the shards. The last little swig of alcohol left in the glass sank into the cuts and I hissed as my brain started to recognize the pain. My hand felt like it was on fire, but all I could do was watch.

My gaze landed on the shards first—scattered across the countertop and glinting in the light, like the fragments of some grim prophecy. Then the blood pooling in my hand, pain points pulsing in time with my heartbeat. The searing pain muted by the strange fascination I found in the crimson streaks slowly winding down my arm.

For a moment, no one moved. The room held its collective breath, the charged silence encouraging me to say something—to lash out, crack a joke, anything to cut through the weight pressing down on me—but all I could do was sit there, helpless against the chaos I'd created.

It seemed like everyone decided to react at the same time —Ana's wide-eyed stare cut through the haze, her lips parting like she wanted to say something but wasn't sure how I'd react. I caught the soft click of the guest room door as Hadley peeked out, her paled face disappearing just as quickly. Gretta cursed under her breath, her words cutting through the tension as she whispered something to Kate, who kept flicking her gaze between me and the floor, her hands twisting nervously at her sides.

Finally, Scheff moved. His steady presence cut through the fog, and I looked up as he reached for me. A wet cloth was in one hand, the other gently cradling mine. I didn't flinch. The first sting of the cloth against my skin was sharp enough to jolt me back into my body.

Ana's hand hovered near her mouth, horror widening her eyes, but she stayed rooted in place. Kate and Gretta stood huddled in the corner, Gretta's arm waving passionately in my direction. None of it mattered now—not the whispers, not the stares—just Scheff's hands working dilligently to extract the shards.

"That hurt," I whined.

"Don't go breaking glasses like you're Superman and it wouldn't hurt." He let out a huff of frustration before asking Ana to hold her phone flashlight over my hand. "You're lucky none of these went too deep."

Gretta pulled herself from a clearly shaken Kate, only to slam a plate of food down in front of me. "When he's done? Eat."

She turned, ripping the apron from her waist before setting to work, dumping her dinner masterpiece into various take-out containers. Leave it to Gretta to bring to-go boxes from the restaurant. Leave it to me to force her to use them prematurely.

I reached my free hand for the bourbon, my fingers brushing against the neck of the bottle right as Ana swiped it away, "You're *done*." And leave it to the only parent present to rip my salvation away like I was a spoiled baby.

"Do you want me to take you to the hospital to get stitches?" Scheff asked as he gingerly wrapped gauze around my hand.

"Where did you get that," I asked, confused by the magical bag of medical supplies that had found its way into his lap.

"I found it in a med kit hidden away in the linen closet." No doubt stocked by the same assistant that was now avoiding my gaze, barricaded behind the island.

"Someone's always taking care of me, huh?" I asked, looking up at him through eyelids weighed down by bourbon.

"Maybe one day you'll see it for what it is," Scheff replied, heaving a sigh as he pulled himself up from the floor. "Now, hospital or shower?"

I ignored whatever he was trying to imply, hopping off the stool and chancing one more glance around the kitchen. Ana's hands were clenched into fists, her knuckles white against her dark skin, her eyes betraying the softness of guilt beneath her anger. Gretta busied herself at the sink, her motions jerky and angry, while Kate simply stood still, a hand pressed to her mouth as though holding back words that wouldn't come. "Shower. I want to watch it heal."

None of them met my gaze as I walked down the hallway,

their eyes heavy and judgmental. I let the shower run for a few minutes before hopping in, hoping that the delay would give everyone time to leave. I let the water run over me, trying to keep my bandaged hand from getting wet. I didn't know if Scheff would still be around to wrap it back up.

I left the steamy room, drying my hair with a towel as I walked back to the kitchen. The door to the guest room was slightly open, the room spotless and free of Ana and Hadley's belongings. The pulsing in my hand was grounding. A sharp, insistent reminder that I was still here, still alive, even when I didn't deserve to be. The pain was cleaner than the tangled mess of emotions in my head, simpler. It was something I could hold onto, something that didn't ask me to be okay. It reminded me of when I first moved in—an empty house that gave me room to breathe. The same loneliness that scared me then echoed with every step I took away from my room.

Scheff stood by the door, his jacket tucked under his arm and his hands buried in his sweatpants' pockets. He looked me over slowly, his eyes lingering like there was an answer to his problems hiding somewhere on my body. For a moment, his brow furrowed, a final show of worry pursing at his lips before his mask of indifference slipped back into place.

"I'll come check on you tomorrow," he said, his voice too steady, as though he were already halfway out the door. I nodded, the only confirmation I could give him before he turned and walked out of the door.

As soon as the latch clicked, I raced to the liquor cabinet, pulling a fresh bottle of bourbon from its hiding spot behind an empty box of peanuts. I don't know why I hadn't thought to have a drink earlier in the week—the alcohol was a salve against the warring sides of my brain. I paused, reaching for a glass before damning that idea. *Who's gonna wash it tomorrow?*

I tilted the bottle against my lips, letting the cool rim rest against my mouth before I began chugging it.

There was a game Scheff and I used to play in undergrad —something to do with counting down from five like we were children. The first person had to drink for five seconds before passing the bottle to the other who had to then drink for four seconds, the cycle continuing until we made it to one second each.

Scheff wasn't here but I could still play.

Five...*Aisha's dead, and today was her funeral, and, somehow, Armatta found a way to ruin it. She's good at that— ruining things.*

Four...*Ana jumped ship. It's like I'm fifteen again, utterly helpless as she storms out of the apartment without a second glance.*

Three...*Kate's feelings toward me were clear, the disgust she felt clinging to her like a bodycon dress.*

Two...*Scheff made a mysterious return and could potentially end up with Ana.*

One...*Armatta is back.*

The moon beamed through the gossamer curtains, highlighting the emptiness that coated the apartment once everyone left.

"Take me to the river, I wanna go." I drunkenly sang the words that my aunt had loved. My voice was raw and the sounds of misplaced notes grated against my throat as my thoughts mixed with the heady alcohol. It should've been me instead of Aisha. *She* should be here. Nobody needs me—not like they needed her.

I climbed into the king-sized guest bed, letting the smell of my sister wrap around me, clinging to the bourbon like a newborn to a bottle. Silent tears dampened the pillow under my head as the voice in my mind quieted to nothing more than a mumble. I focused on a spot on the wall until I lost the fight against consciousness, my eyes slowly blinking toward a heavy sleep.

I could've sworn it was Aisha's voice luring me into the deep, black pit.

You gotta be your own light now, baby.

ELEVEN

JUNE

Releasing my grip on the bottle that had become my cuddle buddy the night before, I groaned and rolled to my back. Scheff was making good on his promise to check in this morning, the sound of the key in the lock rousing me from my fitful sleep in the guest bed.

"Fuck," I groaned as I covered my face with my hands. I could feel the overwhelming brightness that was waiting for me once I pulled my swollen eyelids apart.

"Asha?" Scheff's voice rang out from the kitchen.

"Present," I moaned. I would've hidden the bottle under the pillow or something but the overwhelming need to stay still took precedence. *I will not throw up in this bed.*

"Someone had a good night." Scheff sounded like he was closer, so I opened one eye, lifting my hand enough to see him leaning against the door frame. He looked so odd in yesterday's gray sweatpants with a tight black shirt, its sleeves pushed up to his elbows. How he managed to make simple athleisure somehow *formal*, I'd never know. I covered my eye again, replacing my hand in an attempt to return to my envelopment of painless dark.

"I think we have different definitions of *good*." I drew in a breath, trying to keep the nausea at bay. "Help me?"

The words came out in a whine as I rallied my energy to sit up. I held my free hand up in the air and waited for him to come to my aid. I stayed in that position for a few seconds before cracking my eye open again. Scheff remained against the doorframe, chuckling as he raised a hand to his chin, brushing a new growth of stubble.

"I just want to be clear. *Now* you want help?"

"I do believe those were the words that *just* left my mouth."

"Ask *nicely*," he teased, his voice lilting in the same singsongy way his nieces would when we babysat them in our undergrad days.

"Scheeeeeff."

"It's one measly word."

"Help me, *please*." I paused, waiting for his hand to connect with mine. He obliged as I added, "Before I drag myself from this bed just to beat your ass."

"At your service." He laughed, the sound deep, and rich—an invitation to come back to the land of the socially functioning.

Scheff rubbed my back as he pulled me up. I focused on breathing through the nausea and the stabbing pain radiating at the base of my skull. "I brought you some breakfast. I wish I could stay and watch ultra-hungover Asha try and get through the day, but I have a few things that I need to handle. Are you gonna be okay?"

"Why wouldn't I be?" I said sarcastically as I tried to shuffle out of the bed but the oversized white duvet had twisted around my feet, effectively trapping me.

I groaned as Scheff laughed, my back feeling the abandonment of his hand as he moved to free my legs from the cover. I threw them over the side of the bed as soon as he finished, pain knocking in my head at the sudden movement.

"*Fuck,*" I hissed as I pressed my hands to my temples.

"You'll be fine. You used to drink way more in college."

"Yes, Scheff, but that was six years ago. I'm not the young, spry, undergrad eager to drown in bottles of alcohol anymore."

"You sure?" The words were clipped with accusation as his eyes pinned to the bourbon resting behind me. I ignored the mortification that heated my cheeks as I looked at my bandaged hand.

"Whatever. You said something about food?"

"Yeah, just a few things I grabbed from the hotel."

"Busy man today," I said as I tried to stretch the heavy feeling of sleep away.

He hesitated a moment, swiping at something on the bedside table before lifting his head, his focus turning to something in the hallway. "*Someone* has to keep the office running, Asha dear."

I didn't miss the note of accusation, letting out a frustrated breath before pushing myself off the bed and heading for the kitchen. I looked at the sad take-out box he brought from the hotel—an unremarkable trio of biscuits, eggs, and bacon tucked inside.

"What, no coffee?" I mused, trying to add some levity to the room.

"I figured you'd make some here," he said as he followed me into the kitchen. His feet stepped in time with the, now vibrating, phone in his pocket, stealing his attention from me. "I gotta run though, looks like Kate needs me to pick something up on my way in."

"There is no way you're going to the office looking like that," I said as my stomach roared. While the food was utterly unappealing, the smell had my appetite growing. *It* had *been a week since I ate a full meal.*

"See, that's kind of the perk of owning the company. I can show up however I want," he said with a wink. "And I'm not staying long anyways. Just dropping something off and picking up a few files Kate wants me to look over."

The acrid taste of jealousy filled my mouth as I realized that Scheff was doing *my job*. Just a few weeks ago I was complaining about how many intake files I had to thumb through and now, here I was, wasting my days away in my personal, apartment-sized isolation chamber.

'They don't need you. They never have.'

"I might not make it over for a few days, but I'll check back in when I can." His hand wrapped tightly around the front door handle—his fingers twisting around it in a way that made me miss how they felt tangled with mine.

I waited for him to say something else but no words came out as he huffed a laugh, and shook his head, opening the door and stepping through. It slammed behind him, leaving me to my thoughts and the uninspired box of food waiting for me on the counter.

I opened the container, reluctantly grabbing a biscuit before taking a bite. I choked down the stale hunk of dough while thinking about the fluffy orange scones Scheff had baked for me just a few days ago.

§

I hadn't seen Scheff in a week—not since he brought me last Sunday's budget breakfast—and found myself reduced to a daily text check in and a lunch delivery. Anxiety started to build as I worried that he'd finally replaced me, wondering if he'd managed to forget about me all ready. Sometimes I'd wait a few hours to respond to his welfare texts, just to see if it would entice some type of reaction out of him.

It didn't.

'*Maybe you're not worth his precious time after all,*' the voice said.

I spent a lot of time staring out of the sunroom window, an imprint of my ass starting to form on the couch that lounged in front of it. My body was starting to itch from boredom, but I couldn't find the energy to do anything. So, I continued to rot.

The small trash bin I had placed by the couch in the sunroom—filled with tissues that were soaked with tears from the last few days—overflowed, an avalanche piling up on the floor beside me. Disgusted words whispered in my head when I looked at it, disappointed reminders of how weak I was.

Half-drank cups of earl gray tea—Aisha's favorite—congregated on the coffee table, mocking me. The ever-present voice in my head screaming about how lazy and dirty I was.

An abandoned stack of dirty dishes—from last Saturday's dinner and show—still rested on the counter next to the sink. The food scraped off by my friends left streaks of sauce and small chunks of debris that had crusted over since. When I passed by the ceramic graveyard, I heard echoes in my mind about how horrible and selfish I was.

On Monday, two weeks after she and Hadley abandoned me, Ana texted but only to say that I was needed for a meeting with Aisha's lawyer the following week. The words were curt. Clearly she was still mad.

On Tuesday, Scheff sent a bouquet of flowers to my door, the note tucked inside holding only a small heart with a scrawled 'S' beside it. The elaborate mix of lilies and lavender quickly found its way to the trash as the haunting image of Aisha, surrounded by peonies, overwhelmed the sincerity of the gesture.

By Wednesday, I *knew* the strain of isolation was getting to me. When Aisha haunted me from my dreams, I'd wake up and trudge to the kitchen before making another cup of tea, settling into my cozy corner on the couch—content with turning my brain off while I watched life continue outside. She never stepped a foot in this apartment and yet I could still feel my aunt's touch in everything around me.

The afternoon sun was warming my face when a whiff of Aisha's perfume shocked my senses. The smell was so strong. The distinctive combination of lavender and honeycomb took me back to when I was five—pressed against her chest as she gave me one of her warm hugs. Tears burned my eyes, but I blinked them away.

"Sometimes I think I'm going crazy, Aisha. I know it's not real, it couldn't *possibly* be real. But it feels like you're here. It's like I can feel the dip of the couch, like you're sitting right next to me. And if I lean over, I *know* your perfume would drive me insane." My voice cracked, raw after days of not speaking. *Yeah, definitely going crazy.* "I ordered some more earl gray from your favorite tea shop. I try to make it like you would, but I can never get the right amount of honey. You were always good at that—making everything perfectly sweet." I cleared my throat, taking another sip of the scalding tea as I tried to get my muscles to relax. I pulled on the ring still hanging from the chain around my neck, letting the bite of the prongs ground me as I squeezed.

"Do you remember when I was like, seven? Maybe eight? Armatta was in Vegas for a week, and we were staying with you." I rolled my neck, enjoying each *pop* as I realized how stupid I was in waiting for a response.

The oak trees swayed in the breeze, and a starling dove to the ground. I allowed myself a small smile as the vibrant hues in its wings flashed in the sun. "You took us out of the city to your friend's house. They had a couple of kids my age and they lived on a farm—a couple of acres of land. You told us to, *'Go run and play. I'm gonna be right here if you need anything.'*"

I listened as my sister ran away with the other kids—I think the boy's name was Jakob, and the girl was Jiah, but I couldn't remember for sure—my anxious eyes pinned to Aisha. What if she left us too?

She ran a hand down my face and gave me a wink before turning me toward the field that the others disappeared into. I turned, reluctantly stomping down the steps and away from my auntie.

'Come on, Asha!' Ana called from up ahead. The grass was up to my armpits, brushing against the skin on my arms as I ran, trying to catch up to my sister. Giggles weaved through the weeds as the other kids ran alongside me.

The breeze that danced through the trees cooled the sweat that coated on my back—the air smelling of sunscreen, freedom, and oak trees in July.

"I'm coming!"

We spent hours playing in the field, swimming in the small pond that was tucked in the trees behind the house, and eating some of the ice cream that Auntie's friend made. The summer heat chased us into the evening hours and, after we ate dinner, we hid in the shadows looking for fireflies to catch in jars. After an hour of watching them through the glass, the others went inside, leaving me and Ana sitting together on the front steps, mesmerized by the flickering lights of stars we couldn't see from the city.

"When is Momma gonna come home?" I asked.

"Ain't no telling, Ash."

I leaned forward and plucked a piece of grass from a patch along the walkway, desperate for something to do with my fingers. I rolled it into a small tube before reaching for another, rolling it and tying them together. I repeated the process, working quietly as horrible thoughts ran through my head. I knew I shouldn't say anything—Auntie always said that 'some things are better kept to yourself'—but it was so quiet out here and I knew Ana would keep my secret.

"Sometimes I wish she'd just stay away." Shame crawled up my spine as I mumbled the words that haunted me on the nights we stayed with Aisha.

Ana's shoulder bumped into mine as she leaned forward, reaching for the jar that housed the last firefly. She cracked the lid, releasing a breath before opening it fully, dumping it over to set the small bug free. "Sometimes I wish she would too."

A hard knock at the door tore me from the memory, the feeling of Aisha's presence disappearing from the couch. I groaned as I pulled myself up, setting my teacup on the table.

I looked through the peephole, anxiety swirling in my gut as I reached to unlock the door. I quickly swung it open to find a giant paper takeout bag with TEMITOPE printed on the front.

"Kate?" The words sounded hoarse to my ears as they danced through the hall, bouncing off the walls before seeping into the bricks of the empty corridor. I slowly stepped back inside— locking the door behind me before pulling out my phone. I started to text Kate and had the two simple words typed out but paused, my thumb hovering over the send button. *If she wanted my thanks she would've waited at the door.*

I tucked the phone back into my pocket with a huff of disappointment before moving into the kitchen, ripping into the bag, and pulling out the bounty of take-out containers. Kate's deliberate handwriting labeled each and every one—white rice, pan-fried green beans, roasted chicken, mashed sweet potatoes, and kale. There was enough food here to last me the next three days.

I arranged a small serving on a plate before filling a glass with bourbon, carrying both back to my bedroom. I climbed into bed, folding my legs underneath me as I turned on the TV. I knocked back the liquor, barely tasting the food as I forced myself to eat. It wasn't that the food was bad—Gretta's food was never bad. It was the fact that, as soon as it passed over my lips, it turned to ash and I had to force myself to finish. *Bite, chew, swallow.*

The squeals from some reality show bimbo filled the silence between my bites and I stared at the screen while the mind-numbing buzz took over.

⁂

Scheff had called a few days later, saying I was needed in the office to sign some papers—what I'd call a desperate attempt to get me to leave my apartment. I'd been sitting in the chair opposite him for an hour now, silently observing as he went through the motions, offering me the odd stack of papers now and then.

"How's Kate?" I asked, picking at the patched corner of

the desk in my office. Scheff sat across from me, leaning back in *my* chair with *my* pen pinched between his fingers.

His eyes darted around anxiously as he pulled himself from behind the desk, walking around before sitting on the edge in front of me. "Honestly? She's been drowning the last couple of weeks. She didn't want to tell you because she didn't want to add to what you're going through."

He focused on a loose stack of files, picking through a couple, briefly looking through them before either setting them down or adding them to the group in his hands. After filing through a couple, he turned his attention back to me, his eyebrows pulling together in that worried way that was starting to feel all too familiar.

'*Pity. He pities you.*'

I picked at my sleeve, eager to have something to focus on as I tried to ignore how wrong it felt for me to be here. The plants seemed to be thriving in my absence and I didn't doubt the same could be said for the rest of the office morale as well. I lifted my eyes, looking out on the balcony, wishing for a breeze to rattle through the doors and offer a reprieve from the regret that seemed to be glued to my skin.

"You are withering away right in front of me and all you'll let me do is *watch*. There isn't anything anyone can do about it because you don't trust any of us enough to tell us how to help. You need to make some decisions, Ash." He looked so comfortable perched on the desk—the files of families I had worked so hard to secure pinched in his hand. "Are you going to come back anytime soon? Do we need to work on restructuring? I don't want you to do anything that feels wrong but—"

"I'll come back," I said, the hushed words felt stale in my mouth. "It's time."

He set the papers on the desk behind him, before pulling

my hand into his. His stare lingered on my dry, chewed-up cuticles before those worried ocean eyes met mine. "And you need to talk to someone. It doesn't have to be me, but Ana and I think you should find a therapist. Or just *someone* to talk to."

I ripped my hand from his, the intimate contact suddenly burning at the mention of him and my sister. I shook my head, huffing a laugh while disbelief blew through my nose. "Oh, of course. Whatever *you and Ana* say. You guys know what's best for poor little Asha."

"Just let someone help you."

"There's nothing wrong with me—nothing to help. If any of you saw what I saw, you'd be acting the exact same way."

"No, Asha. I wouldn't give up on living because I saw a dead body."

"My dead *aunt's* body, Matthew."

He laughed, his head tipping back as the sound filled the room. "And now I'm *Matthew*."

"What's wrong with using your name?" I rolled my neck, trying to breathe through the frustration and annoyance that were creeping up my spine.

"You only use it when you want something. Right now, you want me to drop the subject—fine. Consider it dropped. But, as majority owner of the company, I *will* suggest to the shareholders that a mental evaluation be required before you assume your position again."

I froze. "You wouldn't."

"I absolutely would. If it means that you get a sliver of help from someone, I *will* force your hand in this. I don't care how much you hate me."

"Why does it matter? Why do you guys care?"

"If you can't understand that we actually love you, take it

from a selfish point of view. If you don't get your shit together, this entire company, all of those employees out there? Their cushioned lives will fall apart. My investment sinks and Kate loses a job. Ana is your sister and, no matter how far you push her away, she still gives a damn about you. None of us want to see you drown."

My icy glare clashed with the heat and compassion swimming in his eyes. "Then maybe it's time you guys stop watching."

The following Monday, I woke to the incessant *beep* of my alarm. It was the first time in weeks I was able to open my eyes before Aisha's screams sent me crawling for consciousness. I showered, drank an extra-strong cup of coffee—black—and managed a few bites of toast before going downstairs to meet Vlad.

His eyebrows jumped in shock as he glanced over me. My face was bare and framed by still-wet curls that were starting to reach my mid-back. I'd thrown on my softest pair of sweatpants, a baggy hoodie that I could hide under, and, for the first time in *years*, a pair of sneakers.

I hadn't seen Vlad since the funeral but at least he was back to his normal self—the giant ball of excitement and energy I'd grown used to kindly held my morning brew as I settled into the car before he bounced around to the driver's seat. I raised the steaming cup of coffee—and bourbon—to my lips and relished the mix as it swirled in my stomach.

The drink swirled in my hands, a high aided by Vlad's silence and a quick commute.

It wasn't anticipation tying my stomach in knots—just dread as I tried to compose myself in the backseat. If it wasn't for my trusty concoction, I doubted I'd have the nerve to show up in the first place. I forced the door open, mumbling a thank you to Vlad before attempting to walk inside with a modicum of grace. *One foot in front of the other, Ash.*

I waved at the building receptionist, blowing out a steady breath as soon as the elevators closed around me. I counted the seconds as the lift began pulling me toward the office. I could do this—I could be *normal.* The elevator sounded with a ding, opening to reveal what had been my life for the last three years—anxious thoughts rumbling through my head as I pushed the glass doors open and stepped inside.

Everyone seemed to be working diligently—or avoiding me—as I walked through, throwing haphazard smiles to the people who caught my eye.

"No, Mrs. Granders, I'd be happy to get you and your family in as soon as possible. We have quite the waitlist..." Kate's voice greeted me before I could see her, the lilt of her consoling tone weaving through the desks littering the office floor. The sound called to me, making me want to stop and see her bright smile but I was focused on making it to my office first—the promise of privacy waiting if I could just make it across the threshold. "Yes, I know. I would be happy to place you on the list if you could just—"

I turned down the aisle that led to my office, intent on walking by Kate without a glance in her direction. I picked up my pace, the sound of my yoga pants swishing with each step. *Six more steps and you're in your office. You can do it, Ash.*

The comforting buzz from my drink had claimed residence in the back of my head, encouraging a confidence my feet were unprepared for. The toe of my sneaker caught on the corner of Kate's desk, pain radiating from my foot to my head as I doubled over, lightly knocking my forehead against the desk. My teeth sank into my bottom lip as I tried to keep my scream inside, my focus jumping to the mug in my hand —the liquid crashing angrily against the walls of its confinement as it tried to settle back into a calm, rested state.

Once my drink and I found our footing, I looked at Kate, the client on the phone a forgotten memory, as she watched the 'Asha Arlington: One Woman Show.' I silently laughed, swiping my hand across my forehead in exaggerated relief. *I didn't spill.*

My eyebrows dragged together as I looked at her desk— the area, usually overflowing with pictures, tchotchkes, and random mementos seemed...plain. The ray of irritating sunshine that usually surrounded her had dimmed, the only spot of color the bright pink puffball pen that delicately rested between her fingertips.

The small plant she'd named *Petunia*—despite the thing being a pothos—was surely dying in its black and white polka dotted planter. Her corkboard, typically full of bright, color-coded notes and meeting reminders, was bare save for two notes hung from the very bottom—both with writing too light and dainty for me to make out from my place in front of her desk. I made a mental note to ask her about it before putting two fingers to my forehead in salute and marching toward my office.

I closed the door behind me, gliding to the desk to set down my coffee before bursting into a fit of giggles. I kicked my sneakers off and slipped my toes into the comfort of the carpet when Kate came barreling through the door, slamming it behind her.

"Are you *drunk?*" Her shrill voice bounced off the walls of my office as I sank into my chair.

"Drunk? No. Tipsy? Perhaps," I giggled before leaning forward, pressing against the desk as I tried to reach for my coffee cup.

"Oh, no. No, no, no," she said, pulling the mug out of my reach. My head dropped in defeat as she lifted it to her nose and sniffed. "Asha, is there even any coffee in this?"

"A *splash*, one might say." I dug my foot into the ground forcefully, spinning the chair a few times.

"Asha, I can't do this anymore."

"Hmmm," I started, my fingers itching to loop into the handle of the mug Kate was holding hostage in her hands. "Do what, exactly?"

"*This!* You being drunk and me having to cover all the holes that *you* used to fill. *You* insisted on having all client files run by you. *You* insisted on weekly IT meetings to ensure things were up to your standards. You wanted to have input in every department and now everything is *falling apart*. I don't know what to say when they look to me for answers, and I am *drowning* here. I can't keep showing up for someone who has no interest in showing up for herself."

Irritation was enough to sober me up a bit as I Kate picked at the bottom of her blazer—a navy blue number that matched her pants. If she hadn't been on the verge of totally killing my buzz, I would've asked her where it was from.

"Gretta and I have been talking for a while now and—"

"Ah, so that's what you two were whispering about in my apartment. Conspiring against me in my own home." I laid a hand over my heart in dramatic and, albeit feigned, disbelief. "That's low, Kate."

"Conspiring!? I've always wanted what's best for you. I want you to be happy and healthy and this goes back *months*, Asha. *Years*." Tears lined her eyes as her cheeks flushed. "You're so intent on being isolated and depressed that you can't even see how far I've gone to prove how much I care."

"Come on. We both know that the only thing you care

about is that weekly paycheck and your precious writing time. How's that going for you anyways?"

"It would be going a hell of a lot better if my boss held up her end of the deal and actually came to work for once. Fuck, Asha! *This* is what I can't do. I don't *want* to fight with you like you want to fight everyone in your life. If you're so fixed on being sad and alone, then I'm done." Her face scrunched together like she was at war with the thoughts inside of her head.

"I quit."

Twelve

My return-to-work routine relied on steady pours from a secret bottle of bourbon into my coffee cup to defend myself against the sea of people asking endless questions. When the only thing left in my mug was the ring of coffee drying at the bottom, I would sneak away, locking myself in the utility closet responsible for hiding a broom, vacuum, paper towels, and now, my trusty bottle of Bulleit. It took a couple miscalculated attempts, but I had perfected the ratio and timing, able to ride a slight buzz all day without appearing drunk.

Thank God for it too because Scheff had begun to cling to me like a second skin when I was in the office—his refusal to leave me alone since Kate quit, nearing the point of insufferable. I'd gone so far as to tape a vertical line down the middle of my desk, hoping the boundary would ensure him giving me my space.

Seconds after returning from my second clandestine closet rendezvous of the day, I was greeted by Scheff walking into my—*our*—office, fresh from an hour-long meeting with the investors. He plopped into his self-appointed chair—an 'ergonomic' thing that he'd rolled in my first morning back—with a huff, clearly frustrated.

"Rough one?" I asked, sitting in my own chair before taking a sip from my warm, stoneware mug.

"Just lots of questions," he started, tucking his notebook underneath a stack of files. He pitched his voice lower, mimicking the room full of graying hair and fat pocketbooks. "'Are you going to be working in the office full-time? How is Asha doing? Do you anticipate any big shifts or changes this year?'" He blew out a steady breath, his shoulders sinking along with it. "Nothing I couldn't handle, Asha dear."

I chuckled—ignoring the part of myself that was desperate to hear his answers—and turned my attention back to the papers in front of me. Failing to match the organizational skills that Kate had maintained during her tenure, it had been ten days and I still hadn't made a visible dent in the overwhelming stack of nanny files.

"Why would we hire someone like this? She has no childcare references." I paused to look at the file again. "Actually, she has *one* reference, period."

Scheff, crossing the tape boundary, leaned over my shoulder to peek at the file.

"How funny is it that I just pulled a file with a..." he paused, checking the name written at the top. "...Kaia, who happens to live at the *same exact* address and only has one reference."

"Wanna bet that they're each other's reference?"

"It wasn't so long ago that you were asking me to be *your* reference. I remember sitting on that ratty old mattress of yours in Marguerite Hall, talking to—who was it? Pizza Hut's manager?" I stuck my tongue out at him, my face scrunching in faux ire.

"To be fair, I didn't have the familial support of the Scheffters to carry me through job interviews like you did."

His deep, belly laugh filled the room, and I couldn't hold back my smile. I reached for my mug, swallowing the words I wanted to say with the strong brew, and turned my attention to the calendar on my laptop, the millions of brightly colored meeting reminders and to-dos assaulting my eyes.

Since I'd re-assumed my position, my schedule had been packed—a constant torrent of questions and answers from every single department of Arlington Nannies. Today, Glen in HR needed me to look over files, Blake in IT needed my approval on website design updates and a budget increase, and three other people who I didn't remember hiring asked me to set aside time for a "brief meeting."

But Kate was gone. *Gone* gone.

From my first day back, Scheff encouraged me to use a service to find a new assistant, but I didn't want to bring in a *temp*. Nothing about that title suggested that they'd work as hard as Kate did and I needed that level of commitment— especially now.

"I gotta run," I said, reaching for my purse under the desk. Aisha would've had a fit if she saw it on the floor. *Her and her superstitions.*

"What're you getting up to?" he asked, his eyes still roaming over the file in his hand.

"The reading of Aisha's will." I looked at him with a dramatic tilt of the head. "*So* much fun."

He set down the file, turning to reach for my hand. "Are you going to be okay?"

"I'll be fine. The worst part is seeing Armatta." I took a nauseous breath, hesitating before letting him pull me onto his lap.

"Someone's going to see us," I said as I tucked my head into the crick of his neck.

"And?"

"*And*, we're not together so why let any rumors start?"

He bristled at my words, his shoulders rolling as he said, "I'm just consoling my best friend."

"Mmhm. Well, your *best friend's* gotta go. I'll see you tomorrow?"

"I'll be here," he said, with a small, pained smile. I peeled myself from his lap—wishing I could stay wrapped in his arms a little longer. I grabbed my things, flying out the door to meet Vlad on the street.

It took the full thirty minutes to get to Aisha's lawyer in St. Charles and I spent the whole time debating if I should interview the two girls who had submitted applications this week, deciding that meeting them in person would give me a better sense. When we first started the business, I was prone to pickiness—terrified of nannies messing up my reputation, the *company's* reputation, with a bad placement. I'd spend hours trying to match them with the perfect family and I was certain that's why Arlington Nannies became a success. Back then, these two—Kaia and Janice, if their applications were to be believed—wouldn't have made it to the second round of interviews. It was Scheff, reminding me of my own struggles that convinced me to give them a chance.

St. Charles was busy today—the streets full of people excited to spend a summer night outside. Vlad had dropped me off a block away and I was grateful for the few seconds I had to breathe, to shake out the nerves that appeared whenever I was about to see Armatta. After a month holed up in my apartment, the constant swell of people surrounding me was not only its usual nuisance but a pressure I couldn't seem to shake without the help of my doctored coffee. I turned the corner to see Ana and Armatta, waiting outside of the building.

My mother looked every bit of the glamorous woman she pretended to be—no sign of the drug-addled, child abandoner in sight—with her crisp, white linen sundress and lethal, white stilettos, and, the *pièce de résistance*, a navy-blue Birkin bag hanging off her arm. Ana stood awkwardly beside her, irritation pushing her eyebrows down as our mother tried to show her something on her phone. My sister looked effortlessly gorgeous in a comfortable pair of jeans and a blue tee. I walked up to them slowly, drinking in their beauty.

'You'll never be like them.'

"Did you dye your hair?" I asked my sister as the sun, still beaming in the evening sky, caught in her newly auburn curls.

"Yes, Asha, some of us have healthier modes of processing grief."

I rolled my eyes, refusing to play into her inevitable guilt trip when our mother was so close, studying us with her calculating glare. "Armatta," I said, dipping my chin in recognition before she could chastise me for ignoring her presence.

"Oh how lovely it is to be with my girls again," she started and I couldn't help but look at my sister, watching every second of her reaction—or lack of reaction considering the small smirk that had been pointed my way seemed to be glued to her face. Ana crossed her arms over her chest, blowing out a breath so steady that I could hear her voice in my head encouraging me to do the same. "You know, we should really plan a trip together soon. I'll be here until December at least. That gives us plenty of time!"

I held back a gag, forcing a cough into my hand as I

turned my attention to the people-filled streets of St. Charles' Historic District. I listened as my sister, the people-pleasing first born that she was, agreed with her—even going so far as to suggest a few potential locations. I shook my head, hoping they'd figure something out without dragging me into what was sure to be a hell-based vacation. *No fucking thank you.*

A flock of birds, too small for me to name, flew over the brick street, landing on a building across from me. I closed my eyes and let myself drift to another sunny day in June, when Aisha had taken me to Forest Park—just the two of us on a bench under a perfectly blue sky.

"And what's that one called, Auntie?" I asked, lifting the already-dripping ice cream cone to my lips. I swiped my tongue around the edge, quick to catch the sticky mess before it slid onto my hand.

"That one there is a heron. They used to be your momma's favorite when she talked about things like that." It was clear the words weren't meant to be mean, especially when Auntie was watching the bird cross over the water with that special kind of attention—the kind that makes you wonder about life and purpose and stuff.

"Which one's your favorite?" I asked, squinting as I followed the heron, its shadow outlined by the bright noon sun. Aisha looked at me and smiled, running a hand over my braid.

She had twisted it for me when I made it to her house this morning. Auntie all but cursed Momma out when we rolled up to the curb, her words angry but hushed as she asked, "Why does Asha look like a nappy-headed child from round the way when her mother should be teaching her how to keep her hair."

I had tried to comb it down after breakfast but the small rattail comb threatened to break with every pass through my curls. Momma refused to buy any products, saying she'd rather 'waste her money on a bum high than styling shit.'

I sank lower into the passenger seat of the car—wishing I could tuck my ten-year old self into the floorboards but Auntie was already throwing the door open and pulling me onto the street corner. She waved her hand at Momma and wrapped a hand around my shoulder, slipping into the soft Aisha that was always around when Momma wasn't.

"Sparrows," my auntie said, taking a bite from her chocolate sundae. "Something about the simple song always made me feel so happy. It's easy to pick out once you know what you're listening for. It's like getting to listen in on a conversation. Close your eyes, see what you hear." She pointed toward a group of trees and I closed my eyes, trying to find a conversation in the chaos of the park on a nice day.

"I don't hear it," I said, tightening my eyes in hopes I'd be able to pick out Auntie's favorite sound.

"It's okay, baby. One day you will." A drop of cold, sticky cream fell onto my hand and I

opened my eyes. I licked it off before leaning into Auntie's side, her arm wrapping around me as we continued to listen.

A sparrow called, pulling me from the memory just as Ana began to wave her hand in front of my face. I swatted at it, earning a snort from my sister. "We're heading inside, you ready?"

I nodded, taking a single step forward before my mother's icy claws wrapped around my arm, stopping me. Every molecule in my body froze as I looked down at her perfectly manicured hand, the tips of her nails digging into my skin—my brain fighting between the tangible relief the pain brought and the fear of her physically touching me. I wrenched myself free, turning to look at her as she used her now free hand to rifle through her purse. "Let's get a picture first. I don't want to forget this." *Sure, because it's easy to forget your dead sister's will reading.*

I blew a stream of air through my nose, turning to Ana with a look that said, 'can you believe this shit?' before quickly swapping places with her. Armatta held her phone in the air, ensuring the angle was *just right* before she wrapped an arm around my sister, who wrapped her arm around me. A few awkward seconds later, I was sure we were walking into the lawyer's office with a photo that screamed, *"Hi! We're the Arlington's. Don't we look totally insane together?"*

We filed into the office, the brutal heat of the day cut by a chill that rivaled the one surrounding my mother's heart. I wrapped my arms around myself, hoping I could get through the next hour without shivering myself into a pile of dust.

"So, Asha," Armatta started as she sat down in a chair. The lobby of the lawyer's office was vacant aside from a single secretary that scuttled away as soon as we walked in. "What do you say? How about an Arlington girl's trip?"

"Ask me again when hell freezes over."

My mother's eyebrows furrowed, her lips likely fixing to say something about how callous I was but her rebuttal was cut off by the sound of the conference room door creaking open. A short, paunchy man waved us in, a worn leather briefcase dangling at his side.

"My name is Oliver Jefferson," the bald man said, tripping over his words as he secured his place at the head of the table. "Today we'll be discussing Aisha Calloway's will."

Oliver's thin lips set in a tight line as he looked around the room—dramatizing the moment by stopping to stare at each of us. "This outlines her final wishes regarding her estate. Seeing as Aisha has no immediate living family members, we will be referring to her residual beneficiary clauses. I have taken the liberty of including a list of the residual beneficiaries on the second page of your printouts so you can access it with ease." The man passed each of us a stack of papers before hovering awkwardly over his briefcase. His tone was void of any enthusiasm or comfort—like he spent his entire day tending to these kinds of things, droning on and on about who gets what.

He ran a hand over his smooth, domed head, sending dust fluttering through the air. He pulled out an embroidered silk handkerchief—a deep maroon that reminded me of the plump, juicy seeds of a pomegranate—from the breast pocket of his black suit and released a phlegmy cough. The suit itself was a work of art, a Brioni or Kiton if the quality of the wool was any indication. Scheff would've spent an hour talking to the man about the stitching alone. "Now, Aisha requested that those present listen to these notes here in the meeting— the original copies of her words are to be given to you upon conclusion. Any questions before we begin?" *Yes! Why the fuck do I have to be here?*

My sister simply mumbled a small no while Armatta crossed her legs, a cruel, Cheshire Cat-like smile on her face. I rolled my eyes before shaking my head, my eyes focusing on the papers in his hand.

"AnaMarie Arlington. To my dearest Ana, you have been a quiet foundation for our family—never breaking under the weight that was put on your shoulders. There are only a handful of things in my lifetime that I wish I could take back, and that pressure on you is one of them. I leave you what's left in my bank accounts." A tear rolled over the swell of my sister's cheekbone and she quickly swiped it away, looking out the window behind Oliver.

Mr. Jefferson, unmoved by the emotion, cleared whatever was still crawling in his throat and continued. "Let's see here. Ah, yes, Asha Marie Arlington. To the girl who showed us all how to burn bright, I have admired your drive and passion since long before you can remember. You gave our family warmth at a time when we didn't even know we were cold. You were the reckoning. I hope you'll learn how to keep your fire without burning the people closest to you. I leave you my house. It has always been yours as much as it was mine. Please take great care of the things upstairs."

I looked back at my mother just in time to see her shift under the weight of the lawyer's words, slipping back into her poised and perky mask at the same time my heart stopped beating. The faint echo of Aisha's voice in my memory singing, *'Aisha and Asha own a house,'* repeated over and over as my stomach tightened, a wave of nausea crashing over me. I sucked in a deep breath trying to remember the trick Ana had taught me. *What's the fucking trick?*

Panic started rising when I couldn't slow my heaving chest and still, with another obnoxiously unbothered shuffle of the papers in his hands, Oliver continued. "Armatta Louise Arlington. To the woman who showed me what life is like when you bask in the rubble of your own hell, I leave you nothing. Dear sister, you've taken enough from us all."

I locked eyes with Ana, my nostrils flaring as I continued to struggle. Her eyebrows rose in urgency as she pulled in a deep breath through her nose, and blowing it steadily out of her mouth—motioning with her hands for me to breathe with her. *One breath in, one breath out.*

Oliver and Armatta, blatantly unaware of my impending anxiety attack, were fussing over my mother's lack of a bounty —Aisha's insult from the grave enough to bring a small smile to my face, even in the wake of the ever-tightening grip on my chest.

"Well, that just can't be. My sister and I had buried the hatchet. She just visited me in France before all of—" she waved her hand with a flourish, "—this happened. Are you sure she didn't leave a message on your machine to *amend* anything?"

Oliver ignored the twitching of Armatta's face as she tried to bat her eyelashes into Aisha's will. "Even if there was a voicemail, it would be considered void, Ms. Arlington. Your sister is no longer here to give her approval."

"You would have me come down here, just to be embarrassed in front of my family like this? You couldn't have mentioned to me on the phone, 'By the way, your sister didn't leave you anything so don't waste your time'?" She slipped into what Ana and I referred to as the 'rich bitch' voice—her vowels stretching as her temper grew. "Never in my life have I been this embarrassed. Shame on you, Mr. Jefferson."

She snatched her purse from the chair, sending it spinning before stomping toward the door, stopping only to train her heat on me. "Enjoy your *gifts*, girls. We'll see how long it takes before you crumble under the weight of them." My mother was a bullet freed from the chamber, intent on finding her target and making sure her words wounded *someone*—her heels punctuating the statement with each staccato *click* out of the building.

"Ms. Arlington, wait!" Mr. Jefferson called after her, waving a small envelope in his hands. "Your sister wanted you to have a copy of her..." The words faded as they disappeared through the front doors. I didn't realize how far back I'd leaned in my chair, always eager to enjoy an Armatta spiral, until a low groan came from underneath me. The entire situation was ludicrous enough without me breaking a chair that was likely *way* more expensive than it was comfortable.

I pulled myself forward slowly, my fingers turning white as I gripped the edge of the table, the chair literally moaning with each centimeter I moved up. By the time I was upright again, Ana was releasing a belly laugh, so free that I couldn't help the small burst of giggles it pulled from me. I covered my mouth trying to hold them in but lost all control when I looked up to see Ana, a stream of tears running down her face, clutching her stomach. *Leave it to the Arlington sisters to laugh at a will reading.*

It took a good minute for us to calm down, another fit of laughter inspired by a single glance in Ana's direction. I wiped any errant tears from under my eyes before I shoved the papers into my purse and slung it over my shoulder. Ana was beside me in an instant, the two of us more than ready to leave the room and the weight of Aisha's gifts behind for a minute. We passed the secretary's desk and I felt bad for the poor woman who looked disheveled—whether that was because of the wrath of Armatta or it being her general demeanor, who's to say.

Ana's footsteps faltered and I slowed, turning to find that damned worried look scrunching her face. "You can't keep struggling like that, Ash. I know you don't want to hear it, much less from me, but you need help. I don't have to be in your life to want you to have a decent one."

"Oh, just decent then? How sweet."

"I would've opted for 'good' but that depends on you," she said before walking out of the front doors with her head held high, her freshly dyed ringlets bouncing with each step.

'*Perfect, perfect Ana.*'

I huffed a laugh—at least I could count on her to never change. I peered into the conference room, making sure I didn't leave anything behind before I left. Eager to get back to my apartment after a full week in the office. I spun around, nearly bumping into a frazzled looking Oliver. I wondered how hard Armatta laid into the poor guy once we were out of earshot. "Sorry, Ms. Arlington. I was moving too quickly."

"No worries, Mr. Jefferson. Sorry about Armatta. She's...

well she's Armatta." I offered him a small smile because there was simply nothing else to say about my mother—she'd always been in a league of her own.

"Before you go, Aisha left you one more thing." He extended a plain, white envelope in my direction. "Per her instructions, unless she resolved things and asked for it back I am to give this to you. She didn't want me to pass it to you in front of your mother and sister but insisted it be delivered to you as soon as possible."

"Thank you." I dipped my head in a grateful nod.

"She loved you, you know? We only spoke a few times, but she always had something pleasant to say about you."

"She was just nice like that."

His eyes pierced mine in a way that made me feel like he could see right through my carefully crafted facade.

"If you run into any issues with the house, let me know. I'd be happy to help you in any way I can."

I breathed out a "thank you" before giving him a small, awkward wave and heading out the door.

When I stepped outside, I was grateful for the blanket of heat that immediately wrapped around me, replacing the cold of the office. I looked at the thin envelope in my hand, turning it over to see my name written in Aisha's slanted handwriting. My chest squeezed and, ignoring the pain that seemed to have taken up permanent residence, I tucked the letter into my purse replacing it with my phone. I texted Vlad, and he was at the curbside in a handful of minutes.

I slid into the car and Vlad, chipper as always, waited until the door closed before asking, "Home?"

I tried to envision the comfort Aisha seemed to find here—the desire to understand her growing with every day she was gone. It wasn't long before I was itching in my skin, desperate for relief.

"No," I started, the word ashy on my tongue. "Golden Hoosier, please."

As we wove in and out of traffic, the suburb melted into the tight, compact streets of the city proper—counting down the minutes until a glass of smooth bourbon was in front of me. The sun was starting to sink—the bright orange horizon melting into shades of periwinkle and blue, splattered with fluffy, white clouds. By the time we made it back into the city, the evening heat had started to wane, the breeze a welcome respite against the humidity as I walked towards The Golden Hoosier.

I didn't find myself in South City often, opting for bars and restaurants closer to Clayton. Every once in a while, it felt good to venture deeper into the avenues of the St. Louis.

I was welcomed by the bright, neon golden marquee flickering above the unassuming, yellow brick walls of the bar, the distinct hum of electricity buzzing as I passed underneath it, stepping inside. I let the haunting feeling of a building whose bones had outlived most of its patrons settle on my shoulders. The walls—littered with taxidermied animals—seemed to hold their breath, as if waiting for someone to tell their stories. A mortuary of unblinking, glass eyes trailing me as I floated through the room. *How morbidly ironic?*

A brief flash of Aisha's hollow, brown eyes staring at me from across a hotel room stopped me in my tracks, my entire body locking with fear.

'The solution is right *there,"* the voice beckoned, and I forced my stiff legs to keep moving until I was seated at the bar.

The lights that hung above the mirrored backdrop on the wall were warm and dimmed, radiating a coziness that didn't sink in. I tried to keep my mind silent, as I waited for the bartender's attention, opting to look over the menu even though I knew exactly what I wanted.

My phone buzzed in my purse and I pulled it out to find a text from Vlad.

Vlad: Go EASY

"What can I get you?" the bartender—a tall, brute of a man with ginger hair—asked as he made his way over to me, effectively pulling my attention away from the useless warning on my phone. If I could look past the grizzly beard and overwhelming muscles, then he was certainly attractive. He laid a cocktail napkin in front of me, setting a glass of water on top.

"Let's start with two Space Mutts, a shot of your favorite top-shelf bourbon, and a plate of fries," I said.

He stared back at me for a few seconds before letting out a low chuckle with the shake of his head.

"Coming right up..." he said, turning his back to me. *God, those muscles.* "Asha, right?" He looked back at me with a small, knowing smirk that made the hairs on the back of my neck stand to attention. *Who the fuck is this?*

He leaned across the bar, "You don't remember me, do you?" Although his face was inches from mine, I could barely hear his deep voice—the hushed words lost in the thrum of conversations filling the room. He reached under the bartop before placing an empty shot glass in front of me, making sure my eyes were locked on his before he began pouring.

He lifted the bottle into the air, tilting it on its side and letting the amber brown stream into the glass—a trick he'd obviously practiced. He slid the now-filled shot glass closer to me with a wink before turning to mix my other drinks.

I racked my brain for any sense of connection—my mind reeling as I tried to place his unremarkable features—shaking away the confusion before perching the shot glass against my lips, knocking the liquor back with ease. By the time the sting of the bourbon washed over my tongue, the bartender was delivering my next two tickets to salvation.

I reached for one of the Space Mutts, elaborately poured into a tin can for my drinking pleasure. The drink was easily my favorite, a combination of huckleberry vodka, lime juice, and ginger beer, garnished with a charred rosemary sprig—a reminder of holidays crammed around Aisha's dining table. I quickly plucked the herb out and dropped it onto my napkin before sucking the cocktail down quickly, biding my time until that sliver of liquid courage found its way to me.

The bartender, most likely an old fling, moved gracefully behind the bar—his focus now on a rowdy pack of men farther down. He was quick on his feet, but in his head as well, accepting multiple orders without writing a single one down and, seemingly, doling them out without error. I allowed myself to appreciate his muscles one last time before turning back to the second Mutt, sipping slowly—but with intention.

A few minutes passed and another server brought my plate of hot, flaky fries and I dove in, not really caring if the bartender returned while my mouth was full of them.

"My name's Jameson. We met last summer,"

"Oh, yes," I said, swallowing the chewed-up lump of potato. I nodded, pretending I knew exactly what he was talking about. "Right, Jameson."

He laughed, the sound hollow and forced before turning to a new customer, farther down the bar.

As the night wore on, I lost myself in the waves of bourbon and French fries that seemed to satisfy the dread that had taken up residence in my stomach since the will reading. I was content to gorge until Jameson's—I'd taken to calling him Jamie by the end of the night—shift had come to an end. Naturally, I needed a nightcap and invited him back to my place, claiming it would be nice to be reminded of how good his services were.

I called Vlad and we kept ourselves busy against the grim yellow wall, waiting until a honk had me leading Jamie to the car. It was an effort to pull myself off of the giant mass of man and slide into the backseat. Jamie started kissing my neck, his tongue darting out to lick the sensitive spot just beneath my ear. *Well that feels familiar.*

I tipped my head to the side, giving him easier access before meeting Vlad's concerned eyes through the rearview mirror—disappointment poisoning the hazel pools.

'He'll quit too.'

I couldn't bring myself to care as Jamie's hand found its way between my legs, the bitter sting of his comfort drowning the last of my concerns.

THIRTEEN

I couldn't remember the last time I'd slept so hard—too deep in the Sandman's grasp to be bothered by nightmares. I lifted my head, looked around and briefly wondered if the muscled bartender carried me up or if I had enough sensibility to make it in here myself. But Jameson wasn't anywhere to be seen, the only clothes flung about the room were my own. I squinted—the sun too bright and happy for a 'morning after' wake-up call—trying to see what was hanging from my bedroom door. *Bra? Yes, it's definitely my bra.*

I groaned, dropping my head back down on the pillow, hoping the giant man from the night before found his way out of my apartment without robbing me of anything other than the modicum of virtue I pretended remained. The thought had me—begrudgingly—pulling myself upright in the bed to ensure everything was in place. The pile of laundry sat undisturbed in the corner by my closet, and the ever-growing stash of teacups and coffee mugs waited dutifully on the coffee table.

The air-conditioning kicked on, sending a breeze over my

bare skin as I reached for my phone. I slid my thumb over the wake button, just as a loud bang rang out from the direction of the kitchen. My heart instantly started pounding as fear froze me to the bed, afraid to make a sound. *Did the dumbass leave the door unlocked?*

I threw my legs over the side of the bed, reaching for the mockingly small pepper spray bottle I kept hidden in my nightstand. I reached toward the mountain of clothes, grabbing the first thing my fingers grazed which happened to be an oversized sweatshirt. *Thank God it's long.*

I threw it over my body, now covered in goosebumps—from fear or the air-conditioning blasting through the room, I wasn't quite sure—and crept toward the hallway, careful not to alert whoever was dropping pans in my kitchen at six-thirty in the morning.

I crept down the hallway, tiptoeing around the corner with arms locked, ready to spray the shit out of the intruder when, to my surprise, I discovered Scheff lounging in my kitchen. His tall frame leaned against the marble counter as he sipped from a cup of steaming coffee, an apron tightly secured around his waist. *Fucking catalog model.*

"What the fuck, Scheff?" I whined, my shoulders lowering in relief as I dragged myself toward one of the barstools. "You scared the shit out of me."

"Good morning, sunshine," he sang—at a volume *way* higher than acceptable this early in the morning. "I had to send that grossly oversized caveman out when I got here. What the hell were you two up to in there?" He flashed a mischievous grin, his eyebrows wiggling suggestively. His chipper demeanor didn't match the pain that flashed in his eyes.

I ignored him. My eyes—and stomach—focused on the greasy, steaming breakfast waiting for me on the counter next to him. "Are you going to give me that plate or not? How'd you get in here anyway?"

"You're always a pleasure, Asha dear," he huffed with a slight shake of his head. "Here." He slid the heaping plate of food, a glass of orange juice, and three aspirin in front of me.

I reached around him, pointing toward the coffee pot with a pout. He shook his head and, with another small chuckle, stepped forward, filling a cup to match his own before gingerly placing it in my greedy clutches.

He started to scrub the breakfast residue from the pans as I silently wondered what the hell motivated Matthew Scheffter to cook me breakfast this early in the morning—my thoughts quickly replaced with a satisfaction-filled moan drawn from somewhere deep inside my empty stomach.

Scheff crafted a massive breakfast sandwich and sliced it in half for easy eating. The fried egg sat securely between crisp bacon and creamy avocado, all held together by two thick slices of sourdough. Everything was seasoned perfectly, a reminder of Scheff's expertise in every bite. His shoulders shook with his head as he laughed at my enjoyment and I used the beat of silence that followed to take stock of myself, washing the bite down with a scalding hot sip of coffee. I hadn't been able to prepare myself for anyone—outside of an intruder—and knew my hair was a tangled nest of curls, coils sticking out in every direction. My makeup was likely smudged all over my face which meant that my poor, silk sheets were probably covered in it too. I could feel the bags under my eyes and assumed that the pounding in my head matched the scowl that would easily scare most men away. Of course, Scheff could never fall into the category of 'most'.

"Leave me alone. It was a long night," I grumbled before forcing another massive bite into my mouth.

He laughed again, the sound cutting through the groggy

haze of the morning. "I'd say I hadn't noticed but we both know that would be a lie."

My jaw dropped comedically, and we fell into the same rhythm of easy fun we used to have before he started to see me as a problem more than a person. I looked around for something to throw at the smug bastard, my eyes landing on the unused spoon resting next to my plate.

He turned to me and said, "Don't even think about it, Asha Marie."

"Did you just *middle name* me?" I asked, a chunk of breakfast sandwich still hanging from my mouth. My hand was frozen above the spoon when he turned back around—the dishes done and neatly resting in the rack next to the sink.

"I certainly did. You had a long night, and so did I. How horrible would it be of you to capitalize on my weakness?" he asked dramatically, turning to me with a hand covering his heart as he feigned disappointment.

I laughed, turning my attention to the aspirin, swallowing all three with a single swig of orange juice. Scheff found his way to the island and sat, his eyes locked on his own plate of breakfast that waited next to me. The normalcy of the moment stuck to me like a shadow—the haunting idea of what could be. It was as if the years we'd spent shaping into the people standing in this kitchen now, had woven some unspoken bond between us.

Scheff's phone started rattling against the countertop, his morning starting way before I ever intended mine to. He flipped it over and, seeing the name on the screen, pulled himself up from the stool. "I'll be right back."

I watched as he disappeared into the guest bedroom, closing the door behind him. As soon as I heard the latch click, I slid from my seat, making a beeline for the bottle of bourbon I'd taken to storing under my sink—hidden behind a bunch of cleaning supplies that I rarely touched. I unscrewed the cap quickly, pouring the liquor into my coffee cup while I kept an ear on Scheff's voice through the door. As long as he was talking, I was safe. It was too early in the day for a lecture, but I couldn't handle the weird tension I'd created without a little help from the hair of the dog. I replaced the cap, sliding the bottle behind the bottle of bleach before quietly walking back to my seat. I doubted that Scheff would notice but still, I slid the cup back to the same spot—increasingly mindful of how far away it was from my plate—before turning back to glorious breakfast delight in front of me.

The door opened and Scheff came out—his eyebrows pulled together as he continued to look at his phone screen, his thumbs vigorously typing as he walked back to me.

"Everything okay?" I asked, hoping I looked innocent as I reached for my mug, pulling a deep sip from my coffee—made perfect with the splash of *my* expertise—as he made his way back to the stool.

"Yeah, just some...things."

"Anything I can help with?"

I couldn't bring myself to say anything else out of fear that the precariously relaxed silence would shatter the second I did. I shoved the last bite of sandwich into my mouth as he seemed to debate an idea in his head—those blue eyes still lost in thought.

Scheff stood abruptly, dusting crumbs from the counter into his hand before he said, "Yes, actually. We're going out. And no sweatpants. You have thirty minutes to get ready. I will drag you out of here kicking and screaming if I have to and still wave to Frank on my way out."

Matthew Scheffter—ever the red herring.

"Consider it an adventure," he said with a wink, a twinkle alight in his eyes. "Like old times."

I looked out at the water in front of me, Scheff's idea of an adventure being a boat ride around Forest Park. It would've been fine if the boats had motors and didn't require me to use what little energy I had to pedal us around the waterbeds, and through the park.

"Scheff," I whined, drawing out the 'e' for as long as I could. "This fucking sucks."

He laughed, the sound as rich as the birdsong coming from the trees above us. "I just wanted to talk but I knew you wouldn't be able to just sit somewhere. It's supposed to be cathartic."

"We could've talked at my place."

"No, we couldn't have. You would've shut down," he said, the words matter of fact and, even worse, true. I grumbled to myself, wishing I would've hopped back into bed rather than letting him convince me to come out.

"No, I wouldn't have."

"Yes, Asha. There was literally nothing I could do short of trapping you."

A man, about our age, was walking a pack of dogs, a group of chaotic forces dragging him behind. I smiled, turning back to Scheff before the drop of happiness I felt dwindled away.

"Ask your questions then," I started, before pulling my feet away from the footholds. "But I'm done pedaling."

He laughed, a piece of hair flopping into his eyes as his chin dropped to his chest. "Of course you are."

He started pushing again, grunting as we neared Picnic

Island—appropriately named for its expansive grassy areas and the water surrounding it.

"What's it going to take for you to stop drinking?" he said as he continued to push us through the water. We were just passing under a bridge when a turtle slid from its place on a sunken log and into the water, most likely spooked by our proximity. "And don't act like you haven't been sneaking alcohol into everything you drink for the last two weeks. We can all smell you from a mile away."

A mother and daughter walked alongside the waterway, throwing pebbles into the gentle current, ripples reaching all the way out to our boat.

"Just drop it, Scheff." He quit pedaling for a second, letting the force of the water pull us underneath a centuries old bridge. A heron, small and white, studied us from the bank—one beady eye trained on me. My fingers curled in a small wave as we passed by, a silly habit I'd kept since I was a child, eating ice cream on a bench not far away.

"I can't keep dropping it, Ash. Let me *help*."

I spread my legs out, crossing them at the ankles, my hands resting on the back of my head. The heat wasn't unbearable yet—just warm enough to melt the icy shroud that had clung to me in the last week.

Scheff met my refusal to participate with a sigh and continued on, letting the sounds of a morning in Forest Park wrap around us as he *tried* to paddle us back to the boathouse. He was slick with sweat, droplets falling from his hairline, by the time we were walking back to the car.

"When are you going to go to Aisha's?" We started to cross the same suspension bridge we had floated beneath, the metal clanging with each of our steps. "I'm just saying that it would be good for you to have something to do, something to focus on outside of work for a little bit. The house is just *sitting there.* Why not see what you can do with it?"

"I plan to sell it. What is there to *'do'*?" I asked, using my fingers to air quote for emphasis

"Didn't Aisha tell you anything in her letter?"

"How do you know about the letter?" I asked, turning my attention to the family of ducks that lived next to the old, white suspension bridge.

"*Shit,*" he said, the word so quiet that it was nearly lost to the wind. He anxiously rubbed the back of his neck as he kicked his foot against one of the metal posts supporting the bridge's railing. "Ana told me she got one and I just assumed you did too."

Of course sneaky Mr. Jefferson had a few tasks to accomplish on behalf of Aisha.

"Is there something you need to tell me about you two?"

"Yes, actually," he started, clearing his throat and turning to me. His eyebrows knitted together, his bottom lip caught in his teeth in that anxious way of his.

"Oh my god," I wrapped my arms across my chest, my weight settling into one hip. "You're fucking my sister."

"*Whoa,* Asha. Wait a second," he said, his hands slowly rising in defense.

"I mean I get it but *my sister*, Scheff? Was I stupid to think that you would never cross a line like that? Because please, let me know if I'm just walking around like an idiot while my best friend and my sister are shacking up behind my back."

"Asha, it's not like that." He took a step toward me, and I took a step back.

"What is it *like*, Scheff?"

He scoffed, combing a hand through his hair as he blew out a steady breath. "Why can't you call me by my name?"

"What?"

"Why can't you call me by my name?" He turned toward me, taking another step. "It's not hard for you when you want something, so why is it *so* hard every other time?"

"What are you even talking about? We're talking about you and my—"

"We're talking about the things you choose to pay attention to, Asha. You can't see how you manipulate me, and use my feelings for you at your will but have *the nerve* to get jealous when you notice your sister and me talking? Most of the time we're talking about *you*! God, Asha! My life revolves around you and you're so blind to it!" He looked back over the water, his jaw shifting from side to side. "You have been the axis on which I rotate for six years now, and I need to know why." He reached out, pinching one of my curls between his fingers before his hand fell away. "Why can't the reason for which my world turns call me by my name?"

I scanned his face, looking for an out I knew he wasn't going to give me. I retreated once more, offering a slight shake of my head before I turned to flee—the bridge shuttering with every step.

"What's it going to take for you to stop being so fucking afraid!" Scheff called, the words loud enough to ruffle the ducks laying comfortably under the shade of the trees.

I continued my march toward the parking lot, throwing a middle finger over my shoulder, hoping it was aimed in his direction and not some random person walking with their child.

An older man—sporting a rather unfortunately tight set of shorts—walked past me, his hips swiveling as he maintained his speedy walk. "Well, don't you look just lovely today."

"Not today, Grandpa." I said, my steps unfaltering as I

passed him. I didn't have a destination in mind, just anywhere far from Matthew Scheffter.

Of course they thought they could *fix* me—the pair, near equals in their perfection, probably thought they could find the solution to world hunger too. My fists clenched, my nails digging into the palm of my hand enough to distract me from his words, the ones that claimed more than he probably intended.

'Why would he want such a mess?' the voice asked as I stomped over to a bench and plopped down on the wooden planks.

I texted Vlad, who promised me a maximum fifteen-minute wait for a rescue pick-up, depending on traffic, and made myself even more comfortable on the bench—lifting my feet up to rest across the entirety of it. Scheff would know better than to chase me and I was highly doubtful anyone else would be eager to take up the space next to me. Despite the molten rage that was still running through my veins, I closed my eyes and tried to silence my thoughts. *One breath in, one breath out.*

I nodded off, exhausted from the last few days—nothing short of thankful when it was Vlad standing over me as I cracked an eye open—his shadow blocking out the sun and making me feel instantly cold. I followed him back to the car, thankful for his refusal to pepper me with questions. Sometimes it felt like he was the only one who wouldn't. I slid into the comfort of the back seat and let him take me home.

Vlad, merging onto the highway, would veer off in a few exits taking me back to my apartment—where I would undoubtedly pull out a new bottle of bourbon before wallowing in the truth of Scheff's words until I fell asleep.

My best friend's words did what they were supposed to though—needling me into action. I hated the idea of Ana and

Scheff taking control of Aisha's house. I hated the way they talked to each other using me as their point of their connection.

"Vlad," I started, only pausing to make sure I was absolutely certain I wanted to do this. "Will you take me to Aisha's house please?"

He slowly nodded his head—his face lit with an interesting mix of surprise and concern. "Are you sure, Miss Asha?"

I looked out at the sinking sun, trying to enjoy the bright orange hues it cast the world in. *That's exactly how Aisha made people feel—warm and worthy.*

"I'm sure."

❧

'You're nothing more than a coward,' the voice called after me as I stared at Aisha's front door.

My anger from fighting with Scheff had melted, giving way to that sickening guilt that permanently resided in my gut.

I was just starting to make my way down the porch stairs —my focus latched on the crack that ran along the stone balustrade—when a *boom* sounded from inside the house. I froze, my body locking in fear as I realized that, technically, this was my house and there shouldn't have been anyone inside. I turned, my hand dragging against the gritty, stone banister as I started to pull myself back toward the front door. Another suspicious sound from inside had me reaching for the doorknob, only to stop when I heard a chorus of muffled swearing coming from the other side.

The door swung open and I was met by a set of dark-brown eyes peering down at me. "Shit! I'm sorry."

The same inspector I'd met a little over a month ago stood in front of me, his arms filled with a bag of tools and random appliance parts. He'd cut the sides of his hair, letting the wild brown curls grow atop his head. Stubble dotted his cheeks and his full lips were curved in a surprised smile.

"It's fine," I said, ignoring the urge to look around him and into the house—unable to hide from the suffocating pressure that was weighing down on my chest.

'Coward.'

"I'm sorry, I wasn't expecting anyone to stop by today. AnaMarie said it would be vacant for a while." Of course, he'd been talking to my sister and of course she didn't think to tell me.

I nodded, turning my attention to the porch swing that was groaning as it gently swayed in the breeze. I could see Aisha sitting there on an afternoon like this, a cup of tea in one hand and her latest book in the other. I turned back to the inspector, anxiety clouding my thoughts as I tried to remember why I came here in the first place.

"Grayson, right?"

"Yeah, sorry. I know it's been a bit since we first met." He held his hand out to shake mine, the bag of tools resting comfortably between his hip and his bicep. I met his grip, quickly shaking it before wrapping my arms tightly around my body. It was ninety degrees outside and yet I couldn't shake the chill that had seeped into my bones the second I stepped out of the car.

"Did you need something from inside? I was about to lock up and leave for the night, but I can wait if you need to get in." He asked awkwardly, his soft eyes roaming over me— like he was checking to see if I was the same woman that stood in front of him a month ago. *Doubtful. Too much had changed.*

"I have my own key. If I needed to get in, I could see to it myself," I said, knocking my foot against a loose floorboard.

He watched me for a second, his mouth opening and closing as if he was trying to find the right thing to say. "Asha, I'm sorry for your loss. Aisha seemed like a great person."

"Because you would *totally* know what she was like, right? After meeting her once?"

"I just meant that she was kind, and a lot of people seem deeply hurt by her death. It's not hard to tell when someone was loved."

I nodded as I turned to walk down the steps. "She was."

"If there's anything I can do, just let me know."

"I don't need you to do anything besides your job," I said. I was *so* tired of talking to people and didn't even care if he heard me as I stomped back to the car. I'd only been out of my apartment for three hours and, in that time, I'd managed to get into an argument with, not one, but two men. *Universe- 2, Asha- 0.*

"Your sister wasn't kidding when she said you were too caught up in yourself to handle anything right now," he called from behind me, the words rooting my feet to the pebble pathway that Aisha spent hours toiling over.

I turned, digging a small circle into the intricately patterned walk with my heel. "And who the fuck are you to say something like that to me?"

"Me? I'm just a guy, calling it like I see it."

"Funny, I'd say just an *asshole*, sticking his nose where it doesn't belong."

His jaw quirked in annoyance—highlighting how defined it was—as his brown eyes rolled back into his head. '*Keep rolling those eyes and they're going to get stuck in that sassy head of yours,*' Aisha would've said.

"Whatever. Do you want me to keep going through your

sister for updates or are you actually going to respond when I call you?" he asked.

"Oh, so that's who's been calling me non-stop for the last two weeks. Didn't take you for the desperate type. " I'd seen an unknown caller pop on my screen a couple of times but couldn't bring myself to answer—not when my phone felt like a constant connection to the world that didn't belong to Aisha anymore.

The laugh that echoed through the oak trees surprised me, sharp with disbelief, sending the nesting sparrows into the sky. "*No*, you self-absorbed...I told you I'd call you when the water heater was ready. It wasn't until I managed to get ahold of your sister that I even found out that your aunt had passed. *Then* I called to offer my condolences, and I haven't bothered you since."

"Whatever." My cheeks heated as embarrassment crept up my spine. I tore my eyes from him, my gaze dipping in shame. "You can call me for the house stuff."

"Yeah," he turned, stomping his dusty work boots up the front steps. He fished a set of keys from his pocket and went to lock the door. "Whatever."

I turned back towards the car with a huff, overwhelmed and frustrated by the entire trip. A trip that would've been successful if it wasn't for Grayson. I *would've* made it inside if he hadn't come barreling through the door, intent on minimizing my character.

Vlad—distractedly scrolling through his phone—didn't see me approaching. He jumped, his phone fumbling in his hand as I threw open the door with a grunt, sliding into the backseat, my eyes burning with tears I refused to free. I pulled the door closed with a slam, meeting my driver's worried eyes in the rearview mirror. *God, how often does this happen?*

He opened his mouth—words of consolation on the tip

of his tongue, I was sure. I held up my hand to stop him, choking down the sob that was threatening to spill out the minute I tried to speak. I coughed, clearing the feeling from my throat before pressing my fingers under my eyes—pushing any tears that threatened my mascara to the corner and onto my hand, rather than down my face. *One breath in, one breath out.*

I met his eyes in the mirror once more, before nodding my head and pulling out my phone—intent on getting lost in the dozens of emails that had piled up in my inbox over the last week.

"Just drive, Vlad."

I listened to the grass swaying in the open field—the hills alive as the wind swept through the sea of tall, green stalks. I'd had the same dream countless times over the last month but, this time, there was no need to wait for Aisha to reach the crest. For the first time since she'd started to haunt my dreams, she started this scene sitting beside me underneath the towering oak tree.

We sat in silence, my hands twisting long blades of grass into a crown while we listened to the music of the glade. Two sparrows dipped and dived, their silhouettes outlined by the sun that was hanging in its corresponding place in the afternoon sky.

"I haven't been able to enjoy the quiet like this in a long while," Aisha said. My hands froze after I knotted another piece of grass to the growing coronet in my hand. I'd seen her time and time again but she'd never said anything—it was just the same repeating echo of my screams until now.

I finally looked over to my auntie. Her back rested against

the thick, rough trunk of the tree. There wasn't a drop of blood on her and she looked refreshed. Her black hair, streaked in the front with vibrant gray strands, looked healthy. The purple bags under her eyes had disappeared and the twinkle she was known to carry in her gaze was alight once again. I turned my focus back to the dancing hills, scared that she'd revert to her nightmare form if I stared too long.

"Me neither." I reached forward, plucking another piece of grass, my fingers twisting repetitively until the crown was finished. I had so many things to say to the woman next to me, the *healthy* version of Aisha that I was afraid I'd never get to see again. I opted for, "I really miss you. Which, I know, is my fault. I had so much time to talk to you and I was so fixed on being mad. I'm so sorry."

She didn't say anything as her hand reached over, wrapping over mine. I looked at her again, my unburdened auntie still here, her grip on me feeling *so real*. A sad sort of amusement crinkled the corners of her eyes.

"Everybody misses you so much, Auntie. And I don't know how to fix that. I just keep letting them down." She gave my hand another small, comforting squeeze. A single tear slid down my cheek, falling onto our clasped hands. "When does it get easier, Aisha?"

The wind around us began to swell, the field bending in response to the assault as the gust brushed against my face. The leaves above me rustled and the sparrows opened their wings to glide on the current, falling into the waiting arms of the trees when the torrent began to carry them too far.

Aisha reached for the finished crown sitting in my lap, and gingerly placed it on my head. Her hand cupped my cheek, and I looked into her lively gaze. The amused smile that was still tugging at the corner of her mouth sent shivers down my spine—not of fear, but of peace and comfort and a feeling of "everything's gonna be okay." I pulled my gaze away, unable to stomach the promise that her eyes carried, a promise that she couldn't keep.

The wind died down and I listened to the sparrows chattering away in the tree, their lighthearted chirps encouraging me to lean back, to rest against the unfailing support of the oak. A few beats later, the wind picked back up, a whiff of Aisha's floral scent brushed under my nose as the two sparrows leapt from their resting spot once more, pulling a third bird from the canopy and into the sky with them.

Aisha's hand on my cheek slowly faded away, and I looked over to find the space next to me empty. I huffed an incredulous laugh, turning back to the trio of sparrows dancing in the wind, and the sea of grass in front of me—tumultuous waves rooted to the ground, unable to wreak the same havoc of the actual ocean.

Aisha's answer came on the breath of the wind as it wove through the grass and the trees around me.

'When you're ready to make it easier.'

Fourteen

July

There were certain parts of my life I was never meant to return to. Standing on a stage, trapped beneath a spotlight that highlighted every flaw, was one of them. I tried to shake off the ghosts of a past life—the phantom pressure of a forced smile, a well-rehearsed walk, the expectation to dazzle. I silently cursed Scheff for forcing me to hold the attention of a crowd once again. Upon his return to my daily life, he asked Kate to work on a benefit event for the clients and shareholders of Arlington Nannies—a way to 'get to know everybody and show our appreciation,' as he put it. It was nothing more than another obligation that kept me from spending my Friday evening in the way I'd become accustomed to these last two months. Alone, drunk, and in bed.

"Fuck," I said, letting out a deep breath. "I don't want to do this."

Scheff met my complaint with silence, his fingers dancing loudly on the keyboard his sole response. *Someone's* still *pissed.*

"You can't seriously still be upset over the park? People argue. That was weeks ago."

I turned in my chair, barely able to see the grimace that had been stuck on his face all week—at least any time I was in close proximity. "I'm the one who was getting fussed at. *I* should be mad."

His fingers hammered into the keys, the sound ricocheting off of the walls around us as I kneaded at the frustration building in my temples. I had closed the door to give myself a reprieve from the eager buzz that filled the floor over this goddamn benefit but it only made Scheff's irritability more prominent. I pushed away from my side of the desk, my trusty rolly-chair stopping next to him. "Scheff, come on."

"Scheff," I started, poking my nail into the back of his arm. As the youngest in our families, we'd both perfected the art of being impossible to annoy—I just happened to know exactly where he was ticklish. He jumped, giving me the reaction I wanted but then shifted his chair farther away from me, nearly tipping over in the process.

"Scheff."

"*Matthew*," I whined, my last try before giving up on the statue he'd worked himself into. I dug my finger in a little farther, hoping it was enough to drag him back into the world with me.

"Jesus, Asha," he started, his hands abandoning the keys in front of him. "Yes, people argue but I can still be upset. These are not mutually exclusive ideas."

"Fine, be mad." I started, scooting back to my half of the desk. "But can you at least be mad *and* help me with my speech?"

I didn't have to turn around to know he was shooting one of his infamous glares in my direction—two circular beams pointed at the back of my skull. The air filled with a sound of pure frustration, blowing out from the man behind me. "Yes, I will help you." *Success.*

'See how happy you feel when you manipulate him?' the voice called. I shifted in my seat, wiping all traces of amusement from my face.

"I can ask Vlad to take us if that would make you more comfortable."

Curiosity pushed me to turn my chair, and I leveled an assessing glare on the man. "He's just the driver. Why would he make me more comfortable?"

Scheff's eyes narrowed, pinning me to my chair with an accusatory look of his own. "It was just an idea, Asha. I want you to be as comfortable as possible."

"Always or just tonight?" I asked, turning back to the files in front of me.

"If you have to ask, I'm not doing a great job at it, am I?"

I whipped back around, ignoring how blank his face was as he waited for a response that had the potential to break him here and now. "I'll be fine. Vlad can take the night off since I have my trusty Scheff to get me home."

The corners of his mouth perked up, the anxiety melting from his brow as he let out a small breath. "I'll pick you up around seven?"

"And I'll be ready." I offered him a small smile, reaching for the cup I knew was empty, my two o'clock coffee concoction already drained. Right as I moved to go refill it, my phone buzzed next to me—pulling me from my ritual altogether. A message from Grayson, asking if I could stop by Aisha's house tomorrow so he could explain the repairs. The ghost of embarrassment heated my cheeks as his words ran through my head. *'I'm just a guy, calling it like I see it.'*

I sent a thumbs up before slamming my phone on the

desk, snatching the mug and rushing to the closet across the hall—all too aware of my best friend's eyes following me out.

Scheff had secured one of the most beautiful venues in the city for our event, The Fabulous Fox Theater. The last time I'd been there, I'd spent half the show ignoring the stage, captivated by the ornate statues and motifs blooming from every corner of the room. Elaborate chandeliers hung from the ceiling, casting a golden light that heightened the splendor of it all.

Tonight, however, I would be locked away from the extravagance of the stage, forced instead to socialize with the people who kept me paid. *Lovely*.

I had chosen a plum gown, the silk hugging my waist and chest before flaring at the knees and pooling at my feet. The plunging neckline was mirrored in the back, cut to reveal my shoulders while loose, chiffon sleeves covered my arms, tightening at my wrist. Aisha's ring dangled from its resting place on a simple chain around my neck—the small accessory tying the outfit together perfectly. I met my own gaze in the mirror, lingering on this fabricated version of myself. The dress was meant for the theater, for an evening of magic—not this boring excuse for an event. I sighed, slipping on my gold stilettos and stepping out of the closet. I reached for my phone, charging on the bedside table, intent on texting Scheff when I heard the front door of my apartment open.

"Asha?" he called from the kitchen. *Of course, he's already here and of course he let himself in.*

"Do you ever plan on, I don't know, knocking when you come over?"

"No, the idea hasn't crossed my mind once," he replied dryly.

"I'm almost ready," I said, raising my hands behind my ears. I pressed until I felt the pin pricks of four posts digging into my thumb on each side—the pain grounding *and* ensuring that I had put my earrings in. I reached for the small gold clutch I threw on the bed earlier and shoved my lipstick and a pack of gum inside, blowing out one last cinched breath before leaving the room.

Other than occasional excursions to random bars, this is the first night I'd left my apartment without the intention of drowning my grief in a bottle of bourbon—or luring the first hot guy I could from the crowd. I shook out my hands, letting the rhythmic beat of my heels *clicking* against the hallway floors steady me. As I turned the corner, I stumbled—caught completely off guard by how insanely good my business partner looked in a custom tuxedo. He was engrossed in his phone, likely drawn to a problem that needed his particular brand of solution if his scrunched face had anything to say about it.

"Why are you always so perfect?" I asked, the words not as sharp as I intended. His focus jumped to me and I shifted under the weight of his assessment, his eyes twinkling under the warm lights of the kitchen. He swallowed, huffing a laugh as he set his phone on the island.

"I could ask you the *same* thing." I took small, measured steps toward him accepting the small bouquet of roses in his hand as he kissed my cheek. "You are utterly breathtaking, Asha Arlington." He wrapped an arm around my waist, asking if I was ready before leading me to the door. I took one last look at my sanctuary, switched off the lights, and let Scheff drag me into a night of forced gratitudes and preening parents.

We spent the car ride trading gentle touches, his fingers tracing along my spine as I gripped his knee tightly—quietly hoping I could use him as a shield against the crowd that was waiting for us. Grand Avenue was buzzing by the time we made it to the theater, a stream of elegantly dressed people making their way through the front doors as the driver pulled us around to the back. Scheff rushed out of the car, running around to open my door and offering me his hand along with a dazzling smile. I returned it with a quick one of my own before he helped me from the car. I smoothed any wrinkles from my dress and tucked my arm in his, following him through the VIP entrance.

We walked through a dim hallway, and I found myself getting lost in the small, intricate motifs that seemed to exist in every corner of the building. I had no clue where we were going, no clue what room he booked or where I was supposed to give my speech—it wasn't my job to worry about the details this time.

"Will Kate be here tonight?" I asked, hoping the question didn't sound as desperate as it felt.

Scheff clasped my hand in his, tapping it twice before pushing a door open. "She said that she'd try to make it."

I nodded, unwilling to linger on the million different potential outcomes, especially as Scheff pulled me onto the stage. My jaw dropped as I freed myself from his side, spinning in a circle as I took in the opulence of the room.

"What're we doing here?" I whispered, worried that a security guard would pop up from the empty audience and chastise us for being somewhere we *clearly* weren't meant to be.

"Someone told me how much you used to love the theater so I pulled some strings."

"*Someone* being Ana or Kate?" I asked, still drinking in

the enormity of it all—how small I felt from the highest balcony row when I was a child, how I couldn't even find that seat from down here. I fought against a rush of tears, ones that weren't building out of sadness but awe.

"*Someone* being a drunk Asha in our sophomore year. In case you haven't noticed, I pay attention." I laughed, the sound soaring to the rafters of the room as I turned to look at Scheff. I walked over to him, my quick steps punctuated by the acoustics as I held a hand out to him.

"Thank you," I said, pulling him into a hug. It was easy to sink into him, to pretend that, for the night, we were just two players on the stage—a story waiting to be shared with the world.

'Always playing pretend, aren't you?' the voice called, the tone sharp and judgemental enough to make me force Scheff away with a small push.

His fingers laced through mine, tightening as he drew me back—an arm wrapping around me before he kissed me. There wasn't anything calm or patient about it, his lips clashing into mine with a need that overwhelmed me. I sank into it, into *him* and let the comfort silence the voice entirely. I didn't pull away until my lipstick was smudged around his mouth and we were both huffing unsteady breaths.

"Asha—"

"We should find the room." He froze, surprise clear on his face as he searched mine for any understanding—like he could find the answer as to why it was so hard for me to let him in blatantly displayed on my forehead.

"Yeah." He cleared his throat, scrubbing a hand through his hair before gesturing to the door. "The room." He reached for my hand but I pretended not to see it as I walked toward the stage door, 'looking' for my phone in the small clutch.

It took a minute, but we eventually stepped into a new room, the parents of St. Louis dressed to the nines with flutes of champagne in their hands—all raising as Scheff and I walked in. I pasted on a small, delicate smile while Scheff offered a casual wave, one hand pressed to my back as he directed me toward a small group standing near the stage. The hum of excitement sent a pinprick through my head, the start of a headache I'd be able to avoid if I could sneak away to the open bar that was hiding here somewhere. I looked at Scheff —his hand now resting on my hip—and wondered if he planned on playing babysitter all night. He clasped hands with a vaguely familiar man who then reached across and pulled me into a tight hug, spinning me around in a circle. Scheff laughed as my feet found the floor again and I shot to his side.

"Asha, you remember Jace, right?"

"Oh, I'm just the forgotten third in this dynamic duo. Of course she wouldn't remember the guy who spent most of freshman year passed out on the floor while you two plotted, well," Jace raised his hands to the room, "this. An empire."

A brief flash of memories swept through my head and I didn't fight the smile as I remembered him—he was a bit bigger then, his hair long and loc'd with a goofy smile always rounding his cheeks. Scheff and I would peer over the edge of my bed to find Jace asleep, a Four Loko in one hand, an empty notebook 'for studying' in the other. I punched his shoulder playfully before pulling him into another hug. "Of course I remember you. You've just changed a bit."

"A bit?" He jokingly turned to the side, running a hand down the front of his tux as he laughed. "I hope I've changed more than a bit." And he had. The locs had been cut, replaced by a taper fade, his tight curls styled for the night. His smile, still goofy in every regard, reached for his eyes but followed the sharp contour of his cheek bones instead of rounding. Matter of fact, Jace was *fine* now. I caught his eyes—two dark, enticing chocolates—and arched a brow, hoping to entice the man.

As if Scheff could read my train of thought as I looked over our old friend, he pulled me back to his side, leaning down to whisper in my ear. "It's time for your speech."

I nodded, tearing my attention from Jace and our undergrad adventures and directing it toward the stage. My lower back began to sweat as hundreds of eyes pinned to me, watching as I made my way through the crowd. A waitress stood by the platform with a tray of champagne and I snatched a glass from her before Scheff could stop me, climbing the stairs as steadily as possible in heels and a gown. I tried to hold onto a semblance of grace but I'm sure that picture melted away as I turned my back to the crowd, downing the bitter drink before spinning around with a showman's smile.

"Thank you all for coming out tonight," I started, turning away from the mic as I gently coughed—trying to clear the anxiety that was tightening in my throat. "Seriously, it amazes me to be able to look out into this room and see clients who have long since turned into friends."

'Liar, liar.'

"When we started this company, I never imagined that it would grow to this point. Matthew Scheffter and I theorized about this in a dorm room just blocks from where we stand now—grand ideas for a business that was bred out of one simple mission. *To connect.* Through our elaborate models and screening processes, we've been able to match hundreds of families with a nanny *or two*—" I nodded to the Frankshires, both looking utterly relieved to have a night away from their eight kids, "—who were perfect for them. Ensuring that, while your family grows, your nanny is there to grow with you."

The room erupted in applause, surprising me enough that I had to take a step back. My heart dropped into my ass as my heel tugged, ever so slightly, on the bottom of my dress. *You cannot fall up here.*

I reached for the microphone, using the stand to balance myself as the room quieted down. I dipped my chin in a shallow nod, allowing the smile to stay plastered to my face as bright flashes from a camera swallowed my vision. "We've been fortunate enough to not only bridge a gap in St. Louis' childcare needs, but to also craft a beautiful community while doing it. I would be remiss if I didn't give a special thank-you to each and every employee who ensures this company continues to run. You are truly what keeps Arlington Nannies running and I don't know what I would do if it wasn't for you." I raised my glass, sounds of appreciation filling the brief moment.

"To our investors, thank you for taking a chance on two kids with a big plan. I know we might drive you crazy sometimes, but we've been grateful for the guidance you've given us that has helped us to grow. And to my amazing business partner, Matthew Scheffter. There isn't a day that goes by that I'm not amazed that we're still here, making our dreams a reality. I wouldn't have been able to do it with anyone else by my side and I am eternally grateful for that." The room filled with clapping once more, as I blew a small, direct kiss to the man himself, standing front and center. There was something like pride on his face. "And thank you for writing my speech," I added, earning a laugh from the room.

"I won't bore you all much longer, but again, thank you. I

know how many of you had to pay for a sitter tonight so please remember, the bar is open and we're here till midnight!" I finished, allowing the deafening applause to swallow me as I picked up the bottom of my dress and skipped down the side stairs.

I worked through the throngs of people offering me their thanks and congratulations, searching for the tall, blonde who seemed to stick out in situations like this—a crowd already growing around him as I stepped into his side and let his arm wrap around me—his comfort winning over not just me but everyone in the room. He offered me a drink which I took graciously, nodding a silent thanks before all but downing it.

"So, Ms. Arlington," a squat man wearing a toupee that had started to peel away from his sweat-slick forehead began, "that's a beautiful ring you've got there. Did Matthew finally lock you down?"

The champagne I was sipping got caught in my throat, a thousand bubbles coating my airways. I covered my mouth gingerly and turned, coughing to chase the fizzy feeling away. Scheff's hand found my back, his gaze sweeping over me, intent on making sure I was okay. I gave him a shallow nod, waving his care away before turning back to the flock of people still waiting for my answer—their eyes and ears desperate for some gossip. I rolled Aisha's ring between my fingers, letting the sharp edge of the diamond bite into my skin.

"Matthew and I will always be business partners first. This is my late aunt's."

Scheff stilled, his fingers tensing against my back.

"Curious," the same man piped up from the front of the pack. "I would've assumed you'd say *friends*."

"Well, as friendly as someone could be with Asha, Mr. Robertson," Scheff cut in, his voice tight. Slowly, his hand fell away. He turned his head just slightly, and I caught the pain welling in his eyes, the blue pools darkening. His smile, along with the warmth of the evening, slipped in a matter of seconds.

We mingled with the group for a few more minutes, Scheff slipping into the conversation and captivating the audience more than I ever could. His easy going nature made it easy for him to get along with anyone—I envied him for it. A round of laughter pulled me from the bottom of my now-empty glass, and I glanced around for a server. My hands trembled again, and I knew the perfect solution was balanced on a tray somewhere. If I just waited for someone to come by, I wouldn't have to leave Scheff's side and face the rabid gossipers alone. *Be patient.*

But as I leaned into my instincts, I felt him subtly inching away. I brushed my hand against his back, hoping to anchor him.

"I'll be right back," he said with a small smile for the group, before marching out of the room altogether, the sound of his departure swallowed by the chatter of our clients swapping stories about their families and recent trips—the thought of either had me wishing for the alcoholic oblivion to come quicker. I told myself, just thirty more seconds of kindness, and I could politely melt into the crowd and head straight for the bar in the back of the room.

A familiar laugh filled the lull between talking points, a few group members turning to see Scheff laughing next to a tiny, blonde woman—the two of them perfect complements to each other. Jealousy razed a fire that started deep in my toes. I wouldn't have been surprised if someone pointed out steam billowing from my ears as her hand slid down his arm —just before she reached up to adjust his tie. He leaned in and, before I was treated to their inevitable kiss, I bolted—

leaving the room, and the stuffy-ass event, without a second glance.

The warm lights of the theater sign danced on my skin one last time, as if thanking me for letting them shine. I stepped into the humid July night, listening as loneliness beat alongside my heart.

FIFTEEN

I stared at Aisha's house, gravel crunching beneath my heel as I shifted uncomfortably, unable to climb the stairs without bile crawling up my throat. I'd begun to loathe the place. No matter how much joy it brought my aunt, something always seemed to go wrong when I was here.

Thank God for Vlad—who had been waiting outside of my apartment this morning with a freshly brewed, triple-shot Americano, a blueberry muffin, and his inability to leave me alone.

"It's a beautiful house, Miss Asha," he murmured from underneath his newly grown mustache, his nose twitching against the graying hairs.

"It's something, for sure," I murmured into my paper cup, thankful for something to help me keep my sardonic mouth busy.

"Don't you have a key?" Vlad asked, his voice sounding over my shoulder. We'd been standing outside for a few minutes now, waiting for Grayson to pull into the driveway and unlock the door. I shrugged, knowing full well that the key sat in the bottom of my purse alongside Aisha's letter—

the two items hiding in my bag for weeks, their weight never going unnoticed.

Five more minutes passed before the sound of Grayson's truck pulled my attention to the driveway. I watched, annoyed, as he slid from his truck. He took his time fiddling with his tools, packing a bag with them, and gently closing the truck door before walking over to us—his steps somehow filling the space while being excruciatingly slow at the same time.

"Asha," he said, his face twisting into something between a scowl and a glare. It melted away instantly, replaced by a charming smile as he turned, extending a hand toward Vlad. "I've seen you around a few times, but I don't think we've had the pleasure of being introduced. I'm Grayson."

Vlad met his gesture with his usual, overly-chipper, excitement and pulled the man into a hug. His joyous demeanor was infectious—and not in a good way. I took a few steps, moving closer to the house as the two talked, the breeze swelling to take their conversation away. I hadn't heard Grayson's footsteps, his deep voice, creeping over my shoulder, startled me as he asked, "Ready?"

I jumped, muttering curses as coffee spilled out and onto my hands. I squinted at him, my frustration—at the coffee dripping from my fingers, or his general presence, I wasn't sure—threatening to spill over too. I shook my hands, trying to flick off the scalding drink, silently worrying about drops staining my new sweatshirt. I looked at Grayson, an eyebrow arched as I waited for his apology.

"My bad." If it wasn't for the chuckle and asinine smirk on his face, I wouldn't have sent the last, cooling drops of coffee from my hands flying toward his shoes.

I tilted my head, offering him a sickly sweet look before

stomping up the stairs—waiting for him to follow and unlock the door for me. Vlad sent a big wave from the car before he ducked inside, likely excited to listen to some of his book while I was trapped. I rolled my eyes, stepping inside as soon as Grayson pushed the door open, immediately hit by the overwhelmingly familiar scent of Aisha. It was fainter than last time—when she was alive. Still, her floral signature lingered, though no one had been here, outside of the pest standing next to me, in weeks.

"What exactly did you want to show me?" I asked, setting my purse on the bench that Aisha had obsessed over, moving it around the house before deciding it belonged *'right here'*. My heart tightened at the memory, and at the habit that it had built.

"I wanted to make sure you saw the water heater and at least got an idea about how it works," he hesitated, like he was debating whether his next words were worth my reaction. "Do you plan on selling?"

"Yeah."

"Let me know how I can help. I know this can't be...easy." I nodded, wondering what happened to the man laughing at my ire not thirty seconds ago, how he could jump from annoyed to compassionate in that time. I nodded, words difficult the longer the smell of lavender and honey sank into my skin.

"The water heater's in the basement so, lead the way, I guess."

"You can go ahead. I don't really know my way around down there."

I couldn't shake the discomfort that lingered as I followed Grayson downstairs, holding a hand above my head to catch any spiderwebs before they dusted into my face. It wasn't just the house that sent my stomach twisting anymore, but the unparalleled kindness that all but oozed from the man in front of me.

"Watch your head," he said, reaching a hand out in warning. I ducked under a low beam—only to misstep into a dip in the floor. My legs jolted, twisting as I tried to catch myself, but Grayson's arms were already steady around me."Easy there."

My hands tightened around his biceps, and solid muscles tensed in response. I found my footing, quickly distancing myself from the man and mumbling an apology. He stood frozen, his arms suspended in the air as he looked at me like he was trying to sort out a puzzle.

He reached for a light switch, bathing the unfinished, concrete room in a dim, disgusting light. "This," he said, motioning toward the hunk of metal tucked away in the corner. "is your new water heater. It's tankless, electric, and—"

"What does that even mean?" The words were sharper than I intended. *One breath in, one breath out.* I exhaled, trying to soften my tone. "Why does that matter?"

He rubbed a hand against the back of his neck, blowing out a breath before turning to look at me. "Tankless means that there's no limit to the amount of hot water you're getting. Electric is...safer. Doesn't carry the same risks—no gas leaks, no carbon monoxide. Just basic upkeep. The previous model that was in here was gas and ran a limited tank which requires more maintenance and replacements. The old one was running way past its lifespan anyways and gas heaters need replacing every ten years or so. I couldn't find records of anyone maintaining it for your...for Aisha. Wouldn't be surprised if it had been holding on since the house was built."

I chewed on the inside of my cheek, my teeth cutting through the skin allowing blood to fill my mouth. "How long did it take?" The words were quiet, lost in the space between us. "For them to get sick?"

Saddened eyes met mine. "It was a slow leak. The chances of Aisha being exposed before she went to Paris are pretty high, but I think something set it off. A crack spreading, a trip in the venting system, something that made it worse while she was gone. Her making it a week after the funeral was a miracle."

"She was always a stubborn woman." I forced a laugh, the sound flat as I moved closer to the water heater. Grayson cleared his throat, shifting to show me various knobs, and notes, and things I would care to pay attention to if it wasn't for my intention to sell as soon as possible.

Fifteen minutes later, we were climbing the stairs, the comforting smell of Aisha forcing me out the front door. I was already down the stairs, waiting for Grayson on the pebbled pathway, pretending to look at the nearly dead flowers along the walkway. The front door slammed and Grayson skipped down the stairs, stopping once he got to me.

"That's it I guess. Ana told me to send the bill to your office and someone would take care of it?"

"Yeah, that's fine." I nodded, folding my lips into a thin line as I tried to stop my thoughts from spilling out of my mouth—and failing.

"Look," I started, digging the toe of my sneaker into the loose dirt of the flower bed. "I'm sorry for how I acted last time. And this time. I'm not good at...this."

"At what?"

"*This.*" I waved a hand between us. "Socializing. Getting along with others of my species."

Grayson chuckled, swiping a hand under his jaw and behind his neck before looking at me. "Okay. Apology accepted."

"That's it?" I asked, hesitant to believe it was that easy when I'd spent my life jumping through hoops for people's—my mother's—forgiveness.

"What do you mean 'that's it'? There aren't strings attached to my forgiveness, if that's what you're asking. No need to get down on your knees and beg."

We locked eyes, both of us catching wind of an innuendo. Silence swelled between us, thick with anticipation, as we waited to see who would cave to the childish punchline first.

"Unless you want to," he added with a quick wink.

I laughed, the sound fresh and full as it pulled my head back, aiming for the sky.

It had been a long time since I'd walked out of my aunt's house feeling lighter than when I'd stepped in. The last twenty minutes had passed with ease—like the house itself had given me a moment to breathe. I found Grayson's eyes, happy to catch the flicker of surprise that passed over them

"Well, I'm finished for the day. Make sure you lock up before you head out."

"Grayson, wait," I started, hoping I didn't come across as desperate for his attention. I ran my hand over the crack on the stairs, wishing I could get a better sense of Aisha and her grief around it. "Do you...know anyone who could help me with some repairs? I want to fix some things before I put the house on the market but I don't really have any experience with this stuff. And I know you're not a handyman or whatever but do you—"

"If it's just minor repairs, I can help you out," he said, saving me from rambling myself further into embarrassment. "If it wouldn't be weird for you or anything."

"Weird? Why would it be w—" I stopped, catching the weight of his glare—he used every, painfully long, second to look at me, eyes squinting in what I could only assume was an assessment.

"Feel free to text me a list of things you want done and I'll let you know what all I can help with." He hesitated at the door of his truck, glancing back over his shoulder. The fading sunlight played with the perfect planes of his face. "It's nice to see you again, Asha."

I think he actually meant it too.

Sixteen

Fifteen minutes. That's how long I'd been waiting outside of this house, nodding along as the same perky blonde from the benefit gushed about how much she 'loved it.' I dragged my gaze around the neighborhood, admiring how every house looked different as I tried to tune her out. Two staccato vibrations cut through my grip on my phone, saving me from the realtor's yammering. I unlocked the screen, my brow furrowing at the sight of Grayson's name, asking if I could stop by sometime today. I hesitated for a second, my fingers hovering above the screen, before letting him know I'd be free in an hour.

Scheff had asked if I would meet him here and, as I stood outside—impatience growing with every passing minute—I silently cursed him in my head. *Who invites someone somewhere and shows up late?*

I moved to the text thread with my business partner, urging him to hurry. I was eager to have someone else to entertain the realtor—dressed head-to-toe in bubblegum pink, insistent on 'filling me in on the masonry work'. The realtor's voice grew louder with every fact she recited, her enthusiasm teetering on the edge of theatrical. The shrill words became a monologue as my focus shifted to the house itself.

It *was* spectacular. The majority of the place was deep red brick, but thick gray stones replaced the rouge around the door and windows. Together, they formed an elaborate archway and intricate designs that framed the windows. The garage which sat further down the hill was also outlined with the stones, tying the house together with the charm of a deceivingly-large storybook cottage.

"And as you can see, the moulding here is absolutely original. It was restored by—"

"Sherry! It's great to see you," Scheff's voice cut through the realtor's running commentary. *Thank God.*

"*Matty!*" She squealed, running down the porch steps and leaping into his arms, her legs wrapping around his waist as he spun her around. Blatant disgust pulled my lips into a sneer, pursing in reaction to the overwhelming display. *How professional!*

'Disgust? Smells an awful lot like jealousy."

Sherry slid down Scheff's legs, her frame dwarfed in comparison to the tall, muscular man that seemed to tower over her. Clearly, business Barbie and Ken knew each other *quite well*. The utterly perfect duo seemed to skip to me, Scheff pausing briefly to make sure his car was locked. Even the sunshine seemed to taunt me, casting a golden glow on their perfectly wind-blown hair as they climbed the steps together.

I forced my focus back to the house, pretending not to see how easily their fingers fit together. There was nothing to be jealous of, I reminded myself—just two people who belonged to a world I had no place in.

"Hey, Ash," Scheff said, his voice inauthentically casual as he peeled his hand from Sherry's and pulled me into a hug that felt more like an obligation than a greeting. "Sherry and I went to high school together and it only seemed fitting for her to help me in my search for a home."

"We sure did," she drawled, forcing me to exercise every ounce of restraint to keep my eyes from rolling. "And I think this one is *perfect* for you." Her voice was as thick as the jam I spread across my toast this morning. My eyes rolled of their own volition the second she unlocked the door and crossed the threshold.

She turned, her hands running down the front of Scheff's blazer, pulling him closer to her as she said, "Look at this foyer. Isn't it *to die for?*"

I would've gagged if she wasn't right, the outside of the house didn't hold a candle to what was hidden away inside. We were welcomed by high ceilings, and a flight of wrap-around stairs that led to a balcony positioned above us. Abstract stained-glass windows allowed the afternoon sun to light the house in beautiful rays of red and purple, smaller rainbows covering the hardwood floors beneath us. I kept walking, finding a small set of stairs that led to a sunken living room, dark exposed beams crisscrossing above me. I spun, tuning out Sherry and Scheff's discussion about the history of the house, too enamored with the beauty of the room around me.

The air smelled faintly of chocolate chip cookies, the oven sounding from the kitchen might've reminded me of afternoons with Aisha if it weren't for Sherry's squeal shattering the illusion. Her heels click-clacked through the empty house as she raced to rescue them from burning. Scheff stepped into the living room, his movements easy and unhurried as he too spun in place, taking it all in. He let out a long, low whistle, his hands finding their place on his hips. "Now this," he started, his voice steady, "feels like a home."

I froze, my heart tensing at the words. I turned back to the sunken living room, giant windows bathing the room in a beautiful light. It was stunning, everything a house should be. Everything a *home* should be.

"This house is..." I turned again in, eager to drink in the foyer's grandeur again, the words dying in my throat. "Amazing, Scheff. Like...one of the most stunning houses I've ever stepped into." I stopped my twirl, my eyes locking on him as he fidgeted in the doorway, his focus glued to the beautiful floors.

"But?"

I tilted my head, my lips pulling into an unamused smile. "But this house is huge. And it doesn't really seem like *your* style." I raised my eyebrows, inviting him to explain himself.

"I'm just...thinking ahead," he said, finally meeting my eyes as he took a single step forward. He laughed dryly, shaking his head. "Never know when I'll want to start a family." His voice was casual but his eyes—now shifting restlessly—said otherwise.

I nodded, turning—fleeing—from the living room before he could say something he'd regret.

"It's gorgeous. Seriously." My voice echoed around me, dancing in the rafters of the high, exposed ceilings as I stepped into the foyer again, curious about the beauty hiding upstairs.

"I thought you'd like it," he said quietly behind me, the words lost in the space between us.

"But this isn't *my* house, Scheff."

"It could be," he said, closing the gap between us once more and pulling me into his chest. His arms wrapped around me as I closed my eyes.

"Why can't we be happy?" The words were broken,

sounding utterly wrong coming from the man that was holding me. I blew out a deep breath, sinking further into his warmth.

'You'll never be able to make him happy.'

I let the vision of us happily together shatter, pulling myself away from him as the temperature in the room dropped. A chill ran down my spine as I turned to look at him. "You know I can't, Scheff."

"Yes, you've said that many times."

"And you still haven't listened," I said, rifling through my purse in search of my phone. I texted Vlad, confirming he was en route and was grateful for his immediate response. I swallowed my guilt, ignoring the lifeline that he'd slowly grown to be. "Vlad's almost here. I'm going to go see what the repairman's been up to at Aisha's house."

I swung the door open, eager to leave before Sherry found a way to tell me the origin behind each and every piece of brick used to build the house.

"*Matty!*" She squealed, her voice echoing from deep inside the house. "You have to see this kitchen. *Come here!*"

"I can't wait forever, Asha," he said quietly—no doubt so *Sherry* wouldn't hear.

My hand lingered over the handle, his words making me freeze halfway through my escape.

"I know," I said, letting the truth chase me out the door.

I stumbled through Aisha's front door after struggling with the key for a few minutes, muttering a string of curses at it before slamming it shut. Grayson peeked around the corner, splatters of red paint freckling his face.

"Rough day?"

I narrowed my eyes, pointing a finger at him. "Not a word."

He pulled himself around the corner, a paint brush in one hand, a can of paint in the other as he gave me an easy smile and a wink. "Not one."

I tossed my purse onto the bench by the door before following Grayson toward the living room. I was grateful for the return of the playfulness from that first meeting, fighting to ignore just how easy it was. "So, what do you need from me?"

"Well, I was going to ask your opinion on paint colors but you told me to pick whatever so I just started without you." He wiped the back of his hand across his forehead, a drop of paint falling onto the tarp-covered floor. "I thought the deep claret would look nice highlighted by the sun in the evenings. That window over there should hit it *just right.*"

I turned to look at the bay window, one of Aisha's favorite spots to read. One of the last times I saw her, I pulled into the driveway and studied her for a few minutes. I could tell that she was immersed in whatever she was reading, likely some form of smut that she would've been horrified to be caught with. Her eyebrows dipped and arched with each page turn, her body shaking with laughter I couldn't hear on my side of the glass. I had to force myself from my spot on her beloved pathway, and wouldn't have pulled my eyes from her so soon if it wasn't for Junior's voice calling out— *"Cuzzo! It's good to see you!"*

I was already losing the battle—the one that sent me to Aisha's house with ire and angst flaming with each step. I fought the smile that tried to curve my lips as Junior walked over, throwing an arm over my shoulder. I hadn't seen him in months and the time in between had been good to him—his tall frame filling out under the rugged workout regime that was daily football practice in the St. Louis heat.

"Hey," I said, wrapping an arm around him and pulling him close. "How was your summer?"

"It was fine. Super excited to be back on the field though. Grind don't stop, ya know?" he said, mimicking one of the professional athletes he might catch on Sunday's primetime slot.

"Where's Unc?"

"He ran to the store," he started, leading me up the front steps. "Mama's making fish, collards, and cornbread tonight. You should stay!"

I swallowed the lump of guilt that was building in my throat, reminding me of the reason I came here in the first place. "Actually, I just came to talk to your mom for a second," I said, ducking out from under his sweaty arm.

"Asha," he started, his head dropping dramatically as he looked at me through his eyelashes. "Come on. You never come by anymore." And I probably won't be allowed back here after, *I thought.*

"How about you give me a few minutes with your mama, and I'll see about staying for dinner. Yeah?"

"Fine." He huffed a sigh, stomping back outside, a football magically appearing in his hands. I shook off his affection, and stepped into the living room to finally confront my aunt. I hesitated, still reluctant to break the peace she seemed so immersed in.

"Might as well just come in and get it over with, Asha Marie." Her impatient voice sang through the house pulling me out of the shadows with chagrin. I rounded the corner, watching as her eyes continued to dance down the page of her book. She wasn't impressed with me wanting a moment to breathe but made damn sure I was forced to wait until she was ready for me to talk. Typical.

She flipped the page, a clear chapter break open in front of her and, still, she reached for her bookmark begrudgingly, drinking in as much as she could before I could threaten her escape with reality. She closed the book gently, staring longingly at the front cover with a small, demure smile on her face before setting it aside and looking out the window, finally ready to speak. "She offered, Asha."

"You didn't have to accept though."

Her gaze snapped to me, the movement so sharp and sudden I was surprised she didn't hurt her neck in the process. "One day you'll understand why. I shouldn't have to explain to you that, when my only sister reached out in hopes to make amends, I have to try. You're not the only one who's sat by and waited for her to turn her shit around, Ash. She acknowledged *it. That's the first step."* Tears burned at my eyes as I tried to take her words for what they were. She would always *give Armatta another chance, the opportunity to do better. "I don't need your opinion on what I choose to do, Asha. You're* my *niece. I don't even know what possessed you to drag your ass all the way out here to talk about this."*

"Yes, you do. And if you can't understand it, Aisha, then I can't be around you anymore. It hurts too much to see everyone choose her again and again."

"That's fine, Asha. One day you're gonna—"

"I understand." The words came out heavy, half meant for the Aisha in my memory, half for the man in front of me now. "Aisha would've loved it."

"I'm glad to hear it. There's an extra set of coveralls over there," he said pointing to a plastic bag by the fireplace. He shifted to point in another direction, the muscles of his back dancing under his tight, paint-covered shirt. "And an extra paint brush over there."

"You expect me to...paint?"

"I asked you to stop by and help. What were you expecting?"

I nodded, walking toward the bag before pausing, slowly retreating off of the tarp and onto the bare, hardwood floors. I crouched down, pulling the Louboutin sneakers off of my feet before looking for the coveralls. The rustling of the plastic bag as I pulled the denim out was oddly grounding—something to focus on as worries of inadequacy filled my head. "I've never painted anything, let alone a wall before." I said quietly, wishing I could stuff the words into the coveralls bag as soon as they passed my lips.

"That's okay." Grayson laughed, the sound pulling me around to look at him. "A wall is like the easiest thing to paint. We just have to make sure the coats are even." I slid the coveralls over my legs, tightening the straps before pulling them over my shoulders. Concentration furrowed Grayson's eyebrows, a steady hand trailing his brush along the crease of the doorframe. He pulled himself away from the project, his eyes narrowing as he looked at my hair.

I ran a self-conscious hand through it, half-expecting to find a bird poking out by the way he was glaring at me. He set the brush in the can, before putting it on the ground and running—yes, running—out of the room. I heard the echo of the front door closing behind him and looked around, wondering what the fuck just happened.

A few seconds later he was back, a black baseball-cap in one hand and a rubber band in the other. "You'll want to protect your hair," he said, offering them to me.

I muttered a thanks before tightening my bundle of hair into a bun, careful to place it low enough to fit through the small hole of the baseball cap. I looked up at Grayson who smiled, flicking the edge of the hat before picking up his tools and resuming his deliberate strokes against the frame.

I went to grab my own paintbrush, my toe catching on a tray filled with red paint. The world seemed to slow as I looked down to see the tray flicking upwards, the pressure of my toe strong enough to launch the resting liquid and send it flying in my direction. The world resumed its normal speed right as the cold, wet, paint splattered against me, slowly dripping down my body.

Grayson, silently working, was so focused that he probably wouldn't have noticed if it wasn't for the small squeak I let out as I stood frozen, covered head to toe in paint. He turned, horrified, eyes widening as he took in my current state while he fought—hard—against the amusement that contorted his face. "At least you had a hat?" he said as he doubled over in a fit of laughter, the sound filling Aisha's house with a little joy once more.

"Keep laughing, Grayson," I said, the words not as bitter as intended—my narrowed eyes weighed down by paint more so than annoyance. I swiped my hands over my face, using slow, methodical flicks of my hand to clear the paint away. Grayson calmed down, letting out steady breaths as he clutched his stomach. He looked at me again but got a second wind, bending over once more as his laughter wrapped around me. "Grayson, I swear to God. Keep fucking laughing."

My words only pushed him further which, of course, forced my hand. I slowly walked toward him, ignoring the coolness seeping through my clothes and the brief flash of Aisha's cold blood on my hands. I forced my focus back to Grayson and his hunched over frame, waiting until his eyes were closed before pouncing.

I wrapped my entire body around his back, latching onto his shoulders as the paint transferred to him. He yelped, trying to shake me off before falling to the ground in a renewed fit of laughter—my own laughs harmonizing with the sound this time. He rolled, gently forcing my arms to the ground while his hips pinned mine to the floor. "I'm not moving till you promise to be good."

I softened my eyes, pretending to struggle under the weight of his hands on my wrist, nodding my head before giving him a breathy, "Fine."

He slowly freed one of my wrists, pointing a paint-covered finger at me before pulling his weight from me. As soon as I had enough space, I shot a hand toward his face, rubbing it against his cheek and neck while giggling maniacally. He grabbed my wrist again, pulling me toward him and I froze—we both did. Barely an inch separated us, a breath of space separating our lips and his eyes dropped to mine. If he leaned in, I'd let him. We stayed there for a few seconds as I fought against the urge to close the gap, as I waited for him to initiate something, *anything*.

He pulled back abruptly—so fast that I started to fall back to the floor. I closed my eyes, bracing for the shattering impact of my skull against the floor but it never came. Grayson's hand was now resting behind my neck and, before I could say anything, his lips were crashing against mine. I let myself rest against his hand, forcing him to chase the kiss and sink deeper into me. I reached for him, clawing against his shoulders as I pulled him tighter against me.

'Selfish girl. You can never have enough.'

The words echoed in my head, furrowing my brow and causing me to break the kiss. I pushed my hands against his hard, sculpted chest, trying to free myself from the weight that was suddenly threatening to suffocate me. I rolled to my knees, standing abruptly before turning away from the man still laid out on the ground below me.

He groaned, making me turn back, watching as he shifted

to his side before looking at me—his eye-contact confident and unflinching. His jaw flexed just before he said, "I'm sorry. I shouldn't have done that."

I nodded, turning away again before looking down at my body—picking at the paint still running down my skin. "I should go shower before this dries."

I pulled off my socks and coveralls, dumping them on the tarp before ducking out of the room and up the stairs towards Aisha's bathroom. I was probably going to have to borrow something from her or Junior once I was clean and dry. *Is it 'borrowing' if they're dead?*

I tried to ignore the haunting picture-frame outlines still covering the stairwell walls—Grayson clearly hadn't made it this far in the painting process yet. I let my mind imagine a dark, bold color on the walls, something to wipe out any lingering memories of Aisha's family.

I found my way into her room, closing the door behind me before aiming for the shower. I could feel Aisha's hand brushing over mine as I twisted the cold, metal handle—the high pitch squeal of the water rushing forward suggesting it hadn't been used since the last time my aunt was here to haunt the halls.

I shivered, trying to ignore the presence that seemed to be attached to me as I walked into her closet, a new wave of grief stinging at my eyes as I took in a deep breath. It smelt like lavender and honeycombs—like *Aisha*. Her walk-in closet was organized, splitting perfectly in half with her things on one side and Uncle Charles' on the other, a clear balance between the feminine and masculine clothing. I turned to the shelves that held Aisha's shoes, running my hand over a white pair of satin heels that commanded the attention of the room. My finger caught on the sharp, jeweled piece that sat at the top, a small drop of blood rolling off of the tip and onto the pristine stiletto. *God dammit.*

The tears flowed over in earnest, and I rushed to bring my finger to my mouth, stopping the blood from falling onto anything else while also keeping myself from making a sound —I didn't want Grayson feeling concerned. I sank my teeth into my finger, leaning into the grounding bite as I riffled through a drawer, pulling out a pair of sweats and loose-fitting tee shirt.

I rushed into the shower, climbing past the glass doors right as a small sob broke free. I curled into a ball, letting the scalding stream of water—courtesy of the brand-new water heater—rain down on me as I cried silently.

A few minutes passed before I realized I wasn't just crying over the shoes. I couldn't understand why it was so easy to be around Grayson while Scheff—a perfectly good man, with no reason at all to like me—felt like an obstacle I couldn't figure out how to break past.

I waited until my silent sobbing finished before pulling myself off of the shower floor, reaching for a washrag I had snagged from the linen closet. I dug the course material into my skin—relishing how my raw skin burned under the torrent of water—long after the paint had begun to sink down the drain.

I silently hoped that Grayson had run away while I was drowning in self-loathing, the thought wiped out by the cold that pelted my skin as soon as I stepped out of the shower. It was painful in its embrace, threatening to shatter me as I compared it to the warmth that used to grace these halls. I dressed quickly, making sure my eyes weren't red before walking down the stairs—anxiety attacked my gut with each step toward the living room. It was blissfully quiet and, for a second, I wondered if the universe had finally graced me with a winning moment. But instead, as I turned into the living room, I found Grayson lounging comfortably in Aisha's spot —his feet resting on the blue, floral cushion in the bay window while he scrolled through his phone, his eyebrows furrowing and relaxing with every swipe of his thumb.

I paused, stumbling when I saw the sunlight highlight his paint-covered cheeks, dancing along his frame just like it would've if Aisha had been sitting there instead. I couldn't place the feeling twisting in my stomach—something that felt awfully like longing. I struggled to determine if it was longing for the man or the peace he seemed to find in Aisha's favorite nook.

I cleared my throat, trying to hide my laugh as he jumped in response to the sound. "Sorry."

"You're fine," he started. "I should've been paying more attention. Are you okay?"

"Yeah, why wouldn't I be?" I turned, trying to dismiss his concern as I tucked myself deeper into the window, the pressure starting to swell against my chest.

"Have you thought about what you're going to do with the place?" he asked, his eyes wandering around the spacious living room.

"I was going to sell it," I started, unwilling to confront the part of me that fell into an easy comfort here.

"But?"

"But," I said, dragging the word out. "I'm starting to wonder what it might look like if I moved in instead. I don't know. It's probably stupid. I'd be so far from work and there's so much stuff I have to sort through which I *really* don't have time for."

He cracked a small smile, his perfect teeth flashing for a brief second before he eyed me expectantly. "But?"

I let myself meet his unflinching eye contact, trying to sit confidently under his silent scrutiny. "But it feels like home sometimes. I didn't come here often, but I can feel Aisha everywhere. She's practically waiting around the corner. It sounds stupid but—"

"It's not stupid," he said, his hand reaching up to tug on one of my drying curls. "It's okay to feel things, Asha."

I let myself lean into his hand. The rough pads of his palm, crusted over with red and white paint, rested against my cheek as I took in a deep breath. The scent of leather and pine, a distinctly Grayson smell, made its way into my system.

"One day," he started, his fingers gripping my chin—gentle though firm—pulling my gaze to his. "I'll change your mind, and you'll tell me all about it."

"About what?"

"About everything that molded you into this unfiltered powerhouse that crashes through the world."

Any comfort I felt melted away—quickly melting into a slow, simmering pit of anxious anger bubbling away in my stomach. I pulled his hand away from my face, kindly tucking it in his lap before standing up and flying to the other side of the room.

Grayson muttered a curse, running a frustrated hand through his hair before pushing himself up from the window seat, slowly walking toward me like I was some rabid, cornered beast. "Sorry."

"It's fine." *It wasn't.*

"Asha, I didn't mean to push. This afternoon just felt..."

"Different." I finished for him, the word coming to mind easily when I felt the exact same way.

'You don't deserve him,' the voice sang out. The words—repeating on a loop in my head—were the final straw, tears building under the pressure I felt to make myself into something that fit into Grayson's world.

I started laughing as the pools in my eyes, threatening to burst over if Grayson took one more step toward me. "I should go." The words were soft, barely a breath passing over my lips as I scooped up my clothes and grabbed my purse. "Thanks for everything."

"Asha, wait." I heard his footsteps, the stale air of the house threatening to suffocate me the closer he got. I threw open the front door, barreling down the stairs and toward the car before he could say anything else.

'You're nothing but a coward,' the voice called.

I know.

SEVENTEEN

Vlad was used to it now—the silent drive through the city as I asked him to take me to a trail. I sniffled through the ride, only pulling myself together long enough to run into a corner store to buy a bottle of bourbon. I ran my finger along the packaging, catching the lip of branded wrapping that was starting to tear beneath my anxious rubbing. I could feel my driver's stare through the small, rear-view mirror but refused to meet his eyes as evening tugged the light of day under the horizon. I don't think I let out a full breath until we rounded the corner into Laumeier Sculpture Park—a winding connection of trails that highlighted different art installments from various artists. On a good day, one I wasn't intent on burning away with my trusty trauma elixir, I could've spent hours winding through the trees, listening to the crunch of gravel beneath my feet as I lost track of time. Today, however, I knew exactly where I wanted to drown myself—The Hedenkamp Pool.

There hadn't been water in the giant, crumbling, concrete bowl in decades—the pool, once a pond, part of the abandoned land that had been converted into the seventy acre park. At some point, an artist had come through and added patios, stairs, and a wooden path around the structure so people could explore it with ease but none of that mattered to me. Not when I planned to heave myself into the deepest point and wade into the abyss of peace, my trusty support bottle glued to my lips.

Vlad parked the car, shifting in his seat to look back at me with that expectant silence of his. I offered a small smile before pulling myself out of the car and to the nearest trail-head, wondering which path would lead me to the pool today. The park was only open for another hour or so, the threat of darkness pushing me through oak trees, bushes and the occasional interactive sculpture. I didn't touch the seal of the bourbon until my ass was scraping down the wall of the pool, my back supported by the cool edge.

July always felt like the Devil's asshole—warm, sticky, and utterly unpleasant. I sucked down a generous shot, hissing as it sank into my stomach before turning my head to the sky, waiting for the stars to slowly wink into existence.

'Run, run, run, as fast as you can...' the voice called, encouraging another long, disassociated swig from the bottle as I curled against the ruins. I ignored the bits of rock that had started cutting into my face, pushing myself into their sharp edges in an attempt to feel anything other than the shame that seemed to have carved out a home under my skin.

My thoughts meandered as I listened to the night come to life, the sun sinking slowly as if it were trying to give me more time to wallow. I tried to ignore the lingering touch of Grayson's hands on my cheek, and the already fading high of our lips pressed together as I reminded myself that he didn't deserve the inevitable pain I would cause him. An errant tear ran down my face but I didn't—couldn't—move to wipe it away, the salty stream falling from my chin and into a pile of dirt.

I let myself ride the train of thought, unexpectedly arriving at Scheff's house and the tiny bit of warmth I'd let myself feel earlier today. We'd struggled through starting a business together and now he was ready—waiting—to struggle through a life, *a family*, together. And somewhere, deep inside, I wanted to try. To see what letting him support and fix me would feel like. I tightened my eyes, fighting against the rush of emotions as I remembered his arms wrapping around me—as I fought against the safety and security he *wanted* to provide me. Because, despite it all, it was Grayson pulling my eyes to his that sent the entire idea of stability with Scheff out the window.

If it wasn't for the time, slipping away with the heat of the day, I would've let myself fall asleep there—comforted by the chatter of birds and the flicker of fireflies above me. My phone buzzed in my pocket, a ten minute warning from Vlad with a picture attached. The park rangers were already heading into the trails with flashlights, ready to shoo away any last visitors. I groaned, pulling myself off of the ground before resting a hand on the stone, waiting for my head to stop spinning. A dog barked in the distance, yanking me back to the moment and I looked down at my hands—the half empty bottle in one, my phone in the other. For the first time in a long time, I set the bottle down and called my sister.

I walked the diameter of the pool, circling around while I waited for her to answer. An anxiety-riddled giddiness twisting the pit of my stomach each time silence broke through the ringing.

"Asha?" She asked, when the line connected, her voice wavering with concern. "What's wrong?"

A bourbon induced laugh echoed around the pool.

"Something has to be wrong for me to call you?" My cheeks heated as I waited for her response, an unending static buzz carrying through the phone as my amusement fell on its ass. "I just...needed someone to talk to, I guess."

It was Ana's turn to laugh, the cackle so loud I had to pull my phone from my ear. "It's almost like I've been saying that for months now. You're just too stubborn to listen."

My face twisted at her words—a thousand excuses held at the tip of my tongue but I bit down on them. My throat tightened as I tried to pick one out, trying to think of what would manipulate her into understanding. My voice was quiet as I said, "I know."

As if she was stunned by honesty, my sister waited for me to say something else—the only sign she hadn't hung up the phone was the soft breathing I heard coming through the speaker. "Where are you, Ash?" she asked, gentle enough to make my lip wobble. *Lost.*

"Laumeier."

She huffed a small laugh, likely losing herself to the same memories of Aisha leading us up the harrowing stairs of the mound—another relic of history preserved in the park. "What are you doing there? Doesn't it close soon?"

"Do you really want an answer to that?"

She hesitated. "Depends on the answer, I guess."

"Hmm," I started, finally pulling myself out at the shallow end and walking into the wooden terrace that looked over the pool. When I was younger, when things still felt *too* big, I would imagine that this was a lost kingdom—the remains of my own Cair Paravel waiting for lost queens and kings to find their way back. "And if I was halfway down a bottle would that change how much you care?"

"See? That's the problem. Just because you stopped caring doesn't mean I ever did." Any concern in her voice was wiped out by a sharp chortle of understanding. "When are you going to stop punishing yourself?"

"It's not punishment."

"What is it then? What are you running from?" My sister sounded exhausted.

It was my turn to hesitate, to meet her question with an unfair silence. I plopped down on the worn wood, watching as a daddy long-leg—narrowly missing being squashed by my ass—ran down the frames. A strip of caution tape blew in the wind next to me, whipping as the breeze began to build. There were a million answers to her question but I found it easier to say, "Everything."

"That's not an answer. That's a cop-out."

"Forgive me for not pinning down the exact reasoning behind my angst, Ana."

"It's not angst at this point."

"Then what is it, Ana? If you're so fucking knowledgable, then please. *Enlighten me.*"

I'd never met a moment as brutal, as telling, as tangible as this one. My sister, silently diagnosing me from the other end of the phone, just *waited* for me to admit to it—being the problem. "You know, I don't know why I called in the first place. What would *you* know about anything I'm going through?"

Another small, defeated laugh. "Sometimes, you sound just like her."

"And who is that, Ana?"

"Armatta."

My finger ached as it slammed into the small red button, immediately ending the call.

'Asha and Aisha...one and the same...' the voice chased me through the woods. I huffed my way up a hill and into the

parking lot as I tried to ignore the rest of the rhyme Aisha had started when I was younger.

'Though not as similar as the one who gave her the name.'

I'd been sitting on the couch for hours—the bright flashes of the television irrelevant as I turned Ana's words over and over in my head. I'd nearly finished the bottle in the back of the car, Vlad's worried eyes checking on me in that fucking mirror every few minutes. The twenty minute drive left me with a few deep swigs of bourbon—ones I cleared the second I'd locked my apartment door behind me.

Scheff had tried calling but I'd turned off my phone after declining his call. I had no sense of time but the ache in my lower back suggested I'd been planted on the couch, feet crossed under me, for a while. If I cared about anything, I might've dragged my ass to bed. But the voice had long been silenced, replaced by my sister likening me to our mother once again.

I sat there, waiting for my feet to go numb before turning off the TV and stumbling on pins and needles toward my bedroom. I crashed through my apartment, giggling as I knocked over a vase—an extravagant bouquet sent from Scheff earlier in the week. I doubled over, clutching my stomach as laughter echoed through the halls. I looked at the white glass, shards cutting through deep purple lilies and vibrantly red roses. *There's a metaphor in there somewhere.*

I trudged past it, every step of my journey slow and disoriented as I made my way to the shower—the sweet release of pain waiting for me under another scalding rain.

Eighteen

August

I'd spent the last month convincing myself I was fine—burying myself in work, in renovations, in anything that wasn't Grayson. We'd only run into each other a handful of times since we'd kissed which was somehow worse than avoiding him altogether. His inhuman kindness and comfort continued to surprise me—my favorite latte on the kitchen counter when I walked in, a kettle of water warming on the stove on days he knew I'd be there, a book of Aisha's set aside for me as he restored the living room. Grayson had tackled my list of demands with a content smile following him to every project.

The driveway was empty when Vlad and I pulled in, and when I stepped out of the car, a single, stuttering beat of disappointment hit before I could shove it down. I ignored it, climbing the stairs, pausing at the crack she used to complain about—it was a ritual by now, stopping to grieve with Aisha before going into her house.

Except the regret-riddled crack wasn't there anymore. The

wall had been smoothed over, sealed, and painted. The detail that had gnawed at Aisha in her last weeks, erased like it was never there. I ran a hand over it, allowing myself to miss her for a moment before stepping past.

I dug through my purse, my fingers lingering on the worn envelope that had sat in the bottom since June. I abandoned my search for the house key entirely, sliding into Aisha's porch swing before digging her letter out. I ran my fingers along my name, the 'A' leaking down the paper as if it had gotten wet at some point—left to dry in the chaotic mess of my bag. I'd tried to forget about it, to ignore the words that seemed to weigh me down and, even as I sat here—finally willing to look at the damn thing—I still didn't feel like I was ready to hear it. I doubted there was anything inside that would make my life easier.

A flock of geese flew by, enjoying the unbelievably cool day—a brisk eighty degrees on a summer afternoon. I would've been content to spend the day here, swaying in the breeze but my fingers continued their reckless pursuit—the bronze key appearing a minute later.

The key fit into the lock on the second try, my fingers shaking too much to aim. Aisha had always been here to open the door for me. Or Unc, or Junior. Or Grayson.

There had always been someone.

"Gray?" I called as I stepped over the threshold. My voice echoed untouched, seeping into the hollow halls Aisha had left behind. I set my bag on the bench, dropping the key back into the mayhem without a second thought. My fingers were already digging into my side as I walked through the lower level, ensuring I was well and truly alone before stalking upstairs.

My foot crested the top, freezing as I scanned the length of the halls, unsure of why I came in the first place. The house creaked, encouraging me to pop my head into every room before my feet paused in front of the nursery. My fingers dusted over the cool handle, adrenaline coursing through my veins as I waited for my aunt to bust around the corner, fussing at me for being 'so damn nosy.'

Technically, I owned the house. So, *technically*, I wasn't being nosy.

I loosed a breath, shaking my hand out before pressing the handle down, quick to assume I was still locked out. But the latch released, and I stepped through. Grayson must've found his way in if the door had been unlocked but everything in the room was neat, orderly—like he'd been hit by the same wall of grief that slammed into me now and decided to work elsewhere.

My feet were rooted to the floor as I tried to take it all in. The walls were a light shade of blue, various mementos hanging on each one. I stepped up to the nearest item, a tiny pair of crocheted baby socks framed against a white background. My hand hovered over it, wishing I could touch the small booties that Aisha had likely spent hours toiling over. Another step to the left and there was a shelf with a picture of the three of them. The Calloways—an entire family ripped from the world because of an *accident*. A fluke. A simple case of bad luck.

I took my time as I walked through the museum, admiring everything Aisha had hung with intentionality. I tried to lean across the crib, eager to look at the old, yellowed pictures of baby Aisha and Charles that hung above it. I absentmindedly picked at the chipped white paint on the railing—pushing my weight into it in hopes it would give me the extra inches I needed to see the pictures. The crib groaned in response. I hopped back, holding my hands in the air as I waited for it to crumble. My eyes darted to a single ring of bite marks that marred the wooden frame, exposing the wood underneath—my bite marks. It was the same crib that had followed the Arlington women across generations.

I could still hear my Auntie's excitement when she told us she was pregnant with Junior.

"So I'm eighteen weeks now and the doctor says he's growing like a weed," Aisha said, reaching an arm around my shoulder. She tucked me into her side and I leaned in, relishing her warmth. Matta didn't pay the bill this month and had just finished arguing over the phone with the electric company. Despite her cursing, they told her what they always did—the electricity would turn back on when the bill was paid. Ana and I had been alone for a few days, trying to get ahold of her but it wasn't until Aisha had called Matta, telling her she had news, that our mother found her way back to the frozen apartment.

"When's he gonna be here though?" I asked, the words lost as I mumbled them into Aisha's ribs.

She knelt down, pulling my hands into hers before blowing a warm breath into the bundle. "Right around your birthday. Maybe y'all will share it. How cool would that be?"

I offered her a small smile, tuning out her conversation with Matta. I didn't want to share Aisha with someone else, not when we could barely count on her to show up now. I looked at my sister—sitting silently under the blanket castle we'd constructed to stay warm—and detached myself from my aunt, crawling into the fort with her. We listened to the murmured conversation of the adults and, as Ana seethed with disgust and anger, I matched my reaction to hers. If Ana thought this was a bad thing, then surely it was.

It only took a few minutes for the sisters outside of our fortress to start yelling at each other, their raised voices piercing through the layers that surrounded us. "Matta, why can't I have it?"

"Momma didn't give it to you. That's why."

"So, you're telling me you plan to have another kid? You plan to use that crib in the next year?"

"I didn't say that but...well you know. Never know when you're going to get a nasty surprise." The words didn't bother me, not when I knew I was one of the nasty surprises she referred to.

Aisha huffed a disbelieving laugh. "And if that happens, I'll bring it right back over. Charles and I can't afford one right now, Mat. Please.*"*

That horrible sticky feeling filled the apartment, something twisting in my stomach right before the door slammed shut. Matta's voice cut through tension. "All she does is take, take, take. Ana!" My sister jumped as the sound of Matta's ire cut through our sanctuary. "Get your skinny ass in here."

Ana reached for my hand, giving it a quick squeeze before she crawled out and toward our mother, reality waiting for us on the other side of our quilted haven.

I ran my fingers over the marred edge, the damage a much-younger me created when she was still small enough to fit. If Aisha's story was true, she'd come to check on us one morning only to stumble into the apartment to find Ana hanging halfway in of the crib—a six year-old's attempt to free her toddler sister from baby jail. I smiled, turning to find a rocking chair tucked in the corner, a crocheted blanket was thrown across the back, a small table next to it with a journal —open—on top. The house creaked again, as if shifting with anticipation, eager to see what I'd do next.

I relaxed into the cushioned seat, unfolding the blanket with tenderness before throwing it over my legs. I tugged a corner to my nose, inhaling the lavender smell before pulling the dust-covered journal into my lap.

The leatherbound book was held open by an ultrasound,

Charles Francis Calloway Junior was scrawled in thick, curling letters—facts about his birth listed below with a picture of Aisha and Unc, holding newborn Junior at the hospital. I took in another deep sniff before flipping to the front cover, leafing through months worth of notes about her pregnancy. She'd listed everything from her cravings that changed day-to-day, to the ways her energy varied. As personal as I knew this was to her, I couldn't stop myself from flipping through—greedily absorbing the small connection to Aisha and her thoughts. I passed over the ultrasound once more, briefly wondering if the notes would stop there.

I slid my thumb under the thin paper quickly, catching the side and slicing the skin. Blood pulled on the surface and I stuck it in my mouth, too focused on the next set of notes. They were just dates, just weeks counted—a list of things lost before they ever began.

July 3rd, 2009. 8 weeks. Matta had just given me the crib.

February 10th, 2011. 12 weeks.

November 27th, 2012. 16 weeks. I heard the heartbeat this time.

August 4th, 2015. 9 weeks. Didn't tell Charles.

I pressed a fist into my mouth, using the pain as a shield against my building tears.

June 19th, 2018. 20 weeks. I give up.

The rest of the book was empty but the pages were worn too—like Aisha had spent a lot of time leafing through the space she'd hoped to fill. It was agony, pure agony, that ripped through the house as I screamed for her.

Something groaned in the walls. The wood cracking like the house itself could feel it too. None of this was fair, not for Aisha. I pulled the blanket around my shoulders, listening to the stiff cracks of material that hadn't been touched in who knew how long. The air in the room was suffocating again and my headache had its own pulse between my eyes. I ran from the room, my feet leading me to Junior's without a second thought.

I swore there was still a dip in the bed—the outline of Aisha's grief forever imprinted in the mattress. I stumbled over, curling so I could fit in her memory, wishing she was here with her arms around me once more.

"It isn't *fair!*" I screamed, tightening my fist around the blanket, shoving the fuzzy thing in my nose as tears broke out. My ragged breaths filled the space as I realized that, even though I was here, this house was hollow still.

❧

I woke to a rough, calloused hand brushing against my cheek. My lips pulled up at the corners as my forehead creased.

"Hey," a deep, intoxicating voice said from the other side of my closed eyes. A thumb brushed the skin under my jaw, eliciting a small, contented sound from my throat. "Asha, wake up."

I cracked my eyes to find Grayson crouched in front of me, his arm resting on Junior's bed as his hand ran down my cheek—the same hand that shot away as soon as he saw me staring at him. I blinked back into reality, slowly sitting up as Grayson stood up, his tall frame towering above me. My throat was raw, my words dry as I said, "I didn't mean to fall asleep."

"Happens to the best of us. You want some tea?"

"How comfortable have you gotten in here?" I yawned, stretching my arms above my head as I looked around for my phone. I pulled the baby blanket away from my face, slapping my hands against the bed a few times, swiping them in long strides until my hard, brick of a phone collided with my wrist.

Once I realized I'd been asleep for *three hours*, I started to panic, sending my heart beating erratically as I unlocked the screen. No new emails and no missed calls.

I tried to shake the adrenaline that burst through my veins but couldn't. *One breath in, one breath out.*

My hands, shaking hard despite knowing that I hadn't missed anything, danced in my lap. I tucked them between my thighs, hoping Grayson wouldn't notice the tremor.

"Ana told me where to find everything and I've gotten used to hanging out on the porch or under the trees during my breaks." He swiped a hand behind his neck and turned away from me, probably too ashamed to admit that he was finding comfort here. I couldn't blame him—so did I.

"Let me guess," I started, finally pulling myself from the bed. I rolled my neck in a few circles, noticing a new knot that had started to form after hours of laying awkwardly in my cousin's bed. "She has ginger, some assortment of fruit teas, and an insane amount of Earl Grey."

Grayson laughed as he led me out of the room and down the stairs. I ignored the nursery door this time, skittering past it like a terrified little mouse. "Yes, she has all of that and then I brought some oolong and peppermint to round out the collection."

We found a comfortable silence, and I watched as he worked around my aunt's kitchen.

"The honey's almost gone," I started, digging the spoon as deep into the container as I could, scraping as much honey down the sides as I could. "I don't need any if you're used to having it in your tea."

He knocked his knuckles against the counter once before turning, and bolting out the door. "Hold on."

I continued to scrape, waiting for the sound of the front door closing to pull me away from the pot. I looked up to find Grayson with a small honey bear in his hand. The sunlight danced against the chiseled panes of his face, highlighting the excitement and energy in his eyes. "Honey," he started, raising the bear in his hand. My body locked up. "Crisis averted."

I was frozen, trying to process the pause in his words, and overthinking the breath he took after saying honey. *Breathe.*

Anxiety twisted my gut as I opened my mouth to speak, instead filling the air with an unexpected laugh instead. "Thank you."

We waited for the water to finish boiling before taking our steaming mugs out to the porch swing. The sun had started to sink as bugs began to replace birds in the late August sky. I settled into the porch, thankful for the sweatshirt and joggers I'd decided on earlier today—the heat didn't hold as long into the night anymore, a sign that St. Louis was finally dipping into fall.

For the first time in my life, I didn't feel the need to fight for something to say—words incapable of filling the beauty that was happening around us. The leaves rustled in the oaks as an orchestra of crickets started to fill the air. The sky above us was a bright pink, colliding with soft oranges and periwinkles as the night sky began to push against the light of day.

I blew a soft, steady breath over my mug before bringing it to my lips, taking in a scalding sip and allowing it to burn away the anxious word babble that was trying to claw up my throat. Though there was no need when Scheff's sleek, black town car came spinning into the driveway, parking perfectly parallel to Grayson's work truck.

The tall, blonde man I hadn't seen for eight days shot out of the front seat in a flurry, his forehead creased as he locked eyes with me. He shoved a hand through his hair and took a breath before stalking toward us, his cool mask quickly secured. "Asha."

I set my tea on the railing of the porch, ensuring it had enough room to balance before chancing a brief look at Grayson—looking more than a little annoyed. I pushed myself towards the, potentially volatile, bomb working his way up the path. I skipped down the steps, eager to intercept him before he made it to the house. "Hey, what're you doing here?"

"I figured I'd take you to the new house tonight. I thought we could have dinner and drinks but it's clear you have plans."

"No, I don't have plans. I fell asleep in Junior's room and Grayson just woke me up," I said, hoping the energy that seemed to be radiating from him would dissipate at my words.

He took a step past me, directing his attention to Grayson, who was still sipping on his tea, fighting to maintain his own calm disposure. "Did you enjoy watching her sleep?"

"Whoa, Scheff!" I said, trying to catch up to him as he took long strides up the front steps. Grayson met the accusation, setting his tea down before abruptly pulling himself up to stand chest to chest with Scheff. "Grayson! Scheff! What the hell is wrong with you two!"

"I wouldn't call it spying so much as making sure that she's *okay*. What do you know about making her feel okay?" The remaining slivers of sunlight faded against the two of them, twilight weighing down upon us.

"I know a hell of a lot more than you do, *handyman*."

"That's enough! You're both acting like fucking dogs," I said, huffing a frustrated breath before wrapping my hand around Scheff's bicep. I tried to tug him toward the stairs but failed, his feet locked to the ground as the two men continued their silent pissing contest.

"I may be a handyman but at least I know how to *actually* fix shit instead of breaking it further." The pair inched closer, their noses nearly touching as I continued to try and pull Scheff away. I gave one final tug before my hand slipped from Scheff's arm, sending me flying down the stairs. I landed on Aisha's pebbled walkway, the gravel digging into my back.

"Asha!" Scheff cried as he skipped down the steps, gingerly reaching for me. I let him grab my hand, helping me back up as I dusted the bits of rock from my ass.

"I'm fine," I huffed, looking first at Scheff, with his erratic concern, and then to Grayson with his unabashed shame.

I turned for the car, the shock of falling was wearing off and my wrist began to radiate with the call of pain. Scheff helped me into the front seat and, as he walked around to the other side, I turned to see Grayson glaring. He shook his head before turning to the porch swing, grabbing our mugs and disappearing back into the house. He was gone by the time Scheff had dropped into his seat and started the car.

We only made it through fifteen minutes of the drive before Scheff decided the silence wasn't enough. "What was he doing there?"

"He's the fucking contractor, Scheff."

"And?"

"And what? What do you want me to say? You don't get to make rules for me."

He took a deep, shuddering breath, his focus pinned on the road in front of us. "I thought things were changing between us, Ash."

"What? What do you mean? You left me at the party. To be with perky, little Sherry. It's always these games with you."

He laughed, the sound filling the car with a bitter contentment. "I *left*? *My* games?"

"You left, Scheff."

"You pushed me away!" he roared, his hand smacking the steering wheel.

"Why are you so mad!? There isn't anything between Grayson and me! He's fixing Aisha's house before I sell it." I tucked myself further into the corner, willing the cool metal of the door to keep me present.

"So, you just drink tea on the porch and watch the sun set with every painter or contractor who stumbles into your life?"

"Come on, Scheff."

"There is no 'come on, Scheff' about it, Ash!"

"I've been asking you why you came back for months now. It's not my fault if you can't use your words." The city flashed by as Scheff pushed the car to go faster, the engine screaming under the overwhelming pressure to speed.

"I've used my words," he started, running a hand through his hair in a fast, frustrated motion. "And my tongue, and my fingers in that very particular way that you like. I've been by your side for months now, in spite of this self-isolating pit you've dug yourself into. I played the game by your rules and I'm tired of it, Asha. What else do you want me to say?"

I turned my head, blatantly ignoring Scheff's question as I let the window down. I hoped that a breeze blowing through the car would wipe out the tension that was building around my response. But thick, heavy clouds gathered on the horizon began stealing any remaining light—the wind whipping into the car just as suffocating as the conversation inside.

Scheff veered off of the interstate, taking us on a quick drive through residential streets. We were stuck in that uncomfortable in-between—awkwardness all stemming from my inability to talk about the feelings he thought he had for me. He pulled down a quiet street, the thunderheads following us into the driveway of the same, fairy-book home we had looked at with Sherry. He threw the shifter into park, sending the car—and me—jolting into place outside of the garage before running around to open my door. My fingers screamed in protest as he tightened his around mine, tugging me up the steps and toward the elaborately masoned entrance.

"Scheff, stop!"

"We *are* going to talk about this, Asha. I was just trying to give you the decency of a private conversation before I completely lost it in front of my new neighbors." He paused, looking over my shoulder and threw a comedic wave to an elderly woman who was nearly hanging out of her window as she listened to us. *Snoopy old bitch.*

"Scheff, there's nothing to talk about," I hissed, trying to keep my voice low to avoid causing a scene that would spark the elder's gossip fuel for weeks.

"I love you, Asha. I'd say that's something that needs to be talked about. Right now, in fact."

I laughed, the sound cold and callous as I pulled my hand from his, my fingers trembling. "You don't know me. Not really." My voice cracked, but I swallowed hard against the pressure in my chest. "You're in love with someone I've created—an idea of who you want me to be. You need to let go of that." I took a step back, refusing to meet his gaze, the weight of my walls pressed down, solid and unyielding. My chest ached at the thought of him walking away, more than I was willing to admit.

"No, I'm not! I see you. I see *every* shattered, broken, shard that completes you. You think I don't? Then how would I know that you keep me at a distance because of how your mother treated you? Because of how she used you? How do I know that you don't let anyone in because you're scared of them leaving you just like Ana did? I see *you*, Asha."

"No," the word was barely a breath. "I get to choose who

has access to me and I don't want you to care. *You will leave.* Everyone does and I doubt you'll be the exception, Matthew." I sneered at him, the sound of his first name foreign to my lips.

"I won't! You don't get to decide if I care. Stop trying to push me away, Asha!" I stared at him, listening to the powerful clap of thunder that echoed across the sky—the promise of a late-summer rainstorm well on its way.

"Just let me show you at least. Let me prove to you that I won't leave. I've followed your stupid rules for years, Ash. I have held onto every pathetic scrap you've carelessly thrown to me for *six years*. You think I don't care because if I showed you how much I did, you'd lock me out for good." His eyes were stuck to me by now, refusing to give me an easy escape. "I'm tired. Let me try."

I didn't say anything, but his broken voice filled the silence for me. "One for one?"

The small, hesitant words could have brought me to my knees.

'Selfish little Asha. See how far you can push him before he finally breaks.'

I nodded.

"What will it take?" he asked quietly. The wind started to pick up, the leaves rustling.

"Why?" I asked. Both of our questions were laid out in— what had always been—my favorite game of ours.

What would it take for me to let him in? We could've sat there for hours and I still wouldn't have had an answer for him. *I don't know.*

He took a step towards me, pulling my focus from the porch he'd decorated a bit since he'd moved in—a tall fern sat in a giant planter in the corner with a small, wooden bench across from it. "You don't get to run away when I say this," he started, his hands raised defensively while his eyebrows arched. I let out a short, sharp laugh before nodding in consolation.

"I love you," he said, his voice raw, as though the words had been clawing at his throat for years. His grip tightened on my hand, anchoring himself, anchoring me. He'd make me listen this time. "I've loved you for six years, and I *need* you to give us a chance."

I opened my mouth, eager to remind him of my rules or to prove to him that he's wrong about me but he cut me off. "No, I'm talking."

I shot him a sharp look but he continued. "I stood by as you tried to freeze me out. And then you asked me if I would fuck you, no strings attached of course. One, non-committal night with you every year and how could I refuse? Like I said, I was willing, eager even, to take any fucking piece you deigned to give me. I helped you with the business, we built it together and then I provided everything you would ever need to succeed and that's when I realized I fucking love you." His laugh went dark. "So, the world ends up getting pieces of me because all of the ones I would share with someone else, I'm still waiting to give to you. Let me try, Asha. Let me try or...or I need to walk away."

He grabbed my hand again, his grip much looser as he refused to meet my eye. I felt the first drop of rain on my neck, a cool reminder that a storm was close.

Love. He said he loves me. I couldn't stop the calculating side of my brain, the one that screamed, asking what love had ever done for me. Memories flashed—Aisha's laugh, bright and carefree, echoed in my mind as she watched Junior take his first steps. The sound, so full of life, quickly melted into Ana and Hadley's voices mingling in the guest bedroom, a temporary refuge from the loneliness that had taken root since they left. No, they didn't leave—I could still see their faces, shadowed with concern as I pushed them away, the disappointment in their eyes, identical to Armatta's. Another flash and my mother's smile flickered, sharp and cold, like the edge of a knife.

I pulled my gaze back to Scheff, hoping the slick feeling of guilt would dissolve under his steady eyes. I reached my free hand for his chin, gently pushing his gaze to meet mine. I gave him a simple, silent nod and it took less than a second for him to pull me into his arms—our lips meeting in a kiss as intense as it was fraudulent. I moaned, jumping into his arms as I wrapped my legs around his waist, my hands cupping his cheeks. His hands caught under my ass and he pulled me closer to his body, every inch of us meeting in the desperation of the moment. Another clap of thunder drove us apart but only for a second, our lips crashing together once more.

Scheff had just turned to walk us up the porch when the sky finally opened up—a typical Midwest deluge to drench us before we could make it inside the house.

Nineteen

I wasn't exactly used to waking up to someone who was *meant* to stick around past the early hours of the morning. I stared—frozen and unblinking, my eyes locked on my reflection in Scheff's bathroom mirror. I couldn't understand how I'd allowed myself to spend the night, the *whole* night with Scheff. It was already eight in the morning when I reached for my phone on the nightstand, pulling myself from bed to hide here while he slept.

After carrying me into the house yesterday, Scheff and I spent the next few hours reacquainting ourselves with each other's bodies. He took his time, his hands roaming as he kissed me, our naked forms rarely disconnected. We took a small break, and I showered while he went to raid the kitchen for snacks, only for us to fall right back into rhythm as the water rained down on us.

Hours passed and I hadn't caught a wink of sleep, not under the oppressive weight of his arm. Even if he wasn't wrapped around me—tightening every few minutes as if he had to reassure himself I was still there—I'd be suffocating under the pressure of his words from months ago. *'You can't see how you manipulate me, and use my feelings for you at your will...'*

Isn't that exactly what I did here? I fucked the man to pacify him, to keep him close and to keep him from leaving me.

'Selfish, manipulative girl.'

My skin started to warm—slick with shame and the clash of our body heat. I started to lift his arm, the limb heavy and seemingly impossible to move. I held my breath as I shifted out from under him, terrified that if I woke him up, he'd immediately see right through me.

I reached for the silken robe that I'd wrapped around myself last night—the one that had been waiting for me on the bedpost as if Scheff knew I'd cave into him eventually. I tiptoed out of the room, closing the door behind me before slowly releasing the handle. The hallway walls were still bare, entire bedrooms still waiting to be filled with whatever Scheff decided would suit until he was ready for kids. *Kids.*

He bought this house so *we* could build a family. My hands wrapped around my stomach as I stumbled down the halls, trying to avoid the feeling of absence that seemed to linger. I dug my fingernails into my ribs as I stalked through the house, crossing the bridge over the foyer and skipping down the stairs. I forgot about the *creak* that sounded on the second step, wincing as I froze. I waited a few seconds before shifting my weight to my other foot. The same whine slowly released from the stair as I tried to move off of it and, damning it all to hell, I barreled down the rest, stopping again at the bottom to listen for any movement upstairs. I blew out a stressed breath before resuming my journey.

I made it to the kitchen, the morning light shot through the stained glass windows, hues of reds and purples cast on the tiled floors. I quietly tore through the cabinets in a desperate search for a tea kettle, mouthing a silent 'yay' as I pulled one from a lower cabinet, stuffed behind various pans. I threw open a few more cabinets, surprised to find them bare —a couple of plates and glasses gracing the otherwise barren shelves. I pulled open a final door, finding a walk-in pantry on the other side—rows stocked with seasonings, pastas, whatever else a home chef might need, and one measly box of bagged tea. I muttered a string of words, cursing Scheff for having three different types of flour but not a single tin of loose tea leaves.

I pushed back my curls, debating my options when something deep inside told me to go to Aisha's. She had *quality* tea, a kettle and—no matter that my place was closer—I was currently craving the comfort I could only find at my auntie's house. I snuck back up the stairs, stepping over the one that sounded on my way down, and tiptoed back into the bedroom. I let the early hours of the morning light my way, silently rushing to find my own clothes—Scheff's ensemble the only things my hands could seem to find.

I texted Vlad as soon as I was dressed, peeking at Scheff through the cracked door before fleeing fully. Forty-five minutes later, I was outside of Aisha's house.

"Thanks for the rescue, Vlad." I said, sliding out of the car and shutting the door behind me. I skipped past Grayson's truck and up the front porch—pausing to let my heart rate return to normal before stepping inside.

"Gray?" I called as I closed the front door behind me. I slid my shoes off before peeking into the empty living room. "Where are you?"

He didn't answer, but the sound of metal scraping across glass had me walking down the short hall and into the kitchen. "*Hello?* Why are you ignoring me?"

I turned the corner to find him at the small table Aisha

kept by the window. Only two rickety seats could fit around it but that didn't stop her from taking her tea and a visitor here on sunny days. A plate of biscuits and a still-steaming kettle took up most of the tabletop, his mug in hand.

"It seems I don't have anything constructive to say." The words were tight—clipped short as he looked out the window.

"I'm sorry about yesterday, okay? I didn't know he was going to show up."

"You let him drag you out of here like he's someone important to you. I didn't know I'd kissed someone else's woman."

"I'm not...we're not together. He's just..." I looked around the room, ringing my hands as I tried to find the right word. "Scheff."

I went to Aisha's cupboard, reaching for a mug of my own before sitting across from Grayson. I started to make my tea—an Earl Grey blend—when he lightly swatted my hand. "You use too much and make it too bitter. Move."

Only slightly annoyed, I passed him the cup, letting him work his herbal magic. He clearly had it down to a science, and even remembered to add honey before he passed it back to me—the already warm mug comforting as he told me to wait.

I reached across the table, hoping to eat a biscuit while the tea steeped but Grayson slid the plate away as soon as my fingers brushed the flaky tops. "Seriously?"

"Seriously. I can't be sharing my biscuits with a committed woman." He popped a giant chunk into his mouth, his cheeks filling as he chewed. "Gives off the wrong impression."

"I am not *committed*. Stop being like that and give me a biscuit."

He reached for another one, cutting it open with a knife before taking a bite. "No." *Asshole.*

"Grayson, *please* may I have a biscuit?" I asked, bottom lip wobbling in a silent appeal. He simply glared, digging through the pile before tossing the smallest one across the table. I caught it with ease, digging my fingers in so I didn't drop it. Hunks of fluffy dough scattered onto my plate and I turned to Grayson with a bashful look. "Oops."

His angry mask cracked, his cheeks rounding in amusement before he reached for the jam, slathering it on a biscuit of his own. I took a sip of tea, comfort warming my stomach. "You make it just like Aisha did." My words had him pausing, his biscuit frozen an inch away from his face—mouth open and waiting. "It's perfectly sweet. I haven't been able to get it right yet."

He nodded, considering before taking the bite. "I'm glad you enjoy it."

I smiled, he smiled, and then we finished our small breakfast in silence. Afterward, I followed him into the kitchen to help him load the dishwasher—the two of us finally sliding back into the ease of just existing around each other. Grayson had just tucked the butter and jam into the fridge when the front door slammed shut. He looked at me, eyebrows raised, and I shrugged.

"Well, look what we have here. Asha Marie at Auntie's house and no one had to drag you here?" Ana started from the hallway before spinning into the kitchen. "I am *truly* shocked."

I rolled my eyes, my head dropping to my chest. "Hello, sister. What do you want?"

Her focus bounced between Grayson and I, a knowing look spearing both of us—as if she'd caught us doing something nefarious and wanted us to know that *she* knows. I glared, shaking my head before turning to the man. "Sorry, you might not know this but AnaMarie is just as annoying as she is beautiful."

"And Asha is just as infuriating as she is funny," she said, earning a snort from Grayson. I looked between them with my jaw dropped.

"Okay this is *my* house. You guys can't bully me in my own home." I crossed my arms and pouted, playfully nudging Grayson's shoulder with my own.

He wrapped an arm around me, leaned in and said, "You'll survive."

Ana doubled-over, and Grayson's laugh was strong enough to shake the two of us. I ducked out from under him, glaring at Ana one more time before making my way to the living room.

"Okay, so, I probably should've done this before I—" He hesitated at the unamused tilt of my head. "*We* painted but I wasn't thinking fast enough," he started, leading me around the corner and into the dining room. "How would you feel if we knocked this wall down and opened this space up into the kitchen? You could add an island eventually if you decided to, but I think the space could use some more light. More room to breathe."

"So all that work I put into painting was for nothing?" I asked as Ana turned the corner, eyeing the wall like she could already see it gone.

He picked up his tool bag and leaned in close, his breath warm against my ear. "I don't recall you painting anything other than yourself."

I craned my neck to look up at him, the muscles in his jaw tensing with amusement. "I don't think you got much work done that day either."

"*I* think I made progress but," he disappeared around the

corner, popping his head around with a mischievous grin. "Only time will tell." He winked and disappeared once more.

My fists clenched at my side—*one breath in, one breath out*—and followed the insufferable pair into the kitchen. Grayson was knocking on the wall, listening carefully as he did so. I was thankful for the tight-fitting shirt he'd decided to wear today, his back tensing every time he pounded the wall.

Ana walked over to me with an eyebrow raised, saying nothing as she knocked her hip into mine. I gave her a playful glare, flipping her my middle finger with a murmured 'shut-up.' She slapped my hand away and I looked at her, jaw-dropped. I swatted her shoulder, she knocked a hand against the back of my head. I poked her in the ribs, she pressed her heel into my toes. I was just about to dig my fingers into the back of her neck, my face scrunched with determination, when Grayson turned around to acknowledge us. He pointed to a spot on the wall. "I think we can start he—"

Ana and I were standing ramrod straight, hands behind our backs with identical, honey-sweet smiles on our faces. Grayson's eyebrows narrowed as he tore his eyes away. "Here. Who wants the first swing?" He reached a hand into his bag, pulling out a small sledge hammer.

"Considering it's *Asha's* house, I'll let her have the honors." Ana tilted her hand, clapping her hands once before walking toward the carpenter's mask Grayson offered her. As soon as his focus was on securing his mask, I ran up behind Ana and swatted her on the back of the head, pulling the hammer from Gray's hands before she had time to retaliate. I stuck my tongue at her before accepting my own mask— sliding it over my face before raising my hand, weighed down by the weighty metal, and threw all of my weight into the wall. There was now a giant hole in Aisha's house, the thrill of destroying something intentionally filling my body and pushing me to swing again. And again, and again.

The weight of the hammer, the crack of drywall, the rush of impact—I lost myself to the rhythm of it. My arms were weighed down with exhaustion after ten minutes and I looked to my sister, panting as I offered the handle of the tool to her —offering her a taste of the relief I'd found.

She smiled and swapped places with me, wrapping two hands around the handle and raising it high above her head. Grayson stepped forward, pointing to another area and Ana was swinging before he was fully out of the way. The hammer came down with a scream of grief, one I imagined matched the sound of my own just minutes ago.

The three of us spent an hour, taking turns with the hammer—though Grayson didn't fill the room with screams, just deep groans as he swung into the wall. We'd finished tearing it through it, Ana and I now lounging against the wall with glasses of iced tea in our hands.

"I know better by now than to push you but, when you're ready, will you tell me? About that day you found..." *Aisha*. She didn't have to say her name for the grief, the guilt, I'd just released to well back up. I simply nodded, watching through the demolished wall as Grayson continued to pick up scraps, hauling them into a giant trash bag while Ana and I talked. I wondered how much he heard, wondered if I still intrigued him in the same way after I'd taken a chance to really talk to my sister.

A phone began ringing and Grayson dropped the bag, pulling the source from his back pocket. We sat for a few more seconds before the question, still lingering between us, threatened to drown me. I peeled myself from the wall, snatching the garbage bag to pick up where Grayson left off.

Ana was there a few seconds later, helping me to fill the plastic with the broken pieces of Aisha's home.

"There's an emergency at another jobsite and I have to head out a little early," Grayson said, his steps filled with purpose as he looked into his tool bag, securing loose parts before throwing it over his shoulder. "You can leave the mess and I'll get to it tomorrow."

"We got it," I offered, my eyebrows arching in surprise. "I mean, Ana and I can get most of it."

He nodded, his lips pulled into a tightline before he murmured his goodbyes, stalking out of the room.

I walked around her, peeking out of the window by Aisha's reading nook to see if Grayson had already left. He was still out on the driveway, like he was waiting for this moment, his eyes focused on my lookout spot. A smile split across his face as he gave me a wave. I waved back, letting my lips curl to match his before I felt the heat of Ana pressing against my back.

"He's hot."

"Ana!" I quickly moved away from the window, my cheeks heating as tires crunching on the gravel marked Grayson's departure.

"What? He is. Is this tension I see, little monster?"

"There's no *tension*," I said, blowing out a heavy breath of frustration. "And don't call me that."

"Okay, so I need to ask a favor." I turned around quickly, surprised to see my sister anxious—her hands ringing in front of her.

"Okay..."

"I have a conference next month and my babysitter won't be able to watch Hadley." My heartbeat quickened as I waited for her to continue. "Would you be willing to watch her? She loved staying at your place and, despite everything, loves you."

I sat silently, scared to offer the 'yes' that sat heavy on my tongue, the single word choking me. "It would only be a weekend and I've asked around and everyone's busy. I've looked, trust me."

So much could go wrong in three days. "Do you *trust* me to watch her or am I the last resort?"

Her eyes narrowed as she thought about the question. "We both know you're the last resort. And I *want* to trust you."

I filled the now-open space with a bitter laugh. "But you don't."

"Give me a reason to." The challenge wasn't harsh, but once again filled with an exhausted breathiness—like she was begging for me to pass whatever test this was.

Desperate to change the subject, I asked, "How did you even know I was here?"

"Kate gave me access to your location before she quit. You're so attached to your phone, I'm surprised you didn't notice."

"Maybe, when you're in need of my help, Ana, don't make digs."

"It's not a dig," she said, her shoulders raising with the pitch of her voice. "Just an *observation*."

Her eyes narrowed as she took me in, unwilling to hide her blatant assessment of me. "Whatever." She chucked a hunk of the torn-apart wall into the growing pile. "So, can Hadley stay with you?"

My heart skipped again, anxiety spiking at the idea. I swallowed the 'no' that was trying to break free from my throat. "Yeah, sure. Just make sure she has everything she needs because I don't have anything in my house for...kids"

"She's not *really* a kid. She just needs to be fed and stuff.

I'll send her with clothes, a book and her phone. You'll be fine."

"Okay," I rubbed my fingers against my temples, willing my sister-induced headache to go away. "Just send a list of what she likes to eat. Is there *anything else* you need from me?"

My sister settled into her hip and crossed her arms over her chest, pinning me into the corner with the stance—her eyes narrowed as she looked me over, dragging a deep breath in through her nose. "At least you don't reek of alcohol today."

My cheeks flamed—whether in embarrassment or anger, I wasn't sure.

"Hadley is my life, Asha. I do not take leaving her with you lightly."

I looked over at my sister, the sun bouncing off of the dark red walls and into the auburn highlights of her hair. She looked ethereal—an angel in her own regard. I couldn't bring myself to meet her eyes, knowing the fire I'd find swirling in those brown pools.

"I know," I said quietly, letting the anger give way to guilt. I climbed into the bay window seat, letting my head fall into my hands. I didn't like how I felt around the two of them, the way they always seemed to force me under a microscope. Not to mention the pressure of caring for my niece—the fiery ball of passion she'd grown into—that threatened to suffocate me the longer Ana stood over me. I huffed out an understanding laugh looking back up at my older sister with a new clarity. "Thank you for trying to trust me."

"Don't fuck this up, Asha." She lingered, long enough to catch my small nod before turning to leave.

I sat there, shoulders curled in as I toyed with the fear that

I *would* find a way to fuck it up before I even had Hadley in my possession.

TWENTY

I waved to Frank on my way into my apartment building, offering a small smile as music played through my earbuds. I was riding a comfortable high after the afternoon spent with Grayson and Ana and I didn't miss the skip in my step as I stepped onto the elevator. My eyes flickered to Frank after I pressed the button for my floor, barely catching his arm waving to catch my attention as the doors closed on him, marking the ascent to my apartment. Maybe I didn't hear him as I all but floated through the lobby, *Unwritten* by Natasha Beddingfield acting as a soundtrack to my day. *I'll catch him again later.*

I walked down the hallway, mindlessly scrolling through my email and didn't notice the smell radiating from my apartment door until I opened it. The unmistakable scent of vegetables and herbs hit me as I crossed over the threshold.

"Sch—Matthew?" I called out, covering the slip up with a small cough.

"Hey, one second!" His voice sounded from the balcony. I dropped my purse onto the island, peeling off my jacket and draping it over the back of a barchair before turning to look for him—only to be met with the man himself standing right in front of me.

"Hey," I breathed, trying to ignore the anxious tremors that were threatening to take over my hands again.

"Hey." He leaned in, placing a quick kiss on my forehead before bracing my shoulders with his hands. "Where'd you disappear to this morning?"

I looked past him, toward the candles and flowers that decorated the balcony, the evening air turning thick the longer I stared. I snapped my focus back to him, willing the mix of feelings crawling up my throat—guilt, confusion, and clarity swirling together—to go back down. "I was just at Aisha's. Something told me I should be there today and I..." I reached up, wrapping my hands behind his neck before planting a kiss on his lips—gentle, guilty. "I think it was good for me to go."

'Selfish, manipulative girl,' the voice called.

"That's good then, right?" He asked, leaning back to look over my face, as if he needed to be certain I wasn't lying to him about feeling okay.

"Right," I said, lying through the small smile I offered him.

He turned away from me, his fingers twisting with mine as he led me toward the balcony. As the flame battled against the gentle breeze, flashes of silver caught my attention. The table was covered in hundreds of gum wrapper flowers—the same stalks that had once fallen to the floor in a lecture hall recreated.

"Do you remember," he started, pulling out a chair for me. "When I was still just a nervous freshman and I made you flowers to get your attention?"

He sat across from me, pouring water from a pitcher into two glasses. He offered me one, turning his focus to the sunset behind me. He reached across the table, as if he couldn't be disconnected from me for a second—rubbing his free hand behind his neck.

"How could I forget?"

"I think I've loved you since our heads collided," he confessed quietly, avoiding eye contact. I didn't have anything to offer him outside of a lie so I just leaned across the table and kissed him again. He cleared his throat as I sat back down, his next question even softer. "Was, uh, Grayson there today?"

I reached over, rubbing my hand against his smooth palm, trying to ignore the part of me that wanted to compare it to the rough, calloused pads of Grayson's. "No. Ana stopped by though. I'm going to watch Hadley for a few days soon." *A careful lie laced with truth.*

He nodded as if he already knew she was going to ask me, as if he was proud that I'd accepted. The guilt of lying to him stabbed me like a knife—searing hot yet stunningly dull. I leaned forward, pressing my lips to his over the flickering light of the candles' dance.

"This is beautiful, Matty. Thank you." The words twisted the knife further in my gut, so I kissed him again before I could say something that I would regret.

Before I was allowed to keep Hadley next month, Ana made me agree to picking her up and dropping her off for her first week of school. It didn't seem like much of a challenge but I forgot to factor in the hangover migraines I woke up with most days—the morning light blinding as Vlad pulled into my sister's apartment complex.

I sent a text to the groupchat Ana forced me into—the thread hosting the newest trio of Arlington women—letting my niece know I was here. Her only response was a thumbs up that was followed by a five minute silence. I called Hadley, the immediate triple beep suggesting she ignored it the second it showed up on her screen. I huffed, unbuckling and leaning over the console, earning a surprised yelp from Vlad as I laid my hand into the horn. *Thank God it's Friday.*

I pulled away, Vlad shaking his head with a small laugh as I squeezed into the small opening. "So, what's on the agenda for your weekend?"

The question was another surprise to the old man, a relieved look passing over his mustache-covered lip. "Not much Miss Asha. I'll be on call tomorrow and then I'm taking my wife to the movies on Sunday. Maybe some drinks after."

"Trying to get lucky, Vladimir? You fox." I nudged his shoulder, ignoring the cramp that was starting just above my hips.

"I learned long ago that every minute I get to spend with Molly is the luckiest minute yet," he paused, his eyes glazing over. "She's my gift."

I barely recognized it, the pure love blatant on his face— lingering as if he couldn't stop thinking of his wife right now if he tried, if he wanted to. I sat back in my seat, absentmind- edly swiping through emails when the door opposite of me was ripped open.

"She won't let me go to the freakin' party." Hadley huffed, her knuckles turning white around her phone. "All my friends are going, and now I'll be the loser whose mom wouldn't let her stay out past nine."

I fished for words to say, my brain going blank as my niece continued to pout next to me. A frustrated growl filled the car and, as I looked to Vlad for any assistance, his eyes were dutifully glued to the road in front of us—unwilling to tango with the wrath of a teenage girl, seething mad at her mother.

"Hey," I started. The word, meant to comfort her, only directed her fiery gaze to me. I lifted my hands in surrender and leaned farther into the car door. I weighed the words on my tongue—knowing they were the difference between Hadley's sole ire and piling Ana's on top. "Listen, if your mom said no, she likely has a good reason."

"You *would* say that." Her lips twisted in the same way Ana's would when she was about to lay into me. "You're just trying to get back on her good side."

I dropped my arms, shaking my head with a laugh. "I don't know if I'll ever get back on your mother's good side. I just know that she wouldn't keep you from having fun if there wasn't a potential threat to your safety. We live in a city, Hads. It's home to you but bad things can still happen."

She turned toward the door, fingers twitching against her phone as she glared out the window. A sigh, sharp and frustrated, filled the car. Then another. And another.

"Jesus, Hadley. You will not spend this entire drive huffing and puffing. Either talk about it or be quiet."

Her laugh was not kind. "What do you know about talking?" She turned back to the window, her voice soft but still edged with something sharp. "You've been holed up for months."

I looked her over, once again weighing my words before I spoke. "I know enough about your mother to know when to push and when it's stupid to dig in. I will talk to her for you but you have to leave your attitude behind when you go to school. Do you accept my terms?" I held my breath as I reached a hand out to my niece. It was business. Nothing more than a deal.

She stared at my hand, consideration passing over her face before she said, "You'll probably just make it worse."

My hand fell to the seat as I laughed. "You're probably right."

I again looked to Vlad for help, noticing the small—yet fully amused—smile tugging at his mouth. Surprise, and a noticeable hint of something else, bloomed in my chest as Hadley's outstretched hand hovered in my peripheral vision. "I accept your terms."

I shook her hand, my smile growing as we pulled up to her school. My niece hopped out of the car—her usual cool composure already returned.

I looked to the rearview mirror, asking, "Did I just totally fuck that up?"

My driver's cheeks rounded in amusement as he pressed his lips into a tight line. "I wouldn't have done any better, Miss."

He finally met my eyes in the mirror and I laughed, slowly realizing what had started to chip at my heart. Hope.

TWENTY-ONE

SEPTEMBER

"What now?"

"Are you hungry?"

"No, Mom and I ate tacos on the way over." I scrunched my nose at the idea, knowing full well Ana would've pulled into the nearest Taco Bell before grabbing anything from an authentic restaurant.

I'd had Hadley in my possession for barely an hour and I was already certain that she hated me. She probably thought I was the biggest loser she'd ever met. I'd shown her to the guest room after Ana had dropped her off—barely stopping at the curb before Hadley jumped out with a duffel bag—and left her to settle in. But she didn't stay in the guest room. She'd trailed into the living room, a pair of headphones hanging around her neck, looking to me for entertainment. We'd been sitting in silence on my godforsaken couch ever since—the seconds easy to count when the giant clock that hung above the fireplace sounded each passing one with a loud *tick*.

"Okay," I started, huffing out a breath. *Think, Asha.* "I planned to take you shopping tomorrow but why don't we just go ahead and get a head start on that."

"Oh, okay," she said, her focus quickly melting toward her phone. *What kind of girl isn't excited about a shopping spree?*

"I haven't exactly been around in a while," *Duh. She knows that.* "So what do you...want? Or need I guess?"

The lock button on her phone clicked but her eyes stuck to the now-black screen. Her lips twisted as if she was debating her response, her eyes avoidant as she thought. I thought about being her age. How, on the rare occasion she could, Aisha would take me to the store with twenty dollars and no rules. The first few times, I'd only grabbed things we needed at the apartment but Aisha made me stop—had said there were better things to spend my childhood on. After that, I'd used the worn bill to get candy, enjoying a touch of sweetness I couldn't find at home.

"I've never really had someone just spend money on me, so I don't know."

"I'll give you a budget." I said, my mind already made up. "Whatever you want or need, it doesn't matter to me. You can even go into the stores by yourself if you want." An image of Ana—face scrunched in disapproval—popped into my head. "Wait, never mind, that sounds like something your mother would yell at me about."

Hadley laughed. I made my stubborn, precocious niece *laugh*—the sound bright as it bounced around my living room.

"But seriously, you can take your time and make a list, or we can just see what happens. I'll text Vlad to grab us in thirty?"

She nodded with a small smile. "Thanks, Asha."

I dipped my head in her direction before peeling myself from the couch and into my bedroom to get ready. "Shopping will work up an appetite so let's plan on grabbing something to eat on the way home." I remembered how I would've reacted to that statement when I was younger, taking a beat before adding, "And no, the food can't be taken out of a part of your budget!"

Hadley and I spent at least four hours in the Galleria, jumping from store to store. We fell into an easy rhythm and, once she got over how much I was willing to spend on her, she gave into it—eager to buy things for not only herself, but Ana as well. Her thoughtfulness warmed my heart and inspired me to pick out a gift or two myself. I grabbed a stone bookend, shaped like a whale, for Ana, a desk calendar featuring silly animal pictures for Scheff, and a pocket-sized leatherbound notebook for Grayson. I surprised myself with how eager I was to give each of them their gift—even as I ignored another message from Scheff, still afraid of the moment he finally cornered me.

Frank helped us lug Hadley's bags up the stairs—handfuls of clothes that would get her through the next school year without Ana having to worry about it. We stopped by Novel Neighbor, a local bookstore and I let Hadley run around—challenging her with a five minute limit to grab as many books as she could. We finished the night by grabbing a couple of burgers from Hi-Pointe, which we ate while lounging on the couch, watching some trashy TV show Ana would've hated.

Hadley had just turned in for the night when I was getting up to make a fresh cup of tea. As I waited for the water to boil, I double-checked the living room for any lingering trash, and turned out the lights, one by one, leaving the small light over the stove on. I couldn't ignore the voice that was screaming at me, urging me to reach under the sink, and behind the bleach. I was just crouching down to open the cupboard door when Hadley's voice echoed through the halls. "I haven't seen her in a while. But guys, check what we got today."

I pulled myself up and waited for the water to finish boiling, smiling to myself as I filled my cup of Earl Grey. I turned off the light and stalked towards Hadley's door, listening for the energetic spark of a teenage girl's gossip session.

"What's she like? We've all read about her but even the blogs don't know much outside of the pageant stuff," a young girl's voice asked through the speaker of my niece's phone.

'*Selfish, manipulative, bitch,*' the voice listed for me. My stomach knotted as I waited for Hadley to tell her friends what she really thought about me. *What reason does she have to lie?*

"She's..." she started, drawing the single syllable out as if she really had to fight for the right words. I held my breath, waiting for the inevitable gut-punch I was subjecting myself to. "Cool. Like, really cool. I think I want to be like her when I grow up."

"What, rich?" another kid laughed.

"No. She's powerful, and weird but still...kind." Hadley paused before adding, "When she wants to be."

I let out my bated breath, *way* louder than I anticipated, and quickly ducked around the corner, scared she'd catch me eavesdropping. As my stomach twisted under pressure and guilt, I tiptoed down the hallway, and into my own room—eager to stay up, sipping on tea, and listening to my beautiful niece giggle late into the night.

❧

I woke to the sound of my phone buzzing against the nightstand. I flung a hand toward it, pawing around until my fingers graced the edges and brought it to my chest right as the vibrations ceased. I hadn't opened my eyes yet and was about to slip back into sleep when my phone started ringing again, staccato rumbles on my chest. I groaned, cracking my eyes to see a picture of Scheff flashing on my screen. I silenced the call, rolling to my side before unlocking the screen, scrolling through emails before moving to messages—my chest tightening at a new arrival from Grayson, guilt dowsing any anticipation when a new one popped into my thread with my best friend.

I ignored Scheff once more, tapping on the picture of Grayson, Ana, and I from our demolition day. Smiling at the memory, I read his request to take Hadley and I to the hot air balloon festival in Forest Park today. I *may* have mentioned that I'd have Hadley in my care for a few days and he *may* have been interested in meeting the elusive daughter of Ana. I slipped into the guest bedroom, surprised to find Hadley already awake and scrolling on her phone.

"Do you want to go to the hot air balloon thing today?" I asked, pulling my niece's attention from the device in her hand.

"Why not? Do you have anything better planned?"

"Sitting around here and doing nothing?" I offered with a small shoulder shrug. Hadley just giggled and rolled to face the windows.

"What time?"

"Uh, let me ask Grayson."

My niece whipped back around, curiosity alight in her brown eyes. "Who's Grayson?"

"He's working on Aisha's house," I said, tucking a lying lip between my teeth. "He invited us."

"Hmm." She eyed me from her relaxed spot on the bed. "Can we go get coffee first?"

"Your mom lets *you* drink coffee?" I asked, doubtful.

"Since I was six. I can be pretty persuasive. I can't have more than a shot though, that was our deal." It was my turn to stare my niece down, certain she *wasn't* lying to me at all, but was simply a weird ass eleven-year-old instead. I clicked my tongue against my teeth, turning to go back to my room —already texting Grayson back to accept. I offered to have Vlad drive us all but he refused, suggesting he pick us up instead.

My thumbs hovered over the keyboard as I debated the consequences of giving him my address—of letting him into my life even a tiny bit more.

'He won't like you once he truly knows you.'

I typed out the address and sent it before I could second guess the plans altogether—unwilling to brave the festival chaos with Hadley on my own. He said he'd be here around noon, and I yelled the information to my niece in the other room—telling her that, if she wanted coffee she should probably get ready around two.

At three o'clock on the dot, Grayson texted me, letting me know he was outside. I adjusted my crop-top and shorts, making sure everything sat just right on my body before walking down the hall–quick hurried steps to match the knocks on Hadley's door. "Let's go, bug," I said, faltering a second as the nickname I'd forgotten slipped out with ease.

I was still frozen outside of her door when she swung it open, her assessing gaze roaming over me before she deemed the moment uninteresting enough to step past me. I blew out a breath before following her, throwing my purse over my shoulder and reaching for my keys. For the first time in months, I was actually excited to leave my apartment and, as I twisted the key in the lock and turned toward the elevator, I wondered what that could mean.

Once we made it to the curb, Grayson hopped out of his truck and ran around, opening Hadley's door as well as my own—offering me a hand as I climbed in. Once we'd all buckled and he'd pulled into traffic, he said, "So, I heard that coffee was requested. I would love to take you ladies to *my* favorite spot in the city. It's a little drive-thru and it'll take us past the park but I promise it's worth it." He looked to Hadley for approval before me and I appreciated the small effort he put in to make her feel comfortable. She looked at me before nodding, and I wished I could see what was turning through that mind of hers.

"Sounds good," I offered, unsure of how to break the tension that I was likely alone in feeling. Ten minutes later, we were waiting in line at a place called Exit 11, Hadley and I eyeing the menu while Grayson fiddled with the music. The baristas inside the small building—a shed more than anything—moved through the car queue quickly, as if there was a magic well of espresso at the ready for the people pulling in. Grayson pumped his eyebrows at me twice before shifting the car into gear, moving us ahead.

A short woman pushed open the drive-thru windows, her smile so big it wrinkled at the corners of her eyes. "Grayson! It's good to see you. How're you doing?"

"I'm doing good, Candy. How's your morning been so

far?" He sounded comfortable, like seeing her was ingrained in his daily routine.

"It's been *busy*. You just missed the rush. But—oh! You brought some friends today," Candy said, looking around Grayson to wave at me. I smiled, unable to offer the stranger anything more as I watched her interact with Grayson. I wasn't jealous, just purely fascinated with this facet of his life, fascinated with *him*.

"This is Asha and her niece, Hadley, in the back. Coffee was requested before we head over to the festival so I figured I'd introduce them to the best coffee in the city." He smiled at her just as two more women popped their heads into the window. Ever the gentleman, he waved at them both. "Hey Shan, Sara. Where's Mads?"

"She'll be back in soon. You just missed her," Candy said, reaching for a stack of cups by the window. Her salt-and-pepper curls bounced with the movement—just as joyful as her. "It's nice to meet you ladies. Are you getting your usual today?"

"Yes please, and," he looked at me, motioning for me to order but it was Hadley who piped up first.

"An extra-hot, sixteen ounce vanilla latte with one shot, three pumps of flavoring and whip cream on top please. Coconut milk if you have it, almond is fine if you don't."

Shock had me gaping at my niece, any lingering reservations about her possibly lying to me wiped away with her complicated coffee order. I shook my head before turning back to Candy who, to her credit, had already written Hadley's order on the cup and passed it off to one of the others. She looked at me, nothing but kindness in her eyes. "And for you?"

"Just an americano please, thank you." I dipped my head in thanks, reaching for my purse when Grayson's hand covered mine. He was already offering a card to Candy, a content smile on his face. "Thank you."

He nodded and, by the time he slid his card back into his wallet, one of the other girls was passing the drinks out the window—Candy already helping another customer on the other side of the small building. "Here's that americano, the extra-special vanilla latte, and," she paused, looking at the hurried writing on the side of the cup. "Your lavender latte. Have a good day!"

I took a sip of my drink, raising one eyebrow toward Grayson in silent question.

"What? It's good," he said, the tips of his ears burning. I just laughed as he pulled away from the building.

His hand was still resting over mine as we drove, music killing the time as we headed toward The Great Forest Park Balloon Race.

Hadley had finished half of her drink by the time we parked—Forest Park was so full of revelers that we had left it entirely, opting for an open space on a side street a mile away from the festival. I fought against my dismay, pasting on a smile as we started the mile walk back in. There were already some balloons in the air—Hadley's attempt at hiding her awe failed as she all but pressed her face against the car window. At least there were still some childish qualities she hung on to.

"Have you guys done this before?" Grayson asked, a few steps ahead of my niece and me.

"Mom took me once when I was little," Hadley said, unaware of the irony—that she was *still* little.

"It's been years for me," I said, following the path of a PNC Bank balloon as it flew over the city. Aisha had brought us once. Ana and I had spent a good portion of the day arguing over who got to push Junior in his stroller.

"Well, it's one of my favorites. We missed the start of the

race but I'm sure there are still plenty waiting to go up." He lifted his straw to his mouth and I looked away quickly, trying to forget what it felt like to have his lips on mine.

Aside from Hadley's occasional question—Grayson jumping in with answers before I could even process them—we spent most of the twenty minute walk in silence, the three of us following the sounds of revelry to the festival itself. There were balloons and baskets littered throughout the park and one was starting to fill with heat. Two people shot columns of flames into the massive balloon, the fabric swelling as the heat filled its interior. The basket beneath it creaked under the tension, straining against the rope that held it to the ground. With each blast of fire, the balloon inched higher, straining to free itself. The crowd cheered as if the couple's preparation was just as magical as the flight itself.

Grayson turned to my niece and reached a hand toward her, excitement alight in his eyes. She hesitated, looking at me once more before accepting—the two of them running to the front of the crowd with cheers to match the rest of the park. I lost them in a matter of seconds but wasn't interested in pressing through people to find them, opting for a nearby bench instead.

Another handful of minutes passed and the balloon was weightless, aiming for the clouds—the park exploding as it moved farther and farther away. Part of me wished I was up there too, free from the weight of the world and the problems that tethered me to the ground.

The crowd slowly dispersed, moving to the next lift off point and watching as the next pair got ready to take off, fire already coaxed, ready to take them to the sky. I waited on the bench looking for Hadley's bundle of curls to pop out but my eyes landed on Grayson first. His arm was wrapped around my niece's shoulders, the two of them sporting matching grins as they made their way toward me. Once Hadley spotted me, she ducked away from him, running over with a hand stretched toward me. "Asha, come on! They're going to do another one soon."

I stared at her, the moment feeling heavier than it likely was as she wiggled her expectant fingers at me, as if she couldn't imagine *not* sharing this moment with me. I looked at Grayson who was watching us from a few steps behind and, as I tucked Hadley's small hand in mine, I wondered if this was what life was supposed to feel like— love and awe and hope coming together to create an experience. It wasn't until we'd crossed a bridge, leading us deeper into the park that I turned back to realize where I'd been sitting.

I looked across the water to find *the* bench. The one I'd sat on with Aisha, and floated by with Scheff. Any comfort the day had offered collapsed beneath the weight of it, regret hollowing me out. I drifted alongside Hadley and Grayson— silently slipping away as we made our way back to the car.

Hadley walked into the living room, her footie pajamas now zipped against her tall frame, and I held back a laugh as she zipped it to her collarbone. Her hair was wrapped into a bun on top of her head, a respective crown for the queen she was growing into. I patted the couch cushion behind me, a small, but content, smile on my face. I waited, bouncing my knee as she slowly padded over to me—her face scrunched together in a display of feigned grumpiness. I started to laugh as she sank into the cushions of the sofa, leaning into me as I wrapped an arm around her. *Three months ago, I wouldn't have been able to do this.*

"It's your call tonight, Hads. What're you in the mood for?" I asked as the television blinked awake.

She crossed her arms and let out a huff, a sure sign that she was still upset about leaving the festival early—she'd get over it eventually.

"Okay...do you still like Barbie?" I hoped I could provoke her into having a little more fun tonight, even if it was just participating in a bit of banter with her aunt.

She scoffed and turned to look at me, her grumpy face dissolving into one of purely sly intent. "Hmm..." she started, her eyes peeking out from under her eyelashes—a pathetic attempt at begging, I'd assume. "You pick."

"Hmm," I said, mimicking her tone. "One you've seen before or a new one?"

Hadley leaned against the arm of the couch, tucking her feet underneath her as she scratched her chin, silently debating with herself. "Can we do the one with the boy and the music in the city? Mom said you guys used to watch it all the time."

She was referring to a movie my sister and I had watched incessantly one summer. She'd saved up some babysitting money and, on a random trip to Walmart with Aisha, picked it out of the bins of discount movies. The story followed a boy—a musical genius with a gift as boundless as his naivety —who believed that if he followed the music, it would lead him to the parents he had never met. His journey, shaped by six months under the wing of a broken man called the Wizard, became one of connection, resilience, and the quiet thread of hope. Ultimately, he writes a symphony that connects the threads of his life, reuniting him with his estranged parents.

After the end credits rolled through, Ana and I would turn to each other, our knees knocking against each other as we talked about what our birth fathers would be like. Ana always said that her dad was smart, and kind. He could fix anything around the house and, even though he was a boy, he would've played tea parties and dolls with her. I claimed that *my* dad was tall and strong, a force to be reckoned with. Someone who would hold me when the monsters that hid in the night came out to play, and fight them when they came after me. My lips tugged at the thought of the countless nights when we'd fall asleep, our limbs as intertwined as our dreams.

Looks like it's an August *Rush* type of night.

"Thank you, by the way," she started, her eyes still glued to the TV. "For letting me stay. It's been cool."

"Anytime, Bug," I said, the nickname rolling off of my tongue easily—like I had finally earned the right to use it. I pulled myself from the couch, dimming the lights on my way to the kitchen. I ducked into the pantry and pulled out a bag of popcorn, hesitating before grabbing a second. *Just to be safe.*

The music from the opening credits sounded through the apartment. A smile played on my lips as I allowed myself to remember younger days with my knees rubbing against Ana's —trying not to focus on the similar, fragile comfort I had found in these last two days with my niece. I placed the popcorn bag in the microwave and rested against the counter. Comfort wrapped around my body as I heard a giggle come from the living room.

I let her laughter lead me back to the couch, my feet sounding my entrance. Hadley, without pulling her eyes from the screen, reached an expectant hand out, ready for her popcorn. I scoffed, shaking my head before giving it to her— fake-stomping back to the kitchen to make my own bag.

Three minutes passed and by the time I made it back to

the couch, her long frame was tucked into the sofa. My shoulder dug into the door frame as I leaned against it, watching her between bites of popcorn. Her face lit up as the characters bantered on the screen and grew dim when subtle digs were thrown.

I stepped into the room and settled onto the floor beside Hadley, passing her a cherry soda before we got comfortable for the rest of the movie.

As August's parents worked their way through the crowd at the end of the movie, my face was tear-streaked and my sniffles mixed in with the final orchestral procession. I looked down to where Hadley's head rested in my lap, a small smile sitting on her youthful face—sleep having pulled her in long before the movie ended.

I snapped a picture of the two of us, sending it to Ana with a thumbs up before tossing my phone onto the couch and gently shaking Hadley's sleeping form. When she didn't so much as stir, I awkwardly slid out from underneath her, turning to tuck her in with the blanket I kept nearby. I tossed the soda cans into the popcorn bowl, tucking it against my hip as I bent low, reaching to move a fallen strand of hair from my niece's dozing face. Her nose twitched as the strand dragged across it, and I couldn't help but smile at the coziness of a memory in the making.

Hadley wandered into my room before the sun had fully risen, informing me that she was hungry. I couldn't recall my response but she crawled into bed with me and let me sleep a little longer before really insisting that it was *time* to wake up. How the hell does Ana do this every day? Am I even surprised that Ana's fucking child would wake up this early? When did tweens stop sleeping in?

I rubbed my temples as I listened to the popping of grease in the frying pan. Hadley had requested pancakes, which somehow inspired an 'if you give a mouse a cookie' sized breakfast extravaganza. I tried to mimic the comfortability and ease Gretta and Scheff had found in the kitchen—failing as I sipped my coffee and waited for the final pancake to finish cooking. The add-on eggs and bacon, however, were off to a slow start...

"Can't we just eat it how it is now?" the impatient eleven-year-old asked as she picked at the lonely pancake and egg on her plate.

"What sense would it make to eat bacon that's not cooked?" I said with a look of incredulity pasted onto my face. I brought my coffee to my lips, gently blowing on it in an attempt to prevent my lips from getting burnt.

"I'm just saying, bacon doesn't have to be burnt to the depths of hell for us to enjoy it," she said—so matter of factly it sent the hot coffee spewing from my mouth. Rivers of nasal caffeine alongside an insane giggle fit that commanded my body kept me from reprimanding my niece for her language. I tried to compose myself, wiping a paper towel under my nose before peeking at my niece who was failing to hide her amusement. Seeing her—bottom lip tucked away as tears filled her eyes, her shoulders subtly shaking under what I assumed was the pressure of keeping her laugh in—sent me into another fit of giggles. This time, my laughter infected hers, sending us both into a raucous fit.

As if the universe decided to show its comedic hand, the fire alarm soon sounded, reminding me that there was indeed bacon burning to the depths of hell on my stove. A small shriek passed my lips as I jumped for the pan and, not knowing what else to do, rushed it out to the balcony before it could catch on fire or something. Once I was confident that it was securely balanced on the small table outside, I turned back around to find my niece at the intercom, listening intently to what sounded like Frank. She must've heard him buzz while I was preoccupied with the bacon.

"Miss Hadley! How's your mum been?" Frank asked, his voice sneaking through the receiver.

"She's doing great, Mr. Sandusky. Thank you for asking! You missed her when she dropped me off. Did Asha have a delivery or something?" she replied, my niece sounding every bit the mature human she was growing into.

"Yes! With a note! Say, I'll bring this one up myself. I don't know if she'd be able to carry it..." he started. Hadley looked at me, with a spark of amusement lingering in her eyes. "I don't mean to be, what do they call it these days? Anti-feminist? But I would just hate it if one of you got hurt trying to lug this up."

Hadley giggled and gave Frank consent to bring the evidently vast package upstairs and I took a few seconds to check my phone. *I wasn't expecting any deliveries.*

A knock at the door shook me from the minor worry and I heard Hadley greeting Frank. I turned the corner to find them locked in an embrace in the doorway, a massive vase of various flowers hanging off Frank's hip, precariously balanced by his hands.

"Oh! Let me grab those, Frank! You know I could've picked these up," I said, reaching for the elaborate arrangement.

Blue hydrangeas were littered throughout the bouquet, while sprigs of lavender were littered through the random rays of burnt-orange lilies and tiny, bundled blooms of baby's breath. I set it down on the island, leaning in to smell it before searching for the note—Hadley and Frank's conversation melting away from my ears as my fingers brush against the thick edge of an envelope. Tucked delicately between the leaves of a lily, my name was scrawled on a piece of white parchment paper. I hesitated as I reached for the card.

'*What's the worst that could happen?*' the voice crowed from its place in the void.

I took a deep breath, allowing my fingers to pluck the card from its resting place before opening it—carefully pulling apart the glued down flap, listening as the gritty sound of the paper scratched against the envelope.

To:

the girl who notices the sunsets, the bees, the flowers, and trees.

to witness your love of everyday beauty is to be reminded to slow down just enough to notice it.

dinner soon?

—Grayson

My throat felt like it was going to close as my heart tripled in size, tears pricking at my eyes—burning as I refused to let them fall. The sound of Hadley's laugh pulled my attention back to Frank at my door and, while my overly observant niece was focused on her conversation, I dropped the note into the trash. As if she could sense my shift in mood, Hadley ushered Frank out the door—the movement so quick I nearly missed his hurried wave as she closed it on him.

"See you next time!" I yelled as I turned to Hadley, my eyebrows furrowing as I raised my hands in confusion. I sat on a stool at the island, my elbows resting carelessly on the marble slab while I let my head drop into my hands, knowing full well that if Hads was anything like her mother, a lecture was well on its way.

I heard the lid of the trash can open and peaked through my fingers to see Hadley reaching for the note I'd thrown inside. I let out a groan, crumbling even further into my arms.

"Ooo, flowers from Grayson" she teased, in a way that pushed all the wrong buttons.

"He's just being kind, Hads."

"Yeah, because, 'Dinner soon?' is totally just 'being kind.'" The unamused glare she pinned me with was reminiscent of her mother's. "Why is it so hard for you to let us in, Asha?" I stared at her, that now-familiar glare set and assessing me. Her dark brown hair rested lightly on her sun-soaked skin, her frame matching mine in height but carrying grace I still lacked now, in my mid-twenties. She stared me down, her brown eyes likely tucking every detail deep inside.

"What do you mean?" I asked, feigning ignorance.

"Everybody acts like I was so young when you stopped talking to all of us," she said, her passionate stare unwavering. "I had to grow up without you around, but I still had to hear them talk about you as if you were there. I'm not a dumb kid, Asha."

I hesitated to answer, knowing that I could very well fuck up this newfound ease with Hadley that I was so grateful for.

"Hads," I began, pausing to swallow a lump that had found its way into my throat. "There is so much you don't know. Things from my childhood, and things about my relationship with your mom and Matta and...*so* much more. I won't apologize for getting the distance I needed at the time." I turned away hoping that this could be enough for her for now.

"That doesn't mean you can't let other people in. What have I done? What has Grayson done? What did we do to deserve the side of you that refuses to be loved?" she asked, her voice rising slightly.

"Hadley, you don't get it. I–"

"No, Asha. *You* don't get it. You live half a life. I really hope you enjoy being alone. I'm going home," she said, turning to her tote bag that was hanging off of a stool. Her hands ripped through the bag—likely an attempt at finding her house keys that sat conveniently next to me on the counter.

We noticed them at the same time, my determination meeting hers in a wordless race to get there first. I shot my arm out just before she could wrap her fingers around the metal loop, dangling them in her face with a triumphant smirk. She simply rolled her eyes, secured her bag on her shoulder and stomped toward the door.

My chest felt hollow as my mind raced—worried about Hadley leaving and the fight with Ana that would no doubt follow. Counting the unknown dangers that might threaten her when she was supposed to be with me. Organizing a list of reasons why it would be absolutely stupid of me to let her run free through the city streets.

I opened my mouth only to close it again—any worries I wanted to voice were wiped out by the fear that this fragile connection I'd built with Hadley would shatter completely if I forced her to stay.

"Hads, stop. Eat something, please." It was a last ditch effort to get her to sit down, to stay. Maybe some food would help her cool off and allow us to continue on with the day.

She threw her arms across her chest and sent a searing glare my way before reaching for a pancake, shoving the whole thing into her mouth.

"Happy?" she asks, her mouth full of this morning's wasted efforts. She held out an expectant hand.

'*Why even try? You'll just push her to hate you more.*'

"You've made my fucking day," I said, my own unamused smile matching hers. I dropped the keys in her hand, followed by a middle finger flipped in her direction. AnaMarie's child *would* have the nerve to insert her opinion on my life. *One and the fucking same.*

But then I rushed to beat the angry teenager to the door, holding a hand up in an attempt to stop her.

"Don't do anything that I wouldn't do," I said, trying to level an authoritative stare her way. She just scoffed before slinking past me, pancake crumbs still hanging from her mouth as she slammed the door behind her—leaving me to stand in the foyer and stare at the door, the cold bite of loneliness dragging me back into its clutches.

I wasted the rest of the day on the couch with trashy reruns playing on the TV as I waited anxiously by my phone hoping to hear *anything* from Hadley. I'd spent at least an hour berating myself for not demanding that she stay put—or that she at least share her location with me. The crippling feeling of remorse sank deeper into my bones with each *tick* from the clock.

I was just warming up leftovers from the night before when my phone rang, sending me jumping out of my skin. I checked the caller ID, trying to breathe through my building fear of a mother's wrath. A picture of Ana and I covered my phone screen—the photo taken after one of my pageants, smiling and happy, contrasted nicely against the dread pooling in my stomach.

I answered the call, all but gulping before lifting the phone to my ear. "Hey…"

"Hey, Asha? Hey? That's how you want to start a call when I'm three hours away and I get a text from my child, my only child, letting me know that she *rode the Metrolink home?*" Her voice was shrill, stressed, and angry as her words ran together. "Alone! Don't let me forget that she was *alone!* Tell me, Asha. What did you do? How did you fuck it up?"

"I didn't do anything! Hadley just blew up!"

"No. I know my kid and she doesn't just 'blow up.' What happened?" *Persistent bitch.*

"Fuck, Ana," I huffed, dragging myself to the kitching to put the teapot back on the still-cooling stove—eager for even a single, extra ounce of energy to get me through this conversation. "We hung out with Grayson at the hot air balloon thing yesterday and he sent me flowers this morning. She got mad when she saw me throw away his note. Then she stormed out." I rinsed out my mug, double-checking there was no lingering residue before setting it beside the stove and leaning into my hands.

Ana was quiet for so long that I thought she had hung up, the static silence crackled with energy as I waited for her to say something.

"I don't fucking blame her."

"Those are the words you choose, Ana? Not, 'I'm sorry for being angry with you?'"

"Oh, I'm still fucking pissed but at least I get it now. Hadley loves, deeply. It probably hurts her to see you constantly discarding the people you love like we're nothing. So, like I said. I don't fucking blame her."

I tried to decide in the moment if I'd accept her words for the truth they were or discard them too. "Whatever."

I hung up, dipping beneath the sink, fumbling for my hidden bourbon. I sank against the cabinets, pulling the corked lid before resting the cool glass bottle against my lips. I took long, powerful swigs that clawed at my throat and burnt my eyes. The kettle began to steam, its annoying, high-pitched scream filling my self-imposed void once again.

Twenty-Two

October

My heels clicked against the marble floor of the office lobby, echoing through the pristine halls. Most of the staff had departed an hour ago, but I'd been forced to stay in a marketing meeting—finally able to crawl away around five. Scheff was out of town for the week and no one could agree on a plan for this quarter. I'd been forced to play mediator for the first time since I'd been back in the office. I'd been relying less and less on alcohol to get me through the day but, after that meeting, a glass of wine was earned. When I wasn't pouring over placements, marketing plans, IT problems, or whatever else needed my attention, I was trying to solve my family issues.

It had been over a week. Twelve days of my sister, *and* Hadley ignoring me—my calls going straight to voicemail on both of their phones. I stood on the curb, weighing my options while digging around my purse for my sunglasses. I could leave another voicemail, but I knew there was only so much more I could say before my begging for forgiveness was fraught with annoyance and bitter rage. I could change my number, and bypass the block but that seemed like too much work, especially when I could just ask Vlad to take me by my sister's tonight before heading home.

A few minutes passed and the black town car pulled up, Vlad—with his favorite flat cap—bouncing out of the car to open my door. "Thanks, Vee," I said, using the alternate nickname he'd offered when he first started. He hesitated by the door, his eyebrows lifted in surprise. He gave me a small, bashful smile before closing me into the car, rushing back around to his own seat.

"Where to, Miss?" He asked, his cheeks still rounded.

"Ana's."

❧

I'd been standing outside of her apartment for five minutes, relentlessly buzzing the intercom. Her car was parked on the street so I knew that she was home, just choosing to ignore me. I dug my finger into the button again, holding it down. I wouldn't have let go if it wasn't for my sister's exasperated voice coming through the small speaker.

"What the fuck do you want?"

"Come on, Ana. Let me up so we can talk."

"No."

"Ana it's hot out here."

"Good."

I laughed, a curl falling loose with the movement. "If you would've answered my calls, I wouldn't be here right now. This is your fault."

"You wanna talk about faults, Ash?"

"No, wrong word. Sorry." I felt awkward, kicking a pebble on her doorstep while I continued to beg for her to listen to me. "I just want to apologize, Ana. I know I fucked up. I know."

The only response was the sound of the door unlocking and I stepped through before she could change her mind. I climbed through the cramped, dingy stairwell—four flights that twisted around until I was brought to Ana's apartment on the top floor. The door was cracked open, waiting for me to step in and start groveling all over again.

"Where are you?"

"Kitchen." Her voice was flat—the tone leaving little room for any of my antics tonight. *Tread lightly, got it.*

I'd never been inside before, relying on her voice to lead me through the living room. I found a hallway—two bedrooms to the right, a bathroom in front of me—and turned left, hoping the room at the end would host my sister. I found her sitting at a small table, an open notebook and a pile of bills surrounding her. Her hair was frizzy, tufts sticking out around her face as if she'd been pulling them out of her bun in frustration. She didn't look up when I walked in.

I sat across from her, folding my hands in front of me as I tried to catch her attention—going so far to wave a hand in front of her face. "Look, Ana. I'm sorry."

Her pen dug into her notebook. "Obviously. I kinda picked that up from the voicemails."

"Then why are you still acting like this?"

"Acting like you left my eleven-year old to ride the metro home by herself?"

"Hey, I wanted to get her a car but she wouldn't stick around." Her glare could've reduced me to a smoldering pile of ash if she wanted it to. I stood up, turning to look out the small window that sat above her sink. "I didn't mean for her to run away from me, Ana. It's not like I said, 'Hey, kid. Go ride the metro for an hour and then walk twenty minutes to your apartment, all alone, just for fun!' For fuck's sake Ana, she got mad and ran out." We could argue in circles for hours —the air in Ana's apartment as suffocating as the argument itself with the faint smell of this morning's burnt coffee still lingering as I paced around the tiny space.

"And why didn't you follow her?"

"Because that's exactly what you would've done! You smother people when they need space because you're so sure you can fix everything when you can't!"

"You know what happens on these streets to girls like her, Asha. You should've tried harder!" She pushed away from the table with a grunt and turned from the room, leaving me alone in the kitchen.

"I should've tried harder? I should've forced her into the room and made her stay when she was about to explode? Why the hell would I want to do that to her?" I followed Ana through the living room, our steps echoing through her sad, two-bedroom apartment. The walls were a faded cream color —which *almost* matched the carpet that was littered with cigarette burns that certainly didn't come from my sister.

"Because that's what you do when you're a parent!" she screamed, the paper in her hands crumpling as she turned to look at me. The curls framing her face bounced with the hurried patterns of her breath. "Those are the choices you have to make when you have a kid. I would rather her be mad and hate me than to get *any* sort of call that my child was hurt because I was worried about how she'd react to me grounding her."

For the first time in years, I looked at my sister and saw cracks—fissures in the narrative I'd crafted around her expanding with every harsh word we threw at each other. "I said I'm sorry, Ana." The words came out as raw and broken as I felt, desperate to understand and to *fix* this somehow.

"And I said I'm not ready to forgive you. You can accept that or not. Either way, please leave."

I didn't miss the irony of the moment. I stayed rooted to my spot by the worn, flea market table that was barely balancing on the laminate tiles beneath me, if only to needle my sister a little bit longer. She stood up quickly, growling in frustration as she walked away.

"I don't understand why you won't talk to me, Ana! You've *never* talked to me. It's like you woke up one day and decided that I wasn't good enough to be your sister," I said, adding, "Imagine how the fuck that felt!" I tried to breathe through the anger crawling up my spine, through the frustration of trying to understand my sister for once. It felt like the walls of the apartment were slowly caving in.

"What the fuck do you even know, Asha!?" she screamed at me. She crumpled into the couch—like this conversation and her final shout had drained every ounce of energy from her body.

"Apparently nothing, right Ana?" I snapped, already heading for the front door. "Find someone else to watch her next time. You never trusted me in the first place, remember?"

"Asha, wait."

I turned to her, slowly. While I loved to press a button or two, I knew when the weight of a moment called for my silence.

"Matta was gone one night and you were already in bed. I had just turned the TV off when *he* came out of her room." Her throat bobbed, the intensity of the moment seeming to hit its climax. The air in the room went tense, like even the ghosts of her apartment building were waiting for her story, breathless with anticipation.

"He told me that she needed me to fix the dresser drawer, and I didn't think anything of it. She'd asked me to fix it a hundred times before and I thought I could do it fast and then sneak into bed with you. As soon as I got down to fix it, he kicked me. Right in the ribs." She paused, blowing out an unsteady breath before she could continue. "He told me if I screamed or even woke you up, he'd kill us and fix all of Momma's problems right then and there. I didn't want you to wake up so I just...froze. He picked me up and threw me on the bed and I knew what he was going to do. I *knew* it and yet, I just kept thinking that at least it wasn't you. I was so fucking glad it wasn't you, Ash."

She wrapped her arms around herself, letting out a shaky breath. Tears streamed down her cheeks and she rushed to wipe them away. I moved to the couch, sitting close enough that our shoulders kissed, our fingers weaving together like it was second nature.

"At first, I thought he just broke a rib or something," she started again, leaning into me. "But the pain didn't go away and I knew I couldn't talk to Matta about it so I just adjusted to the pain and thought it was my new normal. And then I started getting sick every morning. I would try so hard to get out of the bed without waking you but there was one time you wouldn't let me go. You started bawling and told me you were scared to be alone, and I thought he got to you too. I swore I was going to kill him if he laid his hands on you. I waited till you went back to sleep and I snuck to the kitchen and pulled out the biggest fucking knife I could find." Her hands tightened around mine, skin going white while she faced the truth of her past.

"I walked into her room, crawled up the foot of the bed, and I waited. I waited for either of them to notice I was there, standing above them, ready to get whoever woke up first. I was so tired of her shit and just knew that you and I would figure it out, but they never woke up. I stood over them for

like an hour before I realized that the chaos they created
didn't bother them—didn't hurt them like it did us. So I
brought that knife to our bed, hid it in the side of the
bedframe and curled right back into you. When I saw Matta
later that day, I told her that he needed to go or that I would.
That I would take you with me and she would never see us
again."

I couldn't say anything, the heart aching beat of her story
drawing me in like she was telling me about a fictional hero-
ine, dedicated to protecting her sister and dismantling the
systems of greed that threatened them.

"The worst fucking part is that I knew it was my fault,"
she started.

"Ana, no—"

She held up a free hand to stop me. "It was. I should've
been smarter and I wasn't. I should've waited for her to come
home before I went in to fix the dresser. I didn't want to take
the chance at pissing her off though. Hell, if it came down to
it and I had to do it all over, I would still fix the damn dresser.
If it meant you didn't get hurt the same way, I would do it a
thousand times again."

She sniffed, the sound lingering as she took a deep breath
—one in, one out—just like she'd taught me.

"I hid my stomach for as long as I could. I didn't want to
tell Matta because we both know what she would've done."
Matta always had a knack for hiding the things she was
ashamed of. Probably would've forced Ana into the abortion
clinic herself. "When she did find out I was pregnant, it's
because of stupid Mr. Haskins."

"The gym teacher?" I asked, my eyebrows rising into arcs.
It wasn't all that surprising—Mr. Haskins was sweet but was
prone to sticking his nose where it didn't belong.

She nodded her head. "Yep, called her into the office and made a whole fucking deal about how I was 'a fast little girl and there's something I'd been hiding' from her. You were at pageant practice by the time we got home and that's when I realized that Armatta was the devil. You know what she did instead of asking me what happened? She slapped me. And when that didn't phase me, she punched me right in the stomach. She beat me that night, Asha. Hard. And you know what she said while she did it? She said that *we* were the reason no man ever wanted to be around her. Getting pregnant was my fault because I 'had to go around getting attention from somewhere.'" She pulled her hand from mine to quote the phrase, her tone mocking our mother's—before letting them fall, defeated into her lap. "She never asked me who did it, or if I wanted it. She tried to take Hadley from me before I even got to have her. She tried to beat the best thing about my life right out of me."

Ana wiped at her nose, trying to suck in a snotty breath before she snaked her arms around her waist—rocking herself back and forth in the corner of the couch. Her story filled the room, and I couldn't stop the sob that racked through my body.

"Oh, Ana..." I said before pulling her into a tight hug. I cried for my sister and the burden she'd carried for too long. I cried for Hadley, who would never know that her father was the biggest piece of shit in the world. I cried for our childhood and all the pain that Armatta caused, pain she refused to account for.

"Why? Why wouldn't you tell me, Ana? I'm so sorry." I sobbed. The sounds of our grief began to quiet and our hands found each other once more.

"You were nine, Asha. *Nine.* What could you have said or done? You barely understood where babies came from. As far as I'm concerned, she is mine and only mine. *I* created her, bore her, and raised her. *She is mine.*"

I shifted so that I could look her in the eyes, gingerly placing a hand on each cheek and pulling her face toward mine—wet eyes to wet eyes. "You, Ana, are the strongest person I know. I want to be like you when I grow up." I leaned my head towards hers until we were sitting in a closed embrace, our foreheads kissing. We sat and cried until the pain hurt less, until the world seemed like it might make a little sense again and even then, I refused to let go.

Twenty-Three

A pounding at my apartment door woke me up the next morning—never a great sign when you piss off as many people as I tend to. I groaned, rubbing my hands over my eyes as I tried to wipe sleep's heavy grip away.

Ana and I had stayed up for hours, drinking a cheap bottle of cabernet on her couch and catching each other up on the past six years. I told her about the day I found Aisha—how that moment was a weight I'd shouldered for months, unable to escape the guilt. She sat silently, listening as I described it, wrapping me in a hug when I needed it. It was the first time in months that I wasn't using alcohol to hide but to relax, and, even as the bargain bottle of wine refused to settle in my stomach, I felt lighter than I had in a long time.

She'd drunkenly waved me off as Vlad helped me into the car last night. I smiled, trying not to focus on the ease of it all —chatting with my sister, our child-like giggles weaving together the farther we fell into the bottle. I'm sure the fragile dynamic would shift as soon as I said something to piss her off.

Another series of deep, staccato knocks sounded through

my apartment—pulling me from the warmth of my bed, and the memories we'd laughed over, and towards whoever was intent on sabotaging my peace this morning. "I'm coming!"

I pulled my robe around my body, tying it at the waist before sliding into my slippers and padding down the hall. The fist hit my door again, solidifying my irritation at whoever was so hell-bent on annoying me this morning—and before I'd had coffee too. My eyebrows furrowed as I squinted through the peephole, surprised to find Grayson standing on the other side of the door.

I hadn't texted him after he'd sent those flowers—flowers that incited the emotional hellfire I'd spent last night days smoothing over. I slid the lock free, pulling the door open to let him in—the surprise on his face suggesting that he didn't expect me to actually answer, despite his insistence. I opened the door another inch, tightening my hand on the handle as I debated having this conversation in the hallway.

"Good morning," I started, turning my back to him before heading for the coffee pot, eager for the smell of freshly ground beans and brewing energy to help me through the day.

"Did you get my flowers?" He asked, his question punctuated by the door closing behind him.

I focused on the task at hand, listening to the coffee beans falling into the grinder before letting the awful, grating sound fill the space between us—muting Grayson's footsteps as he followed me into the kitchen.

The room went silent as the water in the machine started to warm before slowly trickling into the pot. I swept my hands down my chest, wishing I could soothe some of the wrinkles that had pressed in my nightgown while I slept. A breath on my neck startled me and I jumped as Grayson's arms wrapped around me, securing me against the counter.

"Hi," I whispered, adrenaline shooting through my limbs from the scare and his proximity all at once.

"Hi, Asha," he said, so close the words were warm on my skin. "What are you running from?"

"I don't run." The words came too quick, too defensive, too obvious a lie. I managed to turn around in the little space he left me, trying to steel my face as I met his.

"Then why didn't you text me after I sent those flowers?"

"I couldn't. Hadley ran away that morning. I was a bit... preoccupied." Much like I was now, my focus stuck to Grayson's lips, entranced with how they moved to form words.

Concern clouded his eyes as he stepped back, breaking whatever spell he had wrapping around me. "Is she okay? What happened?" *What didn't happen?*

"She's fine. She got mad at me about..." I didn't really want to tell him—the honest truth of it all. "You."

"Me?" He stepped farther back, his face going blank with introspection. "I didn't mean to make her uncomfortable at all—I thought we were having a great time at the park."

"Well, not you, *exactly*. She just knows that I can't do relationships so, when she saw your note, she got mad at me about it. She kept going on about how I push people away, even when they don't deserve it." I waved a hand, shrugging off the wisdom immersed in Hadley's words. Enough coffee had dripped through the carafe so I grabbed a mug and watched the rich, brown liquid fill my cup. I looked at Grayson with an eyebrow raised—silently asking if he wanted any—but he shook his head.

"So that's what you're doing then, huh? Pushing me away?"

"It would be evil of me to pretend that I could ever be enough for you. It's just a matter of taking this for what it is."

"And what's that?"

"A fling. A bit of fun. You'll get bored and find someone else eventually and I'll still be Asha Arlington—incapable of love. It's a win-win."

"Except it's too late."

I leaned against the countertop while I tried to battle through every possible thing his words could mean. "What's too late?"

"I see you," he said, gently tucking my hand in his. "I can be patient."

"You'll change your mind. Everyone does and that's okay."

"You're going to have to live with the fact that people actually love you."

"Don't say things you don't mean, Gray."

"I never do, Ash." His eyes were molten, the already lit fuse sizzling between us as I set down my mug, trying to escape the blast zone—lit from both ends and slowly burning towards an explosion I wasn't remotely ready for. I tried to act casual as I stepped into the living room, turning the television on to distract myself from Grayson and his pretty words— only for the man to step in behind me, settling into the couch with an easy comfortability.

"What're we watching?" He threw his arms across the back of the couch, crossing his feet before resting them on my coffee table. I rolled my eyes as he chuckled, clearly intent on spending his morning here if I wouldn't give. I stomped to the kitchen, rescuing my coffee from the island before reluctantly sitting on the couch beside him.

"Hmm, I was thinking *How to Get Away with Murder*," I said, a beast toying with her dinner.

His brow quirked, amusement never far from his innocent eyes. "Should I be worried?"

"Oh, absolutely," I replied, taking a slow sip of my coffee as I side-eyed him. "You've managed to shift the structure of my entire morning—might as well get some ideas on how to handle it." I winked, letting the sounds of the show fill the air while Grayson shifted in his seat, feigning discomfort as I leaned further into his side.

We sat cuddled for hours, the slow start to my Saturday a nice welcome after the hysterics the last week had been filled with. My mind wandered to work for the first time in months, and I found myself eager to solve the problems that had slowly been building in my absence. It had been brought to my attention—through *another* ignored text from Scheff—that some of the employees working on the floor had mentioned some updates that were needed and, while I didn't have a design instinct like Kate, I had been working diligently with department heads to see what we could come up—a new printing station, a coffee bar, and a budget increase for IT were all proposed and, really, didn't seem like too much for me to handle. Yet the uptick in tasks had me drained, lightly complaining on Ana's couch last night.

Grayson had finished with renovations and I thought about asking if he'd want to help with the office too, quickly remembering another life with another man waiting for me. I ignored the guilt pooling in my stomach as I peeked at Grayson—attention locked on the screen as we studied a documentary on the migration patterns of whales, a personal favorite of mine.

He tilted his head in response, as if trying to sneak a glance himself. When he found my eyes instead, he smiled. I pushed myself up, pressing a light peck to the corner of his lips before the intimacy of the moment deterred me. He twisted from his spot, pulling me further onto his lap and wrapping his arms around my waist. I settled into his chest—the steady rise and fall of it was enough to lull me into a peaceful sleep if I let it.

"I'll be beside myself if you don't let me kiss you right now," he said, the words an echo of a conversation at Aisha's house months prior. I had made fun of his wording—the old-school, formal tone of it all. I smiled, pushing myself off of him enough to give him the space he needed. He leaned forward, the two of us waiting for the electric current simmering between us to spark. My eyes dipped to his lips as his hands cupped my face and, suddenly, there wasn't a pair of pliers on earth strong enough to pull us apart.

I sank into him, the two of us clashing together in a kiss that was hungry—indigent. I clawed at his back, trying to be as close to him as physically possible. My breaths were short and needy as he picked me up, my legs wrapping around his waist as I ground against him—hoping to relieve some of the ache that had been growing between us. He carried me to the bedroom, following whatever murmured directions I gave before gently laying me down on the bed. His hands ran through my hair as he peppered kisses along my jawline, down my neck, to my nipples—pebbled beneath the lace of my nightie.

I raised my hands to his chest only for a hand to wrap around my wrists, forcing them back to the bed. "Stay put."

He raised an eyebrow, as if asking if I would comply but I could only manage a simple nod—my focus glued to the fingers that were now rolling my nipple from side to side. I let out a hiss of pain and he stopped. I lifted my head only to be met with concern. "I don't want to hurt you."

"No, good." I dropped my head to the pillow and arched

my back—an offering. He wasn't just giving me what I wanted, he was giving me something I usually took for myself. *Control.* "It feels good."

His lips found my neck, sucking on the tender spot just beneath my ear. "What's the magic word?"

"Please," I begged, the word quiet as it slipped through my clenched teeth.

"What was that?" He pinched my nipple again, hard enough to elicit a moan, my body chasing his fingers as he pulled away.

"Please!" The word echoed around us as Grayson pulled my nightgown over my head, the cool, silk cloth gliding over my skin did nothing to ease the tension building in my body. I reached out for him only for my hands to be pinned down once more.

"I know you don't like to listen but, right now, you're mine and I told you to stay put." I nodded, the acknowledgment rewarded with a kiss pressed hard against my lips. I shifted beneath the man— eager to release the tension building inside—only to be met with the rough material of his jeans against my bare clit. I moaned, sinking further into the bed as he said, "Such an eager girl."

His voice was low, tortured and I didn't miss the hiss of excitement that he released as a single finger ran the space between his body and mine. "*Fuck.* You're already so wet for me, baby."

He dipped a finger inside, another wave of pleasure building through my body as he pushed farther only stopping to curl the single digit before pulling out entirely. His mouth found my nipple as he slid it back in—any worries eddying out of my head as he slipped another finger inside, pumping in and out. "Say my name, Asha. I need to know you're here with me."

The words sent me soaring, my back arching as he curled his fingers, picking up the pace as he pumped his hand faster. *"Please."*

"Everything's just a fucking game to you, Asha. If you wanna play, use your words." His voice was thick, the words growled as he slowed his movements. "What do you want, baby? Tell me what you want?"

"I want to cum," I said, the words lost between my uncontrolled breaths.

"Say my name, Asha." The sound that tore from my lips was purely feral, a frustrated groan that was fed by his fingers, now frozen inside of me. I lifted my head once more, finding his eyes as he flicked his fingers inside of me once. "Say my name and it's yours."

I glared at him, trying to shift myself on his fingers. It wasn't his name that I was fighting against but the implication of everything this moment meant—the realization that I'd given him power over me was the aspect every part of my body fought against.

He shook his head with a small laugh, his free hand wrapping around my neck as he picked up pace once again—threatening to shatter me with a few strokes of his thumb over my now sensitive clit. I couldn't react to the movement, not as his hand tightened around my neck, the restriction only forcing me closer and closer to the edge. I tapped his hand and he freed me in a second, letting me suck down a breath of air before he was kissing me, stealing the air from me again. He pinched my nipple again and a shock wave racked through my body, the overwhelming feeling of pleasure forcing the words from my mouth. "Grayson! Fuck!"

"That's my girl." He pressed his thumb into me, his fingers curling once more, an intense orgasm searing through me. I clawed for him, eager to use his body as a shield from my thoughts as my mind worked to rearrange itself—as I wondered, for a few minutes, why I'd given him the one thing I'd never meant to.

His hands roamed my body, lingering on the crescent scabs on my ribs—physical evidence of the attacks I subject myself to. He pulled himself off of me, twisting my body out of his shadow so he could see what his fingers had found. I let out a small hiss as his fingers rubbed over more recent markings, barely crusted over.

"Why do you do this to yourself?" he asked, his fingers tracing the marks.

"I don't know." He leveled an unamused stare my way. I raised my eyebrows, shaking my head in challenge, only to be met with his expectant eyes. "I started doing it when I was in pageants. It's grounding. It helps me keep my thoughts from running away too quickly."

"Why do you have to hurt yourself though?"

"Sometimes it's the only thing that works."

He seemed to consider it, throwing the silken top my way as thoughts tore away at him. "What about the pain is grounding?"

"Do we really have to talk about this?" I asked, rolling away from him and the shame that seemed to trail its way up my back.

"Color me curious."

I was silent for a while, hoping he'd fall asleep. As his breathing slowed, I dared a look over my shoulder. His eyes were closed, his chest rising and falling in steady pitches. I rolled all the way over, content to stare at him rather than the tiny fleck of blue on my white walls.

His long eyelashes dusted over the skin under his eye, his full, pink lips slightly parted. I dug my nails into my thigh, resisting the urge to reach over and trace my hand over the freckles on his cheek. A battle I lost, my hand freeing itself from the sheets and slowly closing the space between us. My hand was just about to cup his face when his eyes shot open, a smile overtaking his sleepy mask.

I rolled back, my heart threatening to escape my chest. "You're a fucking asshole."

"And you're trying to avoid my questions."

"So?"

"So," he replied, dragging the word out. "Stop running from me."

"I don't think you were complaining a minute ago," I said, hoping that I could distract him away from his curiosities.

He looked at me, a mischievous twinkle in his eye. "Don't ask for trouble, Asha."

I threw the covers off of me, flipping onto Grayson's lap before rolling my hips—keeping the movement steady until I finally pulled a deep moan from his chest. His head tilted back and I nipped at his neck. "I'm *always* looking for trouble."

He offered me a small smile before pinching my chin between his fingers, forcing me to look him in the eyes. "You are still here, Asha. You are here and you are smart, and..." his thumb swiped across my cheek, his throat bobbing. "And simply the most beautiful woman I've ever laid eyes on. You are a masterpiece. I find something new to admire every time I look at you, every time you say something so unbelievably witty and ill-timed."

He huffed a laugh as I hid my face in his palm, unable to look at him, to hear his words, without bracing for the voice, inevitably calling him out for every lie that he told. I pulled myself from his lap entirely when I realized that I was already doing the voice's job for it—counter arguments for everything he'd said already laid out on the tip of my tongue. I pulled the covers over my body, the lingerie I'd chosen seeming childish under the weight of it all. "I'm too broken to be considered a masterpiece. Just drop it."

"Promise me you'll stop hurting yourself."

I didn't offer a response, just a flat, unamused look from my side of the bed before I tucked into his side. We finally closed our eyes to sleep and, as Grayson's arm tightened around my waist, I realized it was the safest I'd felt in years.

ʂ•

"Asha, what the fuck?" Adrenaline forced my eyes open, and I groggily glanced around the room to find Scheff, waiting at my bedroom door with a bouquet of white roses and coffee in hand. Grayson mumbled in his sleep and I worked to free myself from under the comforting pressure of his arm—terrified of him waking up to find my best friend hovering over us.

I held a finger to my lips, trying to convince him to keep his anger in until I could creep across the room and out the door. Long gone was his cold anger, replaced by billowing rage as he turned in a flash, stomping down the hall. I looked back at Grayson, still sleeping peacefully, before I pulled the door closed, inch by agonizing inch. I doubted his restful slumber would last for much longer.

I blew out a breath and followed the trail of flames into the kitchen.

Scheff's back was turned, his muscles tensing the moment I stepped into the kitchen. I took stock of the room, noticing the roses hovering unceremoniously, half in, half out of the trash can. My bourbon-hiding cabinet was open—the booze in question tilting into the paper coffee cup Scheff was damn near throttling in his hands.

"*Him?*" His voice was hushed, as if, even in anger, he couldn't help but do what I asked. The slick feeling of guilt twisted in my stomach as his words, once again, rang through my head. '*You can't see how you manipulate me,*' he had said, the tragic part being that *I could.*

My entire life as it currently stood was thanks to Matthew Scheffter and his love for me, the one thing I knew I would never be able to return to him—and yet.

"We've been fucking other people for years."

"But after I told you I loved you and you told me we could try?" His eyes were nearly black—the darkest I'd ever seen them—his irises like bottomless pits threatening to send me to my doom.

"*You* told me that you loved me. You love me *and* you've known for years that I'm incapable of loving you back. *I tried.*"

"But suddenly you can love him? He can stay the night? What makes him so much better than me?" I watched his face fall. Raw, unrelenting pain was all I could find when he looked at me.

"I don't." The words were small, tentative. I didn't love Scheff, not in the way he wanted. But did that mean I loved Grayson? Or was I just reaching—chasing the illusion of something different, desperate to escape the carnage I'd left in Scheff's arms?

The past few months blurred together—every date, every kiss, every stolen fucking breath with each of them. My chest tightened, the room too small to contain all the truths I couldn't bring myself to look in the eye.

He huffed a laugh as I crossed my arms over my chest. "Scheff..."

"I asked you to stop calling me that." The words were eerily calm, punctuated by him taking a giant swig straight from the bottle. He chased it with the bourbon-infused coffee—well-working his way to some sort of oblivion. He hissed as the liquor settled, running a hand through his hair. "I asked you to stop calling me that and still, it was like hearing you say *my name* was the most painful thing you'd ever said in your fucking life."

"Matty, stop—"

"Don't fucking call me that either!" The words echoed through the apartment, the seal on his carefully kept temper finally bursting.

In six years, he'd never once yelled at me. He'd been mad, sure, but he'd never *yelled* at me. I took a step back, trying to fight the overwhelming anxiety that caused that all too familiar tremor in my hand—cowering into the hallway where my back was met with a strong, solid chest. *Of course, Grayson would wake up now.*

"Don't talk to her like that," he said from behind me, his voice unyielding. I hated how, the moment I felt him behind me, I was at ease.

"Don't act like this conversation has anything to do with you." Scheff's words, spat towards us with a tangible disgust, hit me. His pained eyes locked on the man behind me. There was an ever-present, sarcastic part of me that wanted to argue his point—reminding him that this had *everything* to do with Grayson.

"I don't care if it has jack to do with me. You won't speak to her that way."

Scheff's searing glare jumped to me, and for once, my quippy little mouth didn't have anything to say as I shrank further into Grayson. "You're going to push him away too, Asha. You're going to pull him in, and let him get close, and the second he thinks he loves you? You'll shut it down. It's what you do. You're nothing if not *predictable*. Collecting little toys like your mother."

The words stung worse than the tears now burning my eyes. "Low blow, Scheff."

I wiped at my face—a tear falling free swiped away with a hurried, embarrassed motion. Grayson finally moved in front of me, tucking a protective arm behind his back, his fingers wiggling as if begging for a connection—or he was just painfully aware of how far I was about to fall, eager to provide me the lifeline I was desperate for.

"And sleeping with him wasn't a *low blow?*"

"You know, you want to wake up the whole building with a fight about names? The least you could do is call me by mine. It's Grayson in case you didn't know, asshole."

Scheff laughed, the bitter sound piercing my chest. His hand flexed at his side as if he'd just released an invisible weight he'd been holding for far too long. "You wanna do this, *handyman?*"

"I still don't know why you insist on calling me that name when I told you I'm fine with being the one to fix things. Or was that not clear by how peaceful she looked when you came in this morning? Let me ask, did you enjoy watching *us* sleep?"

Grayson barely had time to shove me out of harm's way before Scheff came barreling after him. The sound of the wall breaking beneath their weight collided with the sound of me crashing into the single picture frame I dared to hang in the entire apartment—a photo of Scheff and me standing hand in hand in our empty office space, years before our business had tripled in size and our relationship shifted into...this. The glass shattered, doing nothing to break my freefall to the floor. A single shard skated against my skin, splitting it open and all I could do was lay there staring at the ceiling as I listened to them fight their way through my home. I couldn't bring myself to watch, not when it felt like two sides of myself—manifested into reality and battling it out in real time.

I listened as they whipped through the apartment, colliding with the furniture and drywall alike. I could feel the vibrations of their anger beneath me as the floor shook with every hit. But nothing really registered past the stinging sensation shooting up my arm, the pain an anchor through the brawl. *I've gotten more scars on my body in this year alone than in the past five put together.*

I don't know what possessed me—some sort of manic demon, lost to the utter insanity and mayhem playing out in my apartment—but I started to *laugh.* The sound bubbled from deep in my stomach, initially a hiccup before spilling out of my mouth and filling the room, drowning out the sounds of my warring lovers. I laughed so hard that my stomach started cramping and I, slowly, rolled onto my side— away from the glass—and pushed myself to my feet. I kept laughing as I lifted my, now-bloodied, hand to the wall, the sound intensifying as red streaked down the white wallpaper, haunting in its contrast.

I turned around to find both men—hair tousled, shirts torn—with faces a mix of confusion and concern. Shocked faces that somehow matched yet were *so,* so different at the same time. Grayson's eyes were still lit with fire, a small quirk of his lips suggested he saw the humor in it all while his thick eyebrows were dipped with worry. Scheff's face seemed to straddle between forced indifference and alarm as he locked onto droplets of blood dotting the shattered picture of us on the floor.

I closed my eyes, trying to compose myself, channeling my inner-Ana. *One breath in, one breath out.*

"Ash?" Grayson started, taking a single, hesitant step forward. "You okay?"

"Of course she's not okay." Scheff piped in.

"So, you speak for her now?"

"Stop," I said, the words quiet compared to the lingering anger still simmering between Grayson and Scheff.

"I've been here for her longer than you have—I'd think I'm the one more in tune to her feelings." Scheff said, his arms crossed in front of his chest with an air of petulance.

"And I'm here now," Grayson replied, their clashing energy renewed, sending them back into a spiral of bickering.

"I said, stop." The words weren't lost this time—punctuated by the *hiss* I released, pain showing it's hand with every movement. "You two don't get to fight over me."

"Asha," Scheff said, taking a step closer. Something primal in me took a step back, something like the acrid taste of fear. I couldn't quell my shaking hand when I lifted it up to stop him.

"You need to leave." The words left my mouth raw, as broken as the look on Scheff's face.

"No, we need to talk about this."

"Not right now. You're drunk and—"

"And acting like you?" He didn't say it in a mean way— his tone leaning toward sad curiosity rather than malice. That didn't mean they didn't hurt all the same.

"Just go get some rest and we can talk later," I started, hating the shattered 'please' that followed. "I need to take a shower."

I turned toward my bedroom without another word, shutting the door on the two of them—unable to care if they decided to go for round two in the kitchen. I turned on the water, the movement a ritual as I pushed the handle as far as it could go, my body buzzing with the anticipation of the needle-like spray raining down on me.

I stripped off my nightgown, rubbing it between my fingers before tossing it in the trash. The black embroidered lace was already stitched with today's memories, too oppressive to ever wear again. I looked at myself in the mirror. *Ugly, hideous, worthless.*

I waited until the steam was thick enough to choke me, stepping underneath the harsh water and relishing the way it burnt against my newest injury. The water mixed with my blood, a peony pink tint coating the bottom of the shower. Time slipped away as I curled into a ball on the shower floor —every movement automatic, ingrained. A single sob broke from my chest and I covered my mouth, sucking in the rest of the cries that threatened to spill free, the pain of preventing release building in my chest.

If Grayson was still here, I didn't want him to hear, to come running in, eager to hold me and to make it better. I *deserved* this pain.

When my skin was flushed and pruny, I pulled myself up, turning the shower handle slowly to let my body cool down with each passing temperature change. I didn't bother with lotion, opting for a pair of sweatpants and a loose shirt that had been sitting on the bathroom floor for weeks instead.

I tried to take a steadying breath before leaving my bedroom, half expecting Grayson to have left along with Scheff—leaving me in the aftermath of my own, fucked up emotional torment. But, as I rounded the hallway corner, now free of glass and no longer bleeding, I found Grayson sitting at the island, a worried look on his face. He pulled himself from the stool, the movement abrupt as he stepped around the corner, slowing like he suddenly remembered who I was, how volatile I could be. He stopped a few steps away, looking me over before letting out a steady breath—as if he couldn't begin to relax until he checked on my well-being.

I didn't ask about Scheff.

"I can fix this," he said, bouncing with anxious energy as he looked at the wall—examining it as thoroughly as he did me the night before. "I just gotta run to the store and grab my tools. An hour tops. Are you going to be okay?"

I gave him a single, silent nod.

"I'll be back in a bit," he started, pulling me closer and placing a gentle, lingering kiss on the top of my head. "Just... Just don't go anywhere. Okay?"

His brown eyes were swimming with worry, as if he was truly afraid that I would bolt—Scheff's words hitting him harder than he wanted to show.

I nodded, sinking further into the couch and my silence, watching as he walked out. I was too exhausted to cry, so I just stared at the stupid fucking hole in the wall—trying to ignore how it seemed to match the one that lived in my heart.

I woke up a couple hours later to the sound of Grayson spreading some type of white goo over the hole in my wall. I laid there silently while he worked—pure determination twisting his lips to the side, his eyes focused on the task at hand. He swiped a hand over the patch before turning around, barely catching my open eyes in his spin, and committing to a double take.

A small, embarrassed smile pulled at his lips as he came to kneel on the floor next to me, trading out his tools for my hand. "I am so sorry."

"It's my fault."

"Asha, it's really not. A lot of shit was said and Scheff and

I pushed it too far. I patched up your arm while you were sleeping."

Scheff wouldn't have done that—not because he didn't care, but because he would've given me the choice between a bandage or letting me torture myself with the open-air risk of infection. For years, I thought that was a kindness. I was only just starting to realize it wasn't.

"Thanks," I mumbled, my words dry after the dramatic start to the morning and my subsequent nap. My body felt heavy with the weight of emotions and understanding crashing together.

"I should be able to paint over the wall tomorrow. It's all patched up for now though."

I slowly pushed myself up, crossing my legs beneath me and wrapping the blanket tighter around my shoulders. "Don't worry about it."

"It's the least I can do," he said as his eyebrows tightened. "Please, it's nothing."

"No, Grayson. Don't worry about it. You can't come back," I started, choking on the words. "He was right."

His grip on my hand tightened, but not in a painful or controlling way. The gesture was full of comfort and reassurance, his warmth shooting up my injured arm. "He wasn't. He wasn't right about any of it. You have to believe that, Ash."

"How would you know? He's known me for six years, Gray. He's right. I can't love you because the only thing I'm good at is breaking people. I'm just like *her* and...and he was right." I laid back down, my head sinking into the couch as tears started to sink into the cushions.

I resumed my glassy stare, the already-fixed hole giving me nothing but another undeserved clean slate, glaring back at me.

"What can I do?" he asked, his steady calm finally breaking with his voice.

'*Nobody can fix you,*' the voice called—the slick, manipulative lilt interjecting now that the rest of the chaos was tidied up.

"Nothing."

His eyes jumped around my face, as if looking for a hidden truth I couldn't give him. He nodded, pulling himself up, his hands wiping against his pants as he took two, painfully slow steps back. "I really thought we could've done it."

"What?"

He huffed a laugh, turning on his heel with his tool bag in hand, and walked out the door.

My eyes were as heavy as the unshakeable pain of failure filled the apartment and I fell asleep not long after—once again surrounded by the wreckage of my choices.

Twenty-Four

Haunting echoes of Grayson and Scheff fighting in my head woke me the next morning—the sounds of my past indecisions reverberating around me before I had the chance to get even a sip of coffee into my system.

It wasn't until noon that I pulled myself from the cushioned depths of the couch, forcing myself to eat the leftover takeout that'd been sitting in my fridge for a few days. I didn't have the energy for social interaction and ordering anything seemed like a waste of the little I had left. Even the taste of cold noodles couldn't wash last night off my tongue.

I had turned my phone off hours ago—Vlad's worried calls had been coming in regular intervals, disrupting the fragile stillness I'd secluded myself to.

'*You don't deserve him,*' the voice called.

I sat for hours, staring at the same spot where Grayson had pinned me to the wall, the lingering feeling of his thumb tracing along my cheek sending me into a fit of tears. The memory of his hands pulling through my hair as he kissed along my neck haunting me as his words echoed in my head, *'Everything's just a fucking game to you'.*

I was too energized to sleep but still too exhausted from the events of the night before to do anything. I hadn't touched a drop of alcohol since my night with Ana, and I fought against the urge to buy a new bottle. I refused to move from the couch—certain that if I did I would wind up at the liquor store—until someone's fist was pounding against my door followed by the *beep* of the intercom.

Frank's voice filled my apartment. "I'm sorry, Asha. I tried to stop him, but he climbed all those stairs. Persistent, I'll give him that."

Dread knotted my stomach. Scheff wouldn't come back after yesterday, would he? Who else would be able to argue their way past Frank?

I rushed to the intercom, dizziness stealing my breath as I shuffled as quickly as I could to the box on the wall.

"Thanks, Frank, sorry," I said before creeping over and peering through the peephole.

"Grayson?" The man standing in front of me looked nothing like the one who had angrily stalked out of my apartment the night before. The same shirt he'd been wearing then was now wrinkled and stained, a five-o'clock shadow grazing his jaw. "Vlad said you were spiraling," he said, the words clipped.

"I'm not spiraling," I said, brushing it off, though we both knew Vlad wasn't wrong. "He should know better by now."

"He said you were ignoring him," he said, glaring at me as though the truth was written on my face somewhere. "But clearly you're fine."

"Yep, *perfectly fine*. What do you want?" I snapped, using

my body to close off any space he could push through—if he came in, I wasn't sure I would let him leave again.

"Fucking Christ." He exhaled a heavy, stress-filled breath while running his hands through his hair. He started pacing in the cramped hallway outside of my apartment and I could see him struggling to regulate his breathing—the irregular rise and fall of his chest as he raised his hands to rest on top of his head. I didn't know what to say, or how to...calm him. There wasn't anything left for me to do.

"Why?" he asked after a minute, letting out a deep breath before leaning against the wall, his chin tilting up while his eyes surveyed the ceiling.

"'Why' what? I didn't ask for him to come over yesterday—"

"But did you choose him?" I could taste the venom in his voice. The echo of the same question not lost on me. Just yesterday, Scheff was asking me the same question: *Why?*

I wanted to scream at both of them. At my family, and at anyone who ever thought that I was nothing more than an object to be owned, and wielded. I had made my own choices —decent ones, at that—for most of my adult life. I owned a goddamn company, and it was successful. I'd grown more in the last year than I had in my entire life and, for once, I refused to let that die because of someone else's desire to *own* me.

"What if I did, Gray?" I asked as I studied every inch of his face one more time. I was glad that I got the chance to map it again after the pained look he'd left here wearing. "What if I chose him? At least *I* made a fucking choice. Scheff asked me the same question about you. Why would I choose you? You wanna know who I want to love, Gray? Myself. I am so sick of everyone coddling me and wanting to take care of me. I want to be able to look in the fucking mirror without the consequences of my choices threatening to suffocate me. Do you even know what it's like to carry that burden? To know that if you hadn't been so fucking selfish, someone who the world *loved* and treasured would still be here, alive and breathing?" His eyes hardened, as if he was finally hearing me. I tried to shake out the nerves running through my hands as he leaned against the wall. "I want to be able to take care of myself. I want to be able to wake up without choking on regret, Gray. I've spent my entire life desperate for someone—*anyone*—to love me. I'm just now realizing how much more powerful it would be if I *finally* figured out how to love myself."

Our eyes met and I could feel myself opening the door for him, my fingers sliding off the handle against my will while we studied each other carefully.

He started to back away, heading for the elevator with painfully slow steps. "Loving yourself doesn't have to come at the expense of everyone else, Asha. Why are you so damn certain you have to be alone to be whole?"

"Grayson…" I started as his hand reached for the elevator button, not sure what the next words out of my mouth might be. "I'm just…I'm sorry."

"Asha Arlington? Apologizing?" He chuckled, shaking his head as he reached for the button, hitting it a few times with a rushed annoyance. "Must be my cue to get the fuck out of your life."

If my heart wasn't already broken, his dismissal of my apology definitely shattered it. *He's right. Asha Arlington* rarely *apologizes.*

I inched the door shut before turning my back to it, sliding against the cool surface until my knees were tucked into my chest. Tears were rolling down my face before the first sob racked through my apartment.

'*You know it's your fault,*' the voice called again, a maniacal laugh echoing through my head. '*You were never going to be enough for him anyway.*'

"Fuck!" I yelled, as my mind raced. I pulled myself up from the floor and stumbled to the bedroom, tears streaming down my face. Ripping off my sweatshirt, I grabbed the first t-shirt in reach. Forget a shower, forget a bra—I needed to turn the world, these feelings, off *now*. I swiped my phone off the counter and called Vlad, putting it on speaker as I shoved my feet into sneakers.

The ringing echoed through my apartment, the silence between each tone heavy enough to crush me. Six rings. No answer.

The reminder was simple and cruel: I was alone, and fixing this was up to me.

I grabbed my phone, ID, and a blanket before rushing out the door. In the elevator, I ordered a car, hoping I could make it across the street to the bodega before the driver pulled up. The cold air wrapped around me as I stepped outside, sharp and sobering, but I paused just long enough to take a breath before bolting into the street.

The automatic doors of the store slid shut behind me, muting the outside world. My eyes locked on the liquor aisle, and I marched toward the bottles waiting like salvation on the shelves.

'*What'll it be today?*' the voice cooed in my head. '*Light or dark? Complacent or destructive?*'

Anything to shut it up. Anything to forget everything that's happened.

My phone buzzed—a two-minute warning from the driver. I reached for the first bottle that caught my eye, barely glancing at it before I bee-lined for the register. Why should I care if they charged me for waiting? *I'm Asha fucking Arlington.*

I sent the driver a message, asking him to wait for me— promising a very nice tip if he did. He replied with a simple thumbs up, allowing me to slow my pace and assess the random bottle in my hand.

Blue Swift Martel. The last time I had cognac I slept through most of the following day. It sounded like the perfect solution. The golden bird—a swift, I'd assume—was what drew me to the bottle. Something about it seemed at peace. *Fucking marketers.*

I grabbed a few random snacks—jerky, an orange, some candy and chips—before striding for the front of the store with my head held high. The cashier barely regarded me as she scanned my items and mumbled the total my way—her atten- tion already flying back to her phone. I tapped my phone against the reader, declined a receipt, and scoffed as she rolled her eyes at the energy she had to waste in throwing it into the trash bin barely a foot away.

I stalked through the doors, playing Frogger to get across the street again and found my driver, waiting patiently outside of my building. I double-checked the license plate before sliding into the cool interior of the car, offering a small smile, and nodding after he confirmed my name.

We quickly merged onto the highway, the Arch disap- pearing into the city's amalgamation of neighborhoods. I ignored everything we flew past, my focus latched on the pint —the glass cold in my hands.

My stomach flipped as we passed the park entrance, the road narrowing so much that a single wrong move could send us flying into the ditch. The driver slowed as another car passed, devouring half the narrow pavement, and we crept down the winding hill. My chest tightened with every twist, but when we reached the bottom, I exhaled a long, steady breath. As soon as we stopped, I flung myself from the car, slamming the door behind me without so much as a 'thank you.'

My feet found the trail with ease and, after a few minutes, I ducked off—meandering through trees and grass, thankful for the sweatpants sparing my legs from scratches. The leaves had started to fall weeks ago, carpeting the ground in soggy piles of reds and yellows while the branches above stretched bare and skeletal toward the sky. I stopped at a tree, resting my hand against its rough bark, and drew in a deep breath before *screaming*. The sound ripped through the still forest, birds scattering as anguish and anger began to harmonize with my grief.

When my voice faded, I trudged forward, stumbling onto a small gravel path. The growing silence around me was oppressive, the only sounds were the crunching of pebbles beneath my feet, and the virtually constant trail of thoughts running free in my head. I let the path guide me, trusting the universe—or apathy—to lead me somewhere secluded, where I could crack open the bottle and drown my feelings in the liquor's unrelenting burn.

It wasn't long before the gravel gave way to a grassy knoll, the trail ending as if I was meant to find my way here all along. I laid out the blanket, dumping my wares haphazardly onto its fuzzy surface, and sat down—the bones in my legs groaning as I crossed them beneath me. Uncapping the bottle, I took a long swig, relishing the chemical-like burn as it seared its way down my throat. Tears blurred the landscape, turning it into a hazy, abstract painting. The breeze curled around me, gentle and indifferent, as I screamed again, my voice swept away in the wind.

Castlewood was expansive, its popularity balanced by the

vastness of its trails. The chances of someone hearing me after I'd walked so far felt slim.

Punishment—that's what Ana called these trips. But what would she know? It's not like she'd ever found time to come with me. I raised the bottle for another swig, eyes on the sky as my last fuck flew off with the golden swift.

I must have sat in silence for at least an hour, wondering when I'd last been able to enjoy it. The haunting voice in my head had gone quiet, most likely from the alcohol's steady hum. Without its sharp, needling truths piercing through, I felt oddly...alone. *Leave it to a figment of my imagination to abandon me too.*

I checked my phone—the cold, hard box in my hand contrasted with my body's heat. Winter's impending arrival would've been more intimidating but the afternoon air stubbornly refused to drop below sixty. It was only half past four, and the sun had already started to set—refusing to take the warmth of the day with it.

My thumb hovered over the ride-share app, ready to order a car but, instead, I locked the screen and laid back on the blanket, enjoying the lavender sky as it stained itself dark blue.

Punishment. How could this be a punishment when it felt like the weight had finally lifted? Everyone has a coping mechanism. Why should it matter that mine was a bottle? I lost myself in a spiral of thoughts, letting it loop endlessly as the world fell deeper into night.

I lifted a hand above me, trailing a wave through the air with my fingers when a single sound broke my blissful quiet —the conversational sound of a sparrow's call. I shot up, head spinning, as I tried to pinpoint which direction it was coming from. Wrapping the blanket around my arm, I grabbed the bottle and started down the path, certain it would lead me to some answers.

The crunch of the gravel under my feet provided a steady rhythm for the sparrow—my search for clarity giving us both a beat to follow.

The thickening darkness pressed in as I stumbled forward, nearly colliding with a tree—the bird's song fading as soon as I stumbled into the parking lot. The empty expanse rotated quickly as I turned in circles, still searching for the damn bird.

I ripped my phone out of my pocket, the screen blinking awake to blind me.

I'd been wandering through the woods for four fucking hours. *Brilliant.*

Six percent battery? *Fantastic.*

"What the fuck do I do now?" I muttered to no one, glancing at the few dingy cars grouped together in the far corner. One engine roared to life, startling a small squeal out of me. I waved frantically at the truck as it crept toward me, no doubt wary of the drunk emerging from the woods.

The window cracked open, revealing a woman about my age. "Are you okay?" she asked, slow and cautious.

"I need an Uber," I said, forcing the words out of my ashy mouth. "My phone's about to die. Could you call one for me? Please?"

She nodded, pulling out her phone. As she tapped away, an incessant *buzzing* started—a swarm of invisible insects droning in my ears. I swatted wildly, stumbling back into the trees.

"Lady! What the fuck are you on?" she called, stepping out of her truck, arms raised like she was approaching a wild animal. I continued my animated dance, unwilling to stop lest the bugs gave up first.

"Hey! I think it's just your phone. You're okay." The sound vanished as quickly as it had come, and I lowered my hands.

"Sorry," I mumbled. "Uber?"

She frowned. "You're too drunk for a driver. Let me take you home. I'll feel better knowing you're safe."

"I don't want to inconvenience you," I muttered, already shaking my head. "Uber."

She stifled a giggle, covering it with a cough. "I'm Tate. I'm heading toward U City anyway. Do you live around there?" *Did I?*

"Clayton," I managed, leaning heavily on her as she guided me toward the truck.

My head swam again, and I looked around, veering for a rusted trash can to unload the acidic contents of my stomach. Tate waited, her concern palpable, as I alternated between puking and trying to catch my breath.

"Let's get you home," she said softly, her kindness radiating as she helped me into the truck. I rattled off my address, curling into the corner where the seat met the door.

When she asked, "Who can I call for you?" I hesitated. *Who would answer?*

Everything in me, down to my bones, screamed for me to go to Grayson but the slick, toxic comfort I'd grown used to won out in the end.

"Scheff," I whispered as I passed her my phone. "Matthew Scheffter. Thank you." She nodded, connecting my phone to a charger before shifting the truck into gear.

"Sorry, I'm a mess," I said, tears running down my face as I wiped at my nose. Tate reached into the glove compartment and passed me a small pack of tissues.

"I've been there. It ain't nothing but a thang," she said, flashing a goofy smile and winking at me. Her gentleness made me laugh despite myself—a soft, pathetic sound that felt foreign after all my screaming. I took the tissues, mumbling a quiet "thanks" before resting my head on the door. I closed my eyes and let her deliver me to the consequences of my choice.

TWENTY-FIVE

For the first time since I'd known him, Matthew Scheffter wasn't at the ready to save me when I opened my eyes the next morning. I'd spent most of the night on the bathroom floor where Frank had left me. *Frank* and not Scheff. Which means that when the girl—Tate —called Scheff, he *chose* not to come. My head ached as I lifted it from the cold floor, a constant thrumming that sent me for the toilet I had been deposited by. *At least Frank didn't leave me in my bed.*

I spent an hour on the floor, the afternoon sun lighting the room behind me as I heaved my regrets into the toilet and flushed them down again and again—embarrassingly losing track of the amount of times my eyes were focused on the base of the bowl. As I, finally, pulled myself from my pathetic ball on the floor, the need to go to Aisha's hit me again. After another hour of nursing my hangover I was dressed and running out of my apartment.

The end of October had welcomed the city with the double-edged promise of change, the leaves finally falling from their place on the trees and slowly decaying into the soil.

A bitter wind swept through the buildings and I wrapped my jacket tighter around my body, wishing I would've brought a scarf and gloves to cover my chill-exposed skin. I'd opted for calling a car again—too afraid to face Vlad while I had Aisha's letter clutched in my hand, determination and hope a dangerous cocktail in my chest.

I looked at the faded envelope, my name written in Aisha's curly scrawl. Despite how thin it was, the letter I'd been carrying with me the last six months felt impossibly heavy. As if Aisha tucked the weight of the world behind the seal placed so delicately on the back—an outline of a single lavender stalk was pressed into the wax, our shared initials, AA, monogrammed in the middle. I ran my thumb over it, slowly embracing the rough edges—like it could give me some sense of the woman who had dripped the wax over it God knows how long ago.

A single beep pulled my attention back to the street, my driver pulling along the curb. I was glad for the cool, late-fall air that was fighting against my nausea with each swaying step I took toward the car. The passenger window rolled down to reveal a young woman confirming that I was, indeed, Asha Arlington.

Whether it was my current state or my general demeanor that kept the driver silent, I didn't care. The thirty minute ride was consumed with my silent thoughts and worries—all centered around what would be Aisha's final words to me, if they would be filled with disappointment alone.

I barely acknowledged the driver as I slid out of the car, slamming the door before walking the path to my auntie's house. The flowers had been dead for a while now, the once-vibrant stalks now dead husks, curling in on themselves. I didn't let them stop me, not as I stomped up the stairs and made my way to the porch swing. I sat down hard enough to throw myself into motion, the back and forth of it doing nothing to keep my lingering nausea and bay.

I looked back to the envelope, digging my finger into the seal and ripping it open. I muttered a curse as I accidentally tore the paper inside, forcing myself to breathe before I ruined the moment in its entirety. I freed Aisha's letter from the envelope's hold, a whiff of my auntie's perfume bringing tears to my eyes as I unfolded it—carefully, slowly, gently. *One breath in, one breath out.*

Dear Asha,

If you finally got your hands on this letter, it means I've passed. If I'm being completely honest, I'm surprised Mr. Jefferson was able to get it into your stubborn hands, and even more surprised you decided to open it. How long did it take you, huh?

Well, either way, the house is yours. It's always been a piece of you __and__ me—even more so than it was your uncle and mine's.

First and foremost, you need to know how sorry I am. I've spent a lot of our time apart realizing that I needed to be there to protect you more. Matta is my big sister, and I failed to protect you from the damage and destruction I'd watched her cause for years. To be honest, I was scared of her—always have been. She's got this way of luring people in and making it seem like, when the world falls apart, it's anyone's fault but her own. You're kinda like her in that way, but I think it's easier for you to hide from accountability rather than facing the truth of it all —that you enjoy the chaos just as much as she does.

Now, when you decide what you're going to do with the house, I need you to be careful with the things upstairs. I've been keeping everything safe for years but don't want you to throw it all out in a fit. And don't let Matta get her hands on any of it either. It's the things we keep in the attic that really burden us, Ash. I hope that you're able to let some of it go, to let the pain go.

It's a beautiful thing, to live. Be worthy, love.
Auntie Aisha

I don't know how long I sat on the swing—knees to my chest, sweats soaked with grief. If it wasn't for a cold wind whipping against my face, I wouldn't have pulled myself up, intent on getting away from the chill. My fingers found Aisha's key with ease, tucking it in my palm before sliding it out of my purse. It was the lock that wanted to be stubborn.

I pinched the head of the key, hard enough for the near-frozen metal to bite through my skin, and rattled the door. It didn't work. I knocked a fist against the door, muttering a string of curses when I opted for kicking it—my toe radiating with pain that wasn't even warranted *because*...it didn't work. I tried to pull the stupid key out once more only to be met with a dull thud that suggested it was, indeed, stuck.

Once I trudged past frustration and dangerously close to rage, I simply unlocked the door and stepped over the threshold.

The slam echoed through the house as the floor rushed up to meet me, my cries harmonizing with the *boom*. I was grateful that Grayson had finished his work and wouldn't be coming back—at least he wouldn't be able to hear the wounded symphony that was building around me. When my eyes were sore from crying and my breath had somewhat steadied, I pulled myself up and went straight for the attic door.

"One day you're gonna understand." Aisha's voice, like her presence, seemed to linger in the halls of her house. She whis-

pered as I climbed the stairs, the ghost of her laugh following as I made my way down the hall. I swear I could feel her hand over mine when I pulled open the hatch, slowly unfurling the wooden steps before climbing a thin set of stairs into the top of Aisha's house.

I peeked my head through, waving a hand to scare away any critters or cobwebs who had it in mind to attack me once I pulled myself through. Using my phone, I cast a light around the room to find boxes and boxes stacked on top of each other—but, thankfully, nothing alive scuttered out to meet me.

The room was a bit warmer than the lower levels of the house, sweat coating my back as I reached for a box that seemed to stick out against the backdrop of memorabilia that had been living up here for years. I peeled it open, coughing as a layer of dust found its way up my nose and into my lungs— the smell of abandonment working alongside a mildewy musk had me tucking the box into my hip, carefully toting it downstairs. I lugged it past the nursery and Aisha's room, ignoring the memory of Ana, Grayson, and me laughing as we hammered holes into the wall. He'd finished it weeks ago, and I still hadn't found the time to see what it looked like finished.

As I got to the first floor, I turned back, realizing that the lingering memory of Aisha's grief had been covered with a fresh coat of paint. The stairwell, once haunted by the lack of picture frames, now matched the vibrant claret in the living room. The setting sun, beaming in through the bay window, highlighted the color—casting the room in an ethereal glow, just like Grayson said it would. I shook off the grip of remorse, the ghosts of Aisha, Grayson, and all the rest of my shitty decisions.

I stepped into the room, slowly making my way to Aisha's cushioned haven, letting the lingering sunrays warm my cheeks as I placed the box next to me—careful to set it down gently.

There wasn't any tape securing it, the flaps elaborately tucked inside each other instead. I easily pulled them apart, the sound of the cardboard edges grating against each other making my skin crawl—just enough to remind me that there very well could be some creepy-crawly hiding beneath the folds. *Fuck, fuck, fuck.*

I pushed myself off the bench seat, running across the room before wiping my sweaty hands down the front of my pants. As intrusive as *everyone* in my life seemed to be, why couldn't any of them be here *now*? *I really don't want to do this.*

"Asha Arlington, if there's one thing your mother didn't do, it was raise a little bitch. Open the fucking box," I said, trying to conjure what little confidence I had in myself as I bounced on my toes. "You can do this. You're Asha fucking Arlington."

I stomped over to the box and threw it open, letting out a deep, relieved breath when nothing jumped out.

"You gotta look in the box," I said to myself, hands shaking as I squeezed my eyes shut. I couldn't remember the last time I'd felt so nervous.

I leaned over—half hoping that I'd been lucky enough to grab the box of ratty, old blankets. I shook it one more time, waiting for a cockroach to finally free himself from whatever memories Aisha felt the need to pack away but, alas, none revealed themselves. I sat back down, and released another deep, healing breath before turning to the box.

A glint of gold caught my eye, and I fished out a first-place trophy from one of my pageants, *Little Midwest Princess* engraved on the base while a—fake—diamond encrusted wand protruded from the top. I set it beside me, admiring the sun that seemed eager to give the prize its moment. *That wasn't so bad.*

I reached in again, pricking my finger on the sharp points of a tiara—one of many I'd been forced to win over my five years in the system. I set it on the floor by my feet before continuing to slowly unpack the rest of the box. Aisha had managed to stuff a lot of things inside—from trophies and tiaras, to sashes and newspaper clippings. I laughed as I looked around at the menagerie of things. She was nothing more than a dragon, eagerly hoarding its gems and gold away from the rest of the world. I fought against the tears that were threatening to choke me, my throat thick with grief.

My fingers danced around the bottom of the box and I thought that I had done it—finally accomplished something post-Aisha—until my eyes caught on a plastic frame. I tipped the box on its corner to find a DVD case left in the bottom. I pulled it out, immediately looking toward the entertainment center across the room. Her television and media player were connected and waiting for me to feed them something to play.

I opened the case, running my fingers over Aisha's handwriting—'A, A, A' written across the silver disc—before sliding it into the player, listening for the nostalgic whir of the processing machine. I pulled the remote from under the TV before walking backwards a few paces, the screen blinking to life as I sat, crossing my legs on top of the hard floor.

A picture of Ana and me flashed across the screen. Seeing the smiles on our young, far-from-innocent faces, convinced me just enough to sit through the full two-hour show of what our lives might have looked like without Armatta.

"Where to, Miss Asha?" Vlad asked from his place in the driver's seat.

It had taken me an extra hour to recover from the panic attack that ensued after the DVD faded to black—the sound of the machine stopping only heightening my response. It felt like I was being forced to confront the very roots of my trauma head on and, worst of all, I did to myself. No one was holding a gun to my head, or holding my eyes open as the scenes passed by. Ana's voice, echoing in my head, reminded me of all of the ways I punish myself. But this? This was true punishment—my childhood passed before my eyes and I realized that, aside from Armatta's obvious neglect—*I* was responsible for most of the pain I felt *right now*.

Every single person I'd pushed away in the past year—hell, the past six years—was because of my inability to accept love.

I tried to keep myself from hyperventilating as the realization hit me all over again, the weight of my choices crashing down as Vlad merged onto the interstate.

"Miss Asha?" I met his eyes in the rear-view mirror, grateful for the calming anchors they were. *One breath in, one breath out.*

I was about to tell him to take me home, the word already formed on my lips when I looked out the window, blinking away the tears when an, albeit hopeful, thought popped into my head. I opened my phone to see if the location was still updated, rattling off the address, and letting hope bloom in my chest once more.

❧

I thought it would be unfair of me to ambush Scheff, especially considering the last few weeks, so I texted him— warning him that I was on my way over to talk. He only responded to let me know that he'd be in Forest Park, 'waiting where everything went wrong.' I would've called him dramatic if he hadn't been right.

I hopped out of the car, Vlad promising to wait for me here as I closed the door behind me. I used my phone as a map, following the path to the small blinking dot that would lead me to my friend—if I could call him that anymore. He wasn't at the bridge like I'd expected but a waterfall nearby, waiting for me on a bench. A flock of birds were rinsing their feathers in the water, a heron watching keenly from a rock above.

"Hey," I said, trying my best not to surprise him. He only nodded in return, his lips pressed into a tight line. I sat next to him, letting the sounds of the splashing water fill the space between us. I knew what I wanted to say—it was the delivery I was struggling with.

"I don't love you," I started, my voice low. "I don't think I ever have, outside of our friendship." The honesty I was offering him was more intoxicating than anything I'd drank over the last year and still, I choked on it. "I don't love you but I still need you. And I know how selfish that is but it's the truth. I don't know what my life looks like if you're not around, not after you came back. I need you to stay and I need you to be my friend. I can't lose you—no. I refuse to." I was blubbering at this point, the words falling past my lips before I could stop them. I looked at him with glassy eyes, noting his focus still pinned across the pond.

"I need time, Ash." The words were quiet, lost in the noise of the park. The waterfall trickled next to us as the birds played in the water at its base—splashing through the reality of my best friend finally tiring of me.

"How long?"

"I don't know," he started, blowing out a breath as he

pushed himself off of the bench seat. "An indefinite amount of time sounds pretty good right now, if I'm being honest, Ash." He leaned down, pressing a gentle kiss to my forehead, and I let myself drown in the comfortable scent of cedar and honey.

"We'll talk soon, then?" I asked, squinting against the light rain now dusting my face, wishing I could say something to make him stay.

"Yeah. Soon." He stuffed a hand in his pocket, retrieving a half-used bottle of cologne, handing it to me with a small smile. *His* cologne, the one whose name I'd been begging after for years now. I wrapped my hands around it, fighting against the growing ache in my chest. Gravel crunched beneath his feet as he turned and slowly walked away with his hands hidden in his jacket—head sinking into his shoulders. I refused to watch him disappear from view, from my life, and turned my attention to the heron that was still studying me from across the bank. The bird opened its wings and pushed itself into the air right as the sun broke through the clouds, a whisper of warmth resting on my cheeks as it took flight. The corners of my mouth curved as the heron rose in the sky, circling around me once before disappearing in the same direction Scheff had.

I asked Vlad to make one more stop before we went home and, as I continued pounding at the front door, the sound of my fist hitting the wood echoed back at me—taunting. "Grayson, *please*."

After a full five minutes of knocking, I sighed in defeat and rested my hand against the frame instead. A drop of wetness fell on my cheek, and it took me a second to realize that it wasn't a tear but the clouds above me threatening to open up. I turned to curse at the sky before sitting on the steps, lifting my head to watch thick, rain-heavy clouds to tumble in.

My stomach turned with guilt and regret—the two feelings bobbing together in my stomach made me feel useless. The truth of it was, I hated myself for fucking things up with Gray. If I hadn't been so selfish, if I had cared enough to be better—to be honest with myself—maybe he would be willing to open the damn door. My hands started shaking as the anxiety of losing him too continued to swell. I clasped them together, digging my fingernails into my skin. The moisture on my face wasn't rain this time.

Fuck... Where was he?

I pulled my sweater tight around my body as I got comfortable, leaning my head against the column.

"A couple weeks ago I would've killed to see you sitting here," he said. The rawness of his words would've been soothing if it wasn't for him scaring the absolute shit out of me. I hadn't heard him open the door. I turned and stood, awkwardly shuffling back and forth on the step—unable to get any closer out of fear that he'd slam the door in my face.

"Grayson, I–"

"Part of me wants to tell you to get the fuck off my porch." He wouldn't look directly at me—his eyes jumping from the flower beds, to the trees, and then up to the sky. My eyes never left him. "And the other part wants nothing more than to take you inside this house and never let you leave again."

The ache building in my chest made it feel like this was the last time I would drink in the details of the man who stood before me. One hand was tucked into his pocket while the other rubbed at the back of his neck. My fingers itched to soothe the ache I knew he had there, the way I would've if I had never ran from my feelings in the first place.

"I waited, Asha."

Warmth—shame, perhaps, at hiding from him—grew in my cheeks as a breeze blew between us, goosebumps crawling on my skin. I tried to pull my sweater tighter, forcing it past its stretching limits.

"Grayson, please let me explain."

"Explain what? You've made it perfectly clear that you never intended to be with me. I was stupid. I fell for you when I shouldn't have. I just don't get why you're here, Asha. I don't get why you *finally* care," he finished, his eyes finally meeting mine. It was like he was challenging me—finally giving me the space to lay it all out.

"I was terrified of you. You are the only person who has wanted to see every aspect of me. You said I was a masterpiece and I thought I was too broken to be and you laughed it off. I get it now, Gray. I get it and I am begging you for one more chance. Please."

His shoulders slackened as I spoke, and a flash of pain crossed his face, barely readable. The warm, deep brown of his eyes sank to black, my hope withering alongside the modicum of light that melted away. "I never thought myself to be a cruel man, Ash. But you're going to have to get the fuck off my porch."

"Grayson…"

"Now."

I took a step down, backing away slowly, "You told me you would change my mind."

"You can't be surprised that someone got tired of you trying to decide. Go see if Scheff cares," he said as he turned and walked in the house without another word.

"I changed my mind, Grayson," I said quietly. I tried to

suck in a breath of air as the weight of the last year pressed down on me. A roll of thunder sounded from the sky and as I fell to my knees, the clouds opened up and it started to pour. "I changed my mind!"

A sob racked through my chest as I curled in on myself, letting the rain fall on me, soaking through my clothes in seconds. None of it mattered when everything—everyone—that I loved had been forced away.

'You still have me...'

I tried to hold it in, but I couldn't any longer. I screamed. I screamed until my throat felt bloody and raw. I probably looked insane from the window I knew Grayson was watching me from.

"Fuck! I said I changed my mind!" I yelled at the house, desperate for him to come out. I pulled myself up, letting one last sob free before I lifted my eyes up to the window. The silhouette of his tall, muscular frame was outlined by a light, a hand raised—in farewell or longing, I couldn't tell—against the window. I flashed my middle finger to him in a goodbye of my own before turning back to the car.

Vlad and I had become accustomed to this part—the pathetic walk to the car, the never-ending silence that tried to suffocate us as we drove away from another one of my meltdowns. The only difference today was that, instead of longing for the peace I could find at the bottom of a bottle, I texted Ana asking if she had time to talk.

I locked the phone screen while the dreadful feeling of rejection—with its scorching grip—wrapped around me. I looked up to catch Vlad's worried eyes in the mirror and I sent a small smile his way. "It just sucks. I fucked it up but I'll be okay."

Relief flooded his eyes. "I've known that for weeks, Miss. I was just waiting for you to realize it."

The tears that released matched the intensity of the rain pounding down on the car. I covered my face in an attempt to hide myself from him as I sobbed—horrifying racks of air bursting from my chest. I listened as the click of the blinker sounded and he pulled over, slowing us down to park. I jumped in surprise when my door swung open, my hands dropping to reveal Vlad standing with his arms outstretched. I caved, leaping out of the car and into his arms. He held me as I let the truth sink in: Asha Marie Arlington was going to be okay.

TWENTY-SIX

NOVEMBER

I f it wasn't for Ana, I wouldn't be trapped in this car, barreling down the interstate toward our mother—the three of us finally committing to the girl's weekend Armatta proposed last summer. She had been at the lavish cabin she rented for a month in the Lake of the Ozarks, entertaining strangers and doing whatever else she fills her endless free time with. *Classic Armatta.*

Ana had offered to drive and, aside from her insisting we 'hit the road' at four in the morning, everything had been going smoothly. I looked over at my sister, watching as the sun, beaming through the sunroof, danced in her hair. It was wrapped up in a messy bun, loose coils springing from the top of her head. The auburn of this past summer had started to fade, leaving a copper hue behind that suited her more than the fiery red curls Aisha's passing had inspired. Her words from that day at the will reading echoed through my head, *'Some of us have healthier modes of processing grief.'*

I thought back to the letter, trying to ignore the hollow feeling in my chest as I *tried*. I was intentionally choosing to be around my family. Aisha should be proud—the fact that I was even in the car, willing to spend two days with Armatta, should've been considered effort enough.

"Who's staying with Hadley?" I asked, reaching down to rifle through the snack bag. Ana had left me in charge of packing things but stopped at a gas station as soon as she saw that I had packed 'health store shit.' My fingers rubbed against the rubbery peel of an orange and I pulled it out.

"Umm," she started, taking a giant bite out of the cheap, gas station meat stick she opted for over the nut and fruit packs I bought. "Kate and Gretta actually."

The mention of Kate's name sent a ripple through me— my fingers digging into the orange peel, sticky juice spreading across my hands. I pretended like the words didn't twist the ever-present knife of guilt deeper in my stomach. "Oh."

Ana was quick to fill the awkward shroud that covered the car, over-explaining while her eyes stayed glued to the road. "I know you guys got into it, but it's not like they're suddenly terrible people. Hadley loves them, and you know they're reliable."

"No, I know," I started, taking a deep breath of the citrus scent filling the car. "How're they doing?"

She shrugged nonchalantly. "Gretta's thinking about opening another restaurant and Kate's been finishing up her manuscript before she starts looking for a new job. I think it's been...good for her to step away."

'Everyone's eager to get away from you,' the voice called.

I nodded, peeling a slice of the orange off and popping it into my mouth, thankful for the burst of juice and flavor that filled my ashy mouth.

"I still can't believe you convinced me to do this," I mumbled through my bite.

Ana laughed, the sound short and sharp. "It's one weekend. What's the worst that could happen?"

"Oh, I don't know," I started, popping another orange slice in my mouth. "I could kill her?"

She laughed again, the car swerving slightly with her jolting shoulders. "You know, I never thought you were above matricide." She held out an expectant hand. "Give me a piece."

I looked at her, letting my lips pull into a brief smile before peeling a few orange chunks off and passing them to her—my fingers brushing against hers as I waited to make sure she had a good grip on them.

"You know what I really want?" she asked, her eyebrows bobbing up and down. "Some filthy, greasy McDonald's."

My jaw dropped in clear and utter disgust, my mouthful of pulp on full display as I tried to recall the last time I had a Big Mac. "Ana, that's so gross."

"Oh, shut up. You used to *love* a chicken nugget Happy Meall," she started, popping through her slices like candy. "Somewhere, deep inside, a little girl is begging for one more bite of a McDonald's nugget, Ash. You should give it to her."

"My stomach will be in revolt for weeks."

"You'll be fine," she said, drawing out the last syllable. "Look!" She pointed in front of us, my eyes following her finger to an information sign proudly displaying all of this exit's finest fast-food dining options—the famous golden, double arches pointing us a mile to the right. Ana all but squealed as she said, "It's meant to be!"

She veered off, taking us through the small, cramped main street of whatever tiny, Missouri town we'd pulled into. She spotted the sign and pulled into the drive-thru, stopping at the speaker before leaning back in her seat. "Make sure you look at everything. I know it's probably been years since you've been here."

"Whatever," I murmured, leaning across the center console to try and get a better sense of the screen. "I just want some fries and a Sprite."

Ana laughed and placed the order while I thought back to similar conversations shared over a half-eaten sandwich and already cooling fries. McDonald's had been a staple for us growing up—easy to access and afford when our mother was flying through life without a care.

We pulled up to the window and, as soon as the bag— already soiled with grease—was in the car, I gagged.

"Asha, stop being so—"

"—*dramatic. We will get some McDonald's after you place first. We never get the reward before we win, selfish girl.*" *My mother said from the driver's seat. We'd finally been able to get a car but it was up to me—a fifteen year old—to make sure we made the payments.*

"I just don't understand why I have to starve all day to place first." *AnaMarie and Hadley had been gone for two months now and I might've missed them if it weren't for the pressure of feeding two more mouths lifted from my shoulders. Momma had somehow been simultaneously nicer and even more mean since they'd left. Every day felt like an emotionally draining war, spent balancing her kind words and hurtful digs.*

"You know that a judge ain't gonna crown a bloated girl the winner. Your scoring dropped last month and I refuse to aid you in your attempt to kill our income."

"I'm not trying to lose, Momma. Maybe I'm just getting too old." Her hand shot up and I flinched against the car door, the metal frame refusing to let me free of her incoming

*swat—but it never came. Just a haunting giggle from across
the car.*

*"You're not too old. You just have more competition now.
You're going to get that sash, and I'll let you have a happy meal
afterwards. Just be grateful."* I let my body uncurl at its own
pace, fear locking me into a ball for a solid thirty seconds. I
looked over to see her hand, resting on the volume control—like
she was waiting for me to see where it went, gaslighting me into
thinking her abuse had always been imagined.

"Sorry," I mumbled, "Thank you."

"I just haven't smelt it in literal years," I said to my sister
quietly.

She pulled the car away, slowly leading us back toward the
impending hell that awaited when we met up with Armatta. *I
can be nice. For Ana.*

I settled into silence, sipping on my soda and nibbling on
my fries as Ana tore into her burger across from me—like the
overly-processed patty dripping with sauce was the most heav-
enly thing she'd ever eaten. My lip curled in disgust and I
turned away, unable to watch the slaughter she was committing while merging onto the highway.

I hadn't realized how far into my own memories I had
fallen until Ana was gently nudging my shoulder an hour
later. "You okay?"

I nodded, clearing my throat. "Yeah, just got...stuck."

"McDonald's hangover?"

"Something like that," I said, offering her a small smile.
"Can I ask you a question without you getting mad?"

She went silent, likely weighing the impact of whatever
words I was going to throw her way next—always one to
employ the Arlington women's book of strategy. She blew out
a steady breath before briefly glancing at me, completing her
assessment. "Hit me."

"Why are we doing this?"

The silence in the car was oddly comfortable, even as she mulled over the question—her mouth working as she got lost in her own train of thought.

"I want to believe she's different," she said, the words soft and vulnerable.

"And if she isn't?"

"Then I need to see it. I need to know that she's the same evil person who raised us."

"Did she *really* raise us?" I asked, sarcasm and humor wiping out the acrid taste of fear. Our eyes met and I flashed her a wink, eager to be the support she needed—despite how I felt. *Growth, right?*

"Well, either way," she started, her voice tight, "at least you and I get to hang out, right?"

"Right." I reached over, a small—genuine—smile pulling at my lips and turned up the volume as we wound through the Missouri foothills. Still, I couldn't shake the feeling that there was a reckoning on the horizon.

&a.

We'd pulled into the driveway of a lavish cabin two hours later, the greasy smell of our road trip pit stop threatening to choke me by the end of it. Ana laughed as I pulled myself out of the car gagging, mentioning something about my 'dramatics.' Whatever easy fun we'd found during the drive shriveled up once I saw our mother, waiting for us on the porch—a glass of wine already clasped in her claws.

"Girls!" She shrieked, the sound inspiring a couple of crows to take flight. "You made it! Come in, come in!" She waved us over, as if this was *her* house and not a rental she was haunting until it was time for her to flee to the next excursion.

I walked around the car as Ana popped the trunk open, pulling our bags from the back of her car. She tossed mine to me with ease, the totebag landing hard in my arms. "You packed surprisingly light."

"I didn't see the point in lugging out a suitcase for three days. Who knows, maybe Matta will get pissed and send me away early."

"For 'disturbing her peace?'" Ana asked, sliding into a perfect imitation of our mother.

"Exactly."

"You'll be fine." She laughed as she said it, pulling her own suitcase out. I peeked into my bag, making sure Aisha's DVD of pictures was still on top.

"Listen," I started, moving closer to my sister. The trunk of her car was still open, giving us a shield from Armatta's prying stare. "I have something to show you later. Once Matta goes to sleep."

My sister didn't say anything, just a small nod before slamming the door. We stood there for a few more seconds, our feet planted to the dirt road until our mother began beckoning us over. "Wanna see how long we can stand here before she gets pissed?" I asked, watching as a small smirk bloomed on my sister's face.

"That's probably the *worst* way to start this weekend," she said, and started the trek toward the house. I followed her, my focus jumping from the line of ants on the ground to the trees towering over us. The house was surrounded by them, and there was only a small opening where the building stood that allowed the sky to peek through. I stomped up the porch stairs behind Ana, listening to her greet our mother with more—faux—excitement than I'd seen the entire drive up.

"How was the drive?" Armatta asked, and AnaMarie turned to me with an expectant eyebrow raised.

"Fine." I rocked back and forth on my heels, trying to find interest in the wrap-around porch instead of the two women staring at me. Ana's eyes widened as if she was begging me to *try*. I rolled my eyes before adding, "How long have you been here?"

"Oh, a couple weeks now." She waved a hand like it was nothing to rent someone's cabin for *weeks* on end. Like it was normal. For my spoiled mother, I guess it was.

"Come, come," she said, motioning toward the front door. "Why don't you girls go pick a room while I shower? We can meet back down here for dinner in say..." she paused, lifting her watch to her face in an exaggerated motion. "Two hours?"

I nodded while peacekeeper Ana launched into a conversation with Armatta, their animated voices disappearing inside the house.

I wandered around for a while, poking my head into the various rooms, trying to balance my disgust over Matta's extravagance with the awe I felt—the house was huge, and old in a way that suggested the walls had hosted their fair share of history. I lost thirty minutes admiring it, another fifteen battling against rage at the expense, and another ten stumbling around looking for a room of my own. I'd found an empty one along the upstairs corridor and threw my bag on the bed, closing the door behind me before deciding to take a shower of my own.

I was quick—letting the water wash away any nerves that were clinging to me before stepping out. Hoping I'd finished before my mother could find me, and rush me to whatever she had planned next.

I had just picked the brush up when Matta made her way into the room—clad in a silk robe and a towel wrapped around her hair—effectively disrupting whatever peace I had scrounged together after the car ride with Ana.

"Let me help you with that, Ash," she said, all but ripping the brush from my hands. I had to fight against my body as it tried to flinch under her hands, unwilling to give her any ammunition to use against me this weekend.

She ran a hand through my curls, catching on a knot. "If you took the time to detangle your hair every day, you wouldn't have a rat's nest to contend with after showers."

There was something childlike to my hesitation. *Fear or rebellion?*

The plastic tines dug into my scalp, the heavy-handed work of a woman with no maternal instincts acting like the simple act of brushing my hair would fix all of the heartache she had caused. I closed my eyes, trying to ignore the twisted comfort I felt as Armatta worked through sections of my hair. The rhythmic tug of the brush, the silence punctuated only by her sighs—it all dragged me back to the one place I didn't want to go and, suddenly, I was twelve again.

Momma had woken us up early in the morning, eager to get on the road.

"The pageant is about three hours away and we have to get there early so you can get a good mirror," she said to me while weaving her fingers through Ana's hair the night before. Now, before even the birds had started singing, she was standing by the door, crowing on about 'getting our lil asses up.'

Ana, ever the appeaser, jumped from the comfort of our shared bed quickly, her footsteps thundering on the cold floor. I listened as she ripped through the closet, hangers banging against each other while she searched for the perfect outfit. I pulled the covers up until I was merely a part of the bed, wishing that I could stay here, hidden, for the rest of my life. I laid there until Momma's ice-cold hands pulled me from my sanctuary, sliding me into a plain blue dress—the front pressed and buttoned, the collar laid perfectly flat around my neck. My pageant wear and makeup were already packed by the door—the suitcase full of everything Momma wanted me to be.

"I don't want to go," I whispered as she sat me in front of her vanity, a brush pulling back the strands of hair on my head, a big glob of gel to lock the fly-away strands down waiting on the back of her hand.

"Speak up," she chided, "no one is going to crown a mumbler."

"I said, 'I don't want to go!'" I yelled, frustration coursing through my body with what might've been a shimmer of pride. Is this what it feels like to stand up for yourself?

Momma stood frozen behind me, my little eyes trailing up to look at her face in the mirror. I watched as she watched me, and I felt the moment shift. She raised the brush in her hand, bringing it down on the crown of my head twice. I yelped as pain radiated, my hands jumping to shield myself from her as she crouched down to meet my face. Her hard eyes met mine as she gripped my chin, forcing me to hold her cold stare.

"Every time you win, we get to keep living in our own apartment. Every time you win, we get to eat another meal. Don't be so selfish, Asha. Think of your family," she reprimanded. I tried to rip my face away only for her to squeeze harder, causing me to whimper. Tears started down my cheeks, cascading over her frozen fingers and down her arm. Her face softened at the emotion, but her grip remained tight.

I managed to nod my head, fear taking permanent residence in my body. Armatta returned her attention to my hair and finished pinning it back in silence. I caught Ana's reflection in the mirror, her eyes wide as she just...watched. I'd long released the expectation that Ana would help me, or that Auntie would make Momma stop. No one was going to save me from her because everyone was just as scared.

She shoved us into the car—Aisha had let us borrow hers for the weekend since we had to drive so far—and we sputtered to the pageant, the sun barely breaking over the horizon. Momma promised a 'nice meal as a family' if I could manage to secure the third runner-up spot or better. That just meant that we couldn't afford it unless I made us some money.

We flew past fields and through cities, and I was happy to succumb to the quiet of the drive before Momma's anxiety surged again. The music drifted softly through the car, weaving between Ana and I tucked together in the back seat.

"This is it," Momma said abruptly. "This is gonna be the one, girls. I just—"

"—know you're one of the most stunning girls I've ever seen, Asha." The overly-sweet tone in her voice made me feel small—the twelve-year-old girl getting admonished under a hairbrush still alive and terrified, controlled by her mother's unpredictable moods.

She set down the hairbrush, the sound making me jump as I tried to shake the trembling anxiety that was rooted in my bones as she stood at my back, her hands resting lightly on my shoulders. "We're going to have salmon for dinner. I found a lovely chef who will come cook for us *here*, in the cabin!" She clapped her hands together, the sharp sound startling me again as she turned, floating out of the room. Her voice trailed down the hallway, as if she never intended for her words to be consumed by an audience anyways.

"*Asha,*" she called, using her rich bitch voice. I rolled my eyes as my body, trained to respond to her shrill commands, moved before I could even process my name echoing through the house. I stopped at the door of the room, my hand tracing over the intricate grooves carved into the frame—a small act of defiance as I stalled, appreciating the time it must've taken to carve flowers into the warm wood. "Asha!" My heart thumped violently against my chest as I crossed the threshold, each stomp of my feet sounding through the cabin, heavy with dread.

❧

True to her lavishly, expensive word, Armatta had a chef come prepare a *seven-course* meal for the three of us, a fare that had me hesitant to hand my card over when hers declined at the end of the night. There wasn't even an ounce of embarrassment in her face as the poor guy asked her to provide another payment—her sly, manipulative eyes sliding to mine with the quiet assumption that I would, of course, take care of it.

"My auntie's like that too," the man said, passing my card back to me. I tucked it into my purse, throwing it back on the counter. "So selfish and focused on appearances, she wouldn't recognize the self-absorbed bitch she'd become if she was staring at her in the mirror."

I felt defensive as I listened to this stranger dig on my mother but let the fuse fizzle out as I realized that, despite how much I *wanted* her to be the perfect mom, Armatta Arlington was, and always would be, far from it. I simply nodded my head, unable to say anything that would benefit the conversation.

"Asha, what is this!" Evil Incarnate called from the living room of the cabin. My head dropped of its own accord, falling to my chest as I released a heavy sigh.

"Good luck," the chef said before sliding a backpack over his shoulders, quickly bolting for the door as Armatta's excitement seemed to grow.

"Oh my god! A home movie? Where did you get this?"

My vision went red—a dark, pooling color that matched the utter rage that boiled over as I realized she went through my bag. *One breath in, one breath out.*

I could do this—get through the next two hours of being awake—for Ana.

"I found it at Aisha's house!" I called, slowly making my way toward the living room.

I turned the corner to see Ana, tucked into the couch, as white as the blanket wrapped around her shoulders. Her eyes were wide with fear—like she knew the boundaries our mother was pushing and was even more terrified of how my reaction would spill over.

"Why would you go through my things?" I said quietly, unable to stand the look of the DVD in Armatta's hands. Aisha's words rang out in my head, *'And don't let Matta get her hands on any of it either.'*

"It was hanging out of your bag anyways, call it curiosity." The words were likely meant to bounce off of me dismissively.

"No, Armatta. Don't go through my shit."

She looked at me, stunned that I had stood up for myself. A familiar glimmer of pride tingled along my spine, and I stood a little straighter as I made my way to the couch, curling into the corner opposite of Ana.

My sister—whose hands were wrapping anxiously in the blanket folds—and I watched silently as Armatta fiddled with the decades-old DVD player. Her hands, barely withered by age, trembled as she pointed the remote at the TV, pressing buttons that didn't respond beneath her heavy-handed touch. While I couldn't speak for Ana, *I* was getting more than a little joy out of seeing her struggle with the device—its distinct arbitrariness as poignant as the woman fiddling with it.

The screen finally flicked to life, a static slate taking over before flashing a picture of Ana and me, damn near babies, holding a bouquet of flowers together. I had to have been 13 or so, my hair pulled back into an elaborate, looping bun, a glimmering first place tiara sitting proudly on my head. The screen blinked and suddenly there was an image of the two of us, splashing at a park wearing swimsuits, followed by one of Aisha and us, crammed together on a picnic bench.

I found myself leaning closer to my sister as we watched the pictures flick by, the only sound coming from Armatta's already disinterested nails tapping away on her phone. I rolled my eyes back to the screen, *totally* surprised that she would cross my boundaries and not have the basic decency to see what she dragged out of my bag.

The screen flashed again, now showing a photo of Ana holding an infant Hadley in her arms at the hospital. I was at her side, a frozen hand swiping the head full of curls to the side as we both smiled down at the small, beautiful girl. I reached over, wrapping my hand around Ana's and accepted the comforting warmth that seemed to shoot through me when she offered a single, tight squeeze in return.

Armatta cooed from her chair in the corner, her attention finally making it to the screen and the childhoods she'd ruined. Her eyes crinkled at the sides, her forehead *almost* furrowing with affection—the filler in her eyebrows would never let her show *that* much emotion. The screen switched again, and our mother laughed at a video of Ana pushing me on a swing set, each sound she made incensing my growing anger and discomfort.

"You don't get to smile over shit like this. You weren't there," I mumbled to Armatta. The smile fell from her face and I was met with a look of crafted horror.

"Asha—"

"No—don't 'Asha' me. The only reason we even have these pictures is because of Auntie and Ana. *You weren't there.*" I was seething as I pulled myself from the couch, aiming for my mother, staring at me in shock from the lonely chair across the room. A tiny part of me was crying out, begging myself to sit on the couch and be quiet—to accept whatever this was for what it was, to accept Armatta for *who* she was. "Where were you when I was four and broke my leg? When Ana had to *carry* me to the bus stop only to use the last few dollars we had to get me to the fucking hospital." I asked, my voice rising steadily. We couldn't even make it through a night together without our tempers flaring and, suddenly, I was thankful for the solitude of the woods surrounding us.

"Where were you when the girls at the pageants would corner me and bruise me until call time? Where were you when the bruises were healing? When *your* fucking boyfriend raped Ana? When Hadley was born? Huh, Armatta? What was more important than us?" I looked my mother in the eyes, noting the brief crack in her composure—a twitch of the lip tugging on her small, demure smile. Hot tears started to roll down my cheeks, two rivers of past unspoken pain cascading down my face—for what felt like the first time in years, I let them flow in front of her.

"When your sister had to lay her husband and son in the ground, where were you? When she was alone, choking to death on her own blood where the fuck were you!?" I turned, looking at Ana who was silently crying in her spot on the couch. Her gaze focused on the wood pile in the corner, far away from the traumatic scene unfolding in front of her.

"Asha, there's so much I wish I could explain," Armatta said, forcing my head to snap back in her direction. The movement sent me into a dizzy spiral—I felt *so* tired.

"There's so much you *don't want* to explain," Ana

snapped, finally pulled from her thoughts. I let her words renew my energy, pulling myself up to stand firmly behind my sister and the couch.

"Look, I'm sorry for how my choices impacted you two but I couldn't have done too bad of a job. Seeing as how one of you owns a company and the other has a beautiful daughter and a wonderful career." She seethed, surprised by Ana's choice to get involved—the perfect daughter who always listened and cleaned up mommy's mess turning on her too.

"You want us to thank you for all of the shit you put us through?" Ana asked in disbelief, I put my hand on her shoulder and squeezed, hoping she felt comfort and found the strength to push through.

"You don't have to thank me, per se. Maybe don't attack me the next time I offer to take you two on a nice getaway," she replied with a tight smile—the cool, collected mask of Armatta Arlington.

Ana laughed, the sound sharp and cold. "The getaway that Asha funded?" Was she finally accepting who our mother would always be? "Just like your entire, luxurious life is funded by Asha. How do you not see the lengths she goes to to make sure you're taken care of? Or do you even care?"

I saw the mask start to break. Armatta's right eyebrow flicked up in surprise while the smile dropped, ever so slightly, on the left side. Her eyes seemed to go distant as she stared at the two of us.

"And you don't, do you?" I asked, the heaviness of the words sinking down to my bones.

"Of course I do," she started, her eyes jumping to meet mine, "You've given me a life I never allowed myself to dream of and I'm grateful for that. I won't apologize for the trials you had to face on the way. It's life. Everything you two have been through, I've been through."

She ran her hands down the front of her dress, the folds of the fabric soaking up the anxiety she was trying to hide from us.

"So because you went through it, we have to? Armatta, that's not the point of being a parent! The point is to do better!" Ana cried, her own experience as a mother shining through.

"Oh, because you know? Your child swears like a sailor and doesn't recognize her place in the world. She's rude and spiteful. It's a surprise that Asha didn't raise her herself." I could see where this was heading, and for once, I hoped Ana wouldn't let her win.

To my surprise, my sister let out another laugh. A full, bellowing sound that filled the entire cabin. I watched her before feeling a giggle build in my throat, the absurdity of the moment pouring through the both of us.

"You...You think Hadley's spiteful? Armatta..." she siad between laughs. "She just *hates* you. "

I let the laughter bubble out of me as I folded over. Armatta, our typically preening and poised matron stood awkwardly on the other side of the room—finally an outsider in her own family.

"I didn't raise you girls to be cruel," she said, as she reached into her purse, her phone emerging wrapped tightly in her claws.

I laughed—short and sharp—the sound causing her eyes to flick to mine. "You didn't raise us at all."

"You," she started, pointing a perfectly manicured finger at me. "You, selfish, selfish girl."

The weight of the world pressed against me as her voice

surrounded me, the sound given a life of its own as it ricocheted through the room.

'Why does everything about you scream worthless?'

'Whatever you can do to make shit easier on yourself, huh Asha?'

'Selfish, undeserving…'

'Maybe you're not worth his precious time after all…'

'See how happy you feel when you manipulate him?'

'You don't deserve him…'

'Selfish, selfish girl.'

"It's you." I looked at Armatta, my eyes burning. "The stupid, controlling voice in my head that mocks *every choice I make?* It's *you.*" The words were a hot venom spilling from my lips as I pointed at her, the realization setting my anger aflame.

"You've taken so much from me. You've forced me to do *so much,* Armatta. And you still can't see what you've done wrong. Or you won't admit it and I don't know which one's worse! You claimed to have named me after Aisha, to have removed the 'i' from her name in hopes that I wouldn't be selfish but, *mother,*" The word tasted foreign and nasty on my tongue. "You are the most selfish person I have ever met."

She had the audacity to raise a hand to her heart, her face twisted in wounded surprise—though her wide eyes flickered briefly with something else. Fear? Guilt? I couldn't tell, and maybe she couldn't either. It was as if the things I was saying were *so* outside her realm of reality that she couldn't believe that I would throw these claims her way. "I might be a selfish bitch, Armatta. But you've always been the blueprint."

The room went tense in silence, Ana's head bouncing between our mother and me as if she had front row seats to the world's most dramatic tennis match.

"Armatta, you have one option as far as I'm concerned." I walked to the center of the room, looking down at her from the regal height she used to mock when I was a lanky teen. "You get the fuck out of here and never contact me again. Keep whatever's in your accounts but after that don't even *think* of my name unless you *genuinely* want to call me and apologize."

"And if I don't?" she asked, evaluating the bed of her nails just like she did her options—thoroughly. "Apologize, that is."

"Don't be dense, Matta. Either own up to it all and say sorry or leave me alone. If you can't handle that, I'll take it all away and you'll go right back to your life in some small, shit town."

She dropped her hand, her jaw falling with it—as if she couldn't believe I'd have the audacity to take her precious, carefully cultivated life away.

"Sounds like a lot of shitty options for you. Maybe you should've been a better parent." Ana quipped from her spot on the couch. I felt a smile pulling onto my lips—doing nothing to hide it as Armatta wrapped her hands around her purse. I'd wasted my life wondering about, if it came down to it, would she choose money or her daughters. This was the first time I felt strong enough to hear the answer. I lifted my chin to the shell of a mother—slowly crumbling—in front of me. Her eyes darted around the room, landing anywhere but on Ana and me. I tilted my head, daring her to pick the right option. Somewhere, deep inside, a little girl was silently begging her to fight for our relationship.

"Well, I guess I don't have much of a choice here," she began, quickly fleeing to the front door. "I'll have my driver grab my things later today."

I felt my heart crack—for the last time at the hands of my mother—as her words sank in. Her hand hovered over the door handle, her head falling as if she was finally struggling under the weight of her consequences. "I really tried to love you two," she said, throwing the door open and stepping into the cold November air. My tears finally released as the door slammed closed behind her, a quick rush of wind filling the house as Ana and I stayed frozen, rooted in place. *One breath in, one breath out.*

I thought back to a far-away summer, my shoulders brushing against Ana's as she released a firefly back into the night. I wondered if the little bug felt the same way when my sister twisted the metal lid off the jar and it spread its wings.

Free.

TWENTY-SEVEN

My bones scream at me as I pull my crossed legs out from underneath me, and the pressure of forty minutes in the confessional. Tears flow down my cheeks, silent rivers working their way down my neck and under the collar of my shirt. I can't bring myself to wipe them away, not when they feel like a badge of honor slowly soaking into my chest.

My eyes lock on Marjorie's pen, watching as she uses my breath-work break to write down any lingering thoughts. I try to keep my mind clear as I listen to her scrawl, the sound working overtime to fill my discomfort.

"So," I start, sniffing hard in an attempt to clear my nose. "I know I'm insane but just how insane?"

Marjorie freezes, her pen digging into the page as she slowly pulls her eyes to meet mine.

"Asha, you are..." she begins, "Well, to be frank, you're someone who's suffered *immensely*. There are things you weren't able to process in your childhood that clearly influenced the way you navigate life now."

I resume my attack on the couch, pulling at threads that

have sprung free from the stitching—unable to meet her eye as anxiety rakes its sharp claws through my gut.

"But—" *There's always a but.* "—you're also someone who has created a life of isolation and chaos for yourself. It seems that you exist in this constant turmoil. Angst that comes and goes in your life that you latch onto and use as motivation for your isolative behaviors. I think that we can work together to break down some of the reflexes you use when it comes to people and the negative way in which you view connection."

I nod my head, fresh tears threatening to fall over at her words. "Okay."

The rustle of the beanbag made me pull my head up, only to find Marjorie, on the floor in front of me, reaching for my hand. Her eyebrows arch, as if asking if it was okay for her to touch me, and I nod again—unable to speak through my now-racking sobs. Her hands wrap around mine as she says, "Asha Arlington, you are strong. And you're going to be okay."

I let my cries come out in earnest, sinking into Marjorie as she moves from my hands and embraces me in a hug. I shutter as the therapist wraps her hands around my shoulders, the weight of trauma—building over the years—releasing from my bones, my mind, my heart. My sobs fill the room and Marjorie, to her credit, doesn't let go, even as I hiccup my relief into her ear. She doesn't step back until I'm calm, my racking chest quieted into an occasional sniffle. I reach for a tissue, wiping my nose before finally cracking open the water bottle that had waited for me.

"I would love to see you for another session, Asha. That, of course, is up to you though. Just call the office whenever, *if* ever you're ready. Okay?"

"Thank you," I say, reaching for my purse and walking toward the door, eager to flee before I could mess this up too.

"Of course," she says, taking a deep breath before adding, "And Asha...I think it might be beneficial for you to reach out to those who you've cut ties with in the last few months. It sounds like you had a village of people who adored you and I doubt their love for you disappeared in an instant."

I focus on the cool, round knob of the door handle and how it fits so perfectly into my palm—holding my breath in hopes that it would keep the, now calm, torrent of tears from spilling over again. I think about Kate, how my life had been an unorganized gambit since she'd decided to quit—since I'd *forced* her to quit. I wonder if she and Gretta still lived in the shoebox apartment and if Kate finished her manuscript. I think about Scheff, how he'd walked away from me in defeat after years of grueling over the idea of a shared life. And then Grayson, and his refusal to let me burn him out with my issues. Do they still love me? Could I actually convince them that I was *better*? "And what if it did?"

She considers it, laying her pen on top of her now-closed notebook. "Then you work through it. You don't get to decide how they heal from the damage you've caused. All you can do is keep working, keep growing, and keep waiting for the day that they are ready to accept you again. And if they don't," she pauses, as if anticipating my train of thought. "Then hopefully we'll have worked through the tools that will help you deal with it."

I nod my head, muttering one last thanks before twisting the knob in my hand and stepping away from the stifling emotions that linger in the overwhelmingly green room. I give a small wave to the receptionist before stepping outside of Marjorie's office—the weight I had shouldered for most of my life slowly slipping away. I drew in a steady breath, deep and smooth as the chilled air wraps around me—wiping away any lingering dread that I had carried into the office with me.

I fight against the urge to call Ana, to tell my sister about the hour I just spent talking and grieving and...learning about myself. I reach into my bag, my fingers brushing against everything *but* my phone as I push away the sound of my mother —the small echo of her voice in my head—telling me that Ana wouldn't want to hear from me anyway.

"Fuck you," I say, acknowledging it one last time. There is only one thing I wanted to do right now and, as I step into the November sun, I pull out my phone and call my sister.

Acknowledgments

There is something unconventionally daunting about sitting down to write acknowledgements. In all honesty, they're one of my favorite aspects of a book—especially as someone whose debut is in your hands *right now*.

When a world created in someone's head finds its way into the hearts of readers, the text is simply a bridge toward empathy. Where there is empathy, there is connection, and connection is what fundamentally drives us.

When I started writing *Attic*, I was stuck in an intense loneliness that I wasn't prepared to navigate. I was bitter, and angry, and confused about so much in my life and the world in general that I couldn't help but look for answers. I fell back in love with reading and found characters that reflected my feelings, my fears, my wants and wishes. The more I read, the less alone I felt. Writing became a haven, as it does, and I started to toy with the idea of ruthless characters and what makes them so. Asha was born not only out of spite, but out of a will to excavate the 'why' behind our harsh exteriors. She not only gave me space to express my feelings but she inadvertently forced me into connecting with some of the kindest, smartest people I've met—people whose attention to detail, intention with craft, and willingness to care helped me get to where I am today.

Nancy Courtelyou, my lovely editor, I'll never forget our first session where you asked me what level of critique I needed—did I want you to hold my hand while we dismantled my drafts, or did you have free rein to be as direct as possible? A small, fragile part of me wanted to whisper, "Please hold me," but I knew that wouldn't help me. Giving you the freedom to critique honestly (without the fear of hurting my feelings) allowed us to fall into a rhythm that pushed me to be better with every session. I truly enjoyed our sessions, especially the ones where it felt like I was simply catching up with an old friend. This book would be nothing without your touch and guidance. Asha helped me find an editor, a mentor, and a friend in you. Thank you a million times over.

Kourtney Jossy, you were a dream to work with, even as my vision shifted over our collaboration. I wouldn't have the cover I do if it wasn't for your intention, your willingness to pivot with my ideas, and your focus on details in Asha's story. I'm so proud to see her entering the world with the cover that you designed.

Britney, Sephy, and Shelby, you were my first readers and the proof I needed that this story mattered. Without your eyes and thoughts, I don't think I would have had the confidence to get to this point. The fire you lit beneath me gave me motivation to finish and I don't think I could say thank you enough.

Danielle, you saved me in ways neither of us could understand until I felt safe enough to voice them. Our walks and discussions gave me comfort and camaraderie when the world felt too small, too bleak. You are a light in my life and someone I know I can turn to for anything. Thank you for listening to me, for sheltering me, and for being the best hiking partner around.

Tina and York, this book would still be collecting dust in my brain if it wasn't for the time and flexibility you've offered me. Between naps, school pick-ups and drop-offs, crying babies and extracurricular activities, I was able to work on this novel without the fear of upsetting you. Your interest and commitment to my dreams and goals while I work alongside your family means *everything* to me. Thank you so much for giving me the time, space, and occasional office take-over so that I could make this a reality.

Dresden and Caspian, if I could give you boys one thing in life, it would be the joy and laughter you've showered me with in the last five years. Being your nanny has been the biggest blessing of my life and I'm so proud to know you both and watch you grow. You've made my heart feel lighter on the heaviest of days and filled my life with magical memories. To be your friend is to be a better person. I love you both so big!

Bricen, when we started dating, I felt like I was touching peace for the first time in my life. Since then, every minute spent with you has been filled with belly laughs, good food, and kindness I never thought myself worthy of. I will never forget loving how my laugh sounded that night, how it felt like a few hours spent with you helped me find my way back to a care-free little girl I thought I'd lost long ago. Thank you for reminding me how to love myself.

Momma, you are one of the most resilient people I know. I tell people often that any bit of kindness I have is because of you. Thank you for giving me the world when I was small and for allowing me the space to be weird and wild inside of it. You filled my life with books and stories and never discouraged me from adventure. I am eternally grateful for everything you've done and continue to do for me.

Finally, dear reader, let me thank *you* for taking a chance on Asha. I've held her between my ribs for nearly four years now and we've watched each other grow in tremendous ways. I wouldn't see the world, my life, or myself the way I do now if it wasn't for her. I hope she's found a way to lodge in your brain, to give you space to *feel*, to remind you to breathe. The weight we shoulder is a lot sometimes and I hope you can find a safe place to shelve it.

Like Asha, you too will be okay.

About the Author

Kristen Lane lives in St. Louis, Missouri and is drawn to stories that spark hard conversations, and turn over harsh truths, while still leaving room for the tender beads of hope that float alongside tragedy.

photo courtesy of Orville Parker III